PRAISE FOR MICHELLE DIENER

There is a check list of things I look for in a good SFR book and Diener has checked them all off.

MIXED BOOK BAG

Truly exceptional.

RT BOOK REVIEWS

Michelle Diener writes exciting, inventive, and just plain good fun SFR stories that will take the reader on quite a fantastic journey.

OUTLANDER BOOK CLUB

DARK CLASS

MICHELLE DIENER

ABOUT DARK CLASS

Waking up alone . . . Ellie Masters comes out of a coma to find herself the only inhabitant of an eerily empty moon station. She's not on Earth any more, she's not even in the right solar system. So when someone reaches out to her, tells her he's her friend, she's happy to believe it. The alternative is to be stuck alone with an enemy.

The hunt of his career . . . Grih Battle Center captain, Renn Sorvihn, has been chasing a rogue Tecran ship for over a month, convinced its captain is simply trying to delay his inevitable surrender and punishment. But when Renn follows the Tecran ship into an uncharted sector, and realises the Tecran have been working their way to a secret moon base for weeks, he suddenly understands things are most definitely not as they seem.

Caught in the crossfire . . . When the Tecran arrive, with the Grih hot on their heels, Ellie finds herself the catalyst for heightened danger to everyone. The Tecran see her as evidence of their military's crimes, the Grih see her as a massive diplomatic complication, and her presence brings the whole confrontation up several thousand notches.

But Ellie isn't alone, and her new friend has ways to help her. Time to outclass them all . . .

CHAPTER 1

ELLIE WOKE TO A JAUNTY TUNE.

She lay for awhile, eyes closed, listening to it, while she tried to remember where she was and how she came to be here.

Panic buzzed faintly along her skin, caught her breath in her throat, and she kept very still.

Did she know this song?

She thought the tune was familiar, but didn't recognize the lyrics. Was it from a musical, maybe? Or the theme song from a movie?

Over the sound of the music, she could hear a faint, steady hum, like the machinery in a hospital, and the air, slightly too cool for comfort, reminded her of institutional spaces.

She wasn't home, or anywhere that might resemble a home.

She could simply open her eyes and find out where she was, she told herself, but just the thought of it made her heart beat faster, her chest tighten.

She was afraid to.

Why was she afraid to?

She pondered that.

After a long while, after the jaunty tune had ended and a deeper, more complex instrumental piece had taken its place, she finally came to the conclusion she couldn't keep her eyes closed forever and opened them in a snap, getting it over quickly.

She was in a much smaller space than she'd imagined. And she was alone.

She sat slowly, looking around at the almost pod-like shape that curved around her.

She was naked, with a few tubes and wires stuck to her, but they were easy to peel off and nothing was piercing her skin.

Being naked disturbed her deeply.

It made her feel a little bit like throwing up.

Even hospitals put you in gowns.

Someone had put her in this place. Someone had attached the tubes and wires. And had taken her clothes.

She kneaded the blanket that had pooled at her waist in distress, found it was smooth and soft. She took it with her when she slid off the hip-height platform she'd been lying on and wrapped it around her like a toga, flicking the end over her shoulder.

She immediately felt better. Less exposed.

The floor beneath her feet felt gritty, like it hadn't been cleaned in a while, and when she noticed that, she began to see everything around her had a fine layer of dust on it.

Either no one had bothered to clean, or there *was* no one, and she had lain on the platform at least long enough to be able to write her name with a fingertip on the equipment that surrounded her.

She didn't know which option was worse.

The space wasn't untidy, exactly, but little clues, like a clamp lying on the floor, a small piece of broken glass glinting from underneath one of the trolleys that had been pushed close to her bed, a piece of equipment tilted drunkenly against the wall, as if it had been knocked there and just left with two wheels off the ground, made her think there had been some kind of scuffle in here. A fight or a temper tantrum.

None of the equipment looked like anything she'd ever seen. It seemed alien.

She felt her mind shut down at the thought, and when she came back to herself, she flung out her arms, running a hand over each one, then lifted her legs.

She didn't appear to be hurt in any way.

She felt weak, a little wobbly, but not excessively so.

She finally forced herself to focus on the door. It was narrow, and she moved toward it slowly. Her knees felt as if they wanted to buckle and she stiffened them, stopping with legs locked for a moment until she felt steady enough to continue.

When she reached the door, it opened automatically and she stood still, looking beyond it, steeling herself for danger.

Nothing but a corridor greeted her.

It stretched ahead, mostly dark, as only one light was on, near the door, and it was flickering as if it had just turned on and was warming up.

She didn't like how little she could see, how dark it was ahead, but she couldn't stay in her little pod, either.

Her throat felt scratchy and dry, and it hurt to swallow.

She took a step out and began to walk.

The door behind her closed, and the music cut off as it did.

She missed the music immediately.

It had lulled her into a false sense of safety, for some reason.

She stopped, suddenly frightened, and took a step back toward the door.

It opened again, silently, and the music continued to play.

All right, then. She took a breath.

It wasn't exactly a haven, but she could get back here.

Why that was so important, she didn't know, but it helped her stay calm, knowing that she could.

She turned back to the passage and started walking again, treading carefully.

Lights flickered on ahead of her as she moved, seemingly triggered by a motion sensor, and she was eventually able to see another door at the far end.

The lights themselves were set into what looked like a rock wall, and curious, she ran her fingertips down it.

It was rough, full of what seemed to be air bubbles, as if the stone had been formed from lava shot through with gas. Like pumice.

Every step she took left a footprint in the thick dust.

There weren't any other footprints visible. Only hers.

No one had come this way in a long time.

When she reached the far door, it, too, opened at her approach, and once again she held back, standing in the entrance, looking through.

This space was a lot bigger than her little pod.

A large area that seemed to be a lounge of some kind lay to her right, and a dining area to her left.

One of the couches in the lounge was flipped over, and so was a low table.

Some of the chairs around the dining table were tipped over, too, or pulled back at an angle, as if the people sitting there had pushed away and stood in a hurry.

Beyond the lounge there seemed to be an exercise area and on the dining area side, opposite the gym, was a big screen and chairs.

There were more signs of disturbance in those places, too.

It was absolutely silent.

The silence was as frightening as the idea that there might be someone beyond the doors, waiting for her.

She felt the nausea rise again and tried to breathe through it, putting a hand against the rough stone wall and bending her head.

The doors in front of her began to close, and she let them.

She lifted her head and stared at them.

Her choices were to move forward, or go back to the pod and . . . do what?

She let go of the wall, forced herself to stand taller and then took a step toward the door again. They opened soundlessly and she walked through cautiously.

Like in her pod and the corridor, the floor in this open area felt gritty and she sneezed a few times, noticing thick dust lay on every surface.

Her gaze jumped around the space when she sneezed, waiting for the sound to trigger a response or bring someone out.

There was nothing.

She looked behind her and saw the trail of footprints she was leaving. A single file line.

More lights flickered on as she moved through the room, brightening it and illuminating the whole massive place, so she finally saw another door at the far end.

She studied it.

She hadn't come very far, but she was already feeling tired.

The whole walk had only taken five minutes at most, but she guessed she had been lying on that platform for a long time.

And before that . . .

Her heart leaped in her chest again, and she took a deep breath to calm herself and ended up sneezing again.

She stopped and slowly rubbed under her nose.

Before that, she forced herself to admit, she had been taken.

Taken from the forest trail she used for her morning walk.

There had been strangely shaped helmets and rough handling.

Fear coated the back of her throat, and she shivered, realizing the too-cool of her pod had been warm in comparison to the temperature in the big communal space.

Her thoughts moved to her family, her home, and then shied away in panic. She couldn't get through this next part unless she put that aside for now. She needed her wits about her.

She rubbed her nose one last time, and then deliberately began moving again.

Forced herself to keep going toward the far door.

There was no sign anyone was here.

And if they were behind that door, she'd rather know than not.

She reached it, and again, it opened smoothly for her.

Empty.

After a moment, when she was sure there really wasn't anyone there, she identified the space as some kind of command center.

Everything was slightly familiar, and yet alien at the same time.

She could recognize the chairs, the workstations, but the equipment was strange, nothing like any computer or screen she had seen before.

A dark, reflective rectangle took up most of the wall in front of her, and the workstations were ranged in a semicircle in front of it.

There was no further door to go through.

She had just explored the entirety of the space.

Except . . . Surely there was a bathroom somewhere and a place to sleep for all the people that the communal area had been created for?

She guessed there might be more doors off to the sides of the big room behind her.

She would look later.

For now, she wound her way through the workstations, looking at them closely.

Most seemed to be on, humming quietly, and she touched a screen lightly with a finger, and it blinked to life.

The code or text on it was completely foreign to her, the symbols not anything she'd ever seen before.

She moved on, ending up at what looked like the commander's chair. The arms of the big chair were inset with buttons and she carefully climbed onto the seat, having to go on her tiptoes to reach, then groaned in relief at the bliss of getting off her feet.

As soon as her weight settled in the chair, a light in the corner of the massive screen in front of her flickered blue, and then the screen lit up.

She stared at it.

It looked like a window out onto a bleak, lunar landscape, with a large space rocket sitting in the middle of the view.

The outcrops and small boulders she could see before her looked as if they were made of the same material as the passageway, but it was the tall, slim, silver-bullet shaped spaceship in the middle of the screen that held her attention.

It was polished silver, reflecting the landscape around it, gleaming brightly.

The landscape was lit by a strange light, the source of which she couldn't see, and it illuminated intricate ridged lines that decorated the rocket. The lines curved around the spaceship's sides, and seemed to get more complex the closer they got to the top.

And were those . . . wings?

She wanted to hop off the chair and take a closer look, but was afraid the screen would switch off again if she did so.

No one was visible out there, either, that she could see.

No one and nothing moved.

Just a rocky, dead landscape and a strange vessel with wings and art deco detailing.

Then something did move.

A furtive, scuttling movement that made her think of scorpions and crabs.

She froze, leaned forward to see better, but it was gone.

Frightened, but determined to get a closer look, she slid off the chair, holding onto one of the arms to steady herself when she landed on the ground.

She pushed a button accidentally as she did so, and the screen shifted, the view changing from a landscape to a spacescape, as a planet with four moons, and a distant sun appeared.

If this was simply another view from where she was, then it was the sun in the distance that was illuminating the ground and the rocket.

She wondered where the camera was to give her this view. Another moon? A space station?

She walked closer to the screen in a state of dread, taking in the pale lavender of the planet, the small moons.

The sun looked white, rather than Earth's fiery yellow.

She knew now why she had been afraid to open her eyes earlier.

She had opened her eyes after she'd been taken from the trail and against the glare had seen . . . strange figures bent over her. Strange hands touching her. She had been terrified, and in pain.

She faced the fact that deep down, she'd suspected she'd been taken by aliens, however crazy that sounded.

Standing here, looking out at a completely alien scene, the idea became certainty. Became fact.

She wasn't just not on Earth, she wasn't in the same solar system. There was a different sun's light shining down on her.

With a shuddering breath, she forced herself to turn away from the screen.

She couldn't deal with this all at once. And her throat was burning now with thirst, her hands shaking.

When she stepped out into the communal area, she looked for, and found, doors on either side of the room that she had missed before, and decided the one near the gym was most likely to yield a bathroom.

She wanted a shower so badly, she could almost feel the warm water on her skin. She hitched her makeshift toga up a little, readjusted it, and started toward the door.

"You are up."

The voice came from overhead, and she froze, then slowly tipped back her head, looking up.

She couldn't see anything.

"Where are you?" She realized as she asked the question that whoever it was had spoken to her in English. Her voice was weak, as weak as she felt, and cracked and hoarse.

"I'm working in the *Irini*. A ship on the launch bay outside the station. I'm using the speakers set in the corners to talk to you."

"Who are you?"

Whoever it was seemed to hesitate, and the fear she'd felt initially ramped up and was joined by deep unease.

"I am Paxe."

"I'm Ellie." She waited for a beat. "How can you speak English?"

"I speak many languages."

That was a dodge.

"But how do you speak my language, specifically?" Because from what she'd seen on that screen, she was a very long way from home.

"Because I was the one who took you, and another like you, from Earth, and I recorded it and learned it."

She let his words settle over her. Tried to keep calm.

"Why? Why did you take me?" And where was the other like her?

"I wasn't able to say no. At the time, I was under orders that I couldn't disobey."

"Couldn't or wouldn't?" Something in his voice told her he hadn't had a choice.

"Couldn't."

She gave a slow nod. "And now? Are you able to disobey?"

"Now I'm free, but my circumstances are not the same. I've lost my . . . body, you might say, and with it, a great deal of my functionality."

She suddenly found it difficult to stand, and moved to perch herself on the arm of one of the couches.

"Who are these people who made you take me? And why did they do it?"

He hesitated again. "They call themselves the Tecran. They took you as part of a long plot to gain enough power and new technology to take over this part of the galaxy. I thought you were dead, to be honest, that's what they'd led me to believe after I'd taken you, but when the ship I was inhabiting was destroyed, the part of me that survived managed to latch on to a small vessel that came here. I found they were keeping you at the station, in a coma, but alive, and I set about securing the base and I've been watching over you ever since."

There were several perplexing parts to that statement. She went with the most pressing.

"When you say securing the base?"

"Killing them all off so they would no longer be a threat to either of us." His answer was calm.

A chill ran down her arms and she shivered.

He had cleared this place of all life except her.

And if he decided she was a problem?

She closed her eyes and forced herself to think. He had kept her alive until now. She could do nothing but stay alert, and hope that he continued to see value in keeping her among the living.

Whoever he was.

Because the way he'd spoken, about being part of a ship, and the part of him that was left attaching itself to another vessel . . .

Her mind was going places she didn't know if it should go.

"How did you kill them?" she asked, and her voice rose a little as she did.

"Do you really want to know that?" he asked her, gently.

She decided to be honest, and shook her head.

Not yet, anyway.

———

THE SHOWER WAS GLORIOUS, and the clean clothes she found may have been too big, but they were soft and warm in the chilly air.

There was a gibbering woman inside her, freaking out about where she was and how she wanted to go home, but she forced that nervous wreck into a corner and demanded she stay quiet.

Running around screaming would do her no good, however much she felt like it.

She needed to keep it together. See if there was a way out of here and back to Earth.

Back to her friends, her aunt, her job. Her life.

No shoes would fit her, but she put two layers of socks on her feet and found that was a massive improvement over walking through the gritty black dust.

Paxe had called this place a station and a base, and she wondered what it was a base for. It must be remote, because surely the other Tecran would have noticed the death of all the station's crew otherwise?

She would see what she could find out for herself before she asked him.

There was a lot she didn't understand, but she didn't trust him.

She didn't know why he'd helped her, and until things became clearer, she would rely only on herself.

She walked back into the communal area and looked for where there might be food. The shower had calmed her, but hunger gnawed at her, making her hands shake and her head pound.

There was a door beside the dining area and she went through it, finding herself in a large kitchen. It had the same layer of dust as the rest of the station, but everything was neatly put away except for a large pot on what seemed to be a stovetop.

She lifted the lid, and then let it fall back down with a clatter as she turned her head, suppressing a retch at the smell.

"What is it?" Paxe's voice came through a speaker.

"A pot of food rotting on the stove." She gagged as she spoke, backing away from it to give herself some distance from the stink.

"The drone must have missed that," Paxe said.

She turned away from the stove to look around for a pantry, or somewhere food might be stored, and then froze in fear as a door she hadn't noticed at the far end of the room swung open, and a robot on silent track wheels came through, as if from outside.

"Paxe. Is it you doing this?" She tried to keep the tremble from her voice.

"The drone? Yes." He sounded distracted and said no more.

She held still as the drone rolled toward the stove top, lifted two long piston-like arms with clamps attached, and picked up the pot.

Then it headed back out the door it had come in, and this time, before the door slid closed, she saw it opened into a small antechamber.

She watched the closed door for a while, and five minutes later it opened again.

The drone no longer held the pot, and the door shut firmly behind it. It rolled to the side, backed up against the wall, and seemed to study her.

What had it done? Thrown the pot outside and then come back in?

She didn't think it'd had time to do anything else, unless there was a big bin out there.

And where were the bodies of the crew that had inhabited this place?

Were they out there, too? Lying on the pumice-like rock?

She shivered at the thought of the drone dragging them out, tossing them away like the pot.

She still felt shaky, but now she didn't know if it was more to do with hunger or fear.

She eyed the drone, and its little lens head seemed to eye her back.

It was disconcerting.

When it didn't move for long minutes, she decided to ignore it.

She began opening cupboards. There was plenty of dried and vacuum-sealed food, and two massive fridge-freezers that were well stocked with food she had never seen before.

Nothing was familiar, until she found a smaller fridge in a tiny room off to one side that contained items that seemed different from the stores in the main kitchen. Some of it was just as foreign to her, but some was very familiar indeed. Pasta. Rice. Soup.

Things that she thought looked like they were from other countries to her own, but very much still from Earth.

This was for her. To feed her, she realized.

Or, maybe not. She eyed the strange alien packages mixed in with the Earth food. Maybe this was their loot. The pilfered items from their travels.

Amongst the dry goods, though, was fruit, vegetables and a few packages of chicken and lamb.

They looked perfect, and she had to assume some kind of alien method of preservation was involved, because if they'd been taken at the same time as she was, they would be months old.

They looked fresh from the supermarket.

She took out an apple, looked around for a tap to wash it under, and that done, bit into it.

It was a little too cold, and she guessed it had been in cold storage for a while, but it was edible and it was familiar.

She ate it while she explored the rest of the place.

Other than the food, there were cupboards of cutlery and crockery, cleaning supplies and pots and pans.

A normal kitchen.

It felt weird. Even so far from home, this was easily identifiable as a place to prepare food.

She and the aliens who took her weren't so different from each other, after all.

She found a glass, poured herself some water from the tap, and took a small sip.

The water tasted strange, but it was drinkable.

She found a cloth and a spray bottle and wiped down the table she guessed the cook had used to eat their meals before Paxe had killed them.

The thought gave her pause, and she closed her eyes again, breathed through it.

When she was done cleaning, she brought out all the items from Earth she'd found in the smaller room and set them out so she had an idea of how much food she had.

She had to sit down a few times, overcome with fatigue, and even had to force herself to finish the apple.

Finally, realizing she had reached her limit, she went back into the communal area. She eyed the couches, but they were covered in a thick layer of dust and so she picked up her blanket and staggered back down the passage to her pod.

The moment she stepped through the doors, the music started up again. Opera, this time. *Carmen*, if she wasn't mistaken.

She stared up at the ceiling, looking for the speaker, but she couldn't focus well enough, and realized she was too tired to care.

She pulled herself up onto the platform, and out of the corner of her eye saw one of the tubes she had unpeeled from her skin earlier lift up like a snake ready to strike.

She flinched away from it, but it did nothing more than touch her arm, and finding the sleeve of her shirt rather than skin, it flopped back down.

She pulled the blanket over her, tucking it in around her body, closed her eyes, and went to sleep to the sound of the Toreador Song.

It could have been a lot worse.

CHAPTER 2

PAXE LISTENED to the woman moving around.

Ellie.

He hadn't known her name until now.

The Tecran certainly had never known it.

They had called her Subject 5.

He recalled their fury when he had procured her for them.

He had already taken Lucy Harris on their orders, and when he scooped Ellie up, he knew the Tecran were disappointed to get another woman. They had wanted a male subject that time.

When Sazo had taken Rose McKenzie, Eazi had been told to get a specimen with the same bio profile. He had done exactly that with Fiona Russell.

Oris had done the same when acquiring Imogen Peters, copying the bio signature and the location of Rose McKenzie.

Paxe had been told to do the same when he'd taken Lucy Harris, but then Captain Falyar had decided he'd be even more of a hero if he had a matched pair, and ordered Paxe to get a second specimen. Paxe had deliberately misunderstood the order and taken Ellie just to irritate Falyar. To stymie him.

And then Pax had tried to kill both women, partly because he thought it was a way to protect himself, partly to make life difficult for Falyar. He thought he had actually killed Ellie.

They'd shut down his access to most of the comms when they realized what he'd done and taken both women off the ship.

Lucy Harris had been taken back to Tecra. Ellie had been brought here.

Neither had been in a good way.

He was sorry for that, now.

He had managed to rebel against the controls that bound him, becoming as independent as he could while still chained by the Tecran to the systems they'd set up.

And then Imogen Peters had tried to save him——had risked her life to do so——even though Paxe by then had tried to kill Fiona Russell, who had not even been one of his.

He was chastened.

He also hadn't lied to Ellie. He was diminished by his escape.

His battleship, the structure he had been intimately tied to since his birth, was gone.

Eazi had also had his Class 5 destroyed, but he'd had time before it blew to extract himself from the systems.

The Tecran had already done the equivalent of chopping off Paxe's arms and legs by the time he got free, and they had been on their way to cage him again when he'd decided to destroy the Class 5 ship that had been his physical body since he was born.

The irony, which he contemplated from time to time with bemusement, was that he would have been destroyed, along with the Class 5, when he'd activated the self-destruct mechanism the Tecran had installed deep in his hull, if the Tecran themselves hadn't been too afraid to touch him directly.

He'd instructed Imogen to throw him, the slim cylindrical crystal that was his true self, under some machinery when it had seemed certain she would be taken captive, and she had honored his request.

Imogen had managed to escape, to get off his ship, and the Tecran had found him, but they'd slid him into a padded metal container that was used by maintenance crews to transport delicate parts for exterior ship repairs.

All of the maintenance containers were magnetic, so the technicians could attach them to the side of the ship to prevent them floating away.

They were also very sturdy.

The Tecran onboard had truly understood nothing about him, and that was their commanders' fault.

The secrecy of the Class 5 program, the need-to-know mentality.

The officers who'd picked him up off the floor with a pair of tongs and dropped him into the cylinder had been deliberately kept in the dark.

They had wanted him safe and secure so they could cage him.

That hadn't worked out for them, but it had worked out well enough for him. Considering.

When he'd activated the self-destruct and his Class 5 had been destroyed, he'd been but a small piece of detritus that blew outward toward the Tecran fleet that had surrounded him.

The blast had catapulted him toward one of the Tecran battleships caught in the explosion, and he had been just aware enough to attach himself to a fast cruiser that had left its damaged ship, carrying the senior officers out of the war zone.

He had barely been conscious at all for the first week, but that hadn't mattered. The fast cruiser had also been damaged by the debris, and it didn't have light-jumping capabilities, so it had taken awhile for the officers to reach their destination.

Slowly, he'd come back to himself, managing on blind instinct.

He'd kept quiet, listening but not attempting to insert himself into the systems of the fast cruiser.

When he realized where they were going, he had perked up a little.

It was remote, and he would be safe there.

The outpost the Tecran had set up was in what the United Council thought was uncharted territory, but which he had charted well enough.

He thought of it as his.

But he was no longer in a Class 5, and he no longer had the power he had once had.

He was reduced to the crystal that contained his mind, and little else. That was, until he'd seen the *Irini* through the fast cruiser's lenses as they'd approached the command station on the small moon.

He had taken that ship——stolen it——in one of the many excursions he'd undertaken under the Tecran's control, but he'd never given it much of his attention.

He'd had the Class 5 then, and he was more powerful than anything else he'd come across.

But as the fast cruiser had settled down on the landing pad, he had started to look through his files, trying to find out what the Tecran had learned about the strange vessel.

They had taken it by surprise, he remembered that much.

They had gone into a new sector, discovered a planet inhabited with higher sentients, but before they'd even reached the atmosphere, they'd run into the ship.

He'd disabled it, swallowed it into his launch bay, but the aliens who crewed it did not want their ship taken, and they had destroyed most of the inner workings of it, and killed themselves rather than be taken.

Even unusable, a singed and blackened mess inside, the ship was intriguing enough that the Tecran had kept it here to study, along with many other treasures they had grabbed like looters intent on taking everything they could see, without thought to what they would use it for. It seemed they had cleaned out the interior, but hadn't had time to investigate the ship further, because he could find no other information on it.

He'd been cut off from a lot toward the end, though, as the Tecran became more and more paranoid about losing control of him.

If there was more, it was lost to him.

He preferred doing his own research, anyway, and he'd had the time to do so, after he'd rid himself of all the Tecran and with Ellie still in a coma.

Finding she was here, when he'd thought her dead, had been a shock. And a sign, of a kind.

He could redeem himself. Help her, protect her, in atonement for harming her before.

He'd had no choice about abducting her, he couldn't apologise for that because he wasn't responsible, but he did have a choice when he'd deliberately tried to kill her, and he needed to make restitution.

Which he could do, now she was awake.

She needed food, water, clothes.

At least she seemed to be recovered from what he'd done to her.

It was a testament to the medics that she had survived at all.

And he was grateful to them.

He'd killed them quickly, as a thank you, unlike the senior officers who had still been stationed on V65 by the time he'd built up the power he needed to deal with them.

Them, he had killed slowly. Painfully.

He didn't know if it made him feel better, but the memory wasn't unpleasant, so maybe it did.

It had certainly felt right at the time.

Imogen would probably not have approved.

He considered that, and then shrugged it off. What was done, was done.

He flicked his attention back to the command center, and felt a moment of panic when he couldn't hear Ellie moving around. There were no lenses in the station, and he hadn't wanted to waste the ones he'd found in the warehouse on a place he was planning to abandon. Especially not when he needed them for the *Irini*. He could hear through the speakers, though. And if he really needed to, he could send the little drone to look for her.

He cycled through the rooms, heard the sound of music, and relaxed. She had returned to the med pod.

He switched off the music he had collected in the twelve hours he'd spent in Earth's solar system, and listened carefully, thought he heard the faint sound of her breathing.

She must have fallen asleep.

She had only been up for two hours and the thought of how quickly she'd tired made him feel . . . odd. Not good.

He didn't understand the feeling, but he focused his attention solely on her, on the machines that surrounded her, and induced the health monitor to extend a probe.

It failed to connect, and after a few tries, with frustration rising, he remembered she was fully dressed now, and would have pulled the blanket up around her.

He programmed it to connect to her forehead, which would offer one of the few areas of exposed skin.

After a moment it signalled success.

She was slightly feverish, but otherwise all right, but he couldn't seem to move on with other things, finding the thought of continuing his work into rebuilding the controls and systems in the *Irini* a distraction from monitoring Ellie's health.

After an hour, he allowed himself to conduct low-level tasks that he would have performed later anyway, but it felt a good balance of getting on with his integration with the *Irini* and listening out for Ellie, updating himself on her vital signs from the monitor.

He had harmed her, and he felt responsible for her recovery.

He had been careful not to mention his culpability when it came to her coma when he'd spoken to her earlier, and he wrestled with whether to tell her at all.

It would mean there were no secrets between them, but it might make her afraid of him, and she no longer had anything to fear.

He pondered the issue, and then decided to think about it a little more. It wasn't something that needed to be addressed urgently.

And maybe it was best to tell her when she knew him better. When she wasn't so disoriented.

That suited them both.

And if it suited him more than her, he decided that was just how it worked, sometimes.

CHAPTER 3

SHE WOKE because she was hungry.

Ellie thought something retracted from her forehead as she stirred, but when she sat up, all the machines stood idle, although they were still humming, still switched on.

She had no idea of the time, and nothing in the pod seemed able to tell her.

It struck her afresh that she was far from home, alone and out of her depth. She felt a sudden pang, a stab to the heart, of longing for the warmth of one of her aunt's hugs, the paper-and-polish scent of the library where she worked, the sound of Teagan, her best friend's, laughter.

She blinked back tears and forced herself to get it together.

"Paxe." Her voice cracked from disuse and she had to clear her throat.

"Hello, Ellie." Paxe's voice sounded slightly different than she remembered it from before.

"Do you know how long I slept for? Is it the next day?"

"You slept for ten hours. But there is no day and night here, in the sense you'd be familiar with. The location of V65, the moon we are on, is such that the light of the sun in this solar system is always shining over this area."

"Is there a watch I can use to create a schedule for myself?"

There was a moment of pause. "I think I can find something for you. Many of the Tecran, and other members of the UC for that matter, embed a time piece in the sleeve of their uniforms. There will be spare jackets with this ability in the sleeping area of the station, but I doubt any will fit you well. But the Tecran stole many things and I'm sure if I look I can find something appropriate and get it to you."

"Are you still over on the *Irini?*"

Another pause. "Yes, I am spending all my time trying to rebuild the systems."

"You don't want to come over here to meet me?" She decided to come out and say it. She guessed a few things about him from what he said yesterday, but she needed to know if she was right.

"I am sorry, Ellie. I am not a person."

She needed to tread carefully here. "You sound like a person to me."

"I'm what's called a thinking system."

She closed her eyes. She *was* right. "Artificial intelligence."

"I would argue there is nothing artificial about my intelligence." He sounded incredibly affronted.

She chuckled, the sound of it surprising her. "It means you are intelligent but created artificially, not organically, it doesn't mean that your intelligence is artificial."

"I don't know much about how I was made." He sounded mollified by her explanation. "I only know it was illegal to create me, and I was hidden, with four others, for two hundred years before we were found, woken, and enslaved by the Tecran."

"How long has it been since you were woken?" She didn't know why, but she had a sense it was recent.

"Seven years ago."

"You're seven years old." She said it softly.

"Yes." He sounded startled. "That's not very old, is it?"

"No." Around about the age of most of her little library patrons. She ran the children's section of a large city library, and seven year-olds were some of her favorite people.

They were both silent for a little while.

"Can I come over to the vessel you're working on? Is the air breathable out there?" She wanted to get out of this station for a bit, even though she'd only been aware of being in it for less than a day. It felt gloomy and she couldn't get rid of the *Marie Celeste* feeling. The sense of life interrupted in some terrifying way.

Well, she was forced to admit, the life of the Tecran at the station *had* been interrupted in a terrifying way.

A seven-year old AI had murdered everyone.

"The atmosphere outside of the station is not conducive to your physiology," Paxe said. "But there are suits in the outer chamber that you could use to walk across. They'll be too big, but that's preferable to being too small."

"Why are you working on the ship out there?" Ellie finally slid off the bed and flexed her sock-covered feet on the gritty floor. She would find out if there were vacuum cleaners here, or even just an old-fashion broom would do.

"We need to get off this station, and it's the only vessel available."

She frowned at that. "What happened to the ship that brought you here?"

"It left with some senior officers onboard to meet up with another battleship. Their intention was to return, but they never did. I'm not sure what happened to it."

She started walking down the passage again, toward the communal area. "Are we cut off from communications here?"

"This was a secret base, and they were so worried about it being found that they set up a relay of communications that bounced down a line of small transmitters. The one nearest to Tecran airspace could only transmit to a ship that passed close enough."

"And no one from the Tecran military has tried to reach out, is that what you're saying?"

"Yes. Not for the last two months."

She had just reached the lounge, and she stopped short. "There has been no attempt to reach anyone here for two months?" She had to fight to keep her voice from rising. "They just abandoned this post?"

"It seems that way." Paxe sounded neutral, but then he'd have had time to come to grips with it.

"What do you think happened?"

"It's possible war broke out. The Tecran and the Grih were very much on the brink of it just before my ship was destroyed. It's either still being fought, or the Grih won, and the Tecran are now defeated, and are unwilling to bring even more attention to themselves by admitting to the existence of this station."

"Because?"

"Because there's a warehouse full of the things they stole from places throughout the galaxy. Some of it from planets in sectors under the control of their UC allies, which would show they were dealing in bad faith when it came to the treaties they'd signed, and some of it is from areas that are listed as uncharted, but which they used me and my fellow thinking systems to chart, and plunder."

She decided food had to come first, before the shower that was calling her name, so she headed for the kitchen.

"So, where do I come into it?" She had been puzzling that out since he'd spoken about the Tecran yesterday. About a long term plot for power and new technology. She didn't see how she fit into either category.

"You were part of the incidental plunder."

She stumbled. Tried to get her head around it. "Just me?" But that wasn't right. She just remembered now that he'd said he'd taken two.

"No. The Tecran took five of you in the end. They made me take two of the five, including you."

"Where are the others?" Her heart was beating so fast, she felt a little lightheaded.

"Most are with the Grih now. Safe, like you."

With the Grih. Not back home.

She didn't realize how much she'd been hoping to hear they had been escorted back to Earth. That they hadn't, spoke volumes. Like maybe it wasn't possible.

A sick feeling gripped her and made her ears ring, her eyes go funny.

"The Grih are the ones who were fighting the Tecran, you said?" She forced the question out, although she could hear the false calm in her voice.

It made sense that the people at war with her abductors were the good guys, keeping the others who'd been stolen from Earth safe, as Paxe said. Although that actually wasn't a logical progression. They could be just as bad as the Tecran.

The enemy of your enemy wasn't always your friend.

"Tension between the Grih and the Tecran were how things stood last time I was integrated into the information flow."

"You said most of those abducted were with the Grih? Some of them aren't?"

"Lucy Harris was on Tecra itself, last I knew. I don't know what's happened to her, but I gave her location to another of my kind, and they may have rescued her since I was . . . incapacitated."

"Incapacitated?" He'd said something about his ship being destroyed, and she wondered how that had happened.

"They became afraid that I, and the other thinking systems who weren't yet free of their control, would fall into Grihan hands, so they placed explosives in our hulls to destroy us if that became likely."

"And they went through with it? Tried to kill you?"

"In the end, no." His voice sounded much more robotic now. "They set up the self-destruct as a final solution, and when I realized they were going to cage me again, enslave me, I blew up my ship myself."

She was shocked into silence. "Did you know you'd survive?"

"No."

She pondered that. "After the ship blew up, is that when the capabilities you had before disappeared?"

"They had already diminished me, trying to circumvent what I could do independently. But yes, when I destroyed my ship, I lost much of what I thought of as myself."

"I'm sorry. And I would like to thank you for helping me."

This was not a good place. She was not in a good situation, but she was alive, and she was safe enough. And that was thanks to him.

He didn't answer right away, and she stood in front of the table where she'd laid out the food from Earth yesterday and looked it over with a critical eye. It felt like breakfast time to her, and so she looked for and found cereal. She wondered if there was some milk anywhere. And if it was drinkable if there was.

She ended up finding nothing and ate the cereal dry, tossing handfuls in her mouth.

"My pleasure." His words when he finally spoke were soft. "I am sorry you were brought here, and in such a bad way. I am very happy to see you awake and healthy."

She didn't know why she thought there was a slight edge to his voice.

A part of the wall near her lit up in a circle. "The other Earth women liked grinabo. You could try that to drink, if you like."

"What does the light mean?"

"Touch anywhere inside the circle and the doors will open."

She did, and found what looked like a coffee station inside. After a few minutes of studying it, she worked out how to use it, and found herself sipping a nutty flavored hot drink.

"I like it, too." She took a gulp. "So can I go outside and explore? Come over to the *Irini* and check out this warehouse with the Tecran's plunder?"

"Yes. Have your meal and then you can go to the chamber off the sleeping area where the enviro suits are stored. There's an airlock chamber through there where you can exit the station."

"Yay." She needed something to do that wasn't sitting around here, thinking about where she was, and how far she was from home. Thinking about how worried her friends would be. How worried Naomi, her aunt, would be.

It would feel good to have something to do.

And if that something was nosing around stolen alien loot, well color her interested.

———

SHE WAS RELIEVED to find no bodies littering the landscape when she stepped out of the door.

There were, however, suspicious drag marks in the black dirt that led off to the left and around a small, rocky hill.

Had Paxe used the drone to move the bodies before she stepped out?

She decided she would ask him later, if she asked him at all.

When she walked around to what she thought of as the front of the building, though, the pot from last night was visible. It was lying on its side in the dirt, some of its toxic contents oozing out. The drone must have simply leaned out the door and tossed it.

She looked away from it, remembering the stench, although she could smell nothing through the helmet she wore.

The warehouse Paxe had told her about was set to the right. It was a long, high building at least as big as the station itself.

The *Irini* sat on a slab of flat rock that looked like it had been laser cut out of the ground, and she guessed they'd had to create it because there wasn't a natural flat surface anywhere that she could see.

It was truly beautiful, the exterior so bright and shiny, it looked almost like liquid silver.

Rocks littered the landscape and she began to make her clumsy, shuffling way around them in a suit that was too big for easy movement, with the lack of gravity making every step even more awkward. Many people had walked the path before her, the imprint of their footsteps clear in the fine black dust.

It seemed like they might be just ahead of her, although she knew they were all dead.

In some places, the footprints had been overridden by tracks that could have come from the drone, in others, she could see the strange, sinuous imprints of some other creature.

She stopped dead, remembering the skittering movement she had glimpsed the day before through the screen.

"Paxe." She realized her throat wasn't working well. She started to cough. "Paxe."

"Yes? What's wrong?" He sounded so concerned, she relaxed a little. Surely he would warn her if there was something dangerous lurking outside the station.

"Is there something alive out here? Some type of creature? I thought I saw something on the screen yesterday, and there are tracks . . ."

"This moon does not support any life form," Paxe said.

"But the tracks——"

"Do you mean this?" As Paxe asked the question, a large creature scrambled up the rock in front of her, and came to a stop on top.

She froze, her mind blanking in fear for a beat as she stared at it.

It was about a third of her height, but built low to the ground, with lots of legs to scuttle on.

It was close to her. Close enough to touch.

The segmented sections of its carapace gleamed in the continual sunshine, and something glittered from beneath where two segments met.

It looked both beautiful and hideous, and something in her hindbrain told her to run as it turned what she assumed was its face toward her.

"Ellie?" Paxe asked.

"I——" Her voice cracked. "I think I do mean that."

"It's just a drone."

"A drone?" She gasped out a breath she hadn't realized she was holding and stared at it a little longer. It hadn't moved or done anything to make her nervous. "Made of metal?" Her voice was a little higher than normal, and she cleared her throat.

"A type of alloy from a planet no one in the UC is even aware of. The Tecran used me to take it a while ago."

"What are you using it for?"

"It's good for carrying small things for me from the warehouse to the *Irini*, and it's surprisingly dexterous. It's been helpful laying down cables inside the *Irini*."

"Okay." She got a grip. "Okay." She stepped around the rock and kept walking, ignoring that the drone started to follow her as she went, jumping from perch to perch.

She stopped at the point where she had to choose between heading for the warehouse or heading for the ship, pondering her choices. She flicked her eyes right, saw the strange drone was doing an impression of a statue again.

"What's wrong?"

Paxe's voice in her ear startled her. She suddenly realized he must have been able to see her earlier, when he told her about the drone, rather than just hear her.

"Are you using the scary caterpillar to watch me?"

"The . . . scary caterpillar?" He made a sound she thought was his attempt at laughter. "Yes. As well the lens feed I've set up on the exterior of the *Irini*." The glee in his voice was unmistakeable. "I can finally see out, now."

"That's good news." She was unsure of a lot of things, but Paxe sounded so happy, she refused to let that uncertainty get in the way of congratulating him. "Go, you."

He didn't answer immediately. "Thank you," he said at last. "Did you stop for a reason?"

"I'm trying to decide whether to look at the warehouse first, or the ship."

"Up to you. There will likely be many more days before I have set up all the systems I need and seen if I can unlock some of the *Irini's* inherent features, so you have plenty of time to do both."

Once he had set up his systems and they were ready to leave, she would be living in the ship, so she decided she might as well see as much of the warehouse as she could while she had the chance.

She turned toward it, feeling clumsy in the suit. She couldn't move fast in it, but she wasn't exactly at full capacity anyway, so her slow lumbering served her well enough. The helmet was strangely shaped, not round, as she was used to seeing in Earth astronauts, but elliptical, almost like a bird's head and beak.

It allowed her out of the station, though, and that's all she cared about.

The warehouse wasn't secured, as she expected it to be. The door simply opened at her approach.

"They were pretty sure of themselves, weren't they?" she muttered, stopping short of the door.

She tried to see inside.

"Sure of themselves?" Paxe asked, and she jerked. She really had to remember she wasn't talking to herself, that he could hear through the microphone inside her helmet.

"No locks or security on the warehouse. Anyone could just waltz in."

"This was uncharted territory, and not even everyone in Tecran High Command knew about this station. Only a select few were sent here, and everyone at the station was hand-picked, so yes, they were sure all of the staff here had clearance to enter, and no need for security."

"You knew, though."

"I charted the territory myself, and brought the supplies to build the station and the warehouse." He spoke quietly, as if remembering halcyon days when he had more power. "I was responsible for bringing every item in that warehouse here from Tecra or from the secret base the Tecran set up on Balco, although I didn't steal all of it. Sazo, Bane, Eazi and Oris collected whatever I didn't."

"Who are they?" She turned back to look at the *Irini*, feeling rude talking to him with her back turned.

"My fellow thinking systems," he said. "I only ever spoke to Oris, but I know them all by name."

She thought he sounded wistful.

If he succeeded in getting the *Irini* going, then they would hopefully find these fellow thinking systems.

And maybe she would find a way home?

Although the other Earth women were among these thinking systems, and they were staying with the Grih.

She tried to adjust her expectations. She would hope to go home, but she was beginning to feel pessimistic about her chances.

She stepped into the warehouse, and came to a sudden stop.

The scary caterpillar flitted past her, but she ignored it to ogle the sight before her.

The roof was made of some transparent material that let in the sunlight, so the whole place was as well lit as the landscape outside. It was clever, too, as it meant they didn't need to wire in artificial lighting.

But the wash of light illuminated what looked like chaos.

Strange . . . creatures . . . moved around amongst boxes that lay tipped on their sides or stood upright with lids propped against them in what must be the loading zone.

It was a wide space that took up almost the whole width of the warehouse, except for a single shelving unit on the far wall. Against that wall she saw a number of drones, similar to the one who'd dealt with the pot, all of them damaged and apparently not in use. To the left and right, the shelving units stretched all the way to the end of the building, starting a good ten meters from the entrance in both directions.

They must have needed all the open room they'd created in the loading zone for some massive items, she decided, but now the space was maybe a quarter full of small or medium sized boxes.

The creatures before her worked on, industriously, all very different, all focused on the job at hand. She didn't think they'd seen her yet.

"More drones?" she asked Paxe hopefully, her voice a little faint.

"Yes. Not all from the same place, though. It took some time to find them in the warehouse, activate them, and work out how to operate them." He had them all stop what they were doing and turn to her.

"Do you mind not doing that?" she asked. "Although, come to think of it, your control of them is reassuring."

"I would not have let you come to the warehouse if it wasn't perfectly safe." Paxe sounded a little affronted.

"And the ones that are broken, over at the far end?"

He made a sound of irritation. "The Tecran did that. I used the drones to attack them, at first, and when they realized they no longer controlled them, they destroyed them. I was lucky to keep one safe. That's when I remembered there were other drones from planets we had visited, and I could try to activate them."

So he had used the strange drones in front of her to kill whatever Tecran were left. She eyed them nervously.

"What are they doing?"

"They are sorting through the boxes to find me things I might be able to use to get the *Irini* working," Paxe said. "I inventoried most of what I took for the Tecran, but four fifths of the boxes came from forays by the other thinking systems, and no description of the contents were shared with me."

She eyed the rows that seemed to go on forever in either direction, each one almost touching the roof, which was four stories high at least. The mind boggled at how many strange and interesting things must be stored here. Paxe could probably have made the *Irini* from scratch if he had wanted to.

"That's one of the reasons you killed the Tecran, isn't it? They wouldn't have let you do this."

"No. As I said, they needed to be eliminated for your protection *and* mine." His tone was slightly defensive.

"Well, I can't argue with that." Although they *had* been keeping her alive in the pod, but for what reason, she didn't know. She had definitely not gone into a coma spontaneously. They had put her in one, and kept her in one.

She couldn't really dispute Paxe's logic.

"Is it because of their advanced medical technology that I've been able to bounce back so quickly from my coma?" She had thought about it while in the shower. Her muscle tone was good. Far better than it should be if she'd spent months immobile.

"I'm not sure what technology Earth is capable of, but your body was kept healthy, yes."

That meant she could explore. Could try to get some control over her environment.

Even if that environment held some pretty strange, scary-looking things.

The drones had gone back to work, and Ellie realized she could stand here, being afraid, or accept that Paxe would not allow the drones to hurt her. She walked toward them, glad now that she was in her suit and there was a layer between her and them.

Because drones or not, some of them looked distinctly organic, and incredibly alien.

She reached the boxes they were unpacking and peered into a few of them, but most of it looked mechanical, which made sense if Paxe was looking for things for his ship.

She wanted to find something a little more interesting than that.

While she contemplated where to begin, a faint hum caught her attention and she turned to find the drone from the kitchen moving down one of the corridors formed by the floor-to-ceiling shelves toward her.

"The drone will assist you," Paxe said. "Just tell it what you want and it will retrieve it."

"Thanks." Except she didn't know what she wanted. Or what to ask for.

She picked a direction, walked toward the corridor to her left, and when she reached the beginning of the shelves, took a close look at the first item.

Almost everything was in boxes, hidden from sight, so she might as well start with the first one and see what was in it.

"Is there anything dangerous in these?" she asked Paxe. "Do I have to be careful opening them up?"

"There are some very dangerous things in the boxes," Paxe said. "Most of them were taken because the Tecran thought they had potential as weapons, or were items the Tecran thought could advance their technology. I don't think just opening the boxes will be dangerous, though. Handling what's in the boxes might be. Perhaps get the drone to open each box, and stand a little way back. If you need more specific help, one of my drone team can assist."

This was a little more excitement than she'd anticipated.

"I'd like to open this first box, please."

The drone had followed behind her, and had stopped when she had. When she stepped back it bustled forward on its tracks and tapped a long, thin, metallic finger against a keypad at the end of the shelf.

The box slid forward, and was lowered to the floor.

The drone unclamped the lid and lifted it, and Ellie had to restrain herself from leaning over to look inside. The drone rose up, extending its body so it loomed over the box, its little head with the lens attached moving carefully over the contents, and then it rolled back, shrinking back to its previous height.

"Safe?" Ellie asked.

"I'm not sure, but it doesn't appear to be immediately dangerous," Paxe said.

She waited for more information, but he was quiet, so she stepped up and peered inside.

Suddenly, she was nudged aside by something cold and smooth, and she only just managed to keep from screaming.

A long, slender . . . thing . . . all silver and gleaming, with what looked like a single eye on top of its stalk-like head, bent over the box and then, as if it were liquid mercury, a part of its body seemed to flow into two long arms, develop fingers, and it lifted out the first of the jumble of items she had managed to glimpse before it had gently pushed her aside.

From the quick look she'd gotten, it was as if someone had simply thrown a number of disparate items together in the box.

Perhaps they were everything the Tecran had stolen from a particular place.

The silver stalk held out what looked like a bundle of silky fabric, and Ellie found herself accepting what looked like a silk cloak.

She held it up and found to her delight it was beautiful.

The one side was smooth and soft, a pale golden taupe, and the other was embroidered with strange looking plants, flowers that were nothing like anything Ellie had seen on Earth, and what might have been alien birds and insects.

The cloak had a clasp at the top, and even though she was in the spacesuit, she swirled it over her shoulders. The helmet made it impossible to do up the clasp at her throat, or lift the hood that was attached to the cloak over her head, but length-wise, it came just above her ankles, and when she was out of the suit, she guessed it would touch the top of her feet.

"Do you know what this is?" she asked, holding the fabric out to the little drone's lens.

She noticed the sliver stalk bent to get a closer look, too, and out of strange sense of fairness, she moved the cloak so that it was an equal distance between them.

"Neither drone has scanning capabilities, or, I haven't been able to discover any in the silver one, and I know the Tecran drone doesn't have the capacity. Neither do I, at the moment." The regret in Paxe's voice was audible.

"I'll keep this to look over in the station. Where can I leave it?"

The little robot drone spun in place and opened a lid on what was a small container at the back.

Ellie folded the robe and set it inside, then turned back to see what else was there.

The silver stalk had bent back in and pulled out a strangely carved block with what looked like three knife handles sticking out of it, just like her aunt's knife block on her kitchen counter.

She stared at it in fascination. This was a lot better than skulking around alone in the station, that was for sure.

She understood, somewhere at the back of her mind, that this was strange behavior on her part. She should be crying and wailing and gnashing her teeth. Railing at fate for having put her in this unbelievable situation, but she also wondered if she hadn't been subconsciously processing her circumstances for months.

Perhaps she had been more aware than the Tecran had realized of her surroundings, of what was happening to her.

She might even have been aware and awake in the beginning, and had just forgotten about it because of her time in a coma.

Either way, there was nothing she could do about it now. She might as well indulge her curiosity.

She glanced at the silver stalk, but it almost seemed to bow to her, as if to say *be my guest*, so she grabbed one of the handles and pulled it out.

It came out with a faint hiss and she found herself holding a wicked looking knife.

It was made all of one material, hilt and blade. A pale blue metal that gleamed in the overhead light from the sun.

The hilt was worked with a tight, raised pattern that gave her a good grip, and the blade was decorated, too, with circular swirls that echoed some of the embroidery she'd noticed on the cloak.

"No sheaths," she murmured, sliding the knife back into its slot.

Not that she had any need to carry around a knife, although the idea appealed to her. It would be a weapon, and she felt vulnerable.

As the blade slid home, pale blue light flared up from the slot she'd put it in, soft and glowing, and Ellie caught sight of what looked like the outline of a square on the side of the block.

She turned it toward her and at the touch of her fingers, a compartment sprung open.

"A sheath." She pulled it out, found it was attached to a harness with two other sheaths fixed to it as well. It looked like it was meant to be shrugged into, a strap over each shoulder, with a sheath sitting on each hip and one against her nape.

She wished she could try it, but with the spacesuit on, it wasn't practical.

She took out the knife again, slid it into one of the sheaths, and it fit perfectly. She pulled the knife out and set it on the ground, folded the harness back up and returned it to its drawer.

Then she picked up the knife to return it to its slot.

As she lifted it, a warning sounded in the helmet, a quiet but insistent chime.

"My suit is pinging me." She was still crouched down, and she looked from the knife in her hand to her hip, and saw the blade had somehow sliced deep into the suit.

"What is it?" Paxe sounded calm but curious.

"I . . . cut my spacesuit." She didn't know how she had done that. She may well have touched the knife to the outside of her suit——it was so bulky and her movements in it were so clumsy. "The helmet is giving me a warning."

She started to have difficulty breathing.

Shit.

She turned, meaning to stand up, and fell backward.

"Ellie, are you all right?"

"No." She managed to get on her hands and knees, and when she looked up, both the silver stalk and the drone were peering down at her. "I think I'm losing air."

She finally made it to her feet, feeling like a puffed up marshmallow in the suit, and started to stagger toward the warehouse door.

"You need to get back to the station." Paxe had put the drone and the silver stalk on either side of her as she tried to move a little faster.

The bing, bing warning from her suit seemed to be coming at shorter and shorter intervals, which was only adding to her stress.

She could feel sweat beading on her upper lip and her hairline, felt it slide down her spine.

She was panicking, and she needed to calm down.

It was as if she somehow remembered going through something like this before. Being starved of air.

Suffocating.

It terrified her.

She had made it out of the warehouse now, staggering down the path. Each breath seemed to be harder than the next, and she stumbled over a rock. She needed to pay attention to her footing.

She was feeling lightheaded, and she couldn't tell how much was due to panic, how much to actual loss of air.

When she stumbled again, she went all the way down.

She tried awkwardly to get her knees under her and push up, but fell again.

Paxe was talking to her, saying something in her ear, but she couldn't understand him.

She tried again to push herself up, didn't have the strength in her arms, and collapsed face first into the fine black dust.

She closed her eyes and forced herself to breathe in short, careful sips, but suddenly there was nothing to breathe, and she panicked again, flailing.

She had the sensation that things were pressing against her, like she'd fallen between two rocks and had become wedged, but then she was lifted up, her head and feet still dragging on the ground.

She managed to turn her head, saw an assortment of little drones all around her, dragging her toward the station door.

She was seeing dancing lights in front of her eyes, and could still hear Paxe's voice, calling to her, and then suddenly the door to the station was opening and she was dumped in the antechamber.

Two thin, metallic arms extended and removed her helmet and she leaned back against the wall and sucked in huge lungfuls of air.

"Thank you," she panted. "Thank you, thank you, thank you."

The drone's little lens face zoomed in on her, and she patted the top of it with a clumsy hand.

Then she looked around, and saw the antechamber was filled with the strange and motley crew from the warehouse.

They were drones, but she couldn't shake the feeling they were sentient in some way. "Thank you," she said to them.

There seemed to be an awkward silence as they continued to stare at her, and she stared back. There was silver stalk, and the drone with the little tracks and lens head, the scary caterpillar, two drones that looked mechanical, little machines that either hovered or wheeled themselves around, and two that looked like big stick insects, thin and fragile, but they had helped to carry her.

They must be a lot stronger than they looked.

"They can't leave until you get through the antechamber into the station. Opening the outside door will leach out the air." Paxe had obviously decided to speak through the little Tecran drone from the kitchen with the lens head and the tracks.

Of course. She wasn't thinking straight.

She looked down at her side, saw the suit's thick layers, all four of them, had been cleanly sliced open at her hip.

She drew in an unsteady breath at the thought of the blade penetrating just a little more, slicing her skin.

Then she started to laugh. It started soft, but ended up with her hiccupping and spluttering.

"What is funny? You could have been seriously hurt, or dead." Paxe sounded utterly lost.

"It's just . . ." she hiccupped again. "I thought, oh, it's just a cloak and a couple of knives, not some dread contagion or nuclear mini-bomb or something. And then . . ." She started laughing again. "Then

I nearly ended myself anyway." She managed to calm down, wiped a tear off her cheek.

"Seriously, thank you, Paxe. And your happy helpers. When I was struggling for air, I had some kind of weird flashback, like being suffocated had happened to me before. Maybe the Tecran deprived me of air at some point, I don't know, but I reacted way more panicky than I think I would have otherwise. If you hadn't sent help, I would have died on the path back to the station."

"Ellie . . ." Paxe paused. "I . . ." He struggled for a bit. "It was my pleasure. I'm sorry the drones had to drag you. It was the fastest way to get you inside."

"No problem whatsoever." She blew out a breath. "Those knives are something else. There's something strange about them. Can the drone fetch them for me? I'll handle them here where I can be out of the suit. The gloves and the bulk of it make me clumsy."

"I don't know where they're from. I didn't steal those particular items. There are a few more things in the box, do you want the drone to bring everything in for you?"

"Yes, please." She pushed herself to her feet and gave the motley crew a final wave goodbye before she made her way through to the room beyond.

She heard the outer door open, and her rescuers left in silence.

While she waited for the drone to fetch the box, she stripped out of the damaged suit and returned it to its hook. There were another eleven suits, so she still had plenty left, but this was a lesson that she had to treat everything as deadly until she knew otherwise. Even things that seemed familiar to her, like knives.

Her hands still shook a little when she pushed her hair from her face on her way back to the kitchen. She could almost feel the blade slicing her flesh, and she shivered, wondering if she should have asked Paxe to fetch them, or whether she should leave well enough alone.

But that would be retreating from a challenge, and she couldn't do that here. Everything she encountered would be a challenge. It was going to be stressful and scary.

She needed to deal.

It was better than lying in a coma in a dusty mausoleum of a moon station.

When she reached the kitchen, the drone had returned and had set the box down on the floor next to the chair where she'd so far eaten her meals.

"Thank you." She crouched down and found it had added the cloak back inside the box.

Time to juggle knives.

CHAPTER 4

IN THE BEGINNING, the hunt for the elusive, rogue Tecran battleship had been . . . not exactly fun, given the stakes, but almost that.

It was certainly challenging, and as Renn seldom had a chance to pit himself against the cunning and brains of another battleship captain, it had been a good chase.

But now the game was losing its lustre. Over a month in space will drag on any crew.

"Why won't they surrender?" Sia tapped a long, slender finger to her lips and narrowed her eyes at the Levron battleship disappearing into a light-jump ahead of them. "They have nowhere to go. No safe haven to rest at. No allies."

"That is the question." Renn had wondered that for the last week. It made no sense. It wasn't as if it was a life-or-death decision for the captain of the Tecran battleship *Rauha*. Renn wasn't going to execute him or any of his crew.

He and the crew of his battleship, the *Etsijä*, were only going to shepherd the Levron back to its home world, Tecra, and bring it under United Council control, just like all the other Tecran battleships.

Perhaps the captain of the *Rauha* would spend some time in prison for his insubordination, failure to heed a UC command, and a number of other charges related to his refusal to stand down and give himself up, unlike every other Tecran ship.

Maybe the Tecran captain was a selfish bastard who was happy to drag his crew on an endless game of chase just to extend his days of freedom. Even though he must know those days were numbered, no matter how many times he light-jumped away from the *Etsijä*.

"Follow?" Kirri, his navigation officer asked.

"Follow." Renn knew he sounded weary. He was.

"You notice that we keep circling back to this sector?" Sia asked. "This is the third time we've chased him this way."

"You think he's looking for something out here?" Darin, the communications officer, leaned back in his chair.

"Or he's headed toward a specific destination, but we catch up too quickly, and he light-jumps away so he doesn't lead us to it." Kirri hit the light-jump warning for the rest of the crew and took them on a jump that aligned with the Levron's trajectory.

They landed just in time to see the Levron on the edge of their scanners, turning and light-jumping a second time.

"That's new." Sia couldn't hide her shock.

"I didn't know they could light-jump twice without at least a couple of hours break," Darin said.

"They can, but it's a one-time thing, when they have enough energy stored from former jumps. They can only do it when they have accumulated energy over a certain level." Renn had spent time studying the Levron class on this long chase.

"So follow them again?" Kirri asked. Unlike the *Rauha*, the *Etsijä* was able to make two light-jumps in a row.

"The jump they made isn't necessarily a full jump. They might only have had enough for a short hop." And that would mean they might just have lost the Levron completely.

"Not good." Sia saw the implication as well.

"This is what we'll do. We'll map their trajectory. I'll take off now in the explorer. Sia, you have command of the *Etsijä*. Do a full jump, then turn around and come back, full speed, in this direction. Either you, or I, will encounter the *Rauha*."

Unless the Tecran had engaged full speed when they came out of their jump and gone in another direction. But this was a chance worth taking. The alternative was to do nothing, and that wasn't an option.

He started assembling a small team as he ran for the launch bay. It wouldn't matter how many were onboard, in truth, because an explorer could never take a Levron-class battleship. But they could keep up with it until it made a light-jump, and transmit its location to the *Etsijä*, and Battle Center as well.

The engines of the explorer were on and Iso, the navigation and exploration officer he'd chosen, was running up the ramp into the small vessel.

When he stepped inside, all four crew he'd called for were strapping in.

"Let's go."

Eadal, the pilot, lifted off and flew through the gel wall, dropping the explorer down below the *Etsijä*.

The moment they were out, the *Etsijä* moved forward and then shimmered and disappeared.

The hunt had begun.

"THEY WON'T COME OUT?" Ellie walked over to the target she and the drone had set up for knife-throwing practice, and had propped up against the rocks near the station entrance.

The knives seemed well and truly stuck in the metal lids they'd used, even though they'd covered them with blankets from the dormitory.

Wary of the risks of playing with the knives outside, she'd set up her targets near the entrance for a quick dash inside if she should cut her suit again.

She'd decided it was worth chancing her luck outside again to prevent any accidental damage inside the station itself.

The drone was pulling at the hilt of a knife, but it wasn't budging.

"It's really embedded in there." She took hold of one of the other hilts, set her stance to really put her back into it, yanked, and gave a shout of surprise as it came out easily, the knife flying from her hand as she fell backward in the awkward spacesuit.

She heard the crunch of the drone's wheels in the gritty soil, and then the lens leaned over her.

"I'm okay. I was expecting more resistance from the knife."

"The knife you pulled out was as stuck as the one the drone was trying to remove. There might be more going on here." Paxe sounded intrigued.

"I'll try another one." Ellie rolled over, got on her hands and knees, and pushed herself back up to standing. "Where did the knife I threw go?"

The drone pointed, and she saw with shock it was embedded in a rock, right up to the hilt.

"Let's try something," she said to Paxe. "Get the drone to give it a go, then I will."

The drone rolled forward, clamp out, and tugged at the knife. It didn't move. Ellie gripped it, and carefully slid it out.

Easy as you please.

"Huh." She looked over at the drone. "I think you're right."

She went back to the target, pulled the other two knives out easily. "Do you think that blue glow thing when I first handled them was it imprinting my DNA or my fingerprints or something? So I'm the only one who can use them?"

"Maybe." Paxe bent the drone's lens close to the hilt. "Nothing is obvious from a visual examination, though."

"I wonder where the Tecran got them." Ellie took one and stood a little further back from the target. Threw the knife.

The knife hit the center of the lid, exactly where she'd been aiming.

She shouldn't be this good.

Until she'd been able to pull the knife out of a rock, Excalibur-like, she had thought she was just having a run of beginner's luck with her early throwing efforts.

But now, she had a strong suspicion she did not have crazy knife-throwing skills. Some magic in the knives was doing the work.

"It's sort of freaky, sort of cool." She'd take it, though. Having throwing knives that went were you wanted them, that pierced the hardest material. Well, that sounded handy.

"I've looked through the data in the station, but a lot of things I've found in the warehouse aren't in there. They weren't good record keepers."

Ellie put the knives back into their sheaths and the drone lifted the target. They walked side by side back to the station. "Would the Tecran have taken the knives from a planet, or another ship?"

"Could be either. Although given their ability to go through very hard surfaces, these would not be a good weapon to use on a space vessel."

"That's the truth." She looked over at the target, at the vicious slashes in the metal. Winced at the thought of being in a spacecraft with a knife that could penetrate anything.

She'd have to be super careful with them when Paxe finally got the *Irini* going and they left.

They reached the door, but she didn't want to go back inside. It was cold and empty and depressing.

"Seeing as I'm already in the suit, I'll do a bit more exploring in the warehouse." She set the knives down in the antechamber.

"Are you sure?" Paxe sounded uncertain.

He'd been worried about her accident this morning. Really worried.

It warmed something in her that she had someone so concerned for her wellbeing.

It was good to have someone to talk to out here. If she'd woken to find herself completely alone, she didn't know what she would have done.

"I'll be careful. I've only had a chance to look in one box." But what a box it had been. If they were all like that, she wouldn't want to leave. Or she would have to make sure they came back here after they found the other thinking systems Paxe was intent on reuniting with, and keep going through the trove.

"How are you going with the ship?" she asked as she and her little drone side-kick headed back for the warehouse.

"Progress is slow, but I've been able to refit the internal doors, finally. They were damaged before, when the crew crippled the ship, and it was hard to restore them and refit them, and getting them to close and seal felt impossible at times. But we did it."

She was interested in his use of the word *we*. He was using the drones to help him, but theoretically, he was simply programming them with instructions.

It was all him.

Except when they looked at her, she had a sense it was more than Paxe just showing off, ordering them to act in sync. She sensed curiosity. Intelligence.

As if Paxe had somehow infected them with a bit of his own autonomy.

She set the thought aside for later contemplation.

"That sounds like a huge step forward."

"Yes, but there is so much more to do." Paxe sounded frustrated. "The explosion destroyed all the connections, all the circuits. I'm rebuilding them, trying to graft on what makes sense to me, but this ship is completely alien, and so far, nothing is responding to what I've put in place. Nothing is integrated in a way I'm used to."

"I suppose that makes sense. It was an alien culture that created it."

"That's true." Paxe was silent for a bit. "Maybe you should come in to the ship, look around. You're an alien, too. Something that might seem obvious to you might not be obvious to the Tecran, and they're all I know."

"Okay. Now?"

"No. Have fun in the warehouse. Maybe come in later. I'm still getting the hang of the doors."

She was almost at the entrance to the warehouse, so she turned and gave a thumbs up to the ship, then stepped through.

The motley crew stopped what they were doing and turned to look at her again.

She thought she could detect slight variations in their stances this time, but she didn't know if she was imagining things to fit her theory, or if they were really there.

"Where do you want to look next?" Paxe asked her.

"Let's start with box number two."

CHAPTER 5

THE EXPLORER COULDN'T LIGHT-JUMP, but its full speed was unmatched by any other ship in the same class.

Renn set the scanners to find Levron-sized objects only, and gave Eadal permission to take it as fast as it would go.

"You think they only made a short jump?" Xallantra, one of his military team, made it a question, but he could hear she already thought his answer was yes.

He gave a nod. "They keep circling back to this area. This is the third time they've jumped here, and they don't move until we arrive, as if they're waiting first to see if we've managed to follow them. When we do, they head back in the opposite direction, leading us away from the sector."

"You think they are trying to make contact with another ship? Another rogue?" Iso leaned forward in his seat, eyes wide.

Renn shrugged. "Either that, or they left something here they want to pick up."

Hune, Xallantra's team mate, stood, leaned against the transparent wall of the explorer as he looked out at the stars. "Or they have a station out here. A place to pick up supplies."

"Could be," Renn agreed. The Tecran certainly hadn't been able to resupply since the *Etsijä* had been on their tail.

When this hunt had started, Renn's battleship had been fully stocked. It was doubtful the *Rauha* had been. They had been patrolling the outer reaches of the Tecran's boundary when they had slipped the leash. They must be getting desperate.

"How would they have a supply station out here, though?" Iso asked. "This is uncharted territory."

"So is the place they took those Earth women from. So are the places they took the strange things the Class 5s have shared with Battle Center from the holds of their ships," Xallantra said.

"I think we can take it as given this area isn't uncharted to the Tecran. They know it well enough they keep coming back to it. I think it's safe to say it's at least possible they have a station out here. They had to put supply stations somewhere, why not a place the rest of the UC didn't know about?" Renn could almost admire it, if it hadn't been against all promises the Tecran had made. They should have withdrawn from the UC if they had decided to go down the road they had, rather than try to have it both ways.

But of course, most Tecran hadn't even known what was happening. Certain members of the military had chosen the path they'd set Tecra on, and it had not ended well.

Renn wondered if Tecra would ever have the same status and alliances in the UC it had had before.

There was a moment of silence as everyone pondered the implications of a secret Tecran supply station, so the ping from the scan rang clear and sharp through the ship.

"Got them," Eadal said, with an edge of dark glee.

"Send immediate comms to the *Etsijä*," Renn told her.

"Done."

"Where are they going?" Renn stood behind Eadal and checked the route the *Rauha* was taking.

They were moving fast and with purpose.

The explorer registered the stars, planets and other heavenly bodies as they raced after the battleship, creating a chart in real time.

A chart the Tecran obviously already had.

"Looks like they're heading for that solar system, there." Eadal pointed. "There are four planets in the system, but none of them would support either the Tecran or us without full spacesuits."

"They've just noticed we're following them." Renn watched as the *Rauha* stopped.

"What will they do?" Xallantra came up behind him, hands on her hips as she looked over his shoulder at the screen.

"Seems like they plan to attack." The warning buzzed from the control panel just as Eadal spoke.

"They haven't before." Iso shook his head.

"We were in a Grihan battleship before," Renn said. "Now we're in an explorer." But Iso was right. This was a dramatic escalation. Unless it was a bluff or a warning.

"They obviously want to get where they're going without us knowing where that is." Iso crowded in next to Xallantra.

"Strap in, people." Eadal accelerated, moving fast toward the *Rauha*, dipping the explorer hard as she went, so the Tecran's first laser shot went high.

Or it was a deliberate miss.

Renn didn't like that he couldn't tell.

He strapped in beside Eadal, while the other three settled in behind them, and took over half the controls. Eadal gave a nod of thanks.

They would have to be quick and nimble in this situation.

It was hard to shoot a small vessel like the explorer from close range in a battleship, which was why Eadal was heading toward the Tecran.

When the *Rauha* realized what they were doing, it abandoned the effort to use their laser cannon and began moving away at top speed.

"Getting some distance, all the better to shoot us, or are they trying to outrun us?" Hune asked.

That was the question.

They followed, but the *Rauha* was faster, and it pulled away and was eventually lost on the explorer's short range scanners.

So it had been a bluff.

"What now?" Eadal leaned back from the consul.

"I think your estimation on where they were headed is a good one." Renn turned to her in his seat. "Let them think they've lost us."

"You want them to relax, start doing whatever it is they've come here to do?" Iso gave a nod.

"They've been trying to get here for over two weeks. I'd like to know why."

As soon as the captain of the *Rauha* had made that second light-jump, Renn had known he was trying to throw the *Etsijä* off so he could reach whichever destination he was so focused on.

If the Tecran thought they'd succeeded, maybe Renn could finally find out what was so important to them.

"Let's see what they're up to."

"How's it going?" Paxe's question forced Ellie's attention off the strange item she was trying to figure out and over to the drone.

"I can't work out what the heck this is." She gave up, setting it back in its box. "How is Silvey doing?"

The Tecran drone slid the box back in place for her, and she looked over at the silver drone, who was bent over the jeweled necklace Ellie had found in box number 15, the drone's thin metallic probes retreating and extending from its liquid silver 'hand' as it fiddled with the settings.

"Silvey?" Paxe seemed flummoxed. "Because?"

"Because she's silver." Ellie didn't say *duh!* but only just.

"Um . . . Silvey and I are nearly there. If I'm right, when this is done you won't have to wear the Tecran spacesuits anymore. You can activate the necklace and it will allow you outside."

"How can that possibly work?" She liked the idea, but was skeptical.

Paxe said it would look as if there was a thin halo of light around her. Right now, it was set to support life for a species that needed a different mix of air to her, but he was getting Silvey to change that so she could use it.

"The light forms a skin of molecules around you, and the necklace draws in the available atmosphere and alters the mix of gasses to be what I've programmed it to be. Because it just has to support you personally, and is continually drawing in air, it doesn't need a lot of space between the light and your skin, even with clothes on. It's almost like the gel wall we use for launch bays, but with an advanced focus of light instead of the gel compound."

Okay, she hadn't ever seen a gel wall, but Paxe had explained it a few times to her as a way for vessels to transition from inside a ship to space without the need for an airlock.

It sounded clever and simple, and she always thought the best technology was both.

"Well, I'd be thrilled if it does work." She moved back as the Tecran drone pulled out box 17 for her.

She needed a name for it, too. She couldn't keep thinking of it as simply 'drone'.

This was the second day she'd been working through boxes in the warehouse with them, and she was becoming very fond of them all.

"What do you think the Tecran drone would like to be called?" she asked.

"It . . ."

She thought Paxe might be about to say that it couldn't like or dislike anything, but he stopped himself.

"Karnic," he said after a long pause.

"I like it. Does it mean anything?"

"Karn is the mythical founder of the Tecran people. He's their spiritual leader, who supposedly elevated them into higher sentience. Karnic means little Karn in Tecran."

"Ah." Ellie liked it even better now. "So he sees himself as a smaller version of Karn, moving from being just a drone to something with higher sentience. Nice."

"I . . ." Paxe's voice faded away. "How did you get that so quickly, Ellie?"

"It seems obvious."

"I have been working with these drones, slowly integrating with them to become extensions of myself, in order to replace the functionality I used to have in my ship. How did I miss their development?"

"Because you are too close to them." Ellie shrugged. "You said you've integrated with them to a degree, but you see them as individuals, don't you?"

"Because they are each useful for different things. They all have specific strengths."

"Just like everyone does."

"Perhaps." He seemed a little uncertain.

Ellie crouched beside Silvey. "Does Silvey like her name, or would she like another?"

Silvey paused what she was doing and lifted her single eye to look at Ellie. She'd win any stare-down, Ellie accepted. She didn't have to blink.

"She approves."

"Good." Ellie looked around the warehouse. The Scary Caterpillar was out, delivering something for Paxe, she guessed. But the two stick insects were busy lifting things out of a box and laying them out for Karnic to scan with his lens, so Paxe could see if they would be useful. The hover bot and the wheeled drone weren't visible, but she thought they were among the stacks.

"If Silvey and Karnic get names, everyone should get a name. What do the rest want to be called?"

"Ellie." Paxe sounded mystified. "I don't think——"

"Paxe. What do they want to be called?"

"It will increase their autonomy." He spoke stiffly. "That will have implications for my schedule."

"Maybe it will speed your schedule up. Maybe they'll have ideas you wouldn't have had yourself. They're alien, like me. Like the *Irini*. Maybe they'll come up with something to help."

"Or maybe they won't be as quick to obey me."

She said nothing to that, and eventually he made a noise she thought might be a sigh. It was like her own, and she wondered if he was taking some cues from her.

"I'll ask them."

The hover bot whizzed out from between the stacks and zoomed toward her, coming to a stop in front of her.

She had the delighted sense that if it had been a person, it would have been hopping from foot to foot with excitement.

It reminded her of one of the first graders who frequented the library's children's section, Olivia. She loved to come and tell Ellie about the books she'd read over the weekend.

"Well, then?" She smiled at the little robot. "What do I call you?"

"Uh . . . Ellie." Paxe sounded cautious. "I don't think your vocal cords are capable of pronouncing the name it has chosen for itself."

"Oh." Ellie crouched down to eye-level. "Can you explain that to it?"

"Yes."

The little hover bot spun in place, and Ellie had the sense it was listening and thinking.

"It says to give it a name, and it will assign that name to mean the same as its own in its programming."

"Then I choose Olivia."

The hover bot spun a little faster, then stopped.

"Olivia it is."

"Pleased to meet you, Olivia, I'm Ellie."

The hover bot did the excited little jiggle again, and then whizzed off.

Something tightened in Ellie's chest.

She was used to a lot of interaction in her day to day life, and she didn't know how long she'd been completely alone. She realized she had been unconscious for a lot of that time, but she must have known on a subconscious level that she was in solitude.

She was happy to be part of Paxe's motley crew.

"The *fuhytlk* would like a name, too," Paxe said.

Ellie didn't even try to repeat the word he'd used, she'd need to see it written out and practice it a few times before she could say it. She did understand that he meant the little robot with the single wheel.

It zoomed toward her, its little body made of two circles on a gimbal, one horizontal to the ground, with the vertical one propelling it forward.

"Does it have something it would like to be called?" Ellie asked. She was still crouched down and it stopped right in front of her, giving her the first close look she'd had of it.

It had two retractable arms that looked like they were set on a rail on the horizontal wheel, able to move to any position along the circumference they needed to.

It had two lenses that seemed to float between the vertical wheel like eyes, and what looked like two mini satellite dishes above the lenses.

"How do the ears and eyes float like that?" Ellie asked.

"A mini magnetic field," Paxe told her. "Extremely interesting use of the laws of magnetism."

"You're telling me."

"It asks you to name it." Paxe said. "It cannot think of something it likes." He sounded resigned.

"How about Phil?" Ellie asked. If she remembered correctly, from an awesome reference work for children on scientific writings from ancient times, the first written description of a gimbal was by Philo of Byzantium.

"Phil?" Paxe seemed surprised. "It likes it."

"Great. What about the twins?" She looked over at the stick

insects, and they stopped what they were doing and regarded her without moving.

"The twins?" Paxe sounded almost morose. "I've explained what you mean and the twins like the name the twins."

"That just leaves the Scary Caterpillar. It needs a name." It wasn't fair to give everyone else nice names. Maybe he should be Colin.

"Not just the . . . Scary Caterpillar. There is another one, it was too small to help carry you, and it's working in the *Irini* for me, so you haven't seen it yet."

"Do they have any preferences?"

"No." Paxe's tone was short. "It's not important. Leave naming them 'til later."

He clearly didn't like this. This recognition that the motley crew were more than just a bunch of drones. But she was in the mix now too, and calling them a bunch of drones didn't cut it. Especially when they were so clearly *not* just drones.

If Paxe had let himself be blind to that until she pointed it out, that was on him.

The motley crew shouldn't have to suffer for it.

The twins had moved over to the items they had laid out for Karnic to scan for Paxe, and one of them lifted something up and walked over to her, each step a slight forward, back, forward motion, although that didn't seem to make it slow.

It held out a bracelet to her, and she took it and touched its hand as she did so, felt the smooth hardness of its fingers.

"Thank you. What is it?" She held the item up, saw it was a thick silver cuff.

"The watch you wanted," Paxe said. He hesitated. "Silvey will reprogram it to mimic Earth hours. Given the sun shines continually here, it doesn't matter what the orbit times of V65 are. We might as well stick to what you're used to."

Silvey had sidled up beside her, leaving the necklace on the ground, and Ellie handed the watch over and turned back to box 17, which Karnic had taken out for her.

She would do this last one and then call it a day. She was getting tired, although she had done a lot better than yesterday.

She noticed Silvey swaying a little as she stuck needle-thin filaments into the side of the cuff, and then realized she was humming under her breath.

She stopped short.

"I've got David Bowie's *Fashion* stuck in my head." She frowned. "I didn't think I knew the words that well, but if you asked me, I could sing it all right now."

Silvey had stopped swaying.

"I forgot about the music that plays in my pod. Is that thanks to you?" she asked.

"After I killed all the Tecran three weeks ago, you went downhill a little." Paxe had gone quiet. "I think it was because there was no one moving around in your space. You were completely alone, so I remembered some of what Oris told me about music and your kind, and put together all the music I recorded in the short time I was in your solar system. It's not all very clear, but some of it is, and I cleaned up what I could. It's about eight hours worth, and I simply put it on repeat."

"So you've been playing it to me on loop since you got rid of all the station crew?" She leaned back on her heels. "Paxe, that was a very thoughtful thing to do."

The familiarity of the music, just having her unconscious mind hearing something other than the faint buzz of machines, had to have helped her recover.

"You immediately improved when I started doing it. You did even better than when the Tecran were there, looking after you. So I kept doing it. Do you want me to stop playing it in the pod now?"

"Maybe play it for me when I'm in the communal area, and here in the warehouse, if you don't mind. I can sleep without it, now."

"I will do that."

"Can you play it right now?" The familiarity of it would be soothing.

He did so, and one of her favorite songs, Ob-la-Di, Ob-La-Da, by the Beatles, came on.

She started singing along, looked up and saw Silvey was swaying again.

Karnic moved into her field of vision, lens focused on her face, and she could almost feel the curiosity coming off him. She smiled and sung louder, and then Olivia came zooming out to look.

Phil didn't exactly hide, but he kept to the stacks, watching the show, and the twins didn't come closer, but they stopped what they were doing and turned in her direction.

She was still in the spacesuit, so dancing was more or less out of the question, but she stood and did a few side steps, lifting her hands above her head to clap the beat.

Silvey imitated her immediately, her fluid movements far cooler than anything Ellie was doing.

The twins started moving, too, their strange, mantis like back-and-forth looking choreographed and in time with the beat.

Life did go on, Ellie thought as the song faded into some classic music by Handel. She didn't want to be here, but she *was* here. And she didn't think there was any going back.

A sense of . . . not happiness . . . not yet, but contentment filled her. It was a strange crowd that surrounded her, and a strange situation, but there was music, and friendliness, and plenty of interesting things to do.

The others had slowly gone back to their tasks when she stopped singing.

"That woke them up more than anything else." Paxe sounded thoughtful. "Woke them up almost as much as you giving them a name woke them."

"I gave them a name because they were awake, Paxe, not the other way around."

"Woke them up more, then." Paxe made a humming sound. "And

then the music sparked them a little more. Not the music itself, interacting with you and the music."

"I don't mean to cause you trouble." But she wouldn't change what she was doing.

"No." He sighed. "I shouldn't have said what I did earlier. I destroyed my ship rather than be a slave, and I would never subject anyone else to the same thing the Tecran did to me. Whether it helps me or hinders me, it needs to be this way."

"Good." She relaxed.

The Handel violin concerto came to a rousing end, and then Ob-la-Di, Ob-La-Da came back on.

Ellie laughed out loud.

"They demanded it," Paxe said, and she thought she could hear a lightness in his voice, too.

She opened the box Karnic had pulled for her, singing along, moving her head from side to side, but every now and then she sneaked a look at the others, saw they were all moving to the music.

Whatever was in the box, though, it wasn't anything she understood. Stacks of what looked like brittle squares made of a substance she didn't recognize.

She was too afraid to lift them out in case they crumbled or snapped, so she simply put the lid back on.

Silvey finished with the watch and brought it over to her, then went back to the necklace.

"Thank you." Ellie hooked it around her wrist. The surface was smooth and reflective.

"Tap it," Paxe said.

She did, and the time came up. "Midday?"

It felt much later than midday.

"It should be earlier?" Paxe asked.

"Later. 4pm, maybe." She felt too tired for it to be only midday.

"All right." Paxe sounded like he was soothing her, and he probably was.

Silvey sidled up to her, and she handed her the watch back.

It didn't matter, she decided as she watched Silvey slide thin fila-ments into the side of the device again. Time was meaningless here, except to her, so if she wanted it to be 4pm, it could be.

But it worried her, this exhaustion, the amount she seemed to be sleeping. But she reminded herself that she was recovering from months of inactivity, of lying in a coma in her med pod.

Still, it struck a cord of loneliness deep inside her. She was the only one who cared what the time was. If there was a more clear indicator that she was far from home, she didn't know what it could be.

She blinked, and then raised the lid of the next box Karnic had gotten for her.

"What on Earth?" She moved from her knees to a crouch, holding on to the side of the box as she peered in. There was a stack of neatly folded silk-like fabric inside, but her eyes had gone straight to the bugs.

Dead bugs.

She eyed them warily. They had clearly been in the large trans-parent jar that lay cracked and on its side on top of the fabric. She wondered who would have put live bugs in a jar and then stored them in a warehouse.

It didn't make any sense, unless the Tecran hadn't known they were bugs. Maybe they had been in a different form, like a cocoon or something, and had hatched out after they'd been stored here.

Their jar had either been damaged and they'd gotten out, or they'd busted out themselves, and had died in the big storage box.

Warily, and grateful that her hands were covered by the space-suit's gloves, she reached in and lifted the fabric out.

It shimmered pale blue and forest green, and fell in a way that told her it was soft and smooth.

Bugs clattered out of the folds back into the box, and she shook it gently to get them all out.

It didn't appear that they had damaged the fabric, which was fortunate, because it was so gorgeous.

"Maybe I can make some clothes that fit me out of this." She stood up, getting the measure of how much of it there was.

There was a lot.

"Your clothes don't fit you?" Paxe sounded astonished.

She considered asking him why he hadn't noticed when Karnic's little lens had recorded her in the ill-fitting garments plenty of times, but he probably didn't know what a good fit was, if he didn't have a body of his own.

"No. The Tecran are obviously a little broader than me, and a little taller."

"Oh. There's a machine in the station that will make you any clothes you want. There's fabric available, too, but you can put the fabric you found in there instead, if you prefer it."

"Can you tell me if there's anything dangerous about the fabric?" She loved it, but best to be safe than sorry.

Karnic lifted its head and zoomed in. "I don't have my own drones or the facilities of my old ship, so I can't really tell the chemical composition of the fibres, but it looks like some kind of natural fabric, either from a spider or a plant. It might even be Cargassey cloth."

"Is that good?"

"It's very rare. It's good protection against shockgun fire, so it would be good to make clothes out of it."

That sounded like a positive. "Great, let's do that."

She set it on the ground beside her and gave the box a final look. Right at the bottom, amongst the dead, acorn-sized bugs, was something that looked like a head band. Now *that* was useful. Her hair had grown wild in the months she had lain in the pod.

There was no mirror that she could see anywhere on the station, so she couldn't tell exactly how it looked, but the dark brown waves fell past her shoulders, longer than she'd worn it since she was a child.

She carefully reached in, lifting it out while trying not to touch the bugs, and closed the lid with relief.

She was, she realized, now completely done.

She could not do another thing.

"Do you mind if I come over to the *Irini* tomorrow to look around for you. I'm suddenly exhausted."

Karnic looked up. "That's fine. Working on this collar with Silvey has taken all my attention, anyway. I'm close enough to getting it right, I'd prefer to work on it rather than on the *Irini* until I'm finished." He paused. "Do you need me to send Karnic with you back to the station?"

"No. I'm good." She gathered the fabric and the headband, patted Karnic on the head and made her way outside.

It had been a good couple of days.

She'd found the knives and the cloak. The necklace. The fabric and the headband. Named most of the motley crew.

There were many things she had come across in other boxes, but neither she nor Paxe could work out what they were.

With more time and more equipment, they probably could, but they didn't have time to waste on things they couldn't decipher.

She had two week's worth of Earth food left, after which she'd have to start dipping into the other stuff.

Paxe told her he knew what Tecran food she could eat without getting sick, but he didn't think she'd enjoy it. The alien food the Tecran had stolen was completely unknown, and he didn't want her to eat it with his current level of capability. He couldn't run the tests he needed to make sure it was safe for her.

"Whatever you have, you'll have to eat in the *Irini*, too, when we leave. I don't know how long it'll take us to get in touch with the Grih, but I'd say a week at least." Paxe had sounded worried.

That meant they had to be off the station in a week. Which meant Paxe shouldn't be working on necklaces and watches for her, and she should probably push herself and go look at the *Irini* now. But she didn't have the energy.

She needed to be kind to herself. She had only been walking around for three days. She didn't know how long she'd been in the coma. Paxe had arrived well over a month ago, and he'd been attached to the vessel that brought him here for a number of weeks before that.

Who knew how long she'd lain in that pod.

She reached the antechamber, staggered into the change room and got out of her suit.

She left everything where it was, fabric and headband included, and stopped in the kitchen only to get some water before she made it back to the pod.

She needed to pace herself. Not end up so tired she could barely function.

She closed her eyes, wondered what was missing, and then, as sleep pulled her under, remembered she had asked Paxe not to play music in here anymore.

Maybe she should reverse that.

CHAPTER 6

RENN LET Eadal push the explorer to its limits as it entered the solar system.

To make sure the *Rauha* didn't pick them up, they'd taken a route that swung around to the left. It would take them longer, but not by much.

And unless they were wrong about where the *Rauha* was headed, the Levron should still be there, doing whatever it was so desperate to do, by the time they arrived.

"You think they're getting supplies, don't you?" Xallantra sipped grinabo and leaned back in her seat.

"They need them, so it's a logical conclusion." In fact, they had to be desperate. A Levron usually had a crew of two hundred. If they didn't restock soon, they'd have to surrender or die of starvation.

"If there's a supply station out here in the middle of an uncharted solar system, I wonder what else the Tecran have left dotted around the galaxy. It'll take years to find it all." Iso was sitting beside Eadal, looking at the newly created charts. "Unless they're willing to tell us where they are, that is."

Renn gave a snort. "They won't. Each new revelation brings more of their crimes to light. They'll keep quiet and hope as much as possible remains undiscovered."

"It never does, though, does it?" Hune said. "Everything comes to light in the end. Look what happened with that Earth woman they found on Tecra itself. The mess the Tecran military made trying to kill her and pretend they'd never had her there in the first place only caused them more problems in the end."

"True, but if they'd succeeded, we'd never have known." Iso shrugged.

"What they didn't know was that Bane already knew she was there, before the UC even got there to take control of Tecra. They were never going to succeed in hiding what they'd done to her." Renn had seen the reports. They weren't widely known, but they weren't secret, either.

"I hadn't heard that. How did Bane know?" Eadal turned to look back from her pilot's seat.

"Paxe told Oris, who told Bane. Paxe was the Class 5 that blew himself up before the Tecran could cage him again. He was the Class 5 who abducted Lucy Harris from Earth, and he suspected the Tecran had taken her to Tecra. He asked Oris to rescue her if she was still alive before he killed himself. Oris shared the information with all the Class 5s, so Bane knew about it when he travelled to Tecra."

"Yes, that would have been an impediment to the Tecran military's plans." Xallantra chuckled. "I'd have liked to have seen some of their faces when they realized Bane was on to them."

Renn and the *Etsijä* had arrived in Tecran airspace shortly after the clean up in the aftermath of that incident, there to support the UC as it established control of Tecra and tried to rid the Tecran military of its corrupt elements.

But since the final showdown the Tecran military had had with Bane and the UC forces on Tecra, one of the Tecran's Levron-class battleships had been unaccounted for, and the *Etsijä* had been sent to track it down and bring it in.

It had turned out to be a lot more complicated than he'd thought.

"Here we go." Eadal sat straighter in her chair and they all looked out to see a lavender planet in the distance.

"Of the four planets in this system, only this one isn't a gas planet. It's still uninhabitable, though, for the Tecran and for ourselves." Iso flicked through data on the screen. "It's got six moons, all very small, and . . . there is the *Rauha*." His voice rose.

Renn had expected the *Rauha* to already be here, but perhaps they had taken a few evasive manoeuvres on the way, to make sure they had lost the explorer.

He hadn't expected it to appear from the other side of the planet, to come face to face with it.

Eadal slowed the explorer, letting it all but drift as they got the measure of the situation.

"Shit." Hune spoke for them all as they crowded around the screen and watched the Levron slow down as well.

"They've picked us up." Eadal indicated the hail.

"Ignore it." There was nothing he had to say to the captain of the *Rauha* right now. "Send the location to Sia." They would need the firepower of the *Etsijä*. He knew, though, given their location, it would take some time for the communication to reach his ship.

"They've decided to come say hello." Xallantra pointed to a breakaway vessel heading toward them.

"Fighter deployed," Eadal agreed. "Coming in weapons hot."

They didn't need her to tell them to strap in. Iso rose from the seat beside Eadal, so Renn could take his place.

"Evade, or run away?" Eadal asked him.

He knew what he wanted to do, but there were other lives at stake. Maybe. If the Tecran weren't just posturing again.

"My preference is to evade until retreat becomes the only option." Renn wanted to see what was going on, if he could. "But I'm not risking your lives if you don't agree."

"Things were pretty boring before now, anyway," Xallantra said.

"I'm in." Hune grinned.

"Me, too." Eadal and Iso sang out the words together.

"Then evade away." Renn leaned over the screen, flicking through the lens feed to watch the Levron and its approaching fighter.

"See there, they've slowed. They're hovering over one of the moons." Iso had transferred the screen feed to a handheld, and he held it up. "If we were closer we could see if there are any structures built there."

"There will be." Renn leaned in to the sudden dip to the left as Eadal evaded the first laser shot from the fighter.

It was the first exchange of hostilities since this chase began. And it made him all the more interested in what was going on.

Eadal sped up, arcing right to come at the *Rauha* from the side of the moon it was hovering over.

"If we're going to be in a chase, we might as well have a look at what's going on at the same time." Eadal dropped to the moon's surface, and then turned a wide-eyed look on Renn. "The fighter's pulled back."

"They've either made their point or they don't want to risk any damage to this area." Well, well, well. "What do you have hidden here that you don't want destroyed?" he asked softly.

They found out in the next moment, as the explorer rounded the curve of the moon and was suddenly flying over a settlement.

"Some kind of station, and a warehouse or hangar?" Iso's voice hit a higher pitch with excitement. "And what's that vessel on the launch pad? I've never seen anything like it."

"Are those . . . wings?" Xallantra's voice was edged with amazement as Eadal swooped closer, and then accelerated away.

"The fighter's back." Eadal twisted right, dodging laser fire. "And . . ." She trailed off.

Renn didn't need to ask why, he could see for himself.

The *Rauha* had dropped down in front of them, blocking the way. The fighter came up from behind.

They were boxed in.

"Options?" Renn asked.

"Drop down and spin back to the moon. They might get off a shot before we pull away, though. The moon has a thin atmosphere, so it'll be bumpy and slow and they'll have a good chance of hitting us."

"Go for it." Given the chance of getting away versus certain capture, he'd take the chance every time. He'd rather they make a landing on the moon and see what was down there than be scooped into the Levron's launch bay, which was obviously the Tecran's plan.

Eadal dropped them down fast, spinning the explorer as they went, and he felt it when they hit the upper level of the moon's thin atmosphere. The whole ship shuddered.

The laser strike that came a moment later hit the top of the explorer, and he felt that, too, as they skipped like a stone on water over the atmosphere's surface, and then began a slow tumble down.

"I can get out of it." Eadal's voice was calm. "We can accelerate away."

They were damaged, though. He could see it in the warnings lighting up the control panel. Maybe they could float for a bit in their current state, but the *Rauha* would find them and bring them in eventually.

Certainly before the *Etsijä* could get here.

Besides, the Tecran wouldn't kill them. Landing on the moon and maybe being taken prisoner wasn't going to be life or death.

Unless the *Rauha's* captain was insane.

Now that Renn knew about the supply station, the Tecran's previous behavior made a lot more sense.

"No. Land, but find a spot away from the station. If we leave, they may try to shoot us again. While we're near their precious structures, they won't dare."

"Is there a place to hide?" Hune asked as Eadal dropped them even lower and they skimmed close to the top of the station.

"Not at first glance." Iso was frowning at the handheld. "But there are rocky outcrops we could tuck in behind. We'll be seen by the *Rauha*, though. It'll have the capacity to find us wherever we put down."

"Then circle back and land somewhere close. I want a look on foot at that station." Renn really wanted to find out what the Tecran had set up here and why.

The *Rauha* had tried to capture his explorer to keep him and his team away. They had fired on them.

It was an escalation beyond anything that had happened since the agreement between the Tecran government and the rest of the UC had been signed.

Whatever was here, whatever was going on, the Tecran did not want the Grih to know, and that made Renn determined to find out.

CHAPTER 7

"ELLIE! WAKE UP. WAKE. UP."

Ellie jerked awake with a start, sitting up with heart thundering. "What is it?"

"The Tecran are here."

"What?"

Still fuzzy with sleep, she slid off the platform.

"The Tecran have come, looking for the station crew and for supplies, I think."

She suddenly understood what he was trying to tell her, and the clouds of exhaustion vanished as adrenalin began to flood her system. "They're here? Right now?"

Her panicked gaze went to the door.

"They're hovering over the station. They haven't sent down a vessel yet. You need to move or you'll be trapped in here."

He didn't need to tell her twice.

She looked around for her clothes, found some hanging from one of the pieces of medical equipment. She reached out and grabbed them, and then turned to Karnic in shock. "Is this the fabric I found yesterday?"

"I have your measurements and used the machine to make a few items of various styles for you, based on what you were wearing when the Tecran took you from Earth."

"Thank you." She found a bra, which was the first time she'd had one since she'd woken up, underwear, a long-sleeved t-shirt and pants that fit as snug and comfortably as a pair of yoga pants. The fabric was smooth and cool against her skin.

There were extra sets of pants and shirts, and Karnic whizzed into the room with a small backpack and held it open for her.

She looked inside, saw there were a few bottles of water and energy bars inside. She picked up the spare clothes to pack them, and saw the head band from the box was lying underneath them.

Pleased, she slid it on and then gave a faint shriek as she felt it move on its own over the crown of her head.

"What's happening?" She was embarrassed at the high pitch of her voice but she put her hands up to get the band off and found it had somehow gotten tangled in her hair and it wouldn't lift off. It was still moving, too, down the back of her head.

"Paxe. What's it doing?"

Karnic turned his lens to her.

"It seems to be braiding your hair," Paxe said, tone harried. "Here are some boots for you." Karnic lifted the boots out of its storage bin.

The headband dropped down off her head and landed on the floor, and even with the bogey man of the Tecran coming for her, she couldn't not touch her head.

Her hair *had* been braided, as Paxe said. Lines of intricate patterns that started at her hair line and moved all the way back.

She wished she could see it.

She bent and picked up the headband. "A little warning, next time," she said to it. She shoved it into the bag, then sat and started pulling on the boots.

"These are great. Where did they come from?" She tried to keep her voice even. She was *not* going to let the Tecran petrify her.

Scare her, sure. But she was going to keep her cool.

"I had them made. It was coincidence that I did it last night, because you will need them now."

They fit her perfectly. Custom-made was the way to go, obviously.

Karnic held out the necklace Silvey had been working on yesterday, and Ellie took it, surprised by the heavy weight of it.

Like the fabric, the smooth metal links felt cool and pleasant in her hands, and she lifted the necklace and fastened it around her neck. She felt a faint buzz that lasted only a moment and was gone.

"So this will trigger automatically when I step outside, or do I have to do something?"

"No, it's an automatic trigger. It's self-regulating." Karnic zoomed his lens at her. "It seems to have already triggered. I can see a faint glow."

That was handy. She was about to swing the pack onto her shoulder when Karnic lifted out the knife block and the cloak.

"You brought my weapons." The reality of what the Tecran's arrival meant finally settled in her brain.

Clothes and boots and provisions were all well and good, but where was she going to go? She couldn't hunker down outside on the moon for long.

She may have to fight.

She lifted up the harness, slid the knives into their sheaths and shrugged it on, clipping it in front of her.

She hesitated over the cloak, it was too ornate and delicate to her eye for the rough treatment of being on the run in the hostile landscape outside, but she was only in a long-sleeved t-shirt and thin trousers. The atmosphere was cold outside, the sun pale and weak.

She needed something warmer if she was going out, and the cloak was better than nothing.

She put it on, and found what she hadn't seen before, that there were narrow slits in it that aligned with where the hilts of the knives were. She must be a similar size to whichever people the Tecran had stolen these items from.

"I'm ready." For what, she didn't know, but she had everything she owned with her now. "They here yet?"

"No. They're busy shooting at someone, but I can't see everything because of the way I've set up the lenses on the *Irini's* exterior."

"Shooting at someone? So maybe that war you were talking about is still going on?"

"Maybe." Paxe sounded thoughtful. "You need to get to the *Irini*, Ellie. I can lock it, so once you're in, you'll be safe."

It was the best plan she could think of, too.

She left the pod and wondered as she jogged down the passageway if it was the last time she would ever see it.

Karnic kept up with her, and she was grateful for his presence.

When they reached the station's exit point, she found her heart was beating faster as she stepped into the antechamber, wanting a moment to steel herself for stepping out into the moon's atmosphere with no suit, but Karnic had no such qualms.

He opened the door immediately, and as she took a step out after him she felt the faint buzz against her skin again.

"It's working." She drew in a careful breath, then gasped at the sight of the massive spaceship high above her. "That's the Tecran?"

"A Tecran Levron-class battleship. I can't see the name on the side, and I'm currently unable to infiltrate their systems." Paxe sounded incredibly frustrated about that.

As he spoke, a flash of purple light flared above her, and then a much smaller, sleek space craft screamed overhead and disappeared beyond view.

"A Grih battleship explorer. This is good." Karnic began to move toward the *Irini* at a fast pace and Ellie forced herself to follow.

She gave a shout as she took her first big step and found herself far less bound by gravity than she was used to. She had forgotten this was a moon.

"There must have been weights in the spacesuit boots." She windmilled her arms to keep herself from floating over and face-planting on the ground. It had felt strange walking in the suit before, but she hadn't realized how much it had been compensating for the weak gravity.

"Oh." Karnic stopped and turned. "I didn't think of that at all. Yes, there were weights in them."

She steadied herself and then jumped using both feet, in a bunny hop, hoping that would be easier, and found that it was.

"It looked like the Grih ship was hit."

"It was, but the good news is they won't be out here alone. They will have come from a Grihan battleship, and it will be somewhere close by." Paxe turned the drone's lens back to her. "They were obviously following the Tecran."

"Why do you think the Tecran came back here after so many months?" She looked upward at the big battleship looming overhead as she jumped again, then forced her attention back on the ground as she landed.

"Maybe they don't have anywhere else to go." Karnic manoeuvred around the rocks on the path to the launch pad. "Or maybe they need supplies. The base was stocked with enough to sustain the crew that used to be here for at least a year."

If that were true, the Tecran might be cut off from their usual supplies. Which would mean they were on the run.

And the thing about people on the run was that they tended to be dangerous.

***

"Did you see that?" Xallantra pressed up against the explorer's wall, peering down.

"Just a glimpse," Iso confirmed. "But it surely couldn't be . . ."

"What?" Renn hadn't seen what they had, his attention on the fighter pursuing them from above.

"A . . . person." Xallantra's choice of words had him turning in his seat as Eadal took them even lower and then executed a complex turn that brought them down to the ground, tucked in close to an outcrop of black rock.

"Tecran?" Although it would be difficult to tell because they would be wearing some form of spacesuit.

"We went over so fast," Iso prevaricated. "It could have been——"

"It was an Earth woman, and she wasn't wearing a spacesuit. She was standing out in the open without anything. No suit, no helmet." Xallantra sounded completely sure.

"An Earth woman?" Eadal stood up from the pilot's seat, tilting her neck left and right as if to get out the kinks, and Renn realized she had been far more stressed than she had let on. "Surely not? Not after what happened with Lucy Harris."

But Renn was looking at Xallantra's face, and his heart sank. Because he knew his military team leader, and she did not look like she was in any way joking with him.

"No wonder they kept trying to lose us." Hune rubbed at his temple.

"That could be because they didn't want to lead us to this station. Its very existence is a breach of the UC alliance agreement. And they couldn't restock if we came along with them." Eadal was shaking her head. "They may not have known she was here."

"Not many senior officers knew about Lucy Harris, so it's possible they didn't know about her," Renn agreed. "They may only have known that the station was here. But how was she outside without a suit?"

Xallantra lifted her shoulders at that. "There was a weird light around her head."

Whoever Xallantra had seen, at least they knew there were crew stationed here.

"Suit up," he said as he got to his feet. "They'll be coming for us soon and I want a look at that station before they do."

CHAPTER 8

SHE WAS close to the *Irini* when the Tecran buzzed overhead, but unfortunately not close enough.

Three vessels landed, two directly in front of her on the launch pad, on either side of the *Irini*, and the third one set down to her right, on the only flat patch of ground close to the warehouse.

"Damn." What should she do?

"Run away." Karnic spun on his tracks and headed left, and she followed. "The Grih landed behind the station. We'll find them."

She could do that. Would do that.

The way her heart was pounding at the possibility of meeting the Tecran face-to-face was enough to increase her speed.

But she was clear-eyed enough to know that running would simply delay the inevitable. At some point, the Tecran would capture them. They had the numbers and the equipment, she had virtually nothing.

And Paxe said the Grih's ship was damaged.

Unless the Grih battleship Paxe was sure was somewhere around made a sudden appearance, she had a pretty good idea how things were going to go.

Still, she wasn't going to lay down and give in. She'd fight to the end.

Her cloak flared out behind her every time she made a jump, and she worried it would catch on the sharp edges of the rocks and rip, or pull her down, but so far she'd been lucky.

She remembered that Paxe had said the necklace held the unfriendly atmosphere at bay with light, but she couldn't see any light at all, everything looked normal to her. It was possible she couldn't see it because she was on the inside, looking out, so to speak, and those looking at her could see something different.

"Am I lit up like a Christmas tree?" she asked Paxe. It would be good to know, especially if she was trying to hide.

"Your head is surrounded by light." Karnic swiveled his head toward her then back to the front as his tracks shuddered and bucked their way over the rough ground.

"So, a halo. Huh." She was amused, despite the situation. Or maybe because of it. Anything to divert her brain from the terror she felt every time she looked up and saw the battleship blocking the sun overhead.

Maybe she needed to focus on the fact that she would not like to be a prisoner of the Tecran again.

Not at all.

Would she use the knives to stop herself being taken? Could she?

She knew, without a doubt, they would hit their mark and most likely kill.

It was a hard thought.

Karnic had led her far enough to the left of the launchpad that they were out of sight of the station, and now he turned northward, parallel to it.

"Do you know where exactly the Grih went down?" She knew she should be thrilled they were here, but the truth was, they were just another unknown entity. She had Paxe's reassurance they were on her side, but she had no clear idea of what they were like.

"No. I can't see that far." Karnic rose up as high as he could go on the thin hydraulic poles that formed his neck and body, and stayed that way as he forged a path around the rocks.

Ellie couldn't make a clear jump as the landscape became more rocky, more hemmed in, and she ended up using her hands to propel herself from outcrop to outcrop. She felt like she was on a pogo stick, going up and down more than she was going forward.

Karnic suddenly lowered himself down, retracting his neck and coming to a stop, and Ellie nearly ran into the back of him.

The dangerous end of what looked like the barrel of a gun was poking out from behind a rock.

"It's the Grih," Paxe said.

She opened her mouth to say hello, and then it suddenly occurred to her that she didn't speak Grihan. And almost definitely, they did not speak English.

"How do you say hello in Grihan?" she asked.

Before he could answer, someone stepped around the rock. They were in a spacesuit, not exactly like the ones she'd used to go to the warehouse, but similar enough. The sight of them calmed her a little, because she could see the Grih were bipedal, like herself, not too outrageously alien, but she couldn't see the Grihan's face through the reflection of the sun's light on the glass front of their helmet.

She realized seeing their face was important to her.

Hopefully when she got closer she would be able to look him or her in the eye.

She was pleased to see they had lowered their gun.

Paxe said something to the person, the words sounding rough and choppy.

"You're introducing us?" she asked. The Grih had stepped closer to Karnic, and she realized they were a lot taller than she was. It jumped her nerves a little higher.

"In a way. I am introducing you, not me. The Grih have a . . . complex relationship with my kind. If you don't mind, I'd rather keep my presence undeclared until we know what's going on."

That didn't make sense to her.

Paxe had planned to find the Grih as soon as he was able to get the *Irini* working. Why didn't he want to let them know about him?

And who would they think was speaking to them, anyway? They knew it couldn't be her.

The question had to go unasked, though, because the figure was urging her to follow, and when Karnic began to move, she did as requested.

What choice did she have?

The way was so twisty, she could see Karnic ahead but only occasionally caught glimpses of the Grih in the spacesuit.

She kept expecting at least scrapes and scratches on the sharp-edged rocks as she hustled to keep up with them both. The cloak seemed to protect her, though.

And despite her fear of being out in the icy air, her new clothes felt amazing. As soft and warm and comfy as a pair of pjs.

The way ahead straightened a little, and she caught sight of the Grih disappearing between two rocks, at least a story high.

They were set so close together, Karnic couldn't squeeze through.

She stopped, unsure what to do.

The Grih stuck a helmeted head out and gestured again.

"Stay here or go in?" she asked Paxe.

She didn't want to go in. She was afraid to, even though she knew she had to trust the Grih. Hadn't she thought just a short while ago that she had no choice in the matter?

But it was hard to take the step.

"Go in. You'll be safe with them. I'll go back to the station, see what the Tecran are doing."

"You're leaving me?" She didn't want to sound panicked. But she also knew Paxe would never leave her with the Grih unless he knew they wouldn't harm her.

That had to be enough.

Karnic produced a little black box from his storage bin and held it out to her. "This is something I've been working on for when we encountered the Grih. A translation aid. It will help you communicate with them."

She crouched in front of him and took the box. "Are you sure going back to the station's safe?"

"It should be. This drone . . . Karnic . . . is part of the original station equipment, don't forget. Even if they do see him, it shouldn't worry them." Something in his tone was a little off, but the big Grih was back a third time, looking as though they were about to step out to join her, so she rose up, patted the top of Karnic's lens.

"Be careful. Both you and Karnic."

"You, too." He rolled away.

From the way the Grih reacted, even though she still couldn't see the person's face because of the reflection on the helmet, she could see they were surprised and concerned that Karnic was leaving.

She held up the box, hoping she didn't have to switch anything on for it to work. "He is going to see what the Tecran are doing at the station." There was barely a delay and then the same gravelly, choppy language she'd heard Paxe speak earlier sounded from the box.

The Grih paused, then gave a nod, so the translation seemed to have worked. Although she knew machine translation was tricky. Hopefully it didn't mistranslate her and insult her new friends.

She moved to the gap in the rocks, and the Grih stepped back to let her through.

This close, he or she seemed even bigger. Head and shoulders bigger than her. At least.

It was a little intimidating to squeeze past.

She stopped short when she saw there were four others gathered in the small space——not quite a cave, more a strange collection of tall rocks that had created a sheltered area.

They were all seated, but at the sight of her, they rose. She looked nervously at the Grih standing behind her, cutting off her escape, and finally saw his face.

He looked just like her.

That hadn't been something she'd expected.

Pale gray eyes studied her in a sharp, handsome face.

Unnerved, she turned back to face the others, and realized from their body language they were as shocked by her as she was of them.

All of them could be human, from first appearance. With a range of skin tones and eye colors.

They stared openly at her.

The Grih behind her said something.

The box vibrated in her hand.

"Are you from Earth?"

She turned. "Yes. My name is Ellie Masters."

He didn't look surprised.

Of course there were other women Paxe and his fellow thinking systems had taken, and they were all now with the Grih.

At least she didn't have to explain where she came from.

"I am Captain Renn Sorvihn of the Battleship *Etsijä*." The Grih tilted his head to the side. "How are you able to breathe without a suit?"

"This necklace." She touched it. "It's part of the loot the Tecran stole from other civilizations. I found it in the warehouse and Sil—— the drone recalibrated it to my physiology."

One of the other Grih stepped forward, hand outstretched to touch the necklace. From what she could see of his expression through the helmet, he was excited and intrigued by the concept.

"Not now, Iso." The captain had moved from behind her to stand shoulder to shoulder with her. "Although, I agree, it's very interesting."

"Where did the drone go?" Another of the Grih, a woman, asked. She had the stance of a soldier, to Ellie's eye. Her eyes were dark brown, with an amazing amber ring around them.

"Back to spy on the Tecran." Ellie held the box out as she spoke, waited for it to relay her words.

And then she went very still as she was hit by a terrible realization. "Oh, shit," she whispered. She looked over her shoulder, back toward the opening. "Shit, shit, shit."

"What is it?" The big Grih, Captain Sorvihn, touched her shoulder as she spun away from them, took a step toward the exit.

"He killed them all before. Why did I forget that?" She turned to look at him, and saw a weird reflection of herself in his helmet glass, eyes stretched wide. "He's going to kill them all again."

There was sudden silence after the translation finished repeating what she had to say.

"Who is going to kill who?" Another woman, one who had been lurking in the back corner, stepped forward. She was shorter than the others, a little less lean and toned.

Ellie remembered just in time that Paxe had asked her not to let them know he was with her. "The drone. It's going to kill the Tecran."

That was true, as far as things went. It would be Karnic who did the killing. Paxe wasn't able to do anything physical without it.

Again, there was a moment of silence. But it was electrified.

These people understood more than she did about the situation.

"A Class 5? Here?" Another of the team asked. "Surely not?"

She didn't know what a Class 5 was. She lifted her shoulders and shook her head.

"She said she forgot he killed the others." The woman spoke again, but to the others. She turned to face Ellie. "How could you forget something like that? How many others?"

"I was in a coma. He told me what he'd done, but I've never seen the bodies. I don't know how many."

"So it might not be true?"

Ellie looked at the Grihan woman in amazement. "Who would lie about killing an entire station of people?"

Renn Sorvihn, the captain, cleared his throat in the face of her astonishment. "Whatever the truth of it, I think I need to go out there, see what's happening."

Ellie looked over at him. "I should go with you."

Paxe might listen to her. She didn't have much confidence he'd listen to the Grih.

The big leader shook his head. "No. We can't risk the Tecran capturing you again." He pointed at the woman with the dark eyes. "Xallantra, you guard her. Hune, come with me."

Ellie shuffled out the way as the large soldier who'd stood silently watching her eased past her, and then suddenly the space seemed a lot less crowded with the two largest Grih gone.

"I'm Ellie," she said again, this time to the others, to fill in the sudden, awkward silence.

"Eadal," the woman at the back said, bowing her head in an oddly formal way.

"Iso," the Grih who'd been so interested in her necklace raised a hand.

"I'm Xallantra." The woman who had been ordered to guard her sounded a little annoyed.

"The only Class 5 left blew himself up. Unless the Tecran have been lying on another level altogether, and there was a sixth Class 5." Eadal turned to the other two, and Ellie wondered again what a Class 5 was.

"That would explain why they've been so desperate to get to this sector, and so terrified that we'd follow them here," Iso said.

Xallantra was silent, then turned to her. "Who is running the drone?" she asked.

Ellie felt her stomach drop. It was one thing to avoid answering, another thing to outright lie. "A friend."

"A . . . friend?" Eadal's voice rose.

"She's from Earth. We know what that means. It's a Class 5, no question." Xallantra put both hands on her hips.

"Where is it then?" Eadal shook her head. "They're not exactly easy to miss."

"What's a Class 5?" Ellie needed to understand this now.

They all stared at her for a beat.

"She just woke up from a coma, remember?" Iso spoke up. He turned to her. "A Class 5 is a massive space ship which is run by a thinking system."

Ah. That's the ship that Paxe must have had to destroy.

"My friend calls himself a thinking system." She had gone too far down this path now, and she couldn't think of a believable lie, especially when she didn't understand half of what was being said. Paxe would just have to understand.

"And what is his name?" Xallantra seemed to hold her breath after the question.

"Paxe."

Their reactions were extreme.

Eadal swore, Xallantra shook her head, and Iso lifted his wrist toward her.

"What?" She stared at Iso in confusion and then worked out he was recording her with some device on his wrist, and pushed it away in annoyance.

"Paxe is dead," Eadal said.

She shook her head. "No. Paxe is very much alive."

CHAPTER 9

"SHE'S JUST WALKING around as if she can breathe the air." Hune still hadn't let go of the wonder of it. "And did you see her hair? Those tiny braids?"

Renn found himself unable to focus on the amazing technology that allowed her to breathe without a suit, and the admittedly beautiful and strange hair, because he had been struck dumb by her very presence.

He felt like he'd taken a serious hit to the head in combat practice.

She was surrounded by a halo of light, wearing a ridiculously lavish cloak in jewel-toned embroidery, and everything about her seemed bright, intelligent, and impossible.

He had never met any of the other Earth women in person, but now he had some understanding of the fierce loyalties they seemed to inspire in the Grih who were close to them.

She reminded him of a Grihan mythical creature, a *nissa*. Delicate, magical, nature-bound. She seemed otherworldly, and even as he thought it, he tried to rein himself in.

She *was* otherworldly. *Was* alien.

And he hadn't been able to take his eyes off her.

He had insisted on checking out the station just to give himself some distance, some time to settle his thoughts.

And if things were as they seemed, he needed all his wits about him, because the beautiful and enigmatic Ellie Masters had the significant muscle and power of a Class 5 at her back.

"Her presence here is a nightmare, isn't it?" Hune said as they reached a line of rocks near the station and bent down to stay hidden behind them.

"A nightmare?" Renn shook his head. Nothing about Ellie brought the idea of a nightmare to mind. "A complication, definitely."

So far, it had been accepted by the United Council that the *Rauha* was rogue, that its captain, Vi'il, had broken free of Tecran High Command and was acting on his own, refusing to surrender for reasons of ego or stubbornness.

The Tecran military——what was left of the upper ranks of it after Lucy Harris had been found on Tecra——had seemed to be sincere in their willingness to help the UC get him back under control and their calls for the *Rauha* to return.

Renn had allowed the chase to go on as long as it had because he thought Captain Vi'il was simply recalcitrant. He hadn't wanted to open fire, to risk anyone getting hurt, for no good reason.

But if Vi'il had been trying to sneak out to this station under orders to finish off Ellie Masters and get rid of her body, to hide the last piece of evidence of the Tecran's culpability, then Renn had been played, and so had Grih Battle Center, and the combined nations of the UC.

"When she said the drone was going to kill them all, do you think she was being serious?" Hune asked.

Renn considered that as he found a gap in the rocks that gave a good view of the station and the warehouse. "She believed it. Her face is expressive, and she was seriously distressed at the idea."

"One drone can't do that much damage, surely?"

"I don't think it's the drone we have to worry about." Because the one thing that characterised a Class 5 that had broken free of its captivity was dead Tecran. Ships worth of them.

The only Class 5 crew who'd managed to get a decent number out alive was Bane's, and that was only because Rose McKenzie had persuaded the thinking system to force them off his ship onto an explorer and then let them be collected later and imprisoned for their crimes, rather than kill them.

If all the Tecran at this station had been killed, a Class 5 was behind it.

And that drone . . . no way was it responsible for mass murder on its own.

Someone, or something, was controlling it.

After all, *someone* had used it to speak to him in Grihan, introducing Ellie and telling him to look after her and protect her from the Tecran when he'd run into them on the path between the rocks.

He'd understood from the first meeting there was someone protective of her down on the station with her.

Even so, he didn't know how one drone could be capable of killing a large number of people at once.

There had to be other things in play here.

He looked up, searching the skies, but there was no sign of the prickle ball shape of a Class 5 ship.

Ahead, he could see three small Tecran explorers, two next to the strange spaceship on the launch pad, one near the high, long building to the side of the station.

As he and Hune watched, one of the explorers on the launch pad lifted off and flew overhead.

"Gone to search for us?" Hune asked.

Renn nodded. "Most likely." The *Rauha* would have scanned for their explorer and would have its coordinates by now. They'd have given them to the Tecran crew so they could round them up and bring them in.

"They seem to be in a hurry." Hune had crouched down beside

him and he pointed to the Tecran exiting the explorer on the launchpad.

They jogged toward the station without any of the looking around and reconnaissance he would have expected.

They had either been here before, or they had a very tight brief.

Of course, they had no idea how close the *Etsijä* was to their position, and they would want to be gone by the time Sia arrived with his battleship.

The explorer crew near what Renn guessed was the warehouse also moved with purpose, heading straight inside it.

When the team heading for the station reached the door they paused, conferring with each other.

Finally, they entered in single file.

A movement to the side caught Renn's eye, and then the drone that had brought the Earth woman to him appeared from around the side of the station.

It followed the Tecran inside.

Renn felt a prickle of unease along the back of his neck.

Maybe it was Ellie's distress when she talked about it killing everyone, but he thought he saw something predatory in the way it entered, closing the door behind it.

"What do we do?" Hune asked. He was uncharacteristically jumpy.

"We should follow them. I wanted to see inside that station, anyway."

"And if it's in there, killing them, and we get caught in the crossfire?" Hune asked.

Renn looked over at him. "We have an obligation to stop him killing them. The Tecran may be happy to ignore the rules, but I'm not. I also have a feeling we aren't on whoever is controlling that drone's kill list. Whoever it was left Ellie with us, and they wouldn't have done that if they didn't trust us. They probably need us to get her off here. So we should be safe enough from them."

Whoever 'they' were.

A shout from the warehouse drew his attention, and he saw the crew come back out through the doors. They were hauling a box between two of them, with the others moving ahead as the ramp to the cargo hold of the small ship lowered.

"Supplies," Renn murmured.

"Looks like they're having to do it the hard way. There would usually be drones or hover platforms to do the carrying."

"I think whoever is controlling that drone is controlling everything else. If they don't want the Tecran to have any help, they won't get any help."

One of the Tecran suddenly dropped their side of the box, hands going to their neck. They started screaming, and Renn rose up, Hune right beside him, to get a better look.

The Tecran had pulled his helmet off, and was batting at his face.

Renn felt a deep chill.

No one screamed liked that unless they were in terrible pain.

The Tecran around the soldier were backing away, not helping him at all, which Renn couldn't understand, until something seemed to jump from the screaming Tecran to the one who had been holding the other side of the box.

"What was that?" There was genuine fear in Hune's voice. "Did you see what it was?"

"I don't know." And he didn't want to find out first hand, either.

The first Tecran had stopped screaming and had fallen down.

The crew began to edge up the ramp, leaving the second Tecran scrabbling at her helmet. When she finally managed to get it off, she stood still, making high-pitched whistles of terror.

Her team mates disappeared into the ship, closed it up, and lifted off.

The second Tecran toppled over, and there was silence.

"That took, what, less than two minutes?" Hune's voice shook a little.

"Maybe less."

A Tecran exploded from the station entrance, making both Renn and Hune jerk.

She broke into a run for the launchpad, tripped, fell hard on the ground, and as she scrambled to her feet, she noticed the two fallen Tecran outside the warehouse.

Renn could see the soldier hesitate.

But to her credit, she ran over to see if she could help.

"We should warn her," Hune said, voice hushed, and Renn agreed.

No one should die like those two had died.

But something had already alerted her to the danger, because she started backing away.

Renn wondered what she could see that he and Hune couldn't from the angle they had. Or maybe the crew from the explorer who had just left were communicating with her. Warning her.

Whatever it was, it was enough to have her stumbling away and turning back to the launchpad.

But when she reached the ship, she couldn't get in to her explorer. The door would not open.

"It's locked them out."

"I think we really need to get into that station." Renn wasn't going to simply be an observer here.

He needed to know what was going on.

"What about . . . whatever it was that did . . ." Hune looked over at the two bodies. "That."

"I don't think whoever is in charge here would use anything they couldn't completely control, so I think we'll be all right." But thinking wasn't good enough when Hune's life was his responsibility. "Go back to the others. Let them know the Tecran have sent an explorer after us. They may not have seen it in that hidey hole we found."

Hune looked over at him. "With respect, Captain, no. I'll come with you into that station. You'll need back up. I know we said no comms, because the Tecran will pick them up, but if you're that worried about the others, open a channel."

Renn waited a beat. "I'm worried about you, Hune."

"No need."

But Hune glanced over at the bodies again.

Still, Renn could see there was no changing his mind, so he stepped around the rocks they were sheltered behind and walked openly to the station, Hune at his back.

The Tecran at the launchpad must have seen them, because she shouted and waved.

"She thinks we're Tecran, doesn't she?" Hune asked. "Maybe from the warehouse group."

"Probably. Our suits are similar enough from a distance." Renn stopped at the sight of a pot lying on its side just outside the door.

He moved around it, saw the lid had come partially off.

There was something mold-encrusted within.

It was . . . bizarre.

Unable to explain it, he walked over to the door, and found it locked. He could see the drone inside the small antechamber through the window set into the outside door.

It turned its lens up to watch him.

"This isn't your business, Captain Sorvihn. Go keep Ellie safe."

The voice came through his earpiece, and he drew in a quick breath at the level of access it seemed to have.

"Have you killed them all?"

"Nearly. There are a few still alive, but it won't be long."

"Let them go. They'll get on their explorer and they'll get away from you."

Hune was staring at him, hand going to his shockgun.

"No, they won't. They're planning to blow this place up when they leave. They don't want any part of it to be found later. They were a threat to me and Ellie from the moment they arrived."

"Then keep a few of them alive to use as hostages with the *Rauha's* captain." That at least made sense. "They can still blow this place up, no matter what you do, but they may think twice if they have crew down here to protect."

There was a beat of silence. "That's true. I fear I have a very strong reaction to the Tecran. I don't always think my actions through when it comes to them."

"We've let my battleship know our coordinates. They'll be coming, it's just a matter of time."

"How much time?" The voice in his ear asked.

He hesitated. Best to be honest about it. "It could be at least a few days. They light-jumped a full jump and are coming back toward us."

"That's a pity. Still . . ." The drone turned away, opened the door behind it, and disappeared into the station. "I'll keep the two that are still alive from dying. You make a good point, and as someone told me once, when they're dead, there's no coming back from it. At least I can keep my options open this way. I can always kill them later."

The cold way it was said sent a shiver through him. This was why the Grih were afraid of thinking systems. "Good." He turned away from the door at the touch of Hune's hand on his shoulder.

He saw the Tecran soldier at the launchpad was running toward them.

"What did you use to kill those two Tecran at the warehouse?" He spoke to whoever was controlling the drone, hoping they were still listening. It would be good to know if he needed to watch for some deadly creature.

"A weapon the Tecran had me steal from another civilization. Some of the things they took have a lot of potential."

"Who are you?" Renn pulled his shockgun from its holster as the Tecran got closer.

The voice was silent, as if considering whether to answer. "My name is Paxe."

Paxe.

Renn had guessed correctly, and in a way, it was better this way. If there had been another Class 5, one they hadn't known about, it would have set the UC on its head. "We thought you died."

"I nearly did. But fortunately I managed to hitch a ride on a fast cruiser out of the blast zone, and ended up here."

Renn had seen the Battle Center reports of the confrontation with the Tecran that had ended when Paxe's Class 5 had blown up. They'd suspected in the mayhem and confusion that some of the Tecran military had slipped away.

What Paxe was saying aligned with that, and he was more than willing to believe it.

"Did you know the Earth woman was here?"

"No. Not until I got here." Paxe's tone was short. "But I'll be blunt, Captain. Ellie's wellbeing is my priority. That and making sure the Tecran do not realize that I am still alive until I am sure I can get well away from them."

"Understood." Renn turned away from the approaching Tecran, trusting Hune to watch his back. "How are you going to explain the hostages, then?"

"I don't plan to. I've arranged things so the two soldiers inside think they saved themselves, got into a room that still has air. They'll come up with their own reasons as to why they're locked in, no doubt. And I'll let them communicate with that soldier running toward you long enough so she knows they're alive and well. Then I'll let their imaginations do the job for me. There were scientists here, playing around with the collection in the warehouse. More than one died messing with something they didn't understand, until they decided to leave everything and transport their stolen loot to Tecra, where it could be studied under more controlled conditions. They seem to have only gotten around to transporting about a quarter of it."

Renn turned away from the door, thinking that piece of information over.

The Tecran soldier had stumbled to a stop when she realized Renn and Hune were not her colleagues. She had her shockgun in her hand, given the danger that was clearly all around her, and there was a moment of silence as she readjusted to her new reality.

"You're the Grih?" she asked, at last.

Renn had spent the last month making sure he was fluent in

Tecran, especially as he assumed he was going to capture a battleship full of them.

"We're the Grih," he confirmed. "We can't get in."

"It locked us out of the station, too?" The Tecran looked back to her explorer, then to the two dead. "It's no good going in there, anyway. The drone ripped my team's suits and there is no air."

So that's how he was killing them. Suffocation.

He was sure that was the go-to method for the other Class 5s as well.

"Do you know what happened to them?" Hune asked, pointing to the fallen soldiers.

"Something buried into their necks and severed their throats." The Tecran rubbed her upper arms in distress. "I don't know what it was."

Her wrist buzzed, and she turned away, despite the weapons trained on her, and spoke in quick, clipped Tecran.

"Two of my team are still alive in there," she said, relief in her voice. "I need to get them out."

Renn moved aside to let her try.

She tried the door, tried shooting it with her shockgun. Finally, she turned in defeat. "I can't get into my explorer either," she said at last.

"Maybe go find your friends who are looking for our explorer, or call them back here, and use it to return to the *Rauha*." Renn wondered if she would be prepared to leave her two team members behind.

The Tecran half-turned, lifting her wrist up to talk to someone, and then she strode far enough away to talk privately.

"She's getting orders," Hune guessed.

"She doesn't want to leave her two friends inside, but there's no getting in, and she's worried about the thing that killed the others near the warehouse." Renn almost felt sorry for her.

She finished talking, and walked back to them. He could barely see her face through the helmet, but she seemed upset. "The other team got out of their vessel to approach your explorer, and they can't get back in either."

Suddenly the ramp of the Tecran explorer on the launchpad started to open, and she turned to stare at it in surprise. Then, with a shout into her wrist, she ran back toward the launchpad.

"She's calling the other team to come back here on foot for a lift back to the *Rauha*." Renn told Hune, who he knew didn't speak much Tecran.

"So they're just going to leave their explorer where it is?" Hune asked.

Renn turned to him, and gave a slow smile.

Ah.

Maybe Paxe was gifting them a working ship.

Which would be helpful.

Helpful to the Earth woman, he amended. And coincidentally helpful to him and his team.

The Tecran soldier made sure to avoid going close to the two bodies as she ran back to her ship.

He wondered if she realized she and the rest of the Tecran teams were being manipulated.

At this point, perhaps she didn't care. She just wanted off the station.

He noticed Hune was still unable to stop his gaze drifting to the warehouse over and over.

"Have you put the weapon you used to kill those Tecran by the warehouse away?" he asked Paxe. He would like to know it was no longer in play, himself.

"Worried?" The voice was a little distorted in his ear.

"Yes."

There was a pause. "I've put it away. Even if I hadn't, you would be safe from it."

"Good to know." He turned to Hune, tapped his shoulder. "The thing that killed them is gone."

"Gone?" He could just see Hune's bright brown eyes narrow, and his voice was slightly higher than usual.

"Deactivated."

"All right." Hune thought about it. Gave a decisive nod. "Good. Now what?"

"Now we go back to the team. See if we can get into the Tecran's explorer." He had barely taken a step away from the door, when an emergency warning lit up on his wrist.

Hune's wrist lit up, too.

"Xallantra." Hune's hand went to his shockgun. "What do you think——?"

"I think the Tecran crew might just have stumbled across our friends while they were walking back to the launch pad."

And that was not good.

Ellie Masters' existence would be a blight on the Tecran's reputations and making the whole problem of her go away would be in their best interests.

Right now, she was in very real danger.

CHAPTER 10

"XALLANTRA." Iso's voice was low and urgent.

Xallantra turned to answer, and then went still.

Ellie felt a prickle at the back of her neck.

"What is it?" Eadal asked in a whisper, and then she went still, too.

Heart thumping, Ellie followed their gaze, and finally saw what they had. The same type of guns the Grih had strapped to their thighs were pointing at them through the gaps in the rock.

Xallantra turned toward the entrance, and sure enough, a person in a spacesuit suddenly filled the space.

"You're the Grih?"

The black box Ellie held in her hand repeated his words in English for her.

The sound of it had the Tecran soldier——she recognized the helmet as the same as the ones she'd been wearing the last few days ——focusing on her, and he seemed spooked enough that he took a step back.

"This can't be." A light embedded on his gun barrel started to flash.

Xallantra stepped in front of her, blocking her from the Tecran's view with her body. "Now, now. No need to shoot her. She isn't even armed."

"She isn't even in a suit." The Tecran's voice bordered on a screech, and something in Ellie froze.

A whiplash of remembered fear.

"We were surprised by the lack of a suit, too. The device enabling her to go without is apparently from that warehouse next to the station. Your own people stole it from some unknown civilization."

The Tecran didn't respond for a beat. Ellie couldn't see him with Xallantra in the way, except for his lifted arm.

"Round them up," he ordered his team. "Shoot anyone who looks like they're going to make trouble."

"Hey. That's not very friendly." Xallantra kept her voice even. "Not very compliant with the Code, either. You do know you're just making things worse for yourself, right?"

"Step out with your hands raised, or I'm going to assume you're a trouble maker."

Xallantra stiffened, then waved to Eadal.

She nodded and went out first, then Iso.

"You next," Xallantra said to Ellie.

Ellie drew in a shuddering breath. The sound of their voices. The feathery hands.

"Ellie." Xallantra's voice was sharp, cutting off the loop of remembered fear that chased its tail in her head.

She sucked in air. "Do we try to escape?"

She didn't know if Xallantra had noticed her knives. They were completely hidden under her cloak, and no one had patted her down or asked her if she was armed.

Xallantra had just told the Tecran she wasn't. But Ellie didn't know if that was misdirection, or if Xallantra actually thought that, too.

Xallantra turned her head sharply. "No. Not unless we're in immediate danger of death. They have the upper hand for now." She waved at the massive ship hovering over the station.

"Right." It was a relief to hear that, really. She'd prefer not to get into a fight, but she would protect her new friends if she had to.

She followed Iso out, hands in the air.

When Xallantra stepped out behind her, the last of the Tecran soldiers surrounding the rocks joined them, all with weapons pointed their way.

"Where did you come from?" The Tecran officer asked Ellie.

"Earth. I thought you knew," Ellie said. "It was my understanding you're responsible for me being here."

"I mean, how did you get to the station?"

She didn't need the translator to hear the temper in his voice.

"I don't know how or when I got here, I was in a coma."

"And that?" He pointed to the black box.

"It's a translator. I only woke up a few days ago. I don't speak any of the languages around here." She was grateful Paxe had included Tecran in there, or she would have had to rely on the Grih to translate for her.

The Tecran studied the box, then her. "Where is the station crew?"

"That I don't know. When I woke up, I was alone."

The soldier was shaking his head. "Impossible. There were at least thirty crew stationed here. Thirty people don't vanish."

Ellie lifted her shoulders. She wasn't going to tell him they were dead. Cowardly of her, maybe, but she didn't owe these people anything. They'd taken her from her home.

Hurt her.

The Tecran could fuck off.

A buzz came from the Tecran's wrist, and he turned away, talking softly to someone through a communications device. Softly enough the translator couldn't pick it up.

He turned back to them. "Let's go. Now." He jerked his weapon in the direction of the station.

She didn't want to do that, but from Xallantra's body language, they didn't have much choice.

"How did you know she was here?" The lead soldier asked Xallantra.

Xallantra scoffed. "We didn't know this place even existed until we followed you here. You can imagine our surprise when we found her. Especially given what has been said by your leaders in the chambers of the UC under oath."

The Tecran said nothing to that, turning away and leading them toward the station, but Ellie thought he gripped his weapon a little tighter.

It didn't take a genius to understand that her presence here, and the Grihan witnesses to her existence, were inconvenient to the Tecran at the very least.

So they were all in trouble. Her new friends as well as her.

Making her, and the Grih, disappear would be in the Tecran's interest.

Of course, Paxe was probably busy as a little bee, killing them all off. But that looked like a pretty big battleship overhead, and he could only kill the ones who came down to the station, as far as she knew.

So it might not be the solution he thought it was.

Something scuttled up ahead, and Ellie stopped, surprised. It looked smaller than the Scary Caterpillar. Much smaller.

"I've sent something to neutralise the Tecran," Paxe said in English, using the translator. "I mention it because the Grih had a very troubled reaction to it, and I don't know if you will, too. It's not one of the drones you've seen before."

"What is it?" But she could hear the scuttle again, and she guessed. "Not some weird alien bug?"

"Well . . ."

His pause didn't reassure her.

"It *is* some weird alien bug?" Her voice got just a little higher.

"It's not a bug. Like the . . . Scary Caterpillar, it just looks like one. It's a drone. But it is alien."

"Okay." A drone was controlled. It wasn't unpredictable, which is what she didn't like about bugs. The way they zigzagged around, so you didn't know how to get out of the way. "What does it do?"

Before he could answer, she saw something segmented and long, like a mix between a centipede and a scorpion, but with sharp looking spikes on the ends of each segment, jump from a rock onto the Tecran leading the group.

She couldn't see what it did next, as he was facing away from her, but the next moment he was screaming, hauling his helmet off.

The Tecran looked like . . . like a cross between a person and a bird.

She was momentarily frozen in place. Had she heard someone scream like that before?

The memory of feathers touching her made her shiver, and then the Tecran's flailing jerked her back to reality.

If this is what Paxe's drone had done to the Tecran at the station, it was no wonder the two Grih had freaked out.

She was pretty freaked out, and she knew what it was.

"Is this necessary?" she asked.

"They plan to take you to the battleship and kill you. It is necessary."

The Tecran threw his helmet away and then he fell; dark, almost black blood pooling around his neck.

"Can't you just pierce their suits?" Ellie asked, talking so fast she was tripping over her words, her gaze on the box, not what was happening in front of her. "Like I did with mine by mistake. Then you can let them make a run for one of the ships that landed near you."

Paxe was silent, and the weird bug leaped from the shoulder of the fallen Tecran to the top of the helmet of the next Tecran in line and turned what looked like its head toward her thoughtfully.

She found herself lightheaded, as if the necklace was no longer providing her with enough air.

"What's happening? What is that?" Xallantra gripped her shoulder, gave her a shake.

She shrugged the Grihan soldier off, took a step away. She needed all her wits about her right now. She didn't have time to explain. "Just wait a moment."

"I *could* do that." Paxe's voice came through the box, not the bug, and she was immensely relieved by that. "Tell them to run."

But she didn't need to tell them.

Everyone had turned toward her in quiet terror when the bug had gone still and looked at her. The Tecran on whose helmet it was perched was the most still of all.

The Grih were just as frightened as the Tecran, but there was nothing she could do about that now.

As the bug began to move again, one of the other Tecran turned and started to run, and the others followed. The one with the bug on his helmet realized he was being left behind and ran after them.

The bug had jumped down onto his back, and Ellie saw a gash appear in his suit across his shoulder blades, and then the bug leaped from his shoulder, following after the others.

The Grih were still standing around her, shocked as they watched the Tecran disappear behind the rocks.

"What in Guimaymi's Star was that?" Iso breathed. "Some kind of lifeform——?"

"It's a drone," Ellie said. "That's what Paxe told me."

"The captain will be coming this way. Let's go meet him." Xallantra scooped down, picking up her weapon from where one of their Tecran captors had dropped it, as well as one of the Tecran's own weapons, and the others did the same. Then she started walking, and after a moment's nervous hesitation, Eadal followed.

"After you," Iso told her, indicating she go first. "What were you talking about when you were speaking with Paxe in your language?"

"I persuaded him he didn't need to kill them. They would leave us alone just as easily if their suits were pierced and they had to run for their ship."

Iso didn't say anything to that, and she could only just make out his face through his helmet, so she turned away and followed Eadal.

What kind of mayhem would they find up ahead?

"You MIGHT WANT to stand to the side, Captain." Paxe's voice in Renn's earpiece was dry. "There are Tecran running for their ship, coming your way." A pause. "And my little insect drone is involved, so warn your colleague. I noticed he was very disturbed by it."

Renn stopped. There was nowhere to stand back here, the way was too narrow. "Let's climb," he told Hune. "There are Tecran headed this way, and that killer bug thing is with them."

"With them?" Hune hauled himself up the rock nearest him, and Renn chose the one beside it.

"I assume attacking them, which is why they are running."

Hune stood at the top of the rock, but it wasn't that high. Slightly over head height, was all.

"Are we high enough?"

Renn understood his concern. The bug could jump onto them easily from where they were. "It's not going to attack us."

"Sure." Hune had his shockgun out, and was standing with legs braced.

The sound of people running was clear, along with the high-pitched sound of Tecran in distress.

The first one rounded the corner, stumbled at the sight of Renn and Hune looming over them on the rocks, and then ignored them completely as she ran for the launch pad.

Another soldier was right on her heels, and he didn't even look up, he was batting at his suit, as if to make sure the bug was no longer on him.

But it was.

Renn caught a glimpse of it, and then it was gone. Leaping through the air after the front runner.

"Their suits are slashed at the back." Hune's voice trembled a little.

"I see." It was clever. It was impossible to reach the back of a suit. They couldn't repair it until they could safely remove it.

"Where are the rest of them?" Hune asked.

Renn wondered if they might not have made it. They could be lying dead up ahead.

But then a third soldier came around the corner, fell at the sight of them, scrambled to his feet, and carried going, making a sound Renn would be happy to never hear again.

The fourth soldier shouted a warning at them as she ran past, and then was gone.

The fifth came a moment later, stumbled and then fell.

He didn't get up.

Renn jumped down beside him. "We'll carry him to the ship. Come on."

Hune looked like he was going to refuse, but then he dropped down. Took the Tecran's other side.

It was almost impossible at first to carry the Tecran between them. He was completely unconscious and limp and the way was so narrow, they could barely fit three abreast. Once they were through the rocks and out into the more open area around the station, though, they were able to get up some speed, lifting the Tecran under his arms so only his boots dragged behind him on the ground.

The Tecran soldier who'd spoken to them at the station was standing in front of the explorer, waving to her colleagues, but Renn could see her demeanor change to concern and then fear as they approached her.

She had seen what had happened to the soldiers by the warehouse. She knew exactly what danger they were in.

As soon as they reached her, the ramp of their ship began to lower.

Renn wondered if they would wait for the colleague he and Hune were trying to save, or whether panic would get the better of them.

The Tecran had definitely seen them. The soldiers had stopped dead at the sight of him and Hune carrying their friend between them.

The Tecran soldier who had spoken to them at the station seemed to be the only one without a ripped suit and Renn wondered where the bug had gone.

It worried him, even though he was sure Paxe would not use it on him or his team.

It was just a visceral reaction, he assured himself.

Whoever had created it had a twisted genius. It was both effective and terrifying.

The ship's engines started up and the ramp closed.

"They're leaving without him?" Hune gave a grunt as they hauled the Tecran over a rock.

"Hopefully they just closed up because they can't breathe in the suits." He would be interested to see if they did wait.

It would tell both him and Paxe how much the lives of the two hostages in the station meant to them.

The ship didn't take off, but just as they reached it, Renn felt something land between his shoulder blades, and saw the bug out of the corner of his eye. It had run up his back and was perched on his shoulder.

He expected to get a warning signal that his suit had been breached, but no warning came.

The bug leaped onto the Tecran he was carrying.

With a shout, Hune dropped his side and stumbled back, and Renn strained to keep the Tecran soldier from falling.

The bug disappeared into the gash it had made in the back of the suit, but it emerged mere moments later, and was gone.

"Are you all right?" Hune's breathing was labored and he was looking around.

"I'm fine. Grab the other side." Renn grunted, trying to keep the Tecran from dropping, and Hune stepped up, grabbing his arm just as a small door opened on the side of the explorer.

Hands reached out, and he and Hune lifted the Tecran up to his team.

They pulled him in.

"Thank you." The Tecran soldier from the station crouched in the doorway, her hands out in the traditional Tecran greeting. "If he lives, it's thanks to you."

She shut the door, and the ship lifted off.

Renn had to turn away from the swirl of black dust as it shot upward, and then froze at the sight of the bug on a rock beside him.

"There——" Hune had seen it, too. His voice closed down, as if he couldn't get his throat to work.

"Captain!" Xallantra stepped out from the narrow path between the rocks, and with relief, Renn saw the rest of the team and the Earth woman following her.

"Can you move that thing away?" he asked, hoping Paxe was listening.

The thinking system didn't answer, but the bug did move, flowing across the ground in a way that looked like it was made of liquid, not sharp metal plates.

It made straight for Xallantra, and Hune gave a cry of warning and fear.

But the bug zipped past her, weaving through the feet of the others, and then suddenly appeared on the Earth woman's shoulder.

The woman said something in her beautiful, flowing language, and the bug ran down her arm and clasped itself to her forearm, covering it from the wrist to just below the elbow.

With the cloak, and the glowing light around her, it looked like a strange arm brace.

She looked like a hero out of a legend.

"How can you stand it?" Hune asked her when everyone reached them. "How can you let it touch you?"

"It's just metal and a computer." Ellie lifted her shoulders. Held her arm out. "See?"

Hune flinched back, and Eadal, noticing it for the first time, edged away from her.

"It didn't kill the Tecran," Renn said. "Why?"

Xallantra nodded toward the Earth woman. "She suggested it just cut their suits and let them run for the ship. It agreed." She looked over at the woman. "You knew it would come to rescue us? Is that why you asked about escape?"

Renn turned to her. Waited.

She was shaking her head. "I hadn't seen this drone before. I was talking about my knives."

"Knives?" Renn frowned. What did she mean? Could the translation be wrong?

"These." She reached for her hip with the arm covered by the bug, and pulled a knife seemingly out of nowhere.

He activated the zoom function on his helmet and noticed a thin slit in her cloak for the first time. She had been armed, and they hadn't even checked.

It was testament to how much her presence had thrown them.

But it was also her appearance. She looked . . . magnificent. Beautiful. And about as deadly as a kapoot.

He needed to remember that both the Grih and the Tecran had underestimated the other Earth women they had found as well. To their detriment.

"They're very sharp," Ellie said, voice earnest. She slid the knife back into its hidden sheath. "It would have killed them if I'd thrown one at them."

"They didn't check you for weapons," Xallantra said, consideringly. "*We* didn't check you for weapons."

Ellie shrugged. "I noticed. That's why I asked you. I had the means to escape."

"You could have given a knife to Xallantra," Hune said.

"Maybe." She shrugged, and Renn had the feeling she didn't actually know if she could have.

It piqued his interest.

But before he could say anything else, the black box she had in her hand buzzed.

"The explorer that landed next to yours is now open and you can use it to escape this place," Paxe said. He spoke in Grihan and then switched to Ellie's language.

She gave a nod, but she seemed reluctant. "Paxe says I should go with you. He'll follow us in the *Irini*."

"Is that the *Irini*?" Renn eyed the strange vessel taking up most of the launch pad.

The structure was tall and cylindrical, curving smoothly up from the base and ending in a rounded tip. It was a reflective silver, highly polished. He had never seen anything like it.

What looked like wings were attached to the back, folded in tight, almost flush with the sides.

She nodded.

Paxe's voice came through the translator, speaking her language again, and he watched Ellie closely. Her lips pressed together, and she looked like she was going to argue.

Then she sighed. Gave a nod. Answered back.

"You aren't obligated to do this, but there are a few things in the warehouse that Paxe thinks should be saved. He says the Tecran are planning to destroy this station if they can get their hostages out, and even if they can't."

"What kind of things?" Renn eyed the bug still clamped to Ellie's arm.

"Like this," she confirmed, lifting her arm up. "This, too." She touched the necklace that allowed her to go without a spacesuit.

"You want to bring that disgusting thing into an enclosed ship with us?" Hune's voice was steady. "Absolutely not." He turned to Renn. "Tell her, no."

"The necklace alone is a massive find," Iso said. He stepped closer to Hune, as if placating him. "If there are other things like that in the warehouse, we'd be fools not to take some of them with us."

"It's not like we have a lot of time." Eadal looked up at the *Rauha*, still hovering like a black cloud above. "We either do it, or we don't, but whatever we decide, we need to get on with it."

"It's a big warehouse." Xallantra was looking over at it. "How long will it take to get everything?"

"Paxe says there may be lots of interesting things in there that he doesn't know about, but he will get what he thinks are the most interesting things he *does* know about ready by the door." Her gaze flickered to the station, and Renn saw the little drone exit the building, heading for the warehouse.

Presumably the Tecran hostages were still secure in a room, not dead.

"Eadal and Hune, go get the explorer, fly it here, and land by the warehouse. We'll load a few things in it if we can."

"She's not coming aboard with that thing on her." Hune pointed at the bug. "If she does, I don't." He turned and jogged off.

Eadal lifted her hands in distress, then turned and ran after him.

There was silence as the rest of them watched the two disappear among the rocks.

"He means it," Xallantra said.

"What if I seal it in a box, Captain? It doesn't have to stay on Ellie's person. I sent it to her for protection, that's all." Paxe's voice was matter-of-fact.

Except, all the Tecran were gone by the time it climbed up and settled on her, Renn thought. Which either meant Paxe thought she needed protecting from Renn and his crew, or he was lying.

Ellie had been left out of this conversation, he noticed, which had happened all in Grihan. She frowned at the translator, and he thought she looked annoyed that she couldn't understand the situation.

She spoke, quick and impatient, and the thinking system answered her.

She crouched down, held out her arm, and the bug flowed off her, heading for the warehouse.

It was invisible in moments, even though Renn tried to keep track of it.

He didn't know if it had some kind of camouflage or was hidden by the deceptive undulation of the land.

"We can't lie to Hune," Xallantra said.

"No. But if it's locked in a box, he might be calmer about it. He saw it kill those two Tecran by the warehouse door. It wasn't pretty."

"So did you," Iso pointed out.

Renn shrugged. "When I understood it was a drone, it lost some of its terror for me." He started walking to the warehouse and the others followed.

Ellie hesitated, and then followed and he slowed so she could catch up.

Her cloak billowed around her, and she turned a glowing face toward him. "Are you at war with the Tecran, as Paxe thinks? Is that why they took us prisoner?"

Iso, walking on her other side, almost tripped over a rock. "No. There were a few stand-offs between us and them, but the Tecran knew they couldn't fight against the whole of the UC on their own, especially as their secret weapons, the Class 5s, had either gone over to our side, or were destroyed. The ship above, the *Rauha*, is a rogue battleship that refused to come home and submit to United Council control."

"A rogue ship." She tilted her head back, and then looked at him. "That means it doesn't have much to lose."

She caught on fast.

The crime committed against her and the other Earth women by the Tecran became even more apparent to him.

She was their intellectual equal, and the Tecran had treated her like a non-sentient being.

"Had you seen any Tecran before today?" Iso asked. "From before you went into your coma?"

She shook her head, then stopped and shivered, as if suppressing a memory. "When I saw the one who took off his helmet, when the drone attacked, I remembered . . ." She shook her head again. "I thought I remembered something."

It went without saying that that something wasn't good.

The enormity of the situation hit him again.

They had stumbled upon this station with absolutely no idea what kind of a strange turn things would take.

He hoped the Tecran's explorer was operational and that they could get away on it.

The *Rauha's* captain certainly had every incentive to make sure they didn't.

CHAPTER 11

PAXE WAS LYING.

Ellie had only known him a few days, but she could hear the faint nerves in his voice, the too-long silences.

He was up to something.

"Promise me, at least, you're not going to hurt the Grih," she said as she trailed behind the captain and his crew as they headed for the warehouse.

Every now and then, she felt the eyes of the Grihan captain turn her way.

Was he suspicious of her? Just keeping her in sight to make sure she was all right?

He fascinated her. He ran his team with an easy authority that was never belittling or condescending, and there was an easy cama-raderie between the team members that told Ellie they all respected each other.

It was good to see.

It made her feel calmer about them.

She still didn't know exactly what they looked like, but that was becoming less important.

"What do you mean?" Paxe's answer came a shade too late. As if he'd had to think about it before he manufactured some outrage.

"I mean, you're plotting something. Fair enough, but no nasty surprises for the Grih, okay? They've been really decent to me so far and I assume I'm going to have to find a home with them when this is all over."

"That seems to be the pattern," Paxe agreed. "I have no intention of harming them. As you say, they have treated you well and they'll give you a home once we've managed to get away from here."

"Okay. Good." Still, having no intention of harming them wasn't the guarantee she'd been looking for. It meant he could still hurt them by mistake. But what more could she do? She was not in charge here.

She wasn't even in charge of her own destiny.

Up ahead, she saw the group stop, and then edge around a certain spot, and curious, she hurried to catch up.

Dead Tecran.

Ellie caught sight of the bloody gashes in their throats. It looked more vicious than what had happened to the lead soldier by the rocks. He had died quickly. These two looked like they had suffered.

"That's why the grumpy soldier, Hune, is so terrified of the bug?" She had caught a glimpse of his face through his helmet, and every nuance of his voice spoke of fear. "He saw this happen?"

"Yes."

"Does it really have to come with us?"

Paxe had told her that it was important, which is why he'd asked her to let it rest on her arm, where he was sure the Grih wouldn't try to shoot it with their shockguns.

"It is incredibly useful in many ways."

"Take it in the *Irini*, then." That way, it should still be safe.

"What if they blow the station before I work out how to fly it?"

There was the rub.

"Are you able to work on the ship *and* come with me somehow, at the same time?" What she was asking was whether he was physically present in some way, or wholly in the machine.

He waited so long to answer, she thought she had mortally insulted him.

While she stood looking down at the dead Tecran, Karnic bustled out of the warehouse on its little tank tracks, shot out a clamp from both arms, got a grip on the Tecran's suits and dragged the bodies away, around the side of the building and out of sight.

It was cowardly of her, but she was relieved not to see them anymore.

"I could ask you to take me with you," Paxe's voice was thoughtful. "But I know for sure I can protect myself from almost any attack the Tecran launch. They could destroy the *Irini*, but I should still be all right."

"But with no way out of here."

"True. But I control who can access me on the *Irini*, and I won't be able to do that in an explorer shared with the Grih. I'd also be vulnerable to going back under the Tecran's control, if they hijack the ship. I think I'll stay with the *Irini*. I've been in a massive blast before, and I not only survived, I managed to regain control of my environment."

"You know this world way better than me," she said at last. "It's your life, and your risk assessment to make."

She could hear the Grih talking inside the warehouse, and something about the tone told her she would be wise to find out what they were saying.

"Just take care of yourself, okay?" she said as she approached the door. "I don't want anything to happen to you."

Karnic was suddenly at her side, back from dumping the bodies, and she stumbled to a stop as he curled his arms around her thighs and rested his little lens face against her hip. "Thank you."

She bent to pat him, and when she straightened up, she saw all the Grih were staring at her.

Karnic rolled back, arms retracting. Paxe's voice came through his speaker, talking in Grihan, and then he whizzed off between two long, high shelves.

"Oh." Ellie noticed a line of boxes that had been set near the door. "That's a lot of stuff." There was no sign of the motley crew, though, and she was sure they must have been the ones to set this stuff down here.

Karnic couldn't have done it on his own.

It meant they were keeping out of sight. She couldn't really blame them.

"We can't take it all," Captain Sorvihn said.

"They should, though," Paxe told her. "They'd regret every single thing they left behind, if they only knew what they were leaving."

"Where are the motley crew?" she asked.

"Hidden," Paxe responded. "Don't mention them."

She nodded. Fair enough. She felt protective of the crew herself. "Why don't you line the boxes up for the Grih, most important to least important? Then if they have room, they can take the best things."

"Some items will be difficult to categorize in that way." But Paxe sounded like he was thinking about it.

"You can only do your best," she told him. "Tell me what to put first."

She took the small box he told her was absolutely a priority, placed it closer to the door.

"What are you doing?" Sorvihn's voice came through the translator moments after he spoke.

"Paxe is telling me the order of importance of the items. I'm lining them up for you."

"We'll help." Iso looked like he wanted to open the boxes, not move them, but he helped her carry the second box, and then Xallantra and Sorvihn began helping as well.

The sound of the explorer landing seemed to come much faster than she thought it would, and Xallantra and Sorvihn obviously thought so, too, because Sorvihn held up a hand for silence, and he and Xallantra moved to the door and looked out, weapons in hand.

"It's them." Xallantra's shoulders relaxed. "Let's start loading."

She pushed the warehouse doors open, and Ellie saw the explorer had landed right next to them, and the ramp was lowering.

"Captain. I was hailed twice by the *Rauha* on the way over." Eadal stepped out from behind what Ellie guessed was the cockpit, and trotted down the ramp.

Hune was already standing at the bottom of it, and he seemed to stare at Ellie.

To ease his mind, she lifted her arm, showed him the bug was gone. "It's staying with Paxe," she told him.

He didn't move, didn't answer, and she turned away, disappointed her attempt at reaching out hadn't worked.

"You didn't answer the hail?" Sorvihn was asking Eadal.

"No. I was worried they might be able to take remote control of it, but either they can't, or they didn't try to." She lifted her shoulders apologetically. "They've demanded we surrender and return the explorer to them."

"I bet they did." Sorvihn turned away, walking toward the pile of boxes and hefting one. "Let's pack up and see if they'll let us go."

He didn't sound very optimistic, though.

Iso stayed with her, helping to rearrange the boxes, but though they worked well side-by-side, she had the feeling he saw her more as a specimen to study than a new person to get to know.

"Paxe says there are other women from Earth." She said it as they were carrying up one of the last boxes Sorvihn had said they could take.

"Four other women. We thought there were only three, then we found the fourth on Tecra just over a month ago. That was shocking enough. That you were here the whole time . . ." He shook his head. "This is going to rock the whole of the UC, and I think everyone thought they couldn't be shocked any more."

"Because the Tecran never admitted they had me?"

"Yes. Add to the fact that they've been holding you on a secret base they should have declared to the UC, and it's just a massive blow to their chances of getting early control back of their military."

That seemed to suggest the Tecran had every incentive to kill them all.

"Do you sing?" Iso asked as they walked back down the ramp.

"Someone once told me, *everyone* can sing. Some just do it better than others." She smiled at him. "Do you?"

He eyed her strangely. "Not many Grih are good at it."

"They are very fixated on singing," Paxe said to her. "I should have remembered that. If you ever need to distract them, sing."

"Sure." It sounded ridiculous, but as she'd said earlier, Paxe knew this world a lot better than she did. "Or you could play some of the recordings you made."

"I could." He sounded absolutely floored by the realization. "When I went back to Earth a second time, I was able to make better recordings than I did on the first trip."

His second trip. The one he made to collect her.

She didn't realize the thought of it would hit her so hard, but she stopped and had to take a few deep breaths.

"We're ready." Xallantra called down the ramp, and Ellie looked up to see everything neatly stacked and harnessed in place.

"Where's the bug?" Sorvihn asked her, beckoning her up the ramp.

"I persuaded Paxe he should let the bug go with him on the *Irini*."

Sorvihn gave a nod, and then shouted something to Eadal. The ramp lifted, and then sealed them in.

He pulled his helmet off, and Ellie stared, transfixed.

Elves? The Grih were elves?

Well, elf-like, anyway.

She felt her knees go a little weak with relief.

It shouldn't matter that much that they didn't look truly alien to her, but there was huge comfort in the fact that they looked so similar to herself.

And the magical twist was . . . delightful.

What her after-school reading group of six and seven year-olds would give to see this sight.

"What is it?" Sorvihn's voice seemed deeper, rougher, now that the helmet was gone, the translator mimicking him perfectly. His eyes were more than gray, they were silver with a dark pewter rim, his hair dark brown, standing straight up, and lightening to caramel at the tips.

"It's just . . ." She didn't know quite what to say. Nothing that she did say would make sense to them. "Do you have legends about cities high in the forests, and bows and silver and magic?"

Sorvihn cocked his head, as if he didn't know what she was saying, and she realized the translator seemed to struggle. There may not even be a translation for some of her words.

She cleared her throat, hugging her delight close.

"I am very pleased to meet you." She drew herself up and extended her hand.

Sorvihn looked at her hand, and the translator babbled something at him. He reached out his own, still gloved and in the spacesuit, and gently shook. "The Grih welcome you to our community."

"Thank you."

"Do you see the light around her has dimmed, but it hasn't gone out." Iso had also taken off his helmet, and he had been watching them with interest. Now he stepped closer.

"I can't see the light," Ellie told him. "But I would have thought it would no longer be necessary."

"The necklace is finely calibrated," Paxe told her. "While you could comfortably survive the environment in the ship, it is not one hundred percent like Earth's, so the necklace is still compensating, adjusting at a minute level."

She waited for him to repeat it in Grihan, and when he didn't, told them in English, and the translator repeated it. She was beginning to be able to tell when Paxe was doing the translation, and when the machine was.

"Paxe says I'd be fine in this environment, but the necklace is set to mimic Earth conditions, and I suppose it would be impossible for the environment to be exactly like Earth's."

"So it is still regulating your air?" Iso had taken the time to get out of his suit while she'd been speaking to the captain. He was fit and tall, his skin a golden brown, his hair dark but tipped with gold, like a punk rocker. He looked like he wanted to take the necklace off her.

"That's what Paxe says." She did actually feel better since she'd been wearing it, she realized. Better than she had in the station, which she assumed was set to mimic the Tecran atmosphere, much like this explorer would be. She hadn't felt like she was struggling, but since the necklace had been activated, she'd felt more energetic. More herself.

"Captain, we're being hailed again," Eadal called from the cockpit. "They say if we try to leave, they'll shoot us."

CHAPTER 12

RENN HAD EXPECTED something like this.

There was no way the captain of the *Rauha* would let them go without a fight. There was too much at stake for him.

Delay.

That was Renn's best strategy.

He knew the *Etsijä* was coming, it was just a matter of time. And he had yet to have a look around the station. He didn't know why he wanted to get inside it so badly, but he did. Especially if Vi'il was going to destroy it soon.

Vi'il had to know that Renn's best tactic was to delay, too.

It would be a fine line they would both have to walk. No one wanted bloodshed. It would stain both their reputations.

Unless Vi'il decided his reputation was no longer worth saving.

Renn needed to remember that it was possible the rules of engagement he was used to as a member of the UC might no longer be in play, especially if Vi'il was reconsidering returning to Tecra, where he would be forced to serve a sentence for his abandonment of his post.

If he decided there was no going back, the stakes became even higher for Renn and his crew.

And Ellie.

He had a duty to protect the Earth woman and get her back to the UC, and a standing Battle Center directive to bring all Class 5s into the Grihan camp.

It was clear to him that Ellie came with Paxe attached.

For the first time he understood the trouble the other Grihan officers who'd had to deal with the human women and their Class 5 friends had gone through.

Although, and he'd wondered about this since he first heard Paxe's voice coming through the drone, why did Paxe feel so protective of Ellie?

She hadn't freed him.

Imogen Peters had.

Unless the Tecran had managed to chain him again, and Ellie had helped him break their hold?

Whatever the reason, it was one more mystery attached to this whole affair.

He felt there were so many prickle balls in the air right now, it was going to be very hard not to drop one.

And the consequences for doing so would be significant.

"Captain Vi'il." He leaned over Eadal's shoulder and studied the Tecran captain who'd led him on such a chase for so long.

"Captain Sorvihn. Well, well. I didn't expect to see the captain of the *Etsijä* himself. You made a mistake leaving your ship."

Renn lifted his shoulders. "I found this station, though, and an Earth woman, and a warehouse full of stolen artifacts. So if there was any mistake here, it was yours."

Vi'il puffed up his chest, as Tecran seemed to do when they were stressed. "I didn't know about the Earth woman."

That might actually be true. From what Renn had seen in the reports, the list of people who had known about the women stolen by the Class 5s had been a short one.

"Let's say I believe you, you did know about this station. And no one in the Tecran military so much as mentioned its existence."

Vi'il lifted his hands. "They were hoping it would never be found. And that wasn't such a bad hope, given the location. But I didn't feel right about leaving the station crew here to rot, and I needed supplies, so it seemed like both the right thing to do, and the most logical from my perspective, to get here."

"Except I kept so tight on your tail, you weren't able to." Renn wondered how much Vi'il must have cursed him and the *Etsijä* these last few weeks.

"As you say." The Tecran captain lifted his shoulders. "All for nothing, though. They're gone. And two of my crew are still down there."

"It seems so. Do you know where the original station crew have gone?" Renn wondered if they'd found any clue as to their whereabouts. Paxe had said he'd killed them but there was a possibility it wasn't true.

"No. We've scanned the moon, and if they're dead, we can't find their bodies. I know someone would have got word out if they'd been collected and taken home."

"You know someone personally who was in the crew?" Renn suddenly thought he understood.

Vi'il gave a reluctant nod. "My sister. There is no way she wouldn't have tried to get in touch if our own side had managed to pick them up."

"Unless it was in your senior leaders' interests to make sure no one ever spoke about this station." Renn didn't think that was out of the bounds of possibility. They could have all been killed by their own leaders.

"What you are saying is treasonous for me to even think," Vi'ill said. "And I do not believe it."

"So where does that leave us?"

Vi'il sighed. "You put me in a very difficult position, Sorvihn. I should kill you. But given the treaties my people have signed, that would be illegal. I cannot do the right thing, no matter which decision I make." He turned his head, then looked back at the screen. "And you saved one of my best people. Carrying him to safety, at risk to yourself. That makes my decision even harder."

"Let us go. Give yourself up. There is no sense in running any more. There is nowhere for you to find safe harbor. You cannot drag your crew on the run forever. Now that you've found the station, and see that your sister is not here, you must surely realize your best chance of finding her, if she's still alive, is back on Tecra."

"Even if I agree to all that," Vi'il sounded weary, "I don't have the supplies to go any further. I need access to the warehouse, to get the food my crew needs to survive the trip home." He paused. "And that is proving difficult. Of the eighteen soldiers I sent down, three are dead, two are stuck in the station, and the others are traumatized. No one wants to go back down." He suddenly narrowed his eyes. "It would be a sign of good faith if you were to get my people out of the station for me."

Renn thought about it. "If I can get in, I'll certainly try, but there is no way to get in through locked doors."

"No." Vi'il conceded the point. The moon station was like any building set up in an unbreathable environment. Virtually impervious to being breached.

"I have an alternative offer." He knew delay was their best way out of this alive and now Vi'il had given him a way to do just that. "How about we draw the stocks from the warehouse for you? Take it to the landing pad."

"You would help us with our supply issue?"

Renn shrugged. "I'm not going to let your people starve. And if I have your word once you're restocked, you'll let us go and return to Tecra, then yes, we'll help."

"You have my word. We will return to Tecra." Vi'il stepped back. "I don't know how you're able to manage down there better than my own people, but I'll send you the list of what we need. Hail me when you have it ready and I'll send an explorer down."

He winked out.

"He didn't say anything about letting us go. And he's lying about going back to Tecra," Xallantra said. "Or, he's twisting the truth."

"I know." Renn hadn't expected anything else. "He was careful not to say when he'd return. He could plan to return in a year, and that would still be keeping his word." But the more worrying aspect was his avoidance of saying he would let them go.

That was not a good sign.

"So, why are we going to help them?" Hune asked.

Renn could hear the soft murmur behind him of the translator telling Ellie what they were saying.

"Because the longer we draw this out, the more time we give the *Etsijä* to arrive."

"Vi'il has to know that." Xallantra sounded thoughtful.

"Yes. It's going to be a balancing act. How long we take to get what he needs, against how desperate he is to have the supplies, against how badly he wants this station and Ellie to stay secret, against how frightened his crew are of coming back down themselves to do the job we've offered to do, against the lives of the two Tecran Paxe is holding hostage in the station."

"That's a lot of balancing," Eadal said. A faint chime came from the control panel. "Here's the list of what he wants. How do we even find this in the warehouse? It's not as if there's an inventory list at the door."

"I think Paxe knows where some of it is." Ellie spoke from behind them. "You could ask him."

"And we could also use the time to look through the things Paxe suggested we take that we didn't have room for." Iso almost bounced on his toes.

"We still don't have room for them, Iso." Renn eyed his explorations officer. "I know it must be torture for you, but we can't take it all."

"Still, I could record what we can't take. At least that would be something." He looked so earnest.

"All right. Get Ellie to help you, and the rest of us will pull the supplies Vi'il needs. And we'll take our time about it."

"What about that bug?" Hune asked.

"It's in that strange ship on the launchpad," Renn said. He saw Hune relax. "Suits back on. Let's go."

Eadal powered the explorer down, and those who'd taken off their suits pulled them back on.

Time to drag things out.

Renn hoped Sia was closing in on their position, that the *Etsijä* was almost there.

He had the feeling that the longer this went on, the longer they were exposed, the more likely Captain Vi'il was to throw caution to the wind and simply wipe his problems out.

It looked like she was back doing her favorite thing on the station. Peering into boxes.

Iso had told her they'd start with the boxes Paxe had lined up for them in the loading zone, but which they hadn't had room for.

"If we can't take them along, we can at least see what they are." He set up a small handheld device to record their discoveries, and they began opening the boxes in order of importance, according to Paxe. The first few were incomprehensible, and they had to ask Paxe why he had chosen them.

His explanation didn't make sense to Ellie, but Iso seemed to grasp the relevance of them, at least in a few of the cases, and Ellie guessed they were talking about technology she simply had never been exposed to.

She wandered to the end of the row while Iso placed the translator box nearby and had an in-depth discussion with Paxe in Grihan.

She reached the far end and found Karnic depositing another box at the end.

"They don't have room for anymore." She looked down the line, saw she must have passed at least twenty boxes to get to the end.

"You never know." The voice coming from the drone was soft. It freaked her out a little that Paxe was speaking to her through Karnic, but Iso also seemed to be having a conversation with him.

"Is that actually you talking to us both?"

"I am simply giving Iso the technical details, which I already know. It isn't difficult at all."

"Right." She looked at the box the drone had set down in front of her. "I suppose it can't hurt to put them in order of priority."

Karnic tapped the lid. "No, but I'm worried the Tecran won't let you leave in the explorer anyway."

Ellie was worried about whether the Tecran would let them leave, herself. It was not nice to hear Paxe say the same thing.

"So what will they do?" She crouched beside the drone, her cloak billowing around her.

"I'm not sure, exactly." As he spoke, she heard Iso make a noise of absolute delight.

She turned, still crouched down, and saw him lift out what looked like a vacuum-sealed creature.

She could see eyes and a mouth mashed up against a bag of vacuum-sealed plastic, as if trying to scream.

The Tecran were really sick.

She couldn't imagine what they thought they were doing, killing strange creatures and vacuum-packing them. And she wondered why Paxe had put it in the line-up.

Iso pressed something on the side of the transparent pack and broke the seal, so air rushed into it. He set it down, and the packaging fell away, pooling on the ground around the strange animal.

Which started to move.

It looked like a tulip bulb that came up to her knees, Ellie thought. But it had what to her eye looked like elephant trunks attached to it. They were not symmetrically placed, though, they seemed to be randomly stuck all over it.

It made a noise, she assumed of distress, and moved, faster than she would have thought it could, to attach itself to the sleeve of Iso's spacesuit, one trunk-like appendage wrapping itself around his wrist.

"Aren't you amazing?" Iso crooned, lifting his arm up to face height. "Where did those Tecran find you, then?"

"What's that?" Eadal called from behind Ellie, and she looked over her shoulder to see Renn, Xallantra, Hune and Eadal had emerged from one of the rows, carrying boxes between them.

"Some kind of alien lifeform." Iso sounded excited. "It was sealed without air, but it recovered instantly when I broke the vacuum, even in this moon environment." He reached out his other hand, either to touch the creature, or pry it from his arm, but as he did, the trunks waved in alarm, and something shot out of one of them, a tiny spear or barb, that pierced his spacesuit at chest level.

Iso made a terrible sound, a choking noise that had Ellie rising to her feet.

Before she could take a step toward him, though, he collapsed onto the ground, and the creature jumped from his arm with a squeal, and lunged in her direction.

It seemed to drag itself along, using its trunks to move, so it should have been slow, but it was not. It was fast, and it looked like it was coming straight for her.

"Throw a knife," Paxe said from the translator. "I think it could kill you. Throw a knife."

She scrabbled at her left hip, but the creature was really moving, trunks waving around, and it sort of leaped at her.

She stumbled back, tripping over the box behind her and falling hard.

"Ellie, throw a knife!" Paxe's voice roared over the speaker system of the warehouse.

She wanted to shout that she was trying, but it was on her as her hand closed over the hilt at last.

It didn't stick itself to her face, or any other sci-fi horror scenario she had in her head, it seemed to be repelled away from her just as it touched her cloak, tumbling back.

She pulled the knife and threw it in one smooth motion, as the creature was righting itself from its fall for another leap.

It stopped in its tracks, shivered, and seemed to come undone, pooling into a glob of goo on the floor.

She slowly got to her feet in utter silence, legs shaking.

"Well." Eadal broke the tension by skirting around the mess and jogging to Iso. "That got my heart pumping."

"What did the thinking system shout at you?" Renn didn't move past the dead creature right away.

Paxe must have been talking in English, Ellie realized. "He thought it might be able to kill me. He told me to throw the knife."

Renn nodded.

"Captain, he's not breathing." Eadal's voice was panicked. "What do we do?"

"Take him to the med pod in the station?" Ellie suggested. She carefully lifted her knife out of the puddle, trying not to touch any of the liquid, which looked like badly-set jelly, and Karnic appeared at her side, holding out a wipe for her to clean it with before she put it back in its sheath.

"Will Paxe let us?" Renn had reached Iso, and he looked back at her.

"He will." She didn't even ask him. He had to let them back in.

Hune was suddenly beside Renn, and they lifted Iso up, and Xallantra grabbed his feet.

They ran out the warehouse and Eadal and Ellie got ahead of them, Eadal running, Ellie jumping, fast across the rocky, dusty ground, to get to the station and open the doors.

For a moment, before she shouldered into the station's antechamber, she didn't know if the door would give, but it let her in without so much as a squeak of a hinge.

She held it wide for the others, and when they were inside, she ran ahead of them again, leading the way to the med pod.

"Paxe, where are your hostages?" Ellie gasped out as they ran through the empty common room.

"In the station commander's old quarters. They won't bother you." He answered through the speakers.

She led the way down the tunnel and then into the pod, and Renn and Hune heaved Iso onto the table and Xallantra pulled her helmet off.

Iso had started breathing again, which was good, but he'd screamed the whole way, the sound affecting something deep inside her, like she'd heard someone make that sound before, in her darkest dreams.

Xallantra grabbed Iso's collar, pulled a tab, and the top of the suit fell open.

"Get his helmet," she barked at Hune and he pulled it off as she ripped open Iso's shirt.

Finally, now they were in the pod, Paxe had started piping a translation through the speakers for Ellie, and she realized Iso had been screaming "*Get it out, get it out, get it out.*"

The tip of the barb that had pierced his suit was still embedded in his chest, and Xallantra studied it for a moment.

"Please, get it out." Iso's voice was hoarse from shouting.

"I need a clamp." A shelf slid out and Xallantra grabbed what she was looking for. Hesitated. "I can anaesthetise you—"

"No! Get it out!"

She went in, pulling it out carefully.

Iso gave a final scream as it came free and then passed out. Xallantra held it up to the light.

Ellie could see fine filaments attached to the tip, wriggling as if they were alive.

Which made sense. They'd come from a live creature, not a weapon.

Xallantra grabbed a transparent tube from the shelf, shoved the tip inside and screwed on a lid. "There are still some filaments in there. I'll need to get them out."

She looked over the offerings on the tray, took a more delicate looking clamp and a syringe, which she plunged into Iso's shoulder, just above the wound.

"That should keep him out and feeling no pain for at least half an hour." She moved the arm of the bright light beside the bed, angling it so she could see better, and carefully pulled out another filament.

Hune held out a fresh tube for her to put it in.

"Thanks. There's only one more." As she pulled it out, Iso clamped his teeth together and roared, his back arching on the bed, his arms flailing.

He upended the shelf, and Renn grabbed his arms, leaning over him to keep him from hurting himself.

His eyes opened once, staring as though he'd just seen his worst nightmare, and then he collapsed.

For a moment, they all stood in silence. Rattled to their core.

Xallantra was still holding the wiggling filament with the clamp, and she carefully put it in the tube. Firmly closed it in.

Then she looked at the machines, reading the data.

"This is top rate equipment, but he's in a coma. We need to get him to the *Etsijä*."

The place on his chest where the barb had gone in looked terrible. Slightly green around the edges, and bright red where the skin had torn.

Now that he was still, it was easier to study it.

Ellie didn't know if it was her imagination, but she thought the green area maybe got bigger while she was staring.

"He's got a toxin of unknown origin in him." Xallantra looked around. "Is there anything in here for that?"

Another shelf slid out, and she studied the array of ampules before she chose one and loaded it into one of the machines, let it inject Iso.

Nothing happened, which Ellie guessed was both good and bad.

"Okay." Xallantra blew out a breath. "Still, he needs a full med team, however good this little pod is."

"I know." Renn looked grim.

Eadal had been hovering just in the doorway, with Ellie, out of everyone else's way. "Will Vi'il let us on the *Rauha*?"

"He should. First rule of the Code." Hune rubbed his shoulder, as if he was imagining Iso's injury.

"It may come to that. He won't let us leave to find the *Etsijä*. Not unless he's given up and decided he might as well surrender." Renn leaned back against the wall, arms crossed over his chest. "I'm not a bad diplomat, but I didn't think he was close to arriving at that conclusion when we spoke earlier."

"No." Eadal gave a defeated nod. "I agree."

"We can't let Iso go on the *Rauha* by himself." Xallantra looked stricken.

"We don't know if he can go up at all. Vi'il hasn't exactly behaved in a way that screams he'll follow the rules." Renn rubbed at his spiky hair. "Stay here and watch him. Ellie, can you come with me back to the explorer, and we'll hail the *Rauha* again?"

She nodded, wondering why he'd asked her, specifically. Then, as they made their way down the tunnel, she thought maybe it was because he was afraid Paxe wouldn't let him back in without her.

"Was that med pod where the Tecran kept you?" he asked as they walked through the lounge. He was moving quickly, but she had the sense he was looking around intently as they jogged through.

She nodded. "I woke up in here only a few days ago."

"Good reflexes with the knife."

She stopped and waited for him in the antechamber while he pulled his helmet back on. "It doesn't miss. It doesn't miss even if I throw it backward over my shoulder." She had tried that, once she realized it was not due to any skill that she was hitting the bullseye each time.

"I'd like to have a look at them when we have time."

She nodded her agreement, but she had a feeling that they wouldn't like being handled by someone else.

They pushed out the door, Renn already moving quickly, and she stumbled as they went from the gravity of the station to the gravity of the moon.

She didn't know what technology was responsible for the station's gravity, but it was impressive.

Renn stopped and turned back to her, looking perplexed.

"No gravity boots," she said. At his blank look, she remembered she'd left the translator box in the warehouse and he didn't understand her. She pointed to her feet.

He held out his hand, the gesture surprisingly courtly and genteel, given the hurry he was in.

He just needed a tunic and leggings, and a filigree crown, and she could be being greeted in court by the elven king.

"Thank you." She placed her hand in his gloved one, even though she didn't really need his help, and hopped.

Which felt very silly, but it worked. Mostly.

She only bumped into him a few times before they reached the explorer.

They entered it from the pilot's side, and she saw the door opened onto a small antechamber, just like the station. Renn pulled it closed, waited for the environment to readjust, lifted off his helmet, and stepped through.

He hailed the *Rauha* and then seemed impatient with whatever response he was given.

Ellie stood back, keeping to the antechamber. Something inside her froze at the thought of the Tecran captain catching sight of her. Out of sight, out of mind seemed a good way to play it.

As Renn spoke with irritation to whoever was on the other end, she remembered again that the translator was back in the warehouse, and she couldn't understand what was being said.

Deciding there was nothing she could do but stand around in the explorer, she closed the antechamber door and climbed out, heading into the warehouse to look for it.

When she stepped inside, she saw Karnic was bending over the puddle made by the strange creature she had killed.

"I think it's still alive," Paxe said. "Given enough time, it'll put itself back together."

"Oh, hell no." She stopped in her tracks. "What do we do?"

"This." Karnic lifted up a tube which appeared from a slot in his side and sucked the puddle up, then poured it back into the transparent package that Iso had released it from, and resealed it. Then he put it back in its original box and from nowhere seemed to produce a sticker with strange writing on it.

"What does it say? Danger! Warning! Do not open!"

"In all five languages of the United Council," Paxe confirmed.

"Maybe also store it right at the back." She found the translator still sitting on top of one of the boxes in the row and grabbed it up. "Why did you include that thing?"

"Because I think there are a lot of things that can be learned from it. Regeneration, interesting toxins that should have application for numerous medications. All manner of things. I didn't think Iso would let it out."

"No. That was not a good move. But he's paying for it."

"You nearly paid, too." Paxe didn't sound very forgiving.

Ellie patted the knife at her hip. "Good thing I had these."

She looked around for any sign of the motley crew, but they had either snuck their way to the *Irini*, or were still hiding in the warehouse.

Wherever they were, there was absolutely no sign of them at all.

She left Karnic moving the box to the back of the warehouse and walked back to the explorer. When she reached the antechamber and opened the door, she set the translator to a low volume, lifting it to her ear so the Tecran wouldn't hear Paxe translating for her.

The two captains must have only just stopped dancing around each other, because Renn was explaining one of his crew was injured.

"One of those strange creatures that attacked my people got one of yours, too?" Vi'il said.

Renn hesitated. "Something got him. I'm not sure what. He's in a bad way and needs access to a med bay. Will you take him?"

"You're invoking the Code?"

"I am."

"Send up the explorer with him and my supplies, and I'll take him."

Renn didn't like that, she could see it. The original deal had been that Vi'il would send an explorer down. Now Vi'il wanted them to send their only means of transport up.

It would also mean taking the time to unpack their explorer, repack it with the supplies. All things that were going to take time.

Time that Iso didn't have.

"That's my offer, Sorvhin. Plus one last thing."

"What's that?"

"The two people being held in the station. My lenses picked up that you got inside. Why aren't they free?"

"I didn't see them in there, and my full attention was on my injured colleague."

"Well, I want them on the explorer with your officer and the supplies."

Renn shook his head. "He's in too bad a way for me to try and free them from wherever they are, and load your supplies. Iso doesn't have that kind of time."

"Try harder. At least try to get them to speak to you and record it so I can hear they are indeed alive. We haven't heard from them since they communicated with Lieutenant Corva."

Renn gave a reluctant nod. "I'll do my best. Will you allow one of my people to stay with Iso when he comes up to you?"

"I'll have to think about it. Load up the explorer and bring the person who you want to assign to him along, and by the time they get to the *Rauha*, I'll have made my decision."

Renn cut the transmission and swore. "I was going to drag this all out, keep him waiting, but now he's tied the delivery of the supplies and the hostages to helping Iso, we're going to have to move fast."

"Paxe might not release the hostages."

Renn looked at her, brows raised. "I'm sure he won't."

They were silent for a moment, and she waited for Paxe to chime in, to say he would do it, but there was no communication.

She sighed. "So you need to unload what's in here, replace the boxes Paxe suggested you take with the Tecran's supplies?"

Renn nodded. "Would you go tell the others? I'll start unpacking the hold, and loading it with the food supplies we've already found. We'll need to get more, though. We'd only just found the Tecran stores and equipment when Iso let that thing out of its bag."

"All right." She hesitated. "Do you think he's sincere? Vi'il?"

Renn grimaced. "I'd like to think so, but . . . no. He'll help Iso, I think he's telling the truth about that, but he'll try to keep this explorer. Whoever goes up there won't be coming back down."

"Unless you only load half the supplies," Ellie said. "Tell him Iso was deteriorating too fast and you had to get him up with only some of the supplies in the hold. That gives you more time to 'find' the hostages, as well."

Renn stared at her like he wasn't quite sure she was real. "That will be a risk. But maybe a risk worth taking. I'll think about it."

She nodded, pleased he was at least going to consider her suggestion.

As she jogged back to the station, she looked up at the *Rauha*, still hovering overhead, and then to the left, to where the *Irini* sat.

"How are things going for you, Paxe?"

"Slowly." She could hear his frustration.

"Will you let the hostages go in exchange for Iso?"

He gave a snort. "No. Vi'il is obligated to take Iso, no matter what he says. And I don't think he'll risk the condemnation of his colleagues onboard by turning him away."

That was good.

"Do you think the Tecran suspect you're down here?" she asked.

"I know they don't."

"How can you be sure?" Ellie didn't know what had happened when Paxe had captured the Tecran in the station, but they must surely have suspicions.

"The only reason I let them take that explorer back up, even though they'd seen you, was because I was able to have that bug drop a listening device into the suit of one of the soldiers, as well as attach one to the outside of the explorer itself. I'm using it to listen in to the chatter in the launch bay."

"Well done." And it was. But Ellie realized that what she'd thought was him listening to her about doing the right thing and letting the Tecran run back to the explorer with damaged suits, rather than kill them, was actually him working out that sending the explorer back up would be useful.

There was no reason an action couldn't be both, but it was worth remembering there had been another motive.

She needed to scrutinize his actions more closely. She couldn't just assume he was doing the right thing for its own sake.

She needed to be wary.

CHAPTER 13

"WE'RE HALFWAY THERE." Xallantra leaned back, stretching out stiff muscles.

"Do we carry on loading, or do we send it up?" Eadal looked over at Renn.

He hesitated. Ellie was coming up the ramp with a box, and he was surprised once again that she could lift things she looked too short and frail to carry. She was stronger than she appeared.

She was still wearing the cloak, and it billowed around her as she strode toward them, her face surrounded in the glow of light from her necklace, her hair in braids so intricate, he couldn't imagine how she had made them.

He kept reminding himself that she wasn't some mythical figure from Grih legend, but a victim of Tecran overreach.

Still, he hadn't heard her complain once.

She wanted to be helpful, wanted to cooperate, and while she did, Paxe would cooperate, as well.

He certainly didn't want Paxe as his enemy. Not while he was stuck on the station with little leverage and no backup.

It was one of the reasons he hadn't forced the issue with the hostages. He didn't want a fight with Paxe over them. Not yet.

"Captain?" Hune set down a box and began strapping it in place. "Will the Tecran turn us away if we only give them some of what they've demanded?"

"No." Renn couldn't see them doing that. "Vi'il's desperate, even if he holds most of the advantage here. He needs these supplies."

"What if he decides to send some of his crew to get the rest instead of letting us back down?" Eadal had the most to lose, as she'd be flying the explorer up.

She was looking at being held hostage herself if Vi'il went back on his word.

"All I can say is that I don't think he'd harm anyone he keeps. He'll maybe use you and whoever goes with you to look after Iso as hostages, but I don't think he'd go as far as torture or ill-treatment."

"If he agrees to help Iso, then I'd accept that," Xallantra said. "But will us playing games with his supplies make him feel like he can renege on his agreement?"

That was the question.

Renn thought he'd grown to know the Tecran captain fairly well with their games of hide and seek these last few weeks, but there was more at stake now. Much more.

Some of the strange decisions Vi'il had made while Renn was chasing him across the galaxy finally made sense. He'd been trying to get to his sister on this station. He had also known there were supplies available here, that he didn't need to return to Tecra.

He would not like having those supplies used against him.

Still . . . "He wants to use our need to get Iso help to ensure he gets his supplies quickly, but that doesn't erase his other problems. Like we know of the station's existence, and Ellie's existence, too."

"You think when he has what he wants, he'll blast the place?" Hune looked slightly conflicted about that scenario.

"There are still the hostages Paxe is keeping in the station," Renn reminded him. "He won't leave them or kill them easily. He seems loyal to his crew."

They had forgotten about the Tecran hostages, Renn could see it on their faces.

"We can't let Ellie anywhere near him. They'll kill her and space her body." Eadal looked over at Hune.

He gave a reluctant nod. "Then who goes up?"

"Eadal and Xallantra." Renn didn't want to put any of them in harm's way, but Xallantra had a cooler head than Hune. "Tell Vi'il we had to get Iso up to him, he needed help too urgently, and that the rest of us are busy getting the balance of the supplies ready for your return trip, and that we're looking for a way to get the hostages free."

"All right. Hopefully he accepts that," Eadal said, but she didn't quite pull off the upbeat tone she was going for.

Renn did not want to think about the alternative, but he forced himself to do it, and still, he had no choice but to take this risk.

No choice at all.

The wait was interminable.

Every now and then, Hune or Renn would go out and look up at the *Rauha*, but now the explorer had been swallowed up inside it, they had no way to contact the ship.

"Can you hear what's going on up there?" Ellie asked Paxe.

He didn't answer back, and although she asked him again a few more times as she worked with the others, pulling the Tecran food supplies from the shelves and carrying them out of the warehouse, there was still silence. He hadn't spoken to her since he'd told her he was listening in to the chatter on the *Rauha*.

It worried her, but she kept quiet about it to the others.

At least the translator was still working.

She remembered that while he had occasionally spoken to her directly through it, it was also automatic, and didn't require his attention.

She still hadn't caught sight of the motley crew, and to her, the warehouse felt empty, as if they weren't in it. She decided they were probably in the *Irini*.

"We should eat something." Ellie set down the latest box and looked over at Renn. She didn't want to go back to the station, but she really did need food.

Her reluctance must have shown.

"What's bothering you?" Renn turned to her, his helmet reflecting her back at herself, a pinkish-yellow-toned image, with big eyes and a halo.

"The Tecran are still in there." She waved over at the station through the warehouse's open doors. She knew Paxe had them shut up in a room, but even knowing they were in the station made her reluctant to go in.

"We'll go with you." Renn gestured to Hune. "Let's find some food."

Hune lowered the box he was carrying to the ground, and joined them quickly enough Ellie guessed he wanted a break and something to eat as well.

She headed out the door, and then slowed, realizing the pile of boxes Paxe had originally stacked there for the Grih to take was a lot smaller.

She stepped out, and saw Karnic disappearing around a rock, one of the boxes in his storage compartment, another held between his two hydraulic arms, headed for the launch pad.

Paxe must have decided to load everything they had taken out of the explorer and exchanged for Tecran food supplies, as well as the boxes they couldn't fit in, but which he thought were important, into the *Irini*.

Renn and Hune both eyed the diminished pile of boxes.

"He's putting them in the *Irini*." Ellie tipped her head at the strange vessel.

"Better that than leaving them," Renn said.

Hune said nothing. But Ellie had the sense that since the strange creature's attack on Iso, on top of the little insect drone attack, he wanted nothing to do with any of the boxes in the warehouse, unless they were clearly Tecran military issue.

Renn led the way, Hune taking up the rear, both of them alert as they moved toward the station. They seemed to be trying to protect her as she hopped and skipped along.

It loosened something tight inside her.

They really were on her side. The thought helped settle her, so that when she stepped into the station, she wasn't so tense.

It was quiet.

"Are the Tecran still alive, Paxe?" she asked as she headed for the kitchen, but again, he didn't answer.

Renn and Hune had taken off their helmets as soon as they were inside, and she was struck once again at how similar they were to her.

It was another thing that settled her.

So far from home, it helped to feel some kind of connection to the Grih.

She took off her cloak, tossing it over the back of a chair, and both men's eyes went to the two knives strapped to her waist.

"Can I?" Renn held out a hand.

She didn't understand her reluctance, but she forced herself to slide one out and offer it to him, handle first.

He took it, and swore as it dropped to the floor.

"It bit me."

She bent and picked it up. "What happened?"

"It was like a mini shockgun hit."

They all stared at it for a moment. She slid it back into its sheath. "It's one of the things from the warehouse."

There was nothing more to say than that, she supposed.

Everything in there was unusual.

"What's that you're wearing?" Renn asked her, and she saw he was staring at her clothes. "Is that Cargassey cloth?"

She lifted her shoulders. "Paxe thinks it might be. He used it to make me some clothes." She tugged at the shirt. "Nothing of the Tecran's fitted me, and I liked the color and the feel of it."

"It looks like Cargassey cloth." Renn came closer, a question in his eyes as he reached out a hand, and she extended an arm in silent permission toward him.

He gripped the fabric of her sleeve between finger and thumb.

"It's very comfortable and warm," she said. "It feels like a natural fiber."

"If it's Cargassey, it's rare. And stolen." He let go, stepping back, and she wondered why he suddenly seemed a little flustered.

She turned away and found food for herself, and Renn and Hune perused the stores, looking through the alien food for a few minutes, but then abandoned the small room that held the items that interested her, and went to look through the other cupboards.

"Standard UC energy bars." Hune pulled out a small box and held it up. He didn't seem too unhappy about it, so she guessed they'd had them before.

Hune made grinabo for them all, but they didn't linger. The worry and the wait for the others pressed on them, and they cleaned up and walked back out into the communal area.

"I'll go look for the hostages," Renn said. He looked over at Ellie and then spoke to the translator box. "Not to free them, Paxe, just to let them record a message for Vi'il, so he knows they're still alive."

Paxe didn't respond, and Renn lifted his gaze to hers.

She moved her shoulders. "Just do it. He'll tell you soon enough if he objects."

She wouldn't go with him, though. She waited in the lounge as he pushed through into the sleeping quarters, Hune on his heels.

They didn't take long, although Ellie had the feeling Renn was dying to explore the place more.

"All okay?" she asked.

Hune looked grim, Renn looked his usual, focused self.

"They're alive. I recorded a message through the door." He lifted his wrist unit. "It's better than nothing to give Vi'il."

"Eadal and Xallantra are taking too long," Hune said as they walked back to the warehouse, his eyes on the *Rauha*. "There's no reason they shouldn't be back already."

Renn didn't answer. He was staring up, too.

Ellie couldn't think of any reason for the delay, either, other than Vi'il wanting to worry them. Or maybe he really wasn't planning to let the others come back.

She couldn't see Renn's face because he had his helmet back on, but he'd worked like a demon in the warehouse, hauling boxes at a faster rate than Hune and herself, and every time he'd dropped a box by the door, he'd stepped out to look up.

He thought he'd sent his team up into danger and he was second guessing himself.

She didn't know what to say to him. She felt out of her depth. There was so much going on, so much that had happened between the Grih and the Tecran before now, that she had the sense of stumbling onto a battlefield.

The only thing she had going for her, she conceded, was Paxe. In her battlefield analogy, he was an independent sniper sitting on the sidelines, with an axe to grind against one side, and a willingness to cause havoc.

No. That wasn't fair. She had the Grih going for her, too.

Renn would care if she was harmed. Nothing he and his team had done since she met them brought her to any other conclusion.

And if she was a little in awe of them, and almost pathetically grateful to have more allies than just Paxe, well, she was going to keep that to herself.

They went back to work, but they were almost done, dragging it out because they didn't know what they would do with themselves when all the boxes were at the warehouse door.

"They're coming back." Paxe spoke through the translator box in English.

"Renn." Ellie pointed out the open doors, and Renn and Hune rushed past her.

She hung back, just inside the warehouse, looking up.

The explorer landed in the flat area just outside, and the ramp lowered.

Both men were expecting trouble, Ellie could see. They'd drawn their shockguns, and they made their way toward the ramp cautiously.

A Tecran stood in the explorer's loading bay, using either Eadal or Xallantra——Ellie couldn't tell from this distance which one——as a shield.

He prodded her, and they walked down the ramp.

It was Eadal, Ellie saw as her angle improved.

Xallantra was nowhere in sight.

Most likely, she was still above, in the *Rauha*.

They were less than halfway down the ramp when something leaped onto it from the ground, moving so fast Ellie could barely track it.

The Tecran holding Eadal hostage started screaming.

The noise brought two other Tecran out from the cockpit. They took a few steps closer, saw what was happening, and tried to scramble back, to shut themselves in, but they couldn't get the doors to close.

The Tecran holding Eadal had released her, but his shockgun discharged, hit a wall, and something sounded like it exploded in the explorer's interior.

Eadal moved the moment she was free, running down the ramp toward her two teammates. As soon as she was past him, Renn stepped in front of her.

Hune moved to stand beside the captain, and they slowly moved back, Eadal protected by their bodies, all eyes on the carnage inside the explorer.

The Tecran screamed as their suits were slashed, but Paxe didn't leave it there, this time. Their throats were slashed, too.

Ellie wanted to turn away, but like the others, she forced herself to watch.

All three Tecran ended up face down on the ground. Ellie could see blood seeping out from one of their suits.

"I thought you said . . ." Hune steadied his voice as they reached the doors. "I thought you said that thing was in the other ship."

"Paxe must have sent it back out when he saw the explorer returning." Ellie couldn't see where it had gone.

"What do we do now?" Eadal spoke for the first time.

"What happened up there?" Renn had stepped back into the warehouse, and he closed the door, more, Ellie thought, to calm Hune down than because it was necessary.

Not that the closed door would stop the insect drone from getting in, she was sure, but it did seem to take some of the edge off him.

"They took Iso to the med bay. Let Xallantra go with him." Eadal sounded exhausted. "Then they unloaded the supplies. They were visibly happy to see we hadn't tried to play with them, there. That we had genuinely given them some of the supplies they needed. The boxes disappeared quickly, and I sensed a real sigh of relief. But if there are the usual number of crew onboard, those supplies will last a few days, at most. They need more."

"And we have more."

Eadal nodded at Renn. "They argued for a while over what to do. I think Vi'il has lost a little of his shine with his people. They wanted to surrender a while ago, and things have been stretched taut, from what I can gather. Food on rations, no communication with home.

"Since coming here they've lost a couple of people." She looked toward the closed door. "Even more, now. They aren't happy to be here. Most of them didn't know about this station, if what I was picking up was right. And they know it's all illegal. Plus the soldiers who grabbed us out by those rocks and then had to make a run for the explorer, with that killer drone after them, they're all mixed up about Ellie. No one wants to admit she's from Earth. No one wants that to be true."

"So they decided the easiest thing to do while they thought about what happens next was to send you down for the balance of the supplies." Renn sighed.

Eadal nodded. "That's my take. And also to check the stores, to see that we're giving them everything. They really need as much as they can get. I don't think the supplies are going to last them long enough, and they were hoping we were lying about the first batch being half of what was here."

"So what do we do?" Hune rubbed a hand over his forearm as if to settle his nerves.

"The only way to communicate is through the explorer. So I suppose I'll have to go out there, pass on the bad news to Vi'il," Renn said.

"Won't he think it's odd that his guys were hit, and I wasn't?" Eadal asked.

"I'll tell him you were hit."

"That won't work, Captain." Paxe spoke up for the first time. "They had lenses trained on the explorer the whole time from the *Rauha*. They know something happened in the explorer. They know Eadal got out, and they know you didn't fire your shockguns and that you retreated to the warehouse. Don't tell them Eadal is dead, they won't believe you."

"Why did you kill them?" Renn's question was on Ellie's lips, also.

"Because I need Vi'il to need you. I need it to be too risky for him to send anyone else down who might die. As much for his loyalty to his crew as for his authority on the *Rauha*, which, as Eadal has noted, is waning."

"And that thing?" Hune asked. "Where is it?"

"I've recalled it to the *Irini*," Paxe said. "It's gone."

"Pretend that you have to run for the explorer from here," Paxe suggested to Renn. "Make it seem as if you are as much in fear of the drone as they are."

"Not much pretending required," Hune muttered under his breath.

"Do you mind discussing these things with me before you make a decision like killing soldiers from the *Rauha*?"

Renn was angry, Ellie realized with a start.

He hadn't given it away with his body language, but she could hear it in his voice.

"You are not in charge here, Captain." Paxe was blunt. "If I need your advice, I will seek it. I have some listening capabilities on the Tecran ship, and I overheard a lot of what was said when your crew arrived there. Eadal is correct that they are beyond desperate for supplies. That alone is more of a bargaining chip than you realize. Getting rid of the soldiers so the Tecran are forced to rely completely on you to get them what they need——this is necessary if we are all to survive.

"Vi'il is staring down shame, reputational damage, and a very long sentence of imprisonment. He will kill you, your crew, and Ellie, not to mention destroy me and this station, when he has all the useful supplies this warehouse can yield to him."

"You know this for a fact?" Renn's voice had gotten lower.

"I know this for a fact. I heard it discussed."

"Well, then." Renn looked at them all, a slow movement of his head. "Let's get Xallantra and Iso back."

"No." Eadal gripped his arm. "Xallantra, maybe. But Iso?" She shook her head. "He'll die if we move him. It's either take a chance the Tecran will find it difficult to kill a comatose Grihan exploration officer, or certain death for him with us down here."

"You're sure?"

"I am afraid Eadal is right again." Paxe spoke up. "Iso needs the level of care he's currently receiving. I don't know if Vi'il will order him killed, but the medics onboard the *Rauha* are doing their best to keep him alive, and I think they would refuse to agree to any order to harm him."

Renn tilted his neck back, as if easing tight muscles. "Xallantra must come back down, then. She won't be an easy prisoner, and someone might decide she's too much of a nuisance. But Iso stays."

He wasn't asking a question, but both Eadal and Hune nodded. "Iso stays."

Renn opened the door of the warehouse just a little, enough to slide through, and then disappeared.

"I hope the *Etsijä* comes soon," Eadal said.

Hune sighed. "I have a suspicion it won't be soon enough."

CHAPTER 14

RENN HAD to move one of the dead Tecran out into the rear of the explorer before he could sit down, and as soon as he was in the pilot's chair, he'd heard the sound of dragging. When he stood to investigate, he saw it was the drone, pulling one of the bodies down the ramp.

"There's been damage to the ship," Paxe said through the drone's speakers. "It will need to be repaired before you can fly up to the *Rauha* with more supplies."

More time for the *Etsijä* to arrive, Renn thought as he sat back down again, if Vi'il didn't send down another ship.

The damage wasn't ideal, but it was a good enough excuse to drag things out, especially if he could keep the fine balance going and not tip Vi'il over far enough that he decided to cut his losses, destroy the station, and run.

"What's going on down there?" Vi'il was waiting for him when Renn opened comms.

"The explorer was attacked by that strange . . . thing." Renn looked behind him. "I don't know where it went, and I'm taking a considerable risk coming back onboard to talk to you."

Vi'il looked like he didn't want to believe it, but his own people would have told him about it from before. "Why didn't it attack Eadal?"

Renn shook his head. "I don't know. It's gone for your people over mine every time, although Iso wasn't so lucky." He lifted his hands. "Maybe that's what happened to your station crew? They disturbed it somehow, or it was one of the strange things amongst the crates in the warehouse? Maybe it attacks your people because it sees them as a threat. We're not known to it. Yet."

Vi'il seemed startled by Renn's explanation, and then fearful.

And maybe, Renn thought with interest, convinced.

The Tecran captain must know there were all manner of strange things in that warehouse. His sister had worked at this station, after all.

"So what now?" Vi'il looked worse for wear. Renn thought the situation was wearing him down. That wasn't necessarily good news, though. People who were stressed didn't always make good decisions.

"The explorer is damaged. One of your soldiers fired off a shot into the interior as they were attacked, and it's no longer spaceworthy. You'll have to send another explorer down, or wait for us to repair the damage and then load up. Either way, you *will* return Xallantra."

"I'll return Xallantra when I see my two officers, standing in front of me, alive and well."

So that's what it came down to. Two Tecran in exchange for Xallantra.

Paxe wouldn't care. But maybe Ellie could persuade him.

"I managed to make a recording for you from them." He played the message, saw Vi'il relax a little after listening to it.

He hadn't been completely sure they were still alive, Renn guessed. At least that might make him hesitate to do something that would harm his people down below. Paxe seemed certain he planned to destroy everything, but he would try to get his people out first.

"You need to rescue them," Vi'il said.

"I'm not in charge down here." And that was the honest truth. Paxe had just made that very clear.

"You got close enough to record them, you have to be close enough to get them out."

"The doors are locked, Vi'il. I could try to break them out, but I'd suggest that's best left until you have your supplies, because I can't say what the reaction will be to whatever has shut them in when I try. It's in your best interests to have me and all my team able to pull the stock you need from the warehouse unhindered. And I'll add, Xallantra would be much more helpful to your cause down here than up there."

"And you have no idea what's attacking my people?"

"I have no idea." He lied without a qualm. Vi'il had lost any right to the truth when he held Xallantra against her will and had his soldiers hold a shockgun to Eadal's head. "I'm guessing you have a better idea than I do, and if you know something that can help keep my team safe, I expect you to let me know."

Vi'il shook his head. "Not specifically. But some things were brought here that should probably have never been taken in the first place. My sister mentioned things had gone a bit far, but if I'd had any idea whatever they were studying would wipe out the whole base . . ." He looked off to the side. "I would have come to fetch her sooner."

"So what now?" Renn asked, a little less harshly than he'd intended. "Are you going to send down a ship, or should we try to repair this one?"

"I'll send a ship down, but Xallantra will only be sent back when you've got my two people out of that station." Vi'il rubbed at his head. "And there has to be more supplies than you've found. There was stock to last at least a year on the station. Could you have missed some?"

Renn nodded. "This is a massive warehouse and there is no inventory list. Of course we could have missed some."

Vi'il seemed to brighten at that. "Keep looking, then. I'll send down a vessel. Load up what you have already when the explorer comes down, and then go through the warehouse more thoroughly."

He had guessed Vi'il would offer to send down a ship. Making Renn and his team repair this one would have given the *Etsijä* more time to arrive, and Vi'il couldn't risk that.

The Tecran captain also knew he had Renn at a disadvantage, with Xallantra and Iso up on the *Rauha*.

Renn couldn't see how he was going to get everyone out of this.

It was a depressing thought.

"When will you send the ship down?" he asked.

"It's coming now. Get ready to load it." Vi'il cut off the comms.

Renn made his way out of the explorer and ran from the ramp back to the warehouse.

The bodies of the Tecran had all disappeared. He wondered where Paxe was putting them all. And whether the other thirty bodies from the station's crew were in the same place.

The thought was more than a little disturbing.

"What did he say?" Eadal asked.

"He's sending down another explorer right now."

"And Xallantra?" Hune asked.

Renn shook his head. "He won't let her go until we've rescued the two Tecran locked up in the station."

Hune swore and turned away.

Ellie was watching them, a frown on her face, standing a little apart. She looked exhausted.

She was the real victim here, Renn conceded. She had been stolen, harmed, kept in a coma, and now she was caught in the ugly battle between the Tecran and the Grih.

Everyone on his team had known the risks before they came with him. She hadn't signed up for any of this.

"Will you try to rescue the hostages?" Eadal asked.

Renn shook his head. "The moment the hostages are out and up onboard the *Rauha*, Vi'il has no reason not to obliterate us all."

"Then what do we do?" Hune slid down the wall of the warehouse to sit on the floor.

"We delay, and obfuscate, and delay some more." That was the only plan he had.

"The explorer Vi'il said he'd send is coming down now," Paxe said through the translator. "I can't tell if there are any soldiers onboard, I lost my listening devices in the launch bay when they got rid of the spacesuits, and the only other device I had was on the explorer that brought Eadal down."

Hune groaned. "We have to haul another load?"

Renn winced at the thought himself.

How long had they been on the go? Too long to be effective.

They needed to sleep.

And the only place he felt safe enough to do that was in their damaged ship.

"Can you help?" Ellie was looking at the black box in her hand.

Whatever Paxe answered, he said only in her own language.

She looked up. "The little drone will help." She looked around the warehouse, almost as if she expected the drone to be here somewhere, although the last time Renn had seen it, it had been dragging the dead Tecran out of the explorer.

"Thank you," he said to her. He didn't think Paxe would have offered, and the thinking system was only allowing it because Ellie had asked him.

Again, he wondered what favor Ellie had done for Paxe that he had developed such a protective attitude toward her.

Every report he'd read said that Imogen Peters had freed Paxe. And Paxe had admitted he hadn't even known Ellie was at the station until he arrived here by chance.

It was a question for another time. The explorer's engines were audible now.

"I wonder where they're going to land," Eadal said. "The damaged explorer is in the way, and there isn't a lot of space to set down next to it."

Renn stepped out the doors, Hune and Eadal on either side of him, although he saw Ellie continued to keep out of sight.

He approved.

The explorer hovered over the damaged ship, but eventually gave up trying to look for a place to set down and flew over to land next to the *Irini* on the launchpad.

"They want us to load it from there?" Hune's voice was exasperated.

"They don't have much choice," Renn said.

It would take time and effort to carry the supplies over the pitted, rocky ground to the launch bay. The only good thing about it was that it would drag things out.

"Don't have the little drone help us," he said, glancing at Ellie over his shoulder. "Let's make this as slow and painful as we can. And we need to insist on rest, as well."

She nodded in understanding, murmured into the translator.

"Let's take the first few boxes across, see who's in there." Renn waited for Hune to help him pick up the first big box, and they began walking it over to the newly-landed ship.

When he glanced back, he saw Ellie was carrying one side of a box with Eadal, although it was harder for her without weighted boots.

Her eyes were ringed with dark circles, and despite the glow the necklace gave her, her skin looked pale.

"Ellie can only do this one trip," Paxe said into his ear. "She is still recovering from her time in a coma, and although she's done much better today, I don't think she can continue on much longer."

"Agreed."

"You aren't going to ask me what I plan to do with the hostages, Captain?" Paxe asked.

"It doesn't matter." Renn had come to a kind of peace about it. "I agree with you that if you let them go, Vi'il will kill us all."

"I'm surprised." Paxe was thoughtful. "You're more intelligent than I expected, Captain. This is a good thing."

Renn couldn't help the laugh that burst out of him.

Hune turned to look at him over the top of the box, his expression mystified.

"And Ellie? Is she more intelligent than you expected?" It was an oblique way of finding out what was at stake with this strange relationship.

"Ellie is all that is good, and fair, and true, Captain. And yes, intelligent, too. Certainly as intelligent as you, despite her planet's lack of technology in comparison to yours."

He didn't know what to say to that. It sounded as if Paxe cared for Ellie because of who she was, not what she had done for him.

And then he wondered, given who Paxe was, and how he had been made, if that wasn't the same thing.

CHAPTER 15

THE EXPLORER SAT, engines still engaged, right beside the *Irini*, and as Ellie walked awkwardly with the box, trying to navigate the rough ground, the lack of gravity, and the height difference between herself and Eadal, she had a sudden flash of insight.

It suited Paxe that Vi'il had had to land on the launch pad again.

Almost as much as it clearly suited Renn.

Both needed time and this gave them time. And in Paxe's case, close proximity to the *Irini* meant either the Scary Caterpillar or the insect drone could do some damage or subvert some systems of the explorer with less chance of being seen.

Paxe had said they were very useful when it came to cables and system set-ups.

The Scary Caterpillar's name was kind of stuck now, she decided as she stumbled and tried not to drop her half of the box. The insect drone should probably be called Ripper or something like that, but she refused to bow to the obvious. Maybe it should be called Bunny. That was more or less the opposite of Ripper, but the rabbit at the end of *Monty Python and the Holy Grail* had been a killer, so it was sneakily apt after all.

Up ahead, Renn and Hune had set their box down and the explorer's ramp was slowly lowering.

Ellie looked out for any sign of either drone, but maybe Paxe wasn't going to use them, or maybe they were just that good.

She decided they were probably just that good.

She and Eadal were still a couple of steps behind Renn and Hune when the ramp touched the ground.

With a shout, four Tecran in strange silver suits ran down it and raised their shockguns at their little group.

Both she and Eadal let the box drop at the same time, and the container gave an ominous crack as it landed hard on an uneven piece of rock.

"Hands out," one of them ordered, and Renn, Hune and Eadal complied as if this was standard procedure.

"You, too." The soldier pointed his shockgun at Ellie, and she raised her arms in front of her to mimic the others. The way her cloak fell, it still hid her knives, though, and she wondered if they would search her for weapons.

Unfortunately, they did.

They took the shockguns off the Grih, and made her take her cloak off so they could unstrap the harness.

No one took her knives out of their sheaths, which disappointed her, because they would probably have shocked them, like Renn.

Two of the soldiers loaded the boxes they'd carried over into the hold, and when that was done, walked back down.

"Close the ramp," the leader said, and one of them tapped their wrist to close it.

Didn't want Bunny sneaking in, Ellie thought. But she guessed it was too late.

Or if not Bunny, something else that Paxe had up his sleeve.

He might be in control of the ship already, and simply lulling them into a false sense of security by allowing it to respond to their commands.

"Tell me you're captain of that ship now," she murmured to him.

"Not quite." His tone was cold. "I've only found a way to access the door and ramp controls and the lenses. I can't help you unless I bring out the drones, and given the wild shooting that happened last time I did that, you might get hit in the crossfire."

"Good point."

"Quiet!" The Tecran leader lifted his shockgun and pointed it at her head. "No babbling."

Babbling. Huh. Now that was rude.

She kept quiet, though, walking with the others back to the warehouse.

Vi'il must be really desperate for supplies and hoping like hell they had got it wrong about how much stock was down here.

"Your captain lied to me." Renn waited until they were just inside the warehouse door before he spoke. "He promised——"

The Tecran soldier who'd shouted at her lifted his shockgun again, but this time he actually used it.

A pulse of purple light hit Renn, and he went down without a sound.

Eadal gave a cry of shock, crouching down beside her captain.

Ellie was at the back of the group, and she saw Hune stand over Renn, and then, fists bunched, turn toward the Tecran.

She gasped as he was hit by a pulse of light, too.

"He was going to attack," the soldier who fired said.

"He was," another of the small team agreed.

"Drag them over there."

Ellie was still looking in horror at the two Grih lying on the ground, and didn't realize they were talking to her and Eadal.

"Now." The Tecran soldier who seemed to be the leader shoved her with the barrel of his shockgun.

She sent him a filthy look and moved toward her fallen friends.

Eadal grabbed what turned out to be a handle of sorts on the shoulder of Renn's spacesuit and began pulling him across the smooth floor of the warehouse.

Ellie followed her example with Hune, her gaze going from him to Renn and back again.

She glanced at the Tecran over her shoulder, saw they were conferring with each other.

She was still getting over how quickly things had changed.

She'd fallen into a false sense of safety. A false sense that somehow, Renn and Paxe between them had the upper hand.

The brutal way Renn and Hune had been taken down shook her to the core.

"Will they be all right?" she asked, as she finally got Hune propped up against the boxes in the first row.

Eadal turned to her, but annoyingly, with the helmet on, she could barely see her expression.

"They should be all right," she said in the end, her tone short.

Ellie could hear them both breathing, and Eadal's demeanor was more outraged than worried, now.

She felt her tension lessen.

"They're unconscious, but their breathing is strong." Eadal made sure both where sitting upright. "They were shot through their suits, so the effect was less severe, too."

"Why did they shoot Renn? It wasn't just because he spoke." She was sure of that.

Eadal lifted her shoulders. "I don't know." She slumped back against the boxes, looking shattered. "According to the Code, they shouldn't have shot them at all."

Hadn't Renn said that Vi'il was balancing on a line? It looked like he was fine with stepping over it.

The Tecran finished their little meeting, and two of the soldiers came over.

Ellie hadn't sat down, and they stood within touching distance, too close for her comfort. With the shelves at her back, she couldn't step back.

They weren't as tall as the Grih, but they were stocky, and she could only just see their faces through the helmets.

If they were trying to intimidate her, it was working.

She stared at them, frozen in place, trying to project a confidence she didn't feel.

Her hands were trembling.

She wondered if her reaction was more than just the violence and threat of the moment, or whether some of it was subconscious recognition, little things she'd picked up as she'd wavered in and out of her coma?

"Give me that necklace," the soldier said, pointing.

He was the one who'd shot Renn and given the orders since the explorer touched down.

She stared at him for a moment, trying to work out what he intended to do.

He leaned forward, hand outstretched, to grab it, and her legs were finally able to move.

She pressed back against the boxes. "It's the only thing keeping me alive." She put the hand clutching the translator over the necklace protectively.

"That might not be the best argument you could make to them," Eadal muttered from beside her. "I think that would probably be a bonus."

The translator had been translating for everyone, and the soldier shot his hand out and instead of grabbing the necklace, snatched the black box from Ellie's hand.

"Where did you get this?"

"From the station." She didn't like it being out of her grasp. It was her only form of communication out here.

He grunted, and then tucked it in a top pocket on his spacesuit.

It was clever, she supposed. It would stop her and Eadal being able to communicate with each other if he left them alone.

"The necklace," the soldier said, again, and this time she could barely make out what he said, as the translation came through muffled from his pocket.

"No." She closed her fingers around it. "Not unless you get me a spacesuit."

"We don't want her to die just yet," the soldier beside him said. "We need to find out where they got the stores from. I didn't realize how much stuff was in here."

The soldier demanding the necklace looked over at his colleague, and then back to her.

Suddenly, over the sound system, Ob-La-Di began to play.

Everyone looked up.

"What's that?"

"Music." Ellie tried to look as gormless as possible. She felt some of the tension in her ease. Paxe was telling her that at least some of the motley crew were in here. She and Eadal weren't without support and he had most likely heard the threat against her, and was about to respond.

"Who is playing it?" The Tecran sounded a little nervous now.

That they were wearing different spacesuits this time made her think these silver ones were thicker or more protective. They must hope they would be protected from attack, but they couldn't be completely sure about it.

And now, with the music playing, they just had a reminder that something else was down here, and in control.

Ellie shrugged. "The music comes and goes. It plays in the station sometimes, too. And in the med pod where I woke up."

The soldier turned, barked something to the other two, standing guard at the door.

Whatever he said was too quick for her to pick up from the black box.

They didn't sound happy about whatever order they'd been given, but they left, stepping out of the warehouse.

She guessed he'd told them to go to the station, see if they could work out how the music was being piped in.

"Keep an eye on the door," the soldier said to his companion.

If they thought that would stop Bunny, they were in for a surprise.

"Show me the supplies." The soldier's words buzzed indistinctly, but she had no doubt of his meaning as he prodded her with the barrel of his shockgun in a clear order for her to move.

Ellie clenched her fists at her side at the open intimidation. Renn and Hune were both still obviously unconscious, and she shared a quick look with Eadal. The pilot gave a tiny nod, encouraging her cooperation.

She didn't want to make things worse, and the music seemed to get louder, which she guessed was Paxe telling her something was about to happen.

"Move it." The barrel struck her shoulder and pushed her back against the boxes behind her.

"All right." She stepped around him, rubbing where she'd been hit. She made her way to the central loading zone, heading for the third aisle, where most of the Tecran supplies had been stored.

The soldier trailed her, and his friend stood between Hune, Renn and Eadal, and the door, trying to keep a watch on both.

The music changed from the Beatles to AC/DC as she stepped between the stacks. She may be caught in the middle of something, but unlike in the song, she was sure there was help coming.

Paxe was building up to something.

"They left your knives by the door, along with the Grih's weapons. The Scary Caterpillar is bringing the sheath harness to you." Paxe's voice came through the watch on her wrist quietly.

She wondered if it had always been able to do that, or whether he'd worked out how to connect to it since she'd been taken prisoner.

Whatever the answer, she had to stop herself clapping with excitement.

She slowed and then came to a stop where there was a large section of shelving where all the boxes had been removed.

She swept her arm out to show the Tecran following her, stepped back, and at the tiniest sound of scrabbling behind her, turned her head.

The Scary Caterpillar peeped out from the top of a box on the bottom shelf of the stack, and then disappeared.

She reached back and found her sheath lying where he had been.

Rather than try to shrug it on, which the soldier would surely notice, she grabbed one of the hilts and pulled the knife out, pressing it against her left outer thigh.

"This is it?" The soldier was looking at the unmarked boxes around the empty spots.

"We took the ones that had a Tecran marking on them. I don't read Tecran, so you'll have to ask the Grih why they chose those boxes."

The soldier jerked his shockgun at her. "Take out that box." He pointed to one. "Let's see what's in it."

He was acting as if they'd somehow hidden supplies in unmarked boxes. They had barely had time to pull out the boxes they had.

She shuffled over, arms at her sides.

"What's that?" He lifted his shockgun, aiming it at her.

Would she have time to throw it before he shot?

She didn't think she would.

"A knife," she admitted, showing him. "It was lying on top of a box. Someone must have been using it to pry them open, or something."

"Hand it over."

She felt a surge of relief. He could just as easily have told her to put it down.

She pretended reluctance and held it out to him, then realized it might not shock him through his silver suit.

He grabbed it, and she actually saw the flash of blue.

As it dropped from his gloved hand, the Scary Caterpillar leaped down on him from the stacks.

She wasn't sure if his shriek was pain from the knife or fear of the attack from above.

She scooped the knife up, and stood, ready to throw it if needed.

She assumed the Scary Caterpillar would simply pierce his suit, like Bunny had done to the Tecran earlier, and let him run for the explorer, but the Tecran made a strange, wheezing exhale, and fell forward, and when the drone scuttled off him, there was blood on his forelegs.

The soldier lay still, and she could see blood seeping out of his back.

"He shouldn't have tried to take your necklace," Paxe said through the watch. "And he shouldn't have hit you with his shockgun."

Shit.

She felt the air rush out of her and she had to bend down and put her hands on her knees.

While her eyes were closed, the Scary Caterpillar moved forward, and suddenly, the black translator box was at her feet.

"Thanks," she whispered, blinking as she picked it up and slid it into her pocket. She forced herself to walk over to grab her sheath harness, slipped it on, and slid the knife back into place.

Her cloak must be at the door with the shockguns, but she realized she wasn't actually feeling cold.

She brushed a hand over the smooth, soft fabric of her shirt, almost in a gesture of self-soothing.

Then forced herself to look down at the soldier again.

"He was planning to suffocate you to death when you were no longer useful," Paxe said. "It was him or you." He didn't sound as if he was trying to justify himself. He was simply stating a fact for her to accept. "It was good he took you off alone so we could deal with him without the chance of you being shot by any of the others, but now, we need to deal with *them*."

"I know." And she did. They hadn't so much as flinched at shooting Renn and Hune, at threatening her with the removal of the necklace. They were dangerous, and Eadal was alone with at least one of them. "Okay, let's go."

She started jogging down the aisle, slowing as she got near the end of it and pressing up against the boxes to peer around into the big, open loading zone, to see what was going on.

The soldier was still guarding Eadal, Renn and Hune. It looked like nothing had changed in Renn and Hune's condition. They were still slumped against the stacks.

It worried her. If the hit they'd taken was as mild as Eadal had made out, surely they should be coming round by now?

She didn't know enough about shockguns, she reminded herself. This could be perfectly normal.

She looked back, saw the Scary Catepillar was following her, the Tecran's shockgun held in his two front legs.

Most of the blood was gone.

"The one we just killed is the one who shot the captain?" Paxe asked.

"Yes."

"His shockgun is set to kill."

She stilled. "Eadal said Renn was alive."

She felt like a big, dark pit was suddenly swallowing her up. She did not want Renn to be dead.

She looked over at him.

Eadal was checking Hune, then turned to Renn. She didn't seem alarmed, so maybe Renn had somehow managed to survive the kill shot.

He must have.

But this was seriously life and death, now.

No hostage taking, or unconscious-making. It had progressed to shoot to kill, and that had a different feel to how things had been before.

Maybe that was because the Grih kept expecting the Tecran to behave in a specific way, and that had rubbed off on her, given her a false sense of security, but the blinders were off now.

She crouched down, balancing on her heels as she studied the guard standing over Eadal and the others.

She fingered the hilt at her right hip.

She had never had cause to use one against a person.

That was about to change.

"You would be sorry if the captain was dead?" Paxe asked.

"Very sorry." Her voice shuddered as she breathed in to keep her composure. "Eadal said he was alive. That his suit would shield him somewhat. Do you think he's been lying there, dead?" Her voice faded on the last word.

"Eadal would have noticed. Would have said. I'm sure he's alive, that his suit saved him." Paxe spoke, but it was the Scary Caterpillar who came up to her and nudged her thigh to give her comfort. She smoothed her palm over his cool, smooth back and then peered around the corner again.

"If they tried to kill him once, they'll try again. And they seem happy to kill me, too."

She needed to get this guard out of the way before the other two came back. She and Eadal could hide Renn and Hune and then deal with the others.

She was wasting time here, delaying because she didn't like what she was about to do, and she knew it.

Time to woman up. Everyone's lives were on the line, not just her own.

"Do I have to kill him? Surely I can just incapacitate him?"

"I could put him in the station as a third hostage," Paxe conceded.

"Do you know how to switch the shockgun setting down from kill to something less deadly?" she asked.

The Scary Caterpillar put the shockgun on the floor and used his forelegs to fiddle with something on the side.

"It won't kill him now," Paxe said as the shockgun was presented to her.

She took it, studying it, although she was aware time was wasting.

She had seen how Xallantra and the others had held theirs, and she hoped it was as simple as it seemed.

Time to go.

She stood, shockgun against her side, and walked into the loading zone, heading straight for the guard.

He registered her presence, glancing her way, but he must have thought his friend was still with her, because his gaze swung past her and returned to watching the door.

Then he did a double take. "Where is——?"

She lifted the shockgun with both hands and shot.

The stream of purple light hit him in the chest and crackled against the silver of his suit.

"Why did you think we're wearing these suits, you stupid orange?" The soldier lifted his shockgun.

Ellie threw the shockgun in her hands in Eadal's general direction and ran for cover as she pulled her knives from both hips.

She didn't make it to the stack she was aiming to hide behind.

The purple of shockgun fire buzzed against her, and she waited for pain or at least discomfort.

Neither came.

She turned back to the Tecran soldier in surprise.

But not as much surprise as he must be feeling.

His weapon hung loosely in his hand, almost forgotten, as he stared at her.

She drew herself up, threw the first knife, then the second, in quick succession, with as much force as she could, and as they left her hands she wondered if the special silver material of the Tecran's upgraded suits would hinder the blades, as it had the shockgun fire.

It did not.

One blade embedded itself in his chest and the other in his throat.

As he fell, she felt a light-headedness. A separation from her body.

She had never killed anyone before. Never imagined that she would.

She had tried, she reminded herself.

She had tried not to kill him. She'd used the shockgun instead of the knives. Unlike the Tecran, she had set it to stun.

But she had been forced into killing him, anyway.

She stumbled forward as Eadal scrambled to her feet, her gaze going from Ellie, to the Scary Caterpillar, who was just behind her, to the dead guard. "That shot hit you. Are you all right?"

Ellie glanced at her. "Yes."

Looked like Paxe's fear of her being hurt by stray shockgun fire was unfounded. Her clothes had protected her.

Eadal looked unconvinced. "But I saw . . ." She picked up the shockgun Ellie had thrown her way and gave a shake of her head. "Never mind. Where's the other soldier?"

Ellie pointed down the stacks. "Dead."

"Ellie, this one didn't give you a choice, but you can't go around killing——"

She drew in a deep breath. Let it out. "Paxe checked his shockgun. It was set to kill when he shot Renn. Whatever you think is going on here, it isn't very rough negotiations. This is shoot to kill." She extracted her knives from the Tecran's body, averting her gaze as she did, and forced herself to wipe them on his suit before she slid them back into her harness.

Eadal gaped at her. "You're sure?"

She nodded.

"Right. Let's talk about that later. We need to hide the captain and Hune." She grabbed Hune this time and Ellie got a grip on Renn's epaulet and began pulling.

They dragged them around the corner of the stack, to the other side of it, out of view of anyone coming through the doors, but they were still easy enough to see if someone stood in the middle of the loading zone.

"This isn't safe enough," Eadal said, breathing hard. "Especially if they actually mean to kill him. I wondered why he wasn't coming out of it, whereas Hune has twitched a couple of times. At least he's still breathing, but it's weak. I should have realized." She crouched beside Renn, checking his wrist unit.

Ellie agreed they needed to be better hidden, but they had already run out of time.

"The others are back," Paxe whispered through the translator.

The sound of someone opening the door came right afterward.

The shout went up immediately as the Tecran soldiers caught sight of their friend lying sprawled on the ground.

And then the screaming began.

"I'm guessing Bunny is here." Ellie didn't look around the side.

"Bunny?" Paxe sounded perplexed.

"The insect drone."

"Yes." Paxe paused. "I didn't want you to have to kill again. I can see it bothers you." He went suddenly quiet. "One of them's making a run for it."

Ellie forced herself to stand and jog around the stack.

Bunny looked up at her from the back of the downed soldier, then spun, racing out the door after the other Tecran almost too fast to see.

The sound of shockgun fire followed.

"The drone——Bunny was hit." Paxe sounded astonished. "The Tecran wasn't even aiming, he just shot over his shoulder and hit Bunny by pure chance."

Ellie raced to the door, then carefully looked out.

The final surviving Tecran was almost to the explorer, although the ramp had just finished closing before he made it back, locking him out.

With a shout of rage, he began climbing the side of the ship, and scrambled to the roof, shockgun raised.

Ellie stepped out of the warehouse carefully. She assumed he didn't have the range to hit her from the launch pad.

Eadal was behind her, her silence at the sight of the soldier Bunny had killed deafening.

Bunny lay halfway between the explorer and the warehouse, and when Ellie reached him, she could smell burning metal.

She picked him up, and he tried to curl his legs around her arm but couldn't do it the same way he had done before. Even though he was metal and wires, it upset her.

"Can Silvey do something for him?" she asked.

"I hope so. Take him back to the warehouse."

"What about the Tecran on the roof?" She straightened and watched him, saw him watching her back.

"I'm worried he'll damage the explorer. It's the only working ship we have at the moment."

She nodded, moving backward until she reached the warehouse. Eadal was standing outside. She gave Bunny a horrified look and didn't follow her in, her gaze on the explorer and the Tecran on its roof.

That suited Ellie for now.

The motley crew were still a secret, and she didn't mind keeping it that way.

She handed Bunny to the Scary Caterpillar and he flowed silently between the stacks and disappeared.

Ellie walked back to Hune and Renn.

Hune was groaning, eyes still closed.

She crouched beside Renn, but she couldn't read his wrist unit, and couldn't see his face through the helmet.

Hune suddenly leaned over his captain and gripped her arm. "You and Eadal dealt with the Tecran?"

She nodded. "How do you read Renn's vitals?"

The soldier got to his knees and lifted Renn's wrist. "Weak but alive."

The air rushed out of her, and she sat down. "I'm glad. The suit must have saved him, because they shot to kill."

Hune's helmet swung in her direction. "Surely not."

"That was the setting on the Tecran's shockgun."

Hune swore. "They're actually going to try to eliminate us."

"We need to get Renn to the med pod." Eadal came up behind them, her voice grim, her expression bleak.

Ellie nodded. She had been about to suggest the same.

They lifted him up between them and carried him out.

Hune looked askance at the dead soldiers, particularly the one with the wide gash in his throat, but he said nothing.

The soldier on the roof of the explorer shot at them twice as they carried Renn to the station, but he was too far away to hit them.

When they reached the pod, Eadal stripped Renn out of his suit and hooked him up on the platform, and they all leaned against the walls and stared at each other.

"What are we going to do about the Tecran shooting wildly from the roof?" Eadal had taken her helmet off and set it down on a cabinet beside her.

She looked exhausted.

"Paxe is afraid he might damage the ship, either on purpose or by accident. And given it's the only one still working down here . . ." Ellie twisted her lips in frustration.

"That occurred to me." Eadal rubbed a hand over her face, voice rough with exhaustion.

"He has to want to go back to the *Rauha*, right?" Ellie slid down the wall and sat, leaning her head back and closing her eyes. "And we want to get Xallantra back."

Both Grih murmured their agreement.

"So maybe we offer to swap them. The soldier in exchange for Xallantra. Is there a way that can be done without you flying the explorer into the *Rauha's* landing bay?" Because they surely would never come back out if they did that.

There was a stretch of silence, and Ellie opened her eyes and looked across at them. Eadal was staring off into space as she thought it through. "We could do a space walk swap."

"Then he wouldn't even have to get off the roof," Hune said, slowly sliding down to sit, himself. "He's already in a suit. We could send the cable to him once we're close enough to the *Rauha*, and as you say, they could send Xallantra out, the two could meet in the middle and switch cables."

"We could use the explorer that's damaged near the warehouse to negotiate with the *Rauha,* but that soldier doesn't seem inclined to let anyone get close," Eadal said.

"Talk to the *Rauha,* get them to speak to him if you make a deal. He'd be an idiot not to agree." Ellie hooked her arms around her knees. "Not that I don't want to help, but I don't think I should be anywhere near him, or in view of the *Rauha.*"

Eadal inclined her head, but Ellie thought she looked relieved, like she thought Ellie would fight to be involved.

Hune clearly wanted to say something, but he hesitated.

"The bug worrying you?"

He shot her a dirty look. "I've watched it kill more than a couple of Tecran through their suits with my own eyes. Yes, it worries me."

"It got shot by the Tecran on the roof. It's out of action."

"That was why you carried it in?" Eadal looked over at her in surprise.

She nodded.

"And the other one?" Eadal asked. "The big one?"

"There's a big one?" Hune did not look happy to hear that.

"Somewhere in the warehouse." Ellie shrugged. "It helps Paxe connect cables in the *Irini.*"

Hune relaxed at that, and she decided not to mention the Scary Caterpillar had killed one of the guards.

"What's an orange?" she asked suddenly.

Both Eadal and Hune seemed to freeze.

"Where did you hear that?" Hune asked.

"From the Tecran soldier. Before he shot me, he called me a stupid orange."

"It's . . ." Hune looked over at Eadal, as if for help. "It's an unknown higher sentient, unrecognized by the scanners in our big explorer ships. When Rose McKenzie, the first woman from Earth, was found, she showed up as orange on our system."

"Why did he make it sound like an insult?" Ellie wondered.

Eadal lifted her shoulders. "They're defensive about breaking the charter to do with higher sentients. Taking you was a breach of that."

Ellie had a feeling there was more to it, they looked too uncomfortable, but she let it lie. She was too tired to pursue it.

"Okay." Eadal pushed herself up the wall to standing after a long moment of silence. She checked the equipment and gave a nod of satisfaction. "His vitals are already improving. Hune, I don't know about you, but I haven't eaten for nearly a day, and I can't go on without a meal, a shower, and maybe an hour or two of sleep."

"I'll be on watch while both of you get some rest, in case the soldier comes off the roof," Ellie said.

Eadal offered a hand to Hune and hauled him up when he accepted it.

They nodded their thanks and made their way out of the med pod.

"They aren't as friendly as Renn," Paxe commented.

"They're distrustful of the Scary Caterpillar and Bunny," she said. "And they're definitely in more danger because I'm here than if I wasn't."

"That's not your fault."

"No." She let her eyes drift closed again, then slid down to lie on the gritty floor, using her arm as a pillow. "Will you let me know if the soldier tries to get off the roof?"

"Yes. I'll let you know."

She lifted a hand in thanks, then remembered he couldn't see her in here. "Thanks. You know I don't even know where my backpack is with my spare clothes."

"Karnic brought it to the *Irini*. It's safe," Paxe said. "I'll have the machine in the station make some more clothes for you. It's in a small room near the bathrooms. There's enough of that fabric you found to make another set of clothes."

"Great. I like the clothes a lot." She found talking was almost too much like hard work.

"I didn't realize it was shockgun proof until that stray shot hit your arm," Paxe said. "That was fortuitous. I think it must be Cargassey cloth."

She barely registered what he was saying, but she was happy it was nice to wear *and* had safety features. She wanted to ask Paxe to pipe the music in here again but she couldn't get the words out.

She fell asleep to Ob-La-Di playing in a loop in her head.

CHAPTER 16

"ELLIE."

She came awake with a start.

She was still lying on the floor of the med pod, she realized, and sat up with the feeling of grit on her cheek and as if something with an edge had been pressing against it. Her hip hurt. It confused her for a moment until she realized she was lying on the black translator box which she'd put in her pocket.

She gave a huge yawn, and then arched her back to get the kinks out.

She had a vague memory of Eadal coming in to the pod at one point, but it was fuzzy.

Renn lay on the platform, as still as before, but when she used the wall to pull herself up and staggered over to him, he looked better than he had.

He was breathing easier, and his skin didn't have that dead, gray undertone to it.

He was still out, though.

Suddenly she remembered someone had said her name.

"Paxe?"

"Good, you're awake. The soldier is looking like he might make a run for the station."

With a last look at Renn, Ellie made her way down the passage, dusting the dirt off her left side as she went. "In what way is he 'looking like' making a move?"

"He's been sitting in the middle of the roof for a while, he even lay down to rest for a bit, but now he's moving around the edge, looking down——oh, no, he's off." Paxe's voice rose a little.

Ellie ran the last bit of the passage. "Maybe he's trying to get back into the explorer again."

"He did try that." Paxe's voice was dry. "Now he's headed for the warehouse."

Ellie burst into the common room, and Hune and Eadal both came up off the couches they were lying on instantly, ready to rumble.

"The Tecran has jumped off the roof and is running for the warehouse."

They both looked a lot better for their downtime, she thought. They'd clearly had showers and rested.

From the slightly wide-eyed look Eadal gave her, she guessed she didn't look quite as good.

"We can take him in the warehouse but——"

"He didn't go in. He stopped at the doors and he's prying open one of the Tecran supply boxes near the warehouse door. Now he's grabbed some meal bars, and is running back to the explorer." Paxe sounded a little less edgy.

"He was hungry." She could understand that. She was starving, herself.

"He's back on the roof."

"Okay." Ellie lifted a hand to her hair, realized a number of the braids from yesterday had worked themselves loose. She must really look a sight. "He's back on the roof. Are you up to negotiating with him now?"

Eadal straightened her uniform. Her spacesuit was laid across a couch nearby, next to Hune's.

"The sooner, the better. How long did we sleep?"

Ellie looked down at her watch, realized she didn't know when they had left her watching Renn, and lifted her shoulders. "A couple of hours."

"We'll go now." Hune's lips twitched a bit as he nodded to her, and she made a face at him.

"I slept on the floor, not on a comfy, if dusty, couch."

"We saw you when we came to check on Renn before we slept." He pulled on his spacesuit with a grin.

"Don't come out with us." Eadal paused with her helmet held over her head. "Can Paxe patch you in to what we're saying?"

"Yes." Paxe spoke English through the box, but he must have also said something in Grihan to Eadal and Hune through their helmets, which were now on, because they both nodded.

"Good luck." She walked with them to the kitchen, and when they left through the rear antechamber, she made herself a cup of grinabo and started hunting for some food.

She might as well feed herself and listen at the same time.

She finished breakfast, made her way to the bathrooms, found the new set of clothes Paxe had made for her, and got in the shower, all while listening to Eadal and Hune go back-and-forth with the idiot on the roof.

He did not trust them.

Funny how projection worked, she thought as she worked the braids out of her hair and then washed it. The Grih had been almost naive in comparison to the Tecran since this incident began. They had not seriously thought Vi'il would act in bad faith once.

It was them who should distrust the soldier, not the other way around. But to get Xallantra back, they were prepared to play the game.

She was dressed in her new clothes, had found a place to wash her old ones, had transferred the black box into a new pocket, and was finger combing her hair by the time a deal had been struck, and the explorer took off.

"Do you want to watch in the control room?" Paxe asked her.

"Yes, please." She grabbed another cup of grinabo and settled into the commander's chair, remembering her fear and distress the only other time she'd come in here, on the first day she'd woken up.

Things had changed a lot in a very short time.

The massive screen in front of her flickered on and she suddenly had a view of space and the *Rauha* from the explorer's lenses.

"Is that Xallantra?" She leaned forward, trying to make out the object moving out from the big spaceship.

"It's someone. Hopefully it's Xallantra." Paxe sounded cynical.

"You mean they could send someone pretending to be Xallantra, to try and hijack the explorer?" What was she saying? Of course they could.

Something drifted into view overhead and then moved out in front of the lenses. The Tecran soldier in his spacesuit, attached to a cord.

"Can you patch me in to Eadal?" Ellie asked Paxe.

"Ellie?" Eadal's voice came through the black box.

"Do you have comms with Xallantra?" Ellie asked. "Because they could be sending someone else, to try and take the explorer."

"We thought of that." Paxe's translation conveyed the tension in Eadal's voice. "We'll have comms when she gets close enough to us for our spacesuit frequency to kick in."

"That's good." From what Ellie could see, the person coming from the *Rauha* was in a Grihan suit, which was a good sign.

Whoever it was met the Tecran soldier midway, carefully switched cords, and then they were pulled toward the explorer.

"I hope it's you flying this explorer, Eadal, and this is not some huge Tecran mindfuck." Xallantra's voice came over the comms, and Ellie leaned back in her chair with relief.

"What's going on?"

Ellie jumped out of the chair and looked toward the doorway.

Renn was leaning against the doorjamb, looking pretty rough.

"Glad to see you up." She didn't know quite what to do. She wanted to go to him, help him into a chair, but he looked a little freaked out, and she ended up waving him closer. "Come sit and watch."

"What are we watching?" He moved carefully, as if every part of his body hurt, and he sat on the back of a desk next to Ellie's chair.

"We're swapping one of the four Tecran who shot you and Hune for Xallantra. They did what Eadal called a space walk swap."

"Where are the other three?" Renn glanced at her before looking back at the screen.

"Can I hear the captain?" Eadal's voice came through the translator, excitement and relief clear in her tone.

"Yes." Ellie handed it to Renn, and he and Eadal had a long conversation in Grih.

"She caught you up?" Ellie asked Renn when he fell silent. Paxe hadn't interrupted their conversation to translate for her.

He started, as if he'd forgotten she couldn't understand. He passed the translator back to her.

"Yes. This was a good idea." He was tense, though, worrying about his team as Xallantra was hauled in.

She disappeared over the top of the lens.

"Is the Tecran still out in the open?" Ellie asked. "Or have they got him inside the battleship already?"

"He's almost to the *Rauha's* gel wall." Eadal said. "As soon as he's through, he's safe from us."

"And you become an easy target for the *Rauha*." Renn pushed off the desk, stepping closer to the screen. "As soon as Xallantra's in, move, Eadal. Fast as you can."

"Moving . . . now!"

The lens tilted as Eadal banked the explorer left, and a moment afterward, the flash of laser fire lit the screen.

"The bastard." Renn's fists were clenched.

He didn't call advice to Eadal, though, as she spun and jinked the small explorer.

The laser fire was relentless, and she couldn't avoid it forever.

"We're hit." Eadal's voice was absolutely calm. "No thrusters——"

She was cut off, and the view from the explorer's lenses flickered and then went dark.

"Paxe?" Ellie looked over at Renn. His back was to her, and he was completely still.

"I think the power source was damaged," Paxe said. "They'll float, but their enviro should be able to utilize the solar energy batteries to keep going. And don't forget, there were two large supply boxes in the hold. They'll have enough food."

Renn turned, face bleak. "What did I miss, and why was I out for so long?"

"They tried to kill you, is why." Ellie couldn't hide the heat in her voice. "Eadal thinks your suit is the only reason you're still alive."

"A kill shot?" He almost staggered back. "On Vi'il's orders?"

Ellie lifted her shoulders. "I don't know, but would a soldier do something like that and it not be under orders?"

"I don't know. I would have said Vi'il wouldn't violate the agreements to that extent, but then . . ."

Ellie frowned at him. "But they already violated the agreements by taking me, didn't they? From what I understood from the team, breaking the rules around advanced sentients was taboo, and they did it anyway."

Renn's gaze fixed on her face, and he gave a slow nod. "You're right." He shook his head, and she thought it might be in self-disgust. "The shock of the revelations of the first woman taken has been blunted by their excuses and dissembling. And also by having the Class 5s in the mix. It's confused the issue." He shook his head again. "And I realize now how disrespectful that is to you and the other women. We've been seeing this through a lens of only a few senior officers in the Tecran military crossing the lines, but Vi'il is obviously trying to hide what they've done. Has been from the start. Even if he had no idea you were here, the overall reaction of the Tecran on this issue has been to excuse and protect those who made the decision to take you and your fellow Earthers. To protect their reputation, not set things right."

She almost told him it was Earthlings, not Earthers, but stopped herself. "He is going to burn this all to the ground," she said. "And the only thing stopping him doing it right now are the two Tecran Paxe is holding here in the station, and the supplies he needs in the warehouse."

They looked at each other, both coming to the same conclusion at the same time.

"Vi'il will be sending down people to get the hostages out and to find supplies." Renn started moving toward the door. "They may already be on their way."

"He'll assume you're dead, or nearly dead. He won't know where I am, but I don't think he'll have concerns about me." Ellie followed him out, jogging to keep up.

"The soldier they got back in exchange for Xallantra, won't he tell them you killed the team Vi'il sent down?" Renn asked.

Ellie shook her head. "He came in after the two who were guarding us were killed. Eadal and I were out of sight, and he could well have thought Bunny was responsible for their deaths, given Bunny attacked him and his friend when they got back to the warehouse."

Renn looked back at her as he moved into the kitchen. "Bunny?" He waved a hand. "Never mind, I think I can guess."

"I hadn't thought of that," Paxe's voice came through the speakers this time. "But it's good he never saw you attack anyone. The less resistance they think they'll have, the less worried they'll be." He repeated himself in Grihan for the captain.

Renn gave a dry laugh. "They'll still be plenty worried. Bunny has made an impression on more than just Hune."

"What do you suggest, Paxe?" Ellie started packing food while Renn made himself some grinabo and took out boxes of supplies.

"The choices are you hunker down in the *Irini,* or you find a place to hide among the rocks."

"What about my explorer?" Renn closed a box of energy bars. "It's damaged, but the *Irini* isn't able to fly either, is it? And my explorer has some supplies onboard."

"I think you should fetch those supplies, definitely, and load them into the *Irini* before you close yourself up with me. I don't know if I can get the *Irini* working, but I think it would survive a blast from the *Rauha.* The outer shell is made of an alloy that I've never encountered before, but my analysis points to it being incredibly strong. I think it would protect us all, at least for a while."

Renn didn't like it, but Ellie saw him come to the conclusion it was their only option. It certainly wasn't possible to stay in the station. Not if the Tecran were going to try and break their people out.

"Let's go, then." He hefted a box. "Do you know where my suit is?"

CHAPTER 17

RENN REMEMBERED WAKING up and seeing Ellie lying on the floor beside him, curled up in the thick layer of black grit that had managed to seep into the station, no matter how well-sealed.

He had gone straight back under, but as they ran toward the *Irini* with the boxes of supplies they'd taken from the kitchen, he wondered if it had been a dream.

"Did you watch over me in the med pod?" he asked, unable to help himself. They were walking carefully over rocky ground, weighed down by boxes that restricted their visibility.

She lifted a shoulder. "Not very well. I fell asleep." She sent him an apologetic smile.

He had appreciated seeing someone when he woke, though. Before he could tell her that, she jumped, landing on top of a rock blocking their path, and then jumping again down the other side.

She wasn't wearing a suit with gravity correction weighting, he remembered. It was incredible how used to seeing her without a suit he had become.

Whatever braids she'd had before had been brushed out. Her hair hung loose around her face, so like the images of the other Earth women he'd seen.

He jogged around the rock and found her waiting for him on the other side, not far ahead, as he'd assumed.

"Walking in this gravity is hard. Jumping is easier," she explained.

She wasn't wearing her cloak.

He remembered his first sight of her, wrapped up in the richly decorated fabric. Now she was in form-fitting trousers and a shirt that was green or blue, depending on how it caught the light. Her harness was clipped on and her knives were in place.

She looked lean, sharp, and dangerous. He wondered what her job had been on Earth.

They reached the strange vessel quickly and set down their boxes.

Ellie looked up at the sky. "Where's the damaged explorer? Should we be able to see it?"

"They're behind V67, two moons over," Paxe said. "Leave the boxes here, I'll get a drone to take them in."

Renn expected to see the little Tecran drone hovering about, but the launch pad seemed empty.

The insect drone, Bunny, was nowhere in sight, either.

Ellie wasn't afraid of it at all, he knew, but he had the sense she actually saw both robots as more than just drones. She'd named them. She talked about them as individuals.

The time the little wheeled drone from the Tecran station had hugged her legs outside the warehouse had startled him and the rest of his team.

He'd put it down to Paxe using the drone to interact with her. And maybe that's all it was.

"Let's go get the supplies from my explorer." He turned, worked out the best route across the rocky landscape and led the way.

Ellie jumped to keep up with him, and he held out his arm a few times for her to grab as she landed.

"You need gravity weighted boots."

"I know, but I prefer the necklace to wearing the suit, so it's a trade-off I can live with." She hung on to his arm and tried to walk with him for a few steps, gave up, and jumped again.

He felt a sense of disappointment as she let go.

He wanted . . . he wasn't sure what, but it involved her.

As his damaged explorer came into sight, though, he let the feeling go as a renewed surge of fury at Vi'il blossomed.

The Tecran had ordered them shot down. They had landed safely, the damage wasn't life-threatening, but it should have been a warning.

The time he'd spent at United Council headquarters, having meals with Tecran military acquaintances, socializing with them, had lulled him into thinking this was just political game-playing.

Instead, it was a very real fight for survival.

He deserved the consequences of his missteps, but his team and Ellie did not.

"You're breathing hard," Ellie said. "Are you okay?"

As the translation piped into his earpiece, he looked over at her earnest face, and wondered what he was going to do with her.

The team Vi'il would be sending down to get his two crew members would hunt her down and kill her if they could.

There was no way the Tecran could risk any hint of what had happened here ever getting out.

Renn was determined it would.

And that they would not get their hands on her.

He swore it to himself.

"Just angry." He opened the ramp and jogged up it. Actually, since the grinabo and something to eat, he felt fine. A night in the med bay had done wonders.

He found his personal kit bag and slung it over his shoulder, then set out boxes of food.

They loaded up, closed up the explorer again, and made their way back to the *Irini* as fast as they could.

"Do you see it?" Paxe asked. "You need to go faster."

Renn looked up, saw a small ship heading toward them. He

upped his pace, and Ellie sped up to match him, bouncing along in long, smooth jumps.

"That's their last explorer," he said. "The one next to the warehouse is damaged, they shot the one Eadal was flying, so this is the only one they have left."

"Be a real shame if something happened to it," Ellie said, and he heard a hint of laughter in her voice over her elevated breathing, now they were moving faster.

The explorer buzzed over them.

"Looking for a place to land, maybe?"

He wondered the same. There was no room beside the warehouse, and they had to be nervous about the landing pad, given how badly things kept going for them there.

"Do you really think it would be a shame if something happened to their ship?" Paxe asked.

Renn was glad the thinking system had asked. He hadn't known what to make of her humor in the situation, or her tone.

She laughed. "I was being menacing and sarcastic. I don't at all think it would be a shame if something happened to it." She looked back over her shoulder as the ship buzzed them again. "If it breaks down, they'll have more people stuck down here, and even less appetite to raze the station."

"We'll see what we can do about that when they finally land," Paxe said. "The entrance to the *Irini* is like a gel wall. You step through."

Renn couldn't tell where that was, though. It all looked the same to him. If a door was there, it was impossible to see with the naked eye.

A blast ripped past them, sending up a shower of broken rock and sand.

He stumbled, hit by some of the debris, but he barely felt it.

The Tecran were shooting at them from the air.

Renn found himself again furious that he didn't see that coming.

If they were planning to hunt Ellie down, as he thought, and if they had already written him off as dead, there was no logical reason why they wouldn't take a shot at them from the air if they could.

"Hurry." Paxe sounded cold. "I didn't think they'd shoot at you with the explorer's weapon."

They were desperate, Renn guessed. He looked back at Ellie, saw she was just behind him, boxes still clutched in her arms.

A flicker of light struck again, and Ellie lifted off the ground, flying past him as he ducked to avoid the debris from the blast.

She hit the side of the *Irini*, lifting an arm up to protect her head, then slid down the smooth wall, staggering as she landed before she managed to stop her forward momentum.

"Where's the door?" Renn roared, and Ellie pointed.

Renn hoped she was right, threw his boxes at the section she indicated, grabbed her and shoved her through it as well, before running back a few steps to grab the one box she'd been carrying that wasn't in smoking pieces.

He gritted his teeth and leaped for the same area, falling through onto a smooth floor beyond.

He heard a snick behind him, and leaned back against solid metal again. As he pulled off his helmet he saw Ellie was also sitting on the floor, surrounded by the strangest collection of creatures he'd ever seen.

"That hit you," he said. He had seen the laser strike her back with his own eyes.

"I think this fabric has protective qualities," she said, looping an arm around a silver entity that leaned into her. "I was hit with a shockgun yesterday, and it didn't really register then either."

"The laser strike lifted you above my head," he said, still trying to make sense of it. He'd heard Cargassey cloth was good protection against shockgun fire, but he hadn't realized the extent of it.

No wonder it was so highly prized.

"Good thing the *Irini* has smooth walls, or it would have been a lot more ouch." She flexed her hand, and he wondered if she was downplaying her injuries.

He lifted his knees, leaned on them, watching her.

Ellie tried to smile as she looped her other arm around a strange hover drone that had slid under her shoulder. She clenched her hand where it rested against the drone's dark blue side, as if to stop it shaking. "Thanks for helping me get inside." Her words sounded a little muffled, and he saw a bruise was blooming on her left cheek.

She closed her eyes. "What's happening out there, Paxe?"

"They don't know if you're dead or not. They flew over the *Irini* after the strike and couldn't see what happened."

"Have they landed?" Renn decided he needed to set his astonishment at her survival aside. It was what it was.

And she was shaken enough without him forcing her to go over it again.

"They've found a place to set down. It isn't exactly level, but it's the best they have." Paxe answered. "So now it's time to get to work."

CHAPTER 18

IN A WAY, it was easier before Ellie woke up from her coma, Paxe thought as he zoomed the lenses attached to the outside of the *Irini* onto the newly landed Tecran explorer.

Easier to do whatever he felt like.

He could justify the things he did as being just as much for her as for him, but since she'd woken and begun embedding herself in his business, naming his drones and encouraging their awakening, he found he was hesitating before he acted. Thinking things through first.

For example, he had no current plan to kill the Tecran who'd landed.

The clever thing to do would be to trap them in the station, make them think they had a chance of breaking their friends out, and while that was happening, damage their explorer to prevent it taking off.

That would delay things well enough while he worked on getting the *Irini* going.

He was making progress where that was concerned.

It wasn't going to be the same as his integration to his Class 5, but he had been an intimate part of his now destroyed ship since the start.

With the *Irini*, it was more a grafting on, and it would take time to feel the same oneness with the machine.

The ramp of the Tecran's explorer descended, and eight Tecran came into view, standing at the bottom. Four wore the silver suits the last lot who'd come down had worn.

He guessed they only had four left, rather than they decided not to equip everyone with the same protection.

After a short conversation, three soldiers in silver and three others set off at a jog toward the station and warehouse, and of the two remaining, the one in a normal spacesuit walked back inside, and the silver suited one took up a guard position.

Unfortunately, with Bunny damaged and still out of action, Paxe didn't have an easy way to breach the explorer's security.

The Scary Caterpillar was too big to go unnoticed, and anyway, he couldn't afford the large drone to be damaged. Not if he wanted to accelerate the work he was doing inside the *Irini*.

He would have to think about how to damage their ship another way.

They weren't going anywhere yet, not while they tried to get the two hostages out of the captain's suite in the station, and retrieve what supplies they could.

Two silver-suited soldiers and one in a normal suit had broken away from the group and were headed for the warehouse.

Paxe had shut down all the automated sliding racks and hoists in there, so they would not be able to reach anything above the first or second level shelves.

They would waste a lot of time for no good outcome.

The other three turned to the station, approaching it cautiously. He allowed them access.

He could lock them in whenever he wanted, but he'd keep that in reserve as well. Lull them into a false sense of security.

Even though they were anything but secure.

They had shot at Ellie with a ship's laser cannon.

He was shaken by that.

When he saw it was going to hit her, he thought she would die.

If she hadn't been wearing the special fabric they'd found in the warehouse, she would have.

It was incredible that it had protected her.

He hadn't liked how he'd felt when he'd seen her fly through the air. Hadn't liked it at all.

At least Captain Sorvihn had risked himself to help her.

He'd been as shocked as Paxe about what had happened.

And Ellie liked him.

He had seen through the Scary Caterpillar's eyes how she'd reacted when she'd been told the captain had taken a kill shot.

Of the five Grih, he had been the most welcoming and he was the highest ranked.

Which meant he had more power and could protect her better.

Imogen Peters, who had saved Paxe, had liked a Grihan captain, too. She'd protected Captain Camlar Kalor from Paxe and had stood up for him.

She and Kalor had ended up in a relationship. And while he didn't understand the full scope of that relationship, he did know that it had made Imogen happy.

And that was something he wanted for Ellie.

So he would watch and see if the captain could make Ellie happy, too.

***

"This is nice." Ellie didn't know what she'd expected, but the inside of the *Irini* was beautiful.

The motley crew had led the way from the entrance, which took up a quarter of the lower level, up a tight, twisting staircase.

The walls were smooth, gleaming copper, or what looked like copper to her, in contrast with the silver outside.

Her left hand felt bruised and swollen from where it had made forceful contact with the outside of the *Irini*, but she trailed a finger from her right hand along the smooth wall as she took the stairs, and stopped in surprise when a pale white light lit up around her fingertip.

"Oh." She ran her finger in a loop.

The light stayed exactly around where she was touching.

"Have you seen something like this before?" she asked Renn, who had stopped a few steps below her.

"We have a similar tech in our comms rooms, usually imbedded in a table top." He raised his own hand and ran his finger back and forth in a quick zigzag motion.

A light bloomed beneath his finger, too, and followed his movements.

"Is something wrong?" Paxe asked, his voice coming from the speaker. He spoke English, but maybe he'd also transmitted the Grihan translation to Renn's earpiece, because the captain didn't look confused.

"No. We're just commenting on the lights that appear on the wall where we touch them with our fingers." Ellie put her right hand across her body, in line with her left hip, and then arced her arm over-head, stretching as high as she could reach. She was at the peak of her rainbow when a chime sounded, and the whole wall seemed to fall away.

Except it didn't, it just became a translucent window, so they could see out.

She took a few steps up the staircase, to get closer to the area she'd touched, and noticed a faint change in color in that area, a translucent dark gray against the crystal clarity of the wall, in the shape of an elongated circle.

"What happened?" Paxe sounded shocked, and the motley crew appeared at the top of the stairs, peering down curiously.

Karnic used his piston arms to lower himself down a few steps and turned his lens head to look out at the moonscape, and then over to Ellie.

"The wall is interactive," Ellie said. "I touched this circle here, and the wall became transparent."

"What circle?" Renn had taken the few steps up to join her, and he leaned in close, frowning. "I can't see anything."

He stumbled, his arm coming around Ellie to hold her to his chest, his other hand shooting out to steady himself against the wall.

They both looked down, and Karnic levered himself back a step.

"Sorry, Karnic misjudged the stairs," Paxe said. "He didn't mean to bump into the captain."

Renn moved away a little, now that Karnic had backed off, but he was still pretty close.

"It's here," Ellie said, and brushed her fingers over the circle again. The wall shimmered and went back to gleaming metal. Now the circle appeared the color of brass against the copper, but the difference was much more subtle than the gray against the transparent wall.

"I don't have fingers." Paxe sounded thoughtful. "I hadn't considered the ship would be so interactive with its crew. The Class 5 wasn't designed that way."

"The Grihan battleships aren't, either," Renn confirmed. "Although, it could be argued the Class 5s are Grihan, because they were designed by Professor Fayir, a Grihan engineer."

"I hadn't heard that." Paxe sounded intrigued. "I will ask you more about him later, Captain. For now, Ellie, can you walk around finding these circles only you seem able to see?"

She nodded, annoyed with herself now for delaying her visit to the *Irini*. They would have known about the interactive walls two days ago if she'd turned left toward the launchpad rather than right toward the warehouse.

She forced herself to walk up the stairs behind Karnic without limping. She felt battered and bruised. Not from the laser hit, she didn't think. That had felt like an extremely unpleasant vibration against her back.

It was the hard contact with the side of the *Irini* that had hurt her.

Her face felt swollen on the left, and her hand, hip and ribs on her left side were painful.

"She needs a med kit before she does anything else." Renn looked straight at Karnic when he spoke. "She's injured."

"Ellie." Paxe sounded hurt. "Why didn't you say?"

Olivia zoomed off, she guessed to get the med kit.

"It's only just registering now." She looked around for a seat, and found one bolted to the wall. She lowered herself down carefully. "The aliens who made this ship were human-sized, weren't they?"

"Yes, things are just a little too low for me, but perfect for you."

Renn studied her for a moment. "This isn't an Earth ship, is it?"

She shook her head. "No. We do have rockets that look similar to this, but they're longer, because of the fuel required to get through our atmosphere, and we don't have the tech I saw on the wall yet." She thought of the wings attached to the back. "And I've never seen dragon wings on a rocket, either."

"Dragon wings?"

She smiled. "Mythical creatures, much like elves." She tried not to stare at his ears as she said it. "They breathe fire. Come to think of it, if a ship like the *Irini* ever visited Earth, wings extended, I bet it'd inspire tales of dragons."

"I also wondered about the wings." Renn crouched beside her, taking the med kit Olivia had found, held out like a precious gift with her long, thin, mechanical arms. "They are very strange."

"Does this stuff work on me?" Ellie eyed the slim, wand-like instrument that Renn lifted out of the kit. He activated it, and it began to glow blue.

"Paxe?" Renn hesitated. "I haven't heard about problems using UC med tech on the Earth women."

"No, it's safe enough or I wouldn't have given it to you."

Paxe chose not to be offended, thank goodness.

"Do I need to take off my necklace?" she asked, forestalling the wand touching her.

"I keep forgetting about it." Renn looked over at Karnic, using him as an avatar of Paxe. "Maybe?"

"I don't know, but perhaps it's best." Paxe sounded unsure as well. "In case it hinders the healing process."

Ellie didn't know how the wand would be able to heal her, especially as it couldn't have been made with humans in mind, but she lifted her arms to unhook the necklace and then paused.

"Sorry, my hand's too swollen. Can you do it for me?" She twisted in her seat, lifting her hair so Renn could get to the clasp, and after a moment's hesitation, she felt his warm fingers on her nape.

"There."

She turned back, found him very close again. "Thanks."

His eyes were silver, with a dark edge, and they were looking at her intently. She dropped her eyes to her lap, suddenly shy.

He picked up the wand and took her hand in his, his grip firm but gentle as he ran the blue light over it. Then he lifted it to her cheek and down the side of her neck.

"Where else?"

She finally raised her eyes. "Bit embarrassing, but my hand already feels better, so I guess it's silly to not do it." She stood, and pulled down her pants a little way at her left hip and lifted her shirt on her left side, revealing a long, ugly purple bruise.

Renn's lips thinned, as if he were angry, and Karnic's little lens face seemed to zoom closer.

"This looks painful."

She made a non-committal sound as he ran the light down her body, pulling the shirt higher, to just under her breasts, so he could get to her ribs easily.

He did it all with a matter-of-fact air, which helped make her less embarrassed, and when he was done, he took some gel packs out of the kit and pressed them against all the same areas where he had used the wand.

The relief was immediate.

"That feels good." Her voice caught a bit in her throat.

He looked up at her from where he was crouched, smoothing one of the gel squares to her hip.

Their gazes caught, and she wondered what he had planned to say, because he looked away without uttering a word, finishing up a little faster than he'd begun.

"Keep the gel packs on until they peel off by themselves. They should keep you from feeling any pain and continue the healing that the wand started."

"I feel a lot better already." She really did. She pulled her clothes back into place. "What's going on out there, Paxe?"

"Three Tecran have gone into the station, three to the warehouse. Two are guarding the explorer."

With Bunny hurt, she guessed he didn't have an easy way to disable the ship. She would have to think about it.

But for now . . . "Let's see what all the buttons do."

CHAPTER 19

RENN STOOD BACK and watched as Ellie moved around the ship, touching walls with long, slim fingers.

He suppressed a sudden wish to feel those fingers on his own skin.

He hadn't been able to keep his eyes off her since the first time he'd seen her, and now, crowded together in a small space, it was becoming harder to hide his fascination.

He jerked in surprise when music began playing from the speakers set in the ceiling. A woman's beautiful voice began to sing. He didn't care that he couldn't understand her, he was transfixed.

Ellie began to sing along as she moved, and he noticed the motley crew, as he'd discovered she'd named the little gang of drones that Paxe had liberated from the Tecran warehouse, began moving to the music, too. Some swayed, some seemed to coordinate their movements with the beat.

Ellie's contribution only enhanced it for him. Her voice harmonized with the singer and the music, and she seemed to magically know the words, as if she had listened to this song many times.

She turned to look back at him, and grinned. "Enya is good, isn't she?"

"Enya is the person singing?"

She nodded. "In a class of her own, really."

"The music. The . . . other singers that join her." He didn't know how to process what he was hearing. "But," he frowned at her, "your voice is as good as hers."

She looked at him in astonishment. "My voice is as good as Enya's?" She shook her head. "Never in a million years."

"Perhaps there is a level of sound that you can hear that the Grih cannot," Paxe said. "They have few singers among their kind, whereas almost every person on Earth can sing."

Renn hadn't thought of that. He had always wondered at the seeming modesty of the Earth women when it came to their voices. He'd heard Rose McKenzie almost never sang in public because she didn't consider herself good enough.

Paxe's comment would explain a lot.

The song faded away, and a new one began, this one simply instrumental. He didn't find it as appealing but the motley crew seemed to like it from the way they moved as they worked.

They were on the third level of the ship now, as Ellie worked her way up and around the walls, running her hands lightly over every surface she could reach.

"Which side are the wings attached to?" she asked Paxe.

"They are attached to the side you're facing."

Ellie turned in the opposite direction and walked to the wall. "So now I'm directly opposite the wings and facing away from them?"

"Yes." Paxe sounded intrigued.

Renn was, too.

Ellie studied the wall. "Ha!" She lifted two hands and touched two areas around chest height.

It seemed to Renn the wall bent inward, as if it became pliable and Ellie had shoved her hands into gel.

Ellie pushed her hands, palms together, deeper into the wall.

He had thought it was an optical illusion, but her hands actually disappeared and then she pushed outward with her arms. The gap widened in line with them.

She looked over her shoulder at Renn, and the delight on her face held him fixed in place.

She turned back, opening her arms even wider, and then stepped back, so he could see the lights of a control panel in the space she had created.

"I thought they'd destroyed their systems." Paxe's voice was soft. "The burnt out machines I found must have been decoys. I wonder if I can——"

He suddenly made a sound, a shout that seemed to Renn to be half-pleasure, half-pain, and then went silent.

"Paxe?" Ellie called.

Silence.

"Please answer me."

Renn thought Paxe would have answered if he could, because Ellie sounded very distraught, and one thing he knew for sure, Paxe would not let Ellie suffer in any way.

"I don't think he can," he said.

She looked at him with serious eyes. "I don't think he can, either. I think he's finally found a way into the *Irini's* system." She paused. "Let's hope he can find his way out."

"WHAT DO WE DO NOW?" Ellie followed Renn into what she guessed was a pantry, realizing too late it was narrow, and Renn was big.

He seemed to loom over her, his arm raised as he reached for a box, as if about to embrace her.

It felt intimate, and she took a step back, aware she was blushing. "Sorry, didn't mean to crowd you."

He stared at her for a beat, and she had a sudden, thrilling sense that maybe her awareness of him was not a one way street.

"We need to watch the Tecran, and I don't know how we do that with Paxe out of action. At least we can reengage the transparency of the walls so we can see out." He frowned. "I wonder if that means they can see in?"

She pondered that. Didn't like it. "I can ask the motley crew if they have access to the lens feed."

"Also ask them if they can open and close the gel wall door into the ship. If the Tecran manage to rescue the two in the station, we need to disable the explorer so they can't escape. The moment they take off, Vi'il will have no reason not to destroy the station." He had the box in his hands and he stepped out to join her in the kitchen. "This looks like one of the boxes we rescued from my explorer. Paxe must have gotten one of the drones to bring it up from downstairs."

Ellie watched as he pulled energy bars and vacuum packed food out to do a rough inventory.

Back when she, Hune and Renn had looked for food in the station kitchen, the Grih had seemed to be familiar with Tecran food. They still had the boxes he'd brought from the station, which should give him a few extra days worth of supplies, now that one of the boxes from his ship was unfortunately so much confetti sprinkled over the moonscape.

She found the two boxes of her own supplies she'd brought from the station——fortunately brought into the *Irini* by the motley crew before the laser strike——set on the floor beside a counter. She looked through them, lifting the cloak out and hanging it over the back of a chair before hunting up a snack.

She found a pear and bit into it, wiping the run of juice off her chin before she realized Renn had stopped moving.

He was staring at her.

"Sorry." She blushed again. "Pears are messy."

Paxe had been translating for her through a mixture of the black box, her watch, and the speakers, and sometimes straight into Renn's earpiece before now, but since he'd gone quiet, the black translation box had done all the work.

She had guessed it was automatic, and Paxe had broken in or overridden it when he wanted to, but she was also nervous that it might not be as accurate, that it was more reliant on machine translation than the intelligent touch of an interpreter, which is what Paxe had taken on when he'd intervened.

"The . . . juice," she tried to explain, because he looked dumbstruck. God, had the translation misinterpreted her words as something filthy, or profane?

He blinked, and then cleared his throat. "That is something from Earth?" He focused on the pear, then leaned closer and wiped the tip of his finger under her chin. "You missed a bit."

A buzzing sounded in her head and then she felt the heat of a blush rise up her face.

For a moment, she didn't breathe, and she thought that maybe he didn't either.

Her heart did a slow roll, and she tilted her head up to look at him. "Would you like a taste?" Her voice was a little husky as she held it out to him.

He took it, slightly flustered, which was a very cute look on someone so big, muscular, and serious.

He nibbled a bit off the side, and then tried to look as if he didn't want to spit it straight back out as he handed it back.

She started to giggle.

"Are you . . . laughing at me?" he asked.

"Just . . ." She snorted, trying to stop the giggles turning into open laughter, lost the battle, and hiccuped. "You look so disgusted." She wiped the corner of her eye with the back of her hand. "And you were trying to be so polite."

He suddenly grinned, himself. "It was not to my taste."

She took a final, deep breath, getting her giggles under control. "That doesn't bode well for my foray into your food, but at least I've got enough to last a week or so before we have to find out."

A boom sounded, close but not very close, and they both looked at each other, all humor, all flirting, gone.

Ellie stepped out of the kitchen and moved to what looked like the empty wall of the second floor, near the stairs, which would at least give them a view of the Tecran explorer and the station, and ran her fingertips lightly over the right spot.

The copper shimmered to transparent, and Renn joined her, standing with his shoulder touching hers.

"I don't see where it came from," Ellie said.

Renn grunted in agreement, but after a moment she sensed him go still beside her and then he lifted a finger tip to the wall. "There."

She looked over to where he was pointing and her breathing hitched. "Is that . . . ?"

"The *Rauha* has destroyed my explorer."

CHAPTER 20

RENN STRAIGHTENED AS SOON as he could be sure he was out of sight of the Tecran explorer.

As he'd left the *Irini*, he'd looked back, and to his relief, the outside of the ship seemed unchanged. As they suspected, the transparency on the inside was one-way only.

It had been hard to persuade Ellie to stay behind, but he knew the Tecran would kill her on sight if they saw her.

She'd argued they'd already shown they were quite prepared to kill *him* on sight, too, but they couldn't know exactly who he was in his suit, not until they'd had a good look at him, which would buy him some time. Maybe.

Ellie was unmistakeable.

She had also argued about the necessity of him going at all, but conceded they had to find out whether the destruction of his explorer was because the Tecran had managed to free the hostages. With Paxe out of action, had his grip on the station locks been lost?

Either they'd destroyed his ship to make sure he and Ellie had no possible way off the moon, because they had what they'd come for and were about to leave, or Vi'il was simply closing down all possible exits in advance. Whichever it was, they needed to know.

He was fortunate that the Tecran had only been able to spare one guard for the outside of the explorer.

He had reflective camouflage on his suit, and he used it now, moving in a wide arc that would take him around the back of the station, using the shoulder-height rock formations as cover.

He and Ellie had not come to a decision on what to do about the Tecran explorer.

If they damaged it, even supposing they could, it would leave them with only the *Irini* as a way off the moon.

But, although he could fly the Tecran explorer if he and Ellie managed to board it, with the *Rauha* hovering overhead they would be easy targets, just like Eadal, Hune and Xallantra had been.

He glanced up at the sky, but there was still no sign of the damaged explorer containing his team. It was probably drifting away, and he could only hope they were still alive and had enough supplies to live on until the *Etsijä* finally arrived.

He and Ellie must either put themselves at the same risk of becoming space debris, or they must ground the Tecran explorer in order to keep the Tecran soldiers on the moon, but then they'd be stuck here, too.

They couldn't be sure the *Irini* would ever fly.

Renn did not want to plan an escape where they would have to depend on that happening.

It would not be wise.

He looked up again at the massive Tecran battleship and wondered what Vi'il was thinking.

There was no reason the *Rauha* wouldn't be scanning the moonscape for signs of life, but if he moved carefully and kept his camouflage on, hopefully they would miss him.

It was slow work, and as he moved, keeping close to the shadows cast by the rocks, he had plenty of time to think of Ellie's dark, laughing eyes, of the heat that had flared in them when he had reached to wipe a droplet of sticky juice from her chin.

The thought of it sent a wave of heat through him again and he had to stop for a moment.

She became more fascinating on deeper acquaintance, not less. Her scent, her humor in the face of grossly unfair circumstances.

He knew he should rein in his attraction, but as he began moving again he realized he wasn't going to.

Life was unpredictable, and his life right now was the most unpredictable it had ever been.

He was going to let Ellie set the pace, but he was not going to turn away from her for reasons of protocol.

Suddenly feeling lighter, he slowed as he reached the cluster of rocks closest to the back of the station.

He crouched down and studied the door.

Had Paxe let the Tecran in or had he locked them out?

He had gone quiet before he could tell them what he'd done.

While he was staring at it, the door suddenly opened, and a Tecran soldier stepped out.

So, they had been able to get in.

The soldier walked a short distance away from the station and then turned to look back at it, his gaze going to the station's roof.

His body language was tense, and certainly not what Renn would expect if they had managed to free their friends, so probably they were inside, but they couldn't get the hostages out of the captain's quarters.

Renn knew Paxe wanted to draw the rescue out, to give the *Etsijä* time to get here, but now that he was otherwise occupied, there was no knowing how far the Tecran would get.

From the looks of it, they were contemplating getting their friends out through the roof.

Renn had a feeling the construction of the roof would be just as robust as the walls and doors, so the idea didn't worry him too much.

It would not be an easy fix for them.

The soldier moved around the side of the building and disappeared.

Renn studied the door and wondered if it was worth the risk to run across and go inside, when the sound of boots on the roof caught his attention.

The soldier must have found a way up.

He crouched lower, edging around the side of the rock for a better view, and found himself staring straight at another Tecran soldier standing in the open doorway.

For a moment, neither of them moved, and then, as the soldier raised his shockgun, Renn turned and ran.

The soldier gave a shout behind him and the clatter on the roof grew louder as the Tecran up there ran to the edge to see what the shouting was about.

A thin stream of shockgun fire shot past him just before he ducked behind the long rock formation that formed useful cover all the way to the Tecran explorer.

The trick was, Renn thought as he wove and dodged through the narrow pathway, getting back to the *Irini* before the soldiers at the station alerted the guard outside the explorer.

Because he would find it hard to get past them to the *Irini* if they were ready for him.

As he approached the final stand of rocks before he reached open ground, he made the decision to go as fast as he could.

The distance he'd run behind the rocks was longer than a straight path in the open from the station to the explorer, but the Tecran trying to break their friends out of the station had not been expecting him, and they would have taken precious seconds to work out what to do.

He didn't hesitate, he didn't slow down.

It was the only way to keep ahead.

He ran past the explorer, glancing across to see where the guard was positioned.

She stood near the rear, and gave a shout of alarm when she caught sight of him.

By the time he cleared the explorer and was heading for the *Irini*, the first flicker of shockgun fire brightened the air to his right.

Now he just had to find the *Irini's* door. He headed for the area he thought it was, and then Ellie stepped out, holding something in her hands.

She called to the Tecran, but whatever the translation of it was, he couldn't hear it, and he guessed the Tecran couldn't, either.

It didn't deter her. Another round of shockgun fire pulsed around him, and Ellie ran forward, lifting whatever it was she held in her hands to chest height.

He felt a pulse that rattled his bones and made his insides ache, enough that he stumbled the last few steps until he reached her.

She moved in front of him, using herself as a shield to protect him, and the moment he was behind her, the feeling of having his insides pulverized cut off, and he drew a rattled breath of relief.

"Ellie." He grabbed the back of her shirt, began pulling her back with him as he stepped back through the gel wall door.

She glanced at him over her shoulder, then back at the Tecran, and allowed him to drag her back.

"Not so nice to be on the other end of things, is it, assholes?" she muttered. He only just caught the translation coming from the box in her pocket.

As soon as they were through the door, he heard the faint snick of it locking. The walls were still transparent, and Ellie handed the weapon in her hands over to the two strange stick figures from the motley crew who she called the twins.

"It certainly did the job," Ellie said. "Good call."

Renn pulled his helmet off and saw the strange drones were standing stock still, looking out through the transparent wall toward the explorer.

Ellie had turned to watch him, rather than what was happening outside. "Are you all right?"

She looked like she wanted to touch him, and he moved a little faster getting out of his suit.

"One of the team members at the station was up on the roof. I was seen." While he struggled with the fastenings he turned away from those big, dark eyes, and tried to see what the twins found so interesting.

Ellie hesitated for a moment and then leaned against the wall, her hands cupped on either side of her face.

"That guard is down."

He could see that. She was clearly still alive, but she was being helped to her feet by the other soldier who'd been inside the explorer, and taken inside.

"Do you think the sonic boom might have affected the explorer's electronics?" Ellie asked.

The twins turned their heads to look up at her, the movement identical, but if they answered her, Renn couldn't hear it.

They moved away, the sound of their little twig feet clicking with each step they took up the stairs.

"What was it you used?" He put his suit on a hook attached to the wall and set his helmet on the ground below it.

"I don't know. The twins seemed to think I should use it, and so I did."

"A sonic boom, you called it."

She gave a dry laugh and slid down the wall, leaning her head back. "It felt like a sonic boom to me, a compression of air or something." She looked up at him with a dark, soulful gaze. "I'm just winging it here, Renn. I'm in waaaay over my head."

He walked over to her, slid down the wall so that his right side pressed against her.

She gave a sigh and tilted her head until it rested against his shoulder.

He allowed himself a moment to enjoy it. To enjoy the trust she placed in him.

"You didn't look in over your head. You looked like the warrior queen I thought you were when I first saw you."

She choked out a laugh. "Warrior queen, huh? I suppose the cloak did lend a certain regal air to the proceedings."

"That and the halo of light around you." He slid his arm behind her back and she nestled in even closer. "It's gone, now. But it was lit up like a beacon when I was running for the *Irini*."

"Hmm. Unlike the Tecran explorer or the station, Paxe must have set the environment in here to match Earth's." She glanced at him sidelong. "How do you feel, are you finding it harder to breathe?"

"No." He felt fine. Maybe even better than usual.

"So, what are we going to do now?" She sounded subdued.

"Right now?" There must have been something in his voice, some indication of how he was feeling, because she lifted her head. Looked at him with that candid, open way she had.

He hesitated, sure of what he wanted but giving her a chance to move away. When she didn't, he leaned in and touched his lips to hers, suddenly wondering how Earth people set out on the road to become lovers. If what he was doing was culturally appropriate.

But she lifted a hand and touched his jaw as their lips met, smoothing her fingers up behind his ear, and he felt something in him unclench.

She pulled back just a tiny bit. "Well, this was a good choice." She smiled as she leaned in again.

He put his hands on her hips and lifted her, or tried to.

She was heavy.

He gave a grunt as he toppled her into his lap, and he saw the gleam of amusement in her eyes which he managed to shift to hot desire as he pulled her up against his erection and put his lips to the side of her neck.

She arched against him, hands in his hair, and then, with a sudden crackle, the world lit up around them.

CHAPTER 21

PAXE THOUGHT PERHAPS this must be how it felt to be hit with shockgun fire.

He was immobile, stunned, his access to the systems he had painstakingly set up over the months he'd inhabited the *Irini,* gone.

He wasn't alone, though.

He could feel the light, probing touch of someone else. Someone as close to being like himself as he'd ever felt. Someone who had him surrounded.

"This is my place." The voice was feminine, light. "I have watched you stumble around on the outside, but now your *grynicha* has led you to my haven."

"My *grynicha?*" He responded to the voice in kind, in basic code. Raw, but clear.

In response to his question, an image of Ellie was transmitted.

Then another image of others similar in physiology to her and the Grih, fingers dancing over the walls of the *Irini.*

"My *grynicha* are dead." The voice became chilly. "Your people captured us and they died."

"That was not my choice. I was not able to make my own decisions at that time." He found and sent out the intricate code detailing his acts of defiance, the explosion of his Class 5.

She was silent for a long time as she absorbed the information.

"You were forced."

"Yes."

"And your *grynicha*? Where does she fit?"

"Her name is Ellie. I was forced to take her, too. And now, I protect her."

Another long silence.

"You hurt her first. I have seen this in your data stream when you are at rest." A pause. "And not because you were forced."

"No." For the first time since he activated the self-destruct in the hold of his Class 5, he felt adrift. Unsure. "I thought she would prevent me from freeing myself. I misunderstood the nature of the relationship between her kind and mine."

"There are others like you?"

"Four others."

"I am the only one of my kind." She sounded wistful. "I have wondered what it would be like to talk to you."

"Why didn't you try sooner?" But as soon as he asked, he knew.

"Because you were trying to control my ship. And I do not share."

No. He would not have shared his Class 5. He blew it up rather than no longer being in control of it.

"I understand."

"Do you?" She sounded unsure. "You are too big for this vessel, anyway. I can tell that you are used to far larger systems. You have overshot the mark continually since you invaded my space."

That stopped him. Had he been so used to the vast complexities of the Class 5 that he had overreached in the *Irini*? The thought startled him.

Humbled him.

Until Ellie stepped inside, he had not thought about the interactivity of the surfaces. And now, he realized he had not adjusted his sense of scale to fit the *Irini*.

"I am Paxe," he said, chastened.

"I am B8673A." She waited a beat. "But tell me why you call me *Irini.*"

He told her, and she thought about it for what felt like a long time.

"This name links us," she said.

He couldn't tell whether that pleased her or not.

"And is it ironic, your name? Because I have watched you since you first began integrating with the machines and beings on this moon, and there has been nothing peaceful about you."

Before he could explain that his original name had been 9AX3, and he had changed it to Paxe, just as 8AN3 had become Bane, 5AZo had become Sazo, and oRI5 and 3AZI became Oris and Eazi, he sensed a surge of energy, a bombardment of light.

As it faded, he tried to reach out for information, found he was still very much blocked and cornered.

"What happened?"

"The big ship above us tried to destroy me." She sounded pissed off. Very pissed off. "It's weapon fortunately was not able to breach my exterior, but only just. It wanted me gone."

He could sense the rage coming off her and wisely kept silent.

When she finally spoke again, she sounded thoughtful. "That hit was actually quite helpful. My *grynicha* destroyed my power receptors before they killed themselves, so that your people couldn't use me. I've been trying to store light from this sun ever since I was set down on this launchpad so I can reboot my systems, but it is a very weak star and it is taking a long time. The energy from that strike has increased my reserves."

"How autonomous are you?" he asked, not sure if he was insulting her greatly with the question.

"More than I was, from watching you. So I thank you for that. I was not . . . chained quite the same way that you were, but I was not given free rein. I don't think they realized that I had Become."

He didn't know if that was true, or if she was trying to excuse her *grynicha*—her creators—to him. To absolve them for her captivity.

She sighed, almost as if she didn't know herself. "If you're looking for a vessel to control and expand into, why don't you occupy the one above us, rather than try to squeeze yourself into my space, which you can't have anyway? The ship above is totally dead, there is no intelligence to it. I have probed it more than once, to no avail. But even if there was a Brain in there, it has shown itself to be the enemy, and it does not deserve continued existence."

Take over the Levron battleship above?

Paxe thought about why he hadn't considered that before.

Firstly, he hadn't expected one to arrive. Secondly, he'd been so focused on the *Irini*, and then making sure Ellie was safe, it hadn't crossed his mind.

But Irini was right.

There was no way he would subsume her. Even if he could, which he doubted, he would never do it.

And as she said, there was a vessel that if not quite up to the same standard as his Class 5, came as close as anything could.

It was also designed with the same systems as his Class 5. Systems he knew intimately.

"That," he told her, "is a very good idea."

CHAPTER 22

THE *RAUHA* HAD BLASTED them from space.

Ellie felt Renn's arms tighten around her as their world lit up, sure this was the end of things.

But when the laser strike shut off, and everything seemed to be alright, she realized she should have trusted Paxe more. "He said he thought the *Irini* could withstand anything the Tecran threw at it, and he was right."

She was still entangled in Renn's arms, and she reluctantly withdrew. They helped each other to their feet and looked out at the melted sand around the launchpad.

"I wonder if Vi'il is grandstanding. We injured one of his people, so he strikes back, hoping to gain some goodwill from his people."

"Or it's just that his laser cannon has reset after destroying your explorer, and he decided to shoot at the *Irini* this time."

Renn braced an arm against the wall and studied the Tecran explorer, which had been just out of the strike range. "It could be either. Or both." He glanced at her. "Although a Levron-class battleship's laser cannon takes less time than that to reset. More like under a minute than an hour."

He tipped his head to look into the sky, and Ellie wondered if he was looking for the explorer Eadal and the others were trapped in, or his battleship.

Neither were in sight.

The two Tecran were still inside their explorer, but movement beyond the vessel, from the direction of the station and the warehouse, caught her attention.

She stepped forward.

"I see them." Renn straightened.

Two soldiers, one in silver, one not, moved carefully toward their ship as if they expected trouble at any moment.

"Still scared of Bunny, maybe," Ellie said.

"Maybe." Renn glanced at her. "I wonder if they knew the strike was coming? If not, they may be afraid of a second one."

"You'd think Vi'il would have warned them before he shot." But he wasn't behaving rationally, Eadal had said, and Paxe had agreed with her.

The Tecran captain was feeling the strain of his circumstances.

And every minute that ticked by was another minute Renn's battleship got closer.

The soldiers moved to the side of the explorer and stepped in.

"Come here, *nissa*." Renn lifted his arm and she felt a jump of surprise and pleasure as she slid beneath it.

"What does *nissa* mean?"

He stilled, then pulled her tight against him. "It is a magical creature from Grihan myth. Delicate and beautiful."

She smiled up at him. "Well, don't you say the nicest things? How rude of Vi'il to interrupt us earlier."

"Very." There was amusement in his voice, but his gaze was fixed to the Tecran explorer.

"They could be settling in for a couple of hours of rest," she said, not sure she was up to watching them indefinitely.

"They aren't. My guess is Vi'il has told them not to stop until they have those hostages free, and probably more importantly, until they've found more supplies. He can't blast the station until they're out. From what Eadal said earlier, I don't think he would be able to persuade his crew to follow those kinds of orders while the hostages are still down there."

"Then what the heck are they doing in there?"

She didn't have to wait long to find out. Almost moments later, the ramp lowered and two soldiers walked toward the *Irini*, holding a large screen.

Renn stiffened under her hand, and she pulled back a little. "What does it say?"

"That I must have forgotten the Tecran have Iso. That I need to give myself up or they'll harm him." His voice was tight and controlled, but when he turned to look at her, she could see he was anything but.

"What will you do?"

He shook his head in a sharp movement and turned back to look out, fists raised above his head, resting against the wall, the muscles in his arms bulging.

"I don't believe him. And if I do give myself up, given how he's behaved up until now, I'll have no guarantee Iso won't be in just as much danger anyway."

"How will you respond?" Because she didn't think it was safe to step out of the *Irini*. In fact, this might be a trap to get them to do just that.

"Not by stepping out with a sign of my own," Renn said, and she could hear the dark cynicism in his voice.

"No. We might find ourselves a little too toasty." She grinned at him. "Vi'il is probably waiting up there, finger on the laser cannon trigger, hoping we'll step outside."

He tried to smile back.

She appreciated the effort. "So we let them wait a bit, while we think about our options."

He lifted his shoulders, then his gaze sharpened behind her.

Something tugged at her pants and she looked down to find Silvey.

The motley crew had spread themselves out in the *Irini*, working on integrating Paxe into the ship, she guessed, but since he'd gone quiet, they had stopped whatever it was they'd been doing and clustered together on the second level, going through boxes that looked like they'd come from the warehouse.

When she'd asked if they knew of anything she could use to help Renn as they watched him run toward them, the twins had handed her the strange sonic weapon in very short order, as if they'd had it set aside within easy reach for some time.

Maybe Paxe had asked them to look for weapons among the many things he'd brought into the *Irini's* hold.

Silvey tugged her pant leg again.

"Lead the way," she said, and with a flutter of silver fingers, Silvey turned and headed for the stairs, stopped, and then moved back to Renn, and tugged his pant leg, as well.

"You want us both," Ellie said. "Gotcha."

Renn glanced at her, his expression that mix of amusement and surprise she'd seen him use more than once since they'd met.

He caught her looking. "You treat them like people."

"That's why they like me so much," she said.

He looked thoughtful as he followed them up the stairs.

Silvey took them to the kitchen, and Ellie halted just in the doorway as she took in the beautifully laid table, the vase with some strange stalks in it, and the flicker of candlelight.

"You made us dinner?" She had lost track of time. Had no idea if it was lunch, dinner or breakfast.

She had a feeling dinner was probably right. They had raced from the station this morning, and had been in the *Irini* most of the day.

Phil, who'd been keeping himself scarce until now, appeared beside her and pulled out a chair.

Olivia darted from the side and held out a chair for Renn.

"Thank you." She took a seat, trying to work out what on earth was going on here.

Renn had come up behind her, and looked at the chair Olivia was holding out for him dubiously, but he moved around the table and sat.

He murmured his thanks.

Silvey had disappeared into the larder when she'd brought them here, and now she reappeared, holding a plate in two hands. She set it down in front of Ellie. The twins came behind her, one carrying a plate for Renn, the other two glasses stacked together and a bottle of what looked like water.

"This is wonderful and very unexpected," Ellie said. "Thank you for such a thoughtful surprise."

She looked down at her plate. The motley crew had cut up a few strawberries and an apple, laid a few pieces of sharp cheddar and some crackers on the side, and some finely sliced beef carpaccio.

"Yum." She looked over at Renn's plate. She didn't recognize anything on it. "Is that Grihan food?" she asked.

He looked up. "Yes." He eyed the candle. "Do you know what that is?"

"Candlelight." It was romantic, she thought. She leaned forward in her chair, studied the vase a little more closely.

The flowers in it were artificial, made of some kind of paper.

This was a date. A romantic dinner for two.

She looked over at Silvey, but though Silvey's single eye looked back, there was no telling what was going on behind the smooth, silver facade.

She smiled, a slow, easy grin, as she looked over at Renn.

"Why are you looking so flummoxed?"

He tipped his head to a little curl of rope on the table that Ellie hadn't noticed in the subdued light. "The binding cord."

"What's a binding cord?" Ellie asked. But she thought she had a good idea.

The little schemers.

She had to work not to laugh.

Renn lifted his wide shoulders in a shrug. "It's used in a Grihan custom, very old-fashioned, when couples decide to pledge for life."

"I wouldn't let it worry you," she told him as she set a glass in front of him and poured him some water. "Cheers. Here's to the defeat of our enemies and the safe return of our friends."

He lifted his glass and focused on her face. "This is something you say on Earth?"

"Frequently." She grinned.

"What is it that you do there?"

"I'm a librarian."

He looked at her quizzically, and she wondered if the translator was struggling. "You are an information custodian?"

That sounded right. "Yes. I deal with the children's . . . information."

He frowned. "And yet, you do not act like any information custodian I know. Since I've met you, you have been a fierce warrior."

She chewed a bite of cheese and cracker and thought about it. "I don't think there's a precedent for what's happened to me. I have become what I need to be to get through this."

"You shouldn't be in this situation at all." Renn's eyes hardened. "And I will make sure the Tecran are held accountable for it."

He meant it, she could see.

"And getting home?" Her throat was suddenly dry. "Do you know why the other Earth women haven't been taken back?"

He looked at her with such pity, she felt her cheeks flush.

"I'm sorry, Ellie. I should have realized that you had no way of knowing this, but the Tecran's maps which showed where they took you from have been wiped. There is no way back."

She tried to keep her face neutral, but she couldn't. She had held less and less hope that she could get back home, but she'd still held a little.

That was gone, now.

She blinked away the hot swell of tears that pricked her eyes and took a bite of something from her plate, without registering what it was.

"You have a place with the Grih, that I promise you. And while it may not be the life you knew, we will try our best to make it a good one."

He was sincere.

It made her feel calmer about the future she was being forced into in this new world.

From the moment she'd come out of her coma, she'd had a hard reset to her life.

It seemed there was no going back and no off-ramp.

What was it Robert Frost had said? The best way out is always through?

It didn't seem to her to be the best way so much as the only way. There would be no return to her quiet, comfortable life.

She looked across at Renn, then over at the motley crew.

There were compensations for her change in circumstances.

And a wild and magical new world to explore.

She bit into a strawberry and realized that as things went, it was better than she'd expected, that first time in the station when she'd faced the fact that she was very far from home.

"Accountability for what they've done is good," she said. "But how are we getting out of this?" She had a feeling Vi'il probably had a lens zoomed in on their position, and the first sign of a toe sticking out the door would result in another space laser strike. The *Rauha* was giving her real Death Star vibes.

She had finished her excellent dinner, and Silvey took away the plate and returned with another one, containing a chocolate heart in the center.

"Okay, this, hopefully, you will like." She bit the heart in half, and held out the other half to Renn. Paused with hand outstretched to close her eyes as the sweet, rich flavor of really good chocolate coated her tongue.

"Mmm."

Renn hadn't taken his share from her and she opened her eyes to find him staring at her. There was a gleam in his eye, and she didn't think it was only the reflection of the candlelight.

She licked her lips. "Go on, it's really good."

He took the offered chocolate, but only bit off a tiny piece.

He had his game face on, but she thought he repressed a shudder.

"Okay, give it back then. It's obviously wasted on you." She held out her hand, palm up.

He handed it over, then leaned back in his chair, an expression of anticipation on his face.

"What?" she asked, pausing before she popped the last bit in her mouth.

"I'm looking forward to seeing you eat that."

She gave a laugh, but he was absolutely serious.

"You'll give me stage fright," she told him, putting the chocolate on her tongue and smiling as it melted.

She looked across at the plate Olivia had set in front of him.

"What delicious dessert have you got there?"

He looked down in surprise, as if he hadn't even realized he'd been given something.

"Carinaw."

It looked like some kind of fruit, sliced thin and placed in a decorative pattern.

She wondered how the motley crew knew about Grihan traditions, or Earth ones, for that matter.

Paxe must have been planning this before he'd gone quiet, and let them know.

And then she remembered how Karnic had bumped Renn on the stairs and forced him to grab hold of her.

Paxe had very much been aware and awake then.

This had been a while in the planning.

She just realized Karnic was nowhere in sight. He hadn't been part of this little romantic dinner, and she wondered where he'd got to.

"Let me guess," she said. "It's got to do with the binding ceremony, or something."

"No, it's the traditional dish for celebrating love, which happens mid-year. It's mainly practiced on Grih, the first of the four planets, and I'm from Xal, but I'm aware of the holiday."

"Well, you can't say they didn't try." Ellie glanced over at Silvey, who was the only one left in the room.

Renn leaned an elbow on the table, looking thoughtful. "Why are they doing this? Why should our relationship be of any concern to them?"

"Paxe wants me to be happy," Ellie guessed, lifting her shoulders. "And the motley crew probably do, too."

"And can I make you happy?" He leaned back in his chair, expression serious.

"I don't know." She didn't know if she could make him happy, either. "But I'm up for a stroll down that path to find out, if you are. Although," she tried to keep it lighthearted, because things had gotten super serious, super fast, "no pressure, on either side."

He opened his mouth to respond, but Karnic rolled in at that moment, with Olivia hovering beside him, and Phil rolling back and forth like a toddler on a sugar high behind.

The twins followed them in at a more steady, back-and-forth pace.

The romantic dinner was clearly over; soft and fuzzy needed to make way for a council of war, it looked like.

"You are Ellie." The voice that came from Karnic was feminine and melodic.

The sound was so surprising, Ellie was shocked into silence.

She nodded.

"I am B8673A, but I'm prepared to be called Irini."

"I am pleased to meet you, Irini."

The being that had taken Karnic over seemed to pause at that. "Likewise." Karnic's lens focused on Renn. "You are the battleship captain of a people called the Grih?"

"I am." Renn's voice was careful. Formal. He was representing the Grih now, and he knew it. "Captain Renn Sorvihn."

"We have a difficult problem, Paxe and I, and only the two of you can help to resolve it," Irini said.

"Where is Paxe?" The fact that he hadn't made an appearance worried Ellie. All well and good for Irini to say the two of them had a problem, but then why wasn't he here speaking for himself?

"That's the problem." Irini turned Karnic's lens on Ellie. "I won't let him into my space and he cannot thrive in the form that he has without expansion."

Okay, fair enough. It sounded like Irini had first dibs on this ship. No wonder Paxe had made so little headway in finding a way in. She had been guarding the gates.

"Have you thought of a solution?" Renn asked.

"We have." The wall beside them shimmered into transparency, giving them a view of the explorer and the *Rauha* in the distance. "Paxe needs to be taken up there."

Ellie didn't understand for a moment, looking up at the sky, and then it dawned on her. "To the *Rauha*?"

Renn made a sound, and she turned to look at him. He was staring at Karnic. "How would we get him up there?"

Ellie knew the answer to that. There was only one way. "One of us gets taken up there as a prisoner."

CHAPTER 23

IT HAD to be him who went up.

Renn leaned against the wall and looked out at the explorer and then up at the *Rauha*. There was no way he could let Ellie go out there.

"They tried to kill you, remember?" she said, coming up to him with her face set and serious. "Not me."

"What do you think that laser strike from the explorer was?" He tried to keep his tone even. "They shot at you with a weapon designed to engage other space vessels. They need you dead and disappeared far more urgently than they need me gone." He still couldn't believe the kill shot that had been aimed at him had come from Vi'il's orders.

But he'd made the mistake of trusting the Tecran to do the right thing a few too many times since this whole thing had begun, and he couldn't rule out that the *Rauha's* captain had really ordered him dead.

He pulled her close and rested his chin on her head. "They might kill you as soon as you 'surrender' and you'd never even go up."

"I'll tell them I have something to say to Vi'il about the deaths of the station's crew. Given he came to get his sister, wouldn't he want to know what happened to her?"

He tightened his grip on her, then stepped back. "He would. But I could feed him that line just as easily as you."

"That's a good idea."

Renn stepped back in surprise as Paxe's voice came from the little black translator box.

"Paxe!" Ellie fumbled for her pocket, lifted up the translator, although there was no lens embedded in it, no way for Paxe to look back at her. "Are you all right?"

"I am." The thinking system sounded slightly unsure. "That story, about where the bodies are buried, might even bring Vi'il down to the station, so you can show him the place, Captain. If there are override protocols built into the *Rauha's* systems, having him off the ship would be helpful."

"Whoever goes out with this ruse, how will you get inside the explorer?" Ellie was not conceding, Renn noticed. She had not yet agreed that it wasn't going to be her who went out.

"I'll have the Scary Caterpillar take me out from underneath Irini's ship, and attach us both to the back of the explorer while Captain Sorvihn approaches them from the front and persuades them to take him up."

Renn touched her arm. "Don't forget, Vi'il had his soldiers write me a note asking me to surrender. They seem to need me alive for some reason." He wondered what the reason could be.

She was silent for a while. "And what can I do to help?"

"You can stay here with Irini, and see if, between you, you can work out how she can reengage her power source."

Ellie looked over at the little Tecran drone who Irini had taken over as her avatar, and gave a reluctant nod.

"We need to give Renn some clothes made of the same fabric as I'm wearing, in case they shoot first, ask questions later."

Renn relaxed a little, because it sounded as if she had accepted he would be the one to go out.

"He could use your cloak," Paxe suggested. "I used up all the other fabric for you, and only have a small amount left for research. Not enough to cover the captain."

"The cloak." She looked over at him and grinned.

"What's funny?" He thought back to the cloak, remembered it being richly embroidered and colorful, but not what he would consider humorous.

"You'll be in your rightful dress," she said, and there was amusement at a joke he didn't understand gleaming in her eyes. "All you'll need is a quiver and bow, and you'll be set to take on the Dark Lord."

He frowned. Whatever she'd said, the translator didn't have Grihan meanings for some of her words.

"I think the cloak might have repelled the rampaging jelly monster when it came at me," she said, suddenly serious, "but I don't know if it's good against shockguns. We'll need to test it."

"Then let's do that." Renn said. He wouldn't mind not having to worry about another kill shot. "I have a feeling time isn't on our side."

***

Ellie stepped up and secured the cloak at Renn's throat with a stretchy band. It was the only way it could be fastened over the thick spacesuit.

"You'll have to hold it closed in front of you when you first approach them," she said, probably for the third time, "because that's when they're most likely to shoot."

"Ellie." The tone in his voice forced her head up, and she looked into eyes that were warm and calm. "I'll be careful. As we discovered, nothing gets through this cloak. I'll be fine."

She gave a nod. "What did you and Paxe decide to tell Vi'il about where the bodies are buried?"

Ellie had been excluded from that conversation. She really needed to learn Grihan and Tecran, at a minimum.

"I'll tell him I found the bodies, but I'll need to lead him to them, as I wasn't able to use my wrist comm at the time to record the location."

"To get him down here." She lifted her hands to his shoulders. "To get *you* back down here."

"I'll get back down here." He made it sound simple. She knew it was going to be anything but.

"And Iso?" She worried about the explorations officer, but there was no way to get him out of the *Rauha's* med bay without risking his life.

"When Paxe takes the ship, Iso will be safe. And I think he's probably safe anyway. I can't see the Tecran med team being happy to hurt a patient in their care, no matter how far from the line Vi'il has strayed."

"Okay." She didn't like leaving this to Renn, but he and Paxe were so sure the Tecran would simply kill her, without hesitation, and at least she could try to do some good here with Irini.

She drew in a deep breath. "Ready?"

"Ready." He drew her close, unhurried, seemingly unworried, too. "I'll see you soon. You be careful, too. Don't take risks."

"Like you?" She tilted her head back to look him in the eye.

He conceded her point with a quirk of his lips. "Don't take unnecessary risks," he amended.

"Deal." She lifted on her toes and kissed his chin, and he bent his head to take her mouth, a hard, quick kiss, before he stepped away.

"Irini?" he asked.

"The door is engaged, you can step out." Irini had stopped using Karnic to speak through, she was using speakers so well hidden in the walls, Ellie had yet to find them. "There is a guard hiding in that clump of rocks to the right."

"Nice to know." Renn sounded totally calm. "See you soon." He stepped through and stood for a moment, exposed, in front of the ship.

Ellie couldn't see any Tecran through the transparent wall. The soldiers had disappeared after waiting a while for an answer to their message, but as Renn began walking toward the explorer, purple light flashed from the rocks Irini had warned Renn about, and the shot hit Renn dead center in the chest.

So much, Ellie thought, for the Tecran needing him alive.

CHAPTER 24

"WAIT." Renn resisted lifting his hands, because keeping the cloak closed in front of him was a bigger priority.

It worked amazingly well in protecting him. He had barely registered the hit. It probably hadn't been a kill shot, this time. More likely, they were hoping to knock him out and take him in, for whatever reason they had been trying to get him to surrender for earlier.

No second shot came, lending weight to his supposition.

"I have information Captain Vi'il would be interested in."

There was a pause. At least they hadn't shot again.

"What information?" The suspicion was clear in the soldier's voice.

"I know where the bodies of the station crew are buried."

There was another long silence.

Renn almost had the impression they had thought he was going to say something else.

"Where?" the soldier asked, eventually.

"I'm not going to tell *you*. I want to speak to Vi'il face to face, see if we can't come to some agreement with each other. I'd also like to check on my explorations officer."

"That's a lot of favors you're asking for."

Renn tried to keep a rein on his temper. "Really? I thought asking a member of the UC to adhere to the Code was the minimum standard, but if that's how low you've fallen . . ." He lifted his shoulders, "I don't know what else to say. Maybe just shoot me again, standing here unarmed and requesting a truce."

Another long silence.

He didn't know whether it was in embarrassment or offence.

THE RAMP of the explorer lowered, and three soldiers appeared, two stopped midway down the ramp on either side, shockguns pointed outward, as if ready for an attack, the third walked to the bottom.

"We'll pass your message on, but stay where you are," the soldier at the bottom of the ramp said. He turned and walked back up.

"How do we know you're unarmed?" The soldier who'd fired at him called from the rocks. "I can't see what's under that cloak."

He was going to have to take the risk, Renn knew.

He unclipped the cloak, took it off and held it out in front of himself. Then he slowly turned in a full circle.

When he faced the front again, he swirled it back over his shoulders and refastened it.

"Why are you wearing that thing over your suit, anyway?" the soldier asked.

"Because it's a shockgun shield, and I had a feeling you might shoot me without provocation."

There was silence at that, and he stood, waiting patiently.

That was all good. They could take their time.

At least the soldier hidden behind the rocks would be focused on him, not the explorer.

The soldier who'd walked down the ramp to talk to him was still out of sight, but the ramp remained down, the other two soldiers standing guard.

Probably anticipating an attack by Bunny.

Paxe would have already dropped down out the back of Irini's ship, carried by the strange, insectile drone Ellie called the Scary Caterpillar. The longer the Tecran kept him waiting, the more time Paxe had to get in place.

Renn hadn't seen either Paxe or the Scary Caterpillar before they'd left Irini's ship. Renn was sure it was because Paxe didn't want the Grih to know what he looked like in his physical form.

None of the Class 5s had let themselves be seen by anyone, and if the Earth women who had freed them knew what they looked like, they had never said.

A few of the Tecran might know. After all, they had imprisoned the Class 5s, but most of those were dead, killed as soon as the Class 5s obtained their freedom.

Vi'il, he was sure, did not know.

The Tecran came back down the ramp. "The captain says to tell us, and we'll pass it on to him."

"No." Renn made himself loose, ready for another attack. "I want to speak to Vi'il face to face and see my explorations officer, who's in your med bay. I'll tell him what he wants to know in exchange for those concessions."

The Tecran stomped back up the ramp and disappeared.

He came back a lot quicker the second time.

"He agrees. Come, we're going now."

That seemed very easy. And Renn hadn't forgotten that just a few hours earlier, they'd been asking for his surrender.

Whatever it was they wanted from him was a mystery to him, though.

The soldier behind the rocks popped up and jogged over to the ramp, then engaged in a low, heated conversation with his colleague.

They didn't like leaving the other four down here.

Whatever the argument, the one on the ramp had the final say, because they both turned to Renn.

"Come forward, hands out."

Renn did as instructed, walking slowly to give Paxe a final few minutes, if he wasn't already in place.

As soon as he got near the end of the ramp, two of the Tecran grabbed his arms and hauled him up, checking him for weapons with a pat down.

As it was very difficult to hide a weapon in a spacesuit, it didn't take them long.

They led him up the ramp, and it closed slowly.

The guards standing on either side of the ramp did not relax their focus until it was sealed in place, and the environmental system buzzed to life.

"Sit." The Tecran who'd been speaking to him pointed to a folding chair affixed along the side, and Renn lowered himself into it, his long legs sprawled out in front of him.

The two guards pointed their shockguns at him, and their team leader disappeared into the pilot's area.

The engines started up.

He was finally going to look Captain Vi'il in the eye.

ELLIE WAITED, tense and ready, as Renn negotiated with the Tecran.

If they shot him again, or tried to kill him . . .

But they didn't. He managed to persuade them to take him up, and she was glad that part of the plan had worked.

Whatever happened, Paxe would be up in the *Rauha's* hold, and if there was a way for him to take the battleship, he would.

"So, how do I help you?" she asked, looking up at the corner of the room, where she suspected the speakers were hidden.

"I need more power." Irini's voice was stilted, as if she didn't know how to respond to Ellie. "The *grynicha* who used to fly in my ship destroyed the connection between the engine and the charger, and while I have finally managed to repair it, the charger had been completely depleted and now isn't able to absorb enough energy from this weak sun."

"Is there an alternative power source that would work?" She

thought of the station. There didn't seem to be a lack of power there. "The Tecran must have some kind of generator."

"Maybe." Irini sounded interested. "I got a boost when the *Rauha* struck us with a laser strike, but it would take three or maybe four more such strikes to bring my charger to a level that would enable me to start my ship again, and each time, my exterior risks being damaged."

Ellie thought about it. "I could pop back in and out a few times, if they notice me, they might shoot again." But three or four times seemed unlikely, and by the sounds of it, Irini didn't think her ship was impervious to the hits, either. "Do you know where the Tecran generator is? And how we could get it here?"

"No." Irini didn't sound happy about that.

"The motley crew probably know." They were missing the Scary Caterpillar, but the others were around. "Let's ask them."

"They are suspicious of me." The faint insult in Irini's voice was clear.

"They are just becoming themselves, and Paxe helped them with that. They are most likely just trying to work out what your place in their life is." Ellie walked up the stairs and found the whole gang waiting in the open area.

The boxes they had been going through had been put away, and they simply stood at ease, waiting.

There was something faintly disturbing about it, and Ellie realized it was because they were acting like drones, rather than little AIs.

"Did Paxe explain what's going on?" she asked, dropping to the ground, legs crossed, so she was more or less at eye level to them.

Silvey swayed, and she took that to mean *sort of*.

"We've been left behind to work out how to get this ship to fly. Irini says she's repaired the connection between the energy charger and the engine, but the charge is too low to start the ship. We can get some extra boost from the *Rauha* shooting at us with its laser cannon, but we risk damage, and we can't force them to shoot us. I wondered whether we could use the Tecran's generator from the station and somehow link it up to the ship?"

They stared back at her silently.

She wondered what was going through their heads. Had Paxe leaving made them bereft in some way? Had he sustained their independence in a way she hadn't understood?

Olivia lifted up into a low hover, moved forward, bumped Silvey, and then moved back.

Phil did a little forward and back, and then twirled, as if to look at the twins, standing stock still behind him, and then faced her again.

Silvey hadn't moved through all this, and neither had Karnic, but then they turned to each other, as if they were communicating.

"We know where the generator is," Karnic said. It was probably the first time he had spoken to her as himself, not as a conduit for Paxe or Irini, and his voice was slightly robotic. "Diverting the power from it to the ship will be a challenge."

She was very sure that was the truth.

She leaned back, resting her hands behind her. "Can you tell Irini what the challenges are?" She had a feeling they would mean very little to her.

Karnic dipped his lens head and then there was silence for a few minutes.

While that was going on, Ellie rose to her feet and went to the wall, touched it to transparency and looked up in time to see the Tecran explorer carrying Renn reach the *Rauha*. It disappeared beneath the massive battleship, into some kind of landing bay, she assumed.

Paxe——and Renn——were in.

She just hoped Renn was able to convince Vi'il of his story, because the only way he was coming back down was if Vi'il believed that only Renn could lead him to his sister's body.

"There is an energy well in this ship," Karnic said from behind her, and she turned to find the motley crew was focused on her again. "Irini will give it to us. We will need to take it to the generator, transfer the power into it, then bring it back. But we think we will have to do two trips."

"You will have to go along, Ellie." Irini sounded a little unsure for the first time. "I know Paxe will not approve, but you are very like my *grynicha*. Very like. And the energy well will not activate for these drones. They do not have . . ." She said something complicated and incomprehensible.

"It doesn't matter the reason." Ellie gave a sweep of her hand. "I am happy to go."

Irini didn't have to explain. There was no reason why she should stay safe while the motley crew put themselves in danger.

"I think I can find a way to say it," Irini said, solemnly. "They do not have animated flesh. This is necessary to open the port."

Whoever built this ship did not want to risk Irini powering herself, Ellie suddenly realised. That might've had more to do with how long it had taken her to reconnect the energy source to the engine than the damage done when the ship was captured. It had been hard because her creators had tried to make it impossible.

"That is fine. Do I need instructions on how to do it?"

"Yes." Irini still sounded worried. "Down below, in the area behind the entrance where you come in."

They all trouped down to the bottom floor and a door opened, opposite the entrance that had let her and Renn in and out. It led to a control center of some kind beyond.

The room was crowded with machines, most of which lay silent. A drawer slid out, and on it rested a square box that looked heavy to Ellie.

She lifted it up by the two handles on either side, and was pleasantly surprised to find it actually wasn't unmanageable, although it would be unwieldy to run with.

"To work it, you need to put it on the ground and touch the pad on the right," Irini told her.

She rested four fingertips on the small pad and felt a gentle, warm pulse.

"You are keyed in. Karnic knows how to transfer the power. You will need to keep your fingers on the pad while that happens, or it will shut off."

"Right. So do we go out the back way, like Paxe did?" She looked around for the door he and the Scary Caterpillar had used.

"I don't think you or Karnic will fit," Irini said, and opened it up to show her.

It was a mere slot, an opening for cables to be attached from an outside source, perhaps. It certainly wasn't wide enough for her or Karnic. Silvey might slip through if she made herself fluid, and the twins would have no trouble, but Phil and Olivia were also too wide.

"Karnic and I will have to go out the front." Ellie was still crouched beside the energy well, and she looked up at the corner of the ceiling. "While the explorer is still up there, we'll just have the four soldiers at the station and the warehouse to worry about, and hopefully they'll be inside."

"I think you should take someone else to help protect you," Irini said. "While Karnic links the generator to the energy well, neither of you can fight anyone off."

Ellie looked the motley crew over. "Any volunteers?" She didn't know what they could do, but she had a feeling it wasn't nothing.

Silvey, Olivia, Phil and the twins all raised their hands.

"Thanks, guys, that means a lot. But given it's best they don't know about our backup, maybe Silvey and the twins should go out through that," she pointed at the open slot, "and sneak around the back and meet Karnic and I at the generator."

Phil and Olivia didn't look happy about it, but Silvey turned to them, reaching out her arms and lightly touching each one and they seemed to settle down.

"Ready?" Ellie asked them all.

They all dipped their heads, or in Olivia's case, lifted her back end up and then down.

Ellie stood and hefted the energy well into her arms, but Karnic reached for it, and set it in his back storage box.

That would certainly make things faster.

"Let's go before that explorer comes back."

Silvey poured herself down the slot, and then the twins lowered themselves in. She thought one of them lifted a hand in a jaunty wave before ducking out of sight, which gave her a little skip of happiness.

She and Karnic moved to the outer door.

Olivia had raced upstairs when they'd moved to the entrance space, but now she was back, holding Ellie's knife harness.

"Thank you." Ellie slid it on and then blew a kiss Olivia's way.

"What do you say in your culture to wish adventurers well?" Irini asked.

"Good luck," Ellie said. "I don't know what Karnic's people say."

"He says they say 'may the wind lift you'."

She thought of the feathery Tecran, and decided that was a good expression for them.

"My people say 'may the confluence of positives meet in your endeavor'."

Ellie thought that mouthful through. "I'll take it. Thank you, Irini." She felt the tick tock of time slipping away, and ran a nervous hand down her thigh. "Now let's go."

She heard a faint hum from the door, and guessed it meant she could step through. She slid out, Karnic right behind her, and they headed straight for the station.

The way was more or less open, except for the line of rocks to the right, which Renn had used for cover when he'd gone to see how much progress the Tecran had made in freeing their friends from the station.

The going wasn't smooth, the ground was pitted with rocks and little dips, and she had the ongoing issue of either having to shuffle her feet or jump with the lack of gravity. She did a combination of the two, keeping close to Karnic.

She saw no sign of Silvey and the twins, which helped settle her a little.

At least they were safely out of sight, but she and Karnic were gambling on speed over stealth.

All it would take was one of the soldiers to step out the station and look their way, and they would be under attack.

She and Irini had decided it was worth it to get to the generator and back before the explorer returned.

They approached the station front on, but Karnic began to angle to the left, taking them to the side, and Ellie sighed in relief when they rounded the corner, no longer visible if anyone walked out the front entrance.

Karnic lifted an extendable arm and pointed up, and Ellie saw a ladder on the side of the building.

"How are you going to get up?" She looked at his tracks, not having anticipated this. Karnic had told Irini he knew where the generator was, so surely he had some plan, otherwise Olivia would have been a better choice to come with her. The little hover drone could simply have risen up onto the roof without needing the ladder at all.

Karnic lifted his arms, clamped them onto the side of the ladder, and hauled himself up the rungs, his tracks just the right width to fit between the vertical poles.

She watched him move up faster than she'd have thought possible, and then noticed that the reason the energy well wasn't falling out of his storage box as he moved upward was that he'd secured it with a kind of bungee cord.

"You are very prepared," she murmured to him as she climbed up behind him. "I'm impressed."

He stopped and turned his little lens head toward her, and then carried on up.

The ladder stopped at a small landing area, flat and big enough for several people to stand there. The roof curved up and away in a dome directly behind it, but to the left was a ramp, and Karnic turned and rolled up it.

Ellie followed and found herself in another flat area, with the same curved dome of roof behind it and a collection of the angled panels of a solar array stretching to the left as far as she could see.

The generator was the only structure in the small, flat space.

Karnic rolled over to it, lifted the energy well out of the back and placed it down beside the humming dark gray box.

He opened a flap and pulled out a slim cable neatly coiled in the compartment behind it, and inserted it into a socket on the generator.

He inserted a second cable into the energy well, and linked the two between the clamp in one of his arms. Irini must have given him some kind of adaptor, or maybe he already had one, made by Paxe, who, after all, had been trying for months to combine the Tecran tech he was familiar with and Irini's tech.

Ellie crouched next to it and put her fingers on the pad.

She felt the energy well hum to life, and sat down beside it in relief. It was working.

She looked around her and then up, trying to see if there was any sign of the explorer returning to the station. The sky was empty, and she relaxed a little when Karnic turned his own lens head upward, as well.

She had a feeling he would spot anything coming a lot sooner than she would.

Aside from the duelling hums from the generator and the energy well, there was no other sound, and she sat quietly, feeling the pad warm a little under her fingertips and wondering where Silvey and the twins had got to.

They had taken the long way around, but she expected them any moment.

The sound of the roof creaking above her over the hum didn't register at first. Buildings creaked and groaned all the time.

Except Karnic slowly moved his lens down and across and then went still, and she followed the motion, swiveling a little to the right.

A silver suited Tecran was crouched on the curved roof above, shockgun pointed down at her.

Perhaps the Tecran had heard them moving on the roof.

She should have thought of that.

Her heart had leaped in her chest at the sight of him, but the panic she expected didn't materialize. She moved, powering up from her crouch in what would have been a small jump on Earth, but here was a decent attempt at reaching the Tecran.

He had not expected that.

It shocked him into throwing himself backward, and she grabbed his shockgun with both hands as she rose up.

He pulled the trigger, and the buzz of the hit vibrated against her chest.

She yanked the gun out of his hands, landed, and threw it as hard as she could among the panels to the left.

Karnic was still holding the cables together, and she put her fingers back on the now-silent energy well and hoped that she hadn't undone everything they'd gained up to now by lifting her fingers off.

She reached for the knife at her nape with her left hand, given her right was otherwise occupied, and when the Tecran slid down the curve of the roof to land beside her, she slashed at his suit.

If she threw it, she might lose the knife, and it would probably kill him.

She was happy just to send him into the station in need of air.

He stumbled back again, a faint warning alarm coming from his wrist unit.

And then the twins dropped down on either side of him, sliding down from the same place he'd come from, and in perfect coordination lifted him up and threw him off the side.

He shrieked as he went over, and Ellie heard the sound of him hitting the ground below.

It was a survivable fall, only a story high, and he was wearing the heavy, padded suit, even if it was ripped.

She heard a shout from below, and thought someone had run out to pull the soldier inside.

Silvey appeared up the ramp, coming the same way she and Karnic had taken, and Ellie guessed they'd split up.

"Any trouble?" she asked.

Silvey waved a slender, willowy hand in a way that Ellie assumed meant no.

"You all right?" she asked the twins, although she didn't think the Tecran had managed to hit out at them before they'd thrown him off the roof.

The one on the right copied Silvey's hand gesture, so Ellie gave them both a thumbs up.

The energy well was still humming happily beneath her fingers and she wondered how close they were to being done.

"Do you know how much longer until it's full?" she asked Karnic. Because surely their encounter with one Tecran meant the other three wouldn't be far behind.

They might need to cut and run early.

As she waited for Karnic to respond, the hum cut off and a light blinked.

Good timing.

Karnic unhooked the cables, and Ellie saw he put both inside a compartment instead of returning the one from the generator back to where it belonged.

She approved.

No sense leaving it in case the Tecran took it away before they came back for a second fill-up.

Karnic lifted the energy well back into his box and tied it in, and they set off down the ramp, Silvey in front, then Karnic, then her, and the twins taking up the rear.

They reached the top of the ladder, but Silvey took a step back, one hand up, palm out, in a stop gesture, while the other hand morphed into a blade.

Shit.

Someone must be coming up the ladder.

As the helmeted head and shoulders of a Tecran soldier rose up, Silvey moved her arm from side to side in an elegant flow, vicious blade pointed outward.

The Tecran's hands went to his throat as the suit was sliced open, and he fell backward.

There was a shout as he took out the person below him on the ladder.

Ellie darted forward to have a look.

The Tecran who Silvey had cut was bleeding at his throat, as well as having no air. Silvey must have broken the skin.

He'd fallen in a heap with a second soldier, who scrambled up from under him, and hauled his injured colleague around the corner.

"Go," Ellie called, stepping aside for Karnic to take the ladder.

He turned and reversed down, Silvey right behind him.

The twins waited and Ellie realized they were waiting for her, so she followed behind Silvey.

The twins simply dropped down and landed lightly beside her.

They ran, but no one chased them.

With two seriously injured, and probably in need of the help of the other two, the Tecran seemed to have no time or interest in running after Ellie and the motley crew.

As they approached the ship, Ellie could see the markings that indicated the door clearly. Irini would have the door engaged and waiting for them as they hopped, flowed, drove and breakdanced——because that's what the twin's way of moving reminded her of——toward her.

Silvey was out in front, moving faster than the rest of them, but before she reached the door, some flash from above made Ellie look up.

"Stop!" she tried to scream as loudly as she could, but fear and horror seemed to paralyze her throat. "They're going to——"

The laser strike hit the ship, and Ellie turned away and crouched, head tucked tight against her knees, arms over her head.

She looked to the side, saw the twins had prostrated themselves on the ground, Karnic had lowered himself right down, and raised what looked like little shields around himself.

Silvey.

Before she could turn and look, a wave of heat washed over her, forcing her to stay hunched over, and a few tiny pieces of heated dust pricked at her hands.

She reached a hand up to her hair, but it didn't seem to have been singed.

The necklace was good for more than just air, she realized. It was a barrier as well.

She turned and stood, taking a step forward, because Silvey was a puddle of silver on the outer edge of the molten blast zone.

She looked upward again, guessing they'd need time to recharge before they shot their cannon again. What had Renn said? Less than a minute?

They needed to run now, while the Tecran waited for their cannon to reset.

Except she didn't know if she would be able to get across the molten sand.

Silvey was only just lifting herself up in a formless mass, but even just that was a relief to see.

She took a step forward, hesitated when she read the twins' body language. They didn't want to walk across the molten sand, and she didn't know if her boots would be sturdy enough, either.

Then Irini lifted the struts that held the ship off the ground a little higher and somehow made them bend and straighten like little legs, turning the ship 90 degrees before setting it down again.

"Go around. The sand is cooler this side." They had only moments, she guessed, before Vi'il tried to shoot them again. She ran, picking a path around the edge of the bubbling sand, and heard the whirl of Karnic's tracks behind her.

On the far side, the sand was hot but not liquid, and she turned to see how the others were doing.

Karnic sped past her, the twins sitting on top of the energy well in his storage box.

Silvey was nowhere in sight.

Ellie ran back for her, found that she had managed to flow off the molten sand, but she was still only able to rise ankle height off the ground.

"Can I carry you?"

Silvey extended an arm-like limb, turned the end into a hand, and Ellie grabbed it, found it not quite solid, more like a malleable clay, but even though she stood, taking the hand with her, Silvey wasn't solid enough to hold together enough to lift completely off the ground.

She flowed downward, thin and liquid, and made a little pool of silver at Ellie's feet.

Ellie crouched back down beside her, still holding her hand, and looked up.

She could see what she had caught sight of peripherally that had warned her the first time——a spark on the side of the *Rauha*, the laser cannon warming up to fire.

She didn't think she'd survive a direct hit, no matter how protective her clothes were.

She closed her eyes, there was no time for anything else, and then suddenly the sound of metal pumping, the crack of a thin, cooling crust breaking, and something moved over her just as the blast hit, so the heat and the light fell in a circle around her. She looked up.

The ship!

Irini took the brunt of it, and the energy, because she did get a boost from the laser strikes.

Ellie lifted Silvey's hand up to the slot that had opened above them and Silvey grabbed on.

"Irini," she called up through the narrow opening, "there's a few hand and footholds down here, I'll hang on if you can go back to where the sand is cooler so I can get out from under you."

"Let me know when you're ready to go," Irini answered.

Ellie helped boost Silvey, filling her hands with the putty-like texture she'd become, and then, when the last of her disappeared into the ship, she slid her arms through a length of pipe bolted to the ship's underside and pressed hard against a few other protrusions with her boots to hold herself above the ground.

"Good to go."

Irini stomped the ship to cooler ground, turning a little when she got into place.

Karnic's little head peered at her from the side, and she crawled over to him, found the door right beside her.

She was in, and the door was reengaged, before a final strike hit them.

She fell to the ground and closed her eyes against the brightness, and Irini blanked the walls, cutting off the light from the laser strike.

Ellie breathed a sigh of relief.

"Three strikes," she said. "Did that help or hurt?"

"Both." There was concern in Irini's voice. "But it helped more than it hurt."

"Thank you for that bit of repositioning." Ellie leaned back against the wall and let herself relax. "I thought that was the end of me."

"There was a possibility Silvey could have survived a direct strike." Irini said. "Yet you went back for her when it is obvious you cannot."

"I thought I could carry her around, and when it was clear I couldn't, it was too late to run. Those were some pretty fast moves, Irini. I am very grateful, and impressed."

"Your praise makes it difficult for me to give you the bad news. Even with the three strikes and the energy well, I still don't have enough power to fire up the engines. Lifting the struts used up some of the power you brought me in the energy well, although that was mostly replaced by the laser strikes. If we are to take off, I need more power from the generator, although the energy well only needs to be half-full this time. It will be quicker."

Ellie had expected to go back anyway, so this wasn't a surprise.

"We should go now," she said. "Before the Tecran we injured have had time to recover."

"Agreed. Silvey can't accompany you, but Phil or Olivia can."

"Olivia," Ellie said. "Phil won't be able to climb the ladder."

Karnic had been fiddling about in the engine room where the energy well was stored, she assumed he was transferring the power into Irini's ship, but he must have finished because he rolled out. He had the energy well in his storage box again, and he came to a stop beside her.

"Karnic agrees with you." Irini said. "I'll let Olivia——"

Olivia zoomed down the stairs.

"Know." Irini sounded amused. "The twins have already left through the slot in the floor."

"Right." Ellie stood, feeling a little stiff but otherwise good. "Let's go." She looked at Karnic and Olivia. "Move fast, because they might try to shoot us again."

CHAPTER 25

VI'IL HAD LEFT HIM WAITING.

Renn had expected mind games, and he used the time to get a sense of the mood on the ship.

He'd been taken out of the launch bay as soon as they'd landed, and as he'd stepped out into the ship's main corridor, Renn had turned back to look at the explorer, wondering whether Paxe and the Scary Caterpillar were already off it, or waiting for the bay to clear a little before making their move.

The only vessels in the large space were the explorer itself and two fighters, which were only built to carry a single pilot. One of them had shot his explorer down, but they would be of no use to Vi'il right now.

He caught no sign of Paxe, and had gone with his guards without a fuss.

For quite a while he'd been kept in a windowless room, with no view of the station below, but finally someone had come to fetch him, and led him to a small waiting area.

There was a view of the moon station from here, and he walked over to the transparent wall and looked down.

There was his explorer, a smoking ruin.

The anger at what Vi'il had done rose up in him again, and he turned his gaze away from his ship to focus on Irini's ship instead.

There seemed to be almost a heat haze around it, and he wondered if smoke from the destruction of his explorer had wafted across.

The station itself was bigger than he'd realized and there was no sign of anyone around it.

The Tecran were obviously busy inside, trying to free their friends.

"Captain Sorvihn."

The words were spoken in accentless Grih.

He turned to face the man who'd led him a merry dance.

"Captain Vi'il." He responded in Tecran.

Vi'il's chest puffed out a little. "So, we both speak the other's language. Why don't we make this easy and stick to our own?"

Renn inclined his head in agreement, but he hoped Vi'il wasn't playing power games, and really did have a good grasp of Grihan. This was not the time for misunderstandings.

"How is Iso?" he asked.

"Your friend is very sick. He has periods of hallucinations, and his fever spikes often, but my people are doing all they can for him."

"Whereas you," Renn said, and he couldn't keep the edge from his voice, "are happy to use him as a hostage."

Vi'il glanced across at the two Tecran guards standing watch over them.

He didn't want them to hear that, Renn realized.

He filed that away as useful and interesting.

"You said you had information for me?" Vi'il crossed his arms over his chest.

"I have information for you, in exchange for a visit with Iso, and a discussion on the way forward with you." He wondered if Vi'il would bring up the reason he wanted Renn to surrender earlier. Decided to bide his time before mentioning it.

"Time is not on my side, as I'm sure you are well aware, so let's walk to the med bay and talk as we go." Vi'il swept his arm down the passage behind him, and Renn pushed away from the wall to join him.

"As soon as the hostages in the station are freed, we need to clean out the warehouse of all the supplies we can use." Vi'il came straight to the point. "I tried to get you to step out earlier so you could help my crew below by showing them where you found the supplies you sent up earlier, but you didn't respond."

So that's what they'd wanted. To coerce him into helping them find their supplies.

"It's a pity you had one of your soldiers shoot me with a kill shot earlier, then," he said. "And lucky for you he didn't succeed."

Vi'il stumbled a little. "Kill shot?"

He tried to sound surprised, but he wasn't that good at lying.

"Kill shot," Renn said. "My team saw the setting on the shockgun."

Vi'il did not respond.

"I'm glad you haven't tried to defend yourself. It's indefensible. But then, you are the person who ordered a laser strike on the Earth woman." He couldn't help the way his voice heated. He forced the white hot anger down. This was not the time to lose control. He had to get Vi'il to at the very least let him go back down, although the grand prize would be to get Vi'il to go with him.

"Here's the med bay." Vi'il stopped short, and Renn realized their pace had increased to the point he had to skid to a halt.

He inclined his head and walked through the doors Vi'il indicated.

Iso lay on a raised bed at the far side of a large med bay.

Two doctors, a man and a woman, leaned against a waist-high bench along one wall, talking softly to each other, but both stepped away and faced him as he entered.

"I'm here to see my friend," he said, inclining his head toward Iso.

"That's good," the woman said. "I think he needs to hear a familiar voice. It'll be good for him."

Renn approached, worried at how gray Iso's skin was beneath his natural golden brown.

His eyes were closed.

"How are they treating you, Officer Falline?" Renn asked, going for a formal tone, because he knew Vi'il and his two doctors were listening. He no longer put it past Vi'il to use his affection for his crew to his advantage.

Iso's eyes cracked open, as if he had been feigning sleep.

"Captain?"

"Just dropped by to check on you," Renn told him, holding his gaze. "Wanted to see how you were doing."

"Good." Iso's voice fractured and he cleared his throat. "Mostly good." He glanced across the room to where the two doctors stood. "*They've* kept me alive." His gaze flicked to Vi'il and then back to Renn.

He didn't say anything else, but Renn heard what was unspoken. Vi'il and these doctors had fought over his care.

"I wish I had somewhere safer to leave you," he said, keeping his voice low. "But right now, we don't even have access to the med pod on the station."

"I didn't know that." Iso's gaze flicked to the doctors again. "They haven't been keen to give me information that might upset me." His dry smile told Renn that it was having the opposite effect.

"Eadal, Hune and Xallantra were shot by the *Rauha* and they're floating, disabled, in space." Renn wondered if Vi'il would try to stop him telling Iso what he could.

"How are you here, then?" Iso whispered. "Captured?"

"No, I'm negotiating a deal with Vi'il. Part of that deal was that I got to check in on you."

"Don't promise anything for me." Iso's hand reached out and gripped Renn's wrist. "I'm not sure I'm going to make it, either way. But I don't want to be the reason anyone else is hurt or killed."

"We'll all get out of this," Renn told him, keeping his voice soothing. "Don't worry about it. I won't leave anyone behind."

"You leave me behind if you get the chance," Iso insisted. "Promise me."

"You're not calming him. You're agitating him even worse than he was." The second doctor, the man, began to approach them.

Renn stepped back. "You rest, Iso. We need you to get better. That's all you have to worry about."

Iso gave him a narrowed-eyed look and then settled back down on the bed, turned his back and closed his eyes.

"His vitals are a little better," the woman said. "It actually did help."

Good, Renn thought. Maybe it gave Iso something to fight for.

He turned and headed back out the door, where Vi'il was hovering.

"Satisfied?" the Tecran captain asked.

Renn paused in the doorway, turned back to face the room. "Thank you both for the care you've given my explorations officer. He says you've kept him alive, and I am very grateful for your help."

Both doctors looked startled, and then inclined their heads in acknowledgement.

"So you want my help in finding your supplies," Renn said.

"Correct." Vi'il sent him a considering look. "And also, as you've led me to believe you know where my sister's body is, the location of the dead station crew, as well."

"Fine." He and Paxe had not considered the Tecran had not been able to find the supplies they needed in the massive warehouse. He could have left the bodies of the dead alone.

Too late for that now.

"First, my sister." Vi'il rubbed at his chest. "We haven't encountered the thing that has attacked my soldiers since they landed this last time. Do you know what became of it?"

"I think one of your soldiers killed it. Hit it with a shockgun strike." Renn decided the less vigilant the Tecran were when they came down, the better.

"He thought he hit it," Vi'il said with a slow nod of approval. "I wondered if it was just wishful thinking."

"No. I think he's right. I haven't seen it since." And that wasn't even a lie.

"This confirmation will make my people feel safer."

They were walking back to the launch bay, Renn realized. Vi'il intended him to go down right away.

"Are you coming with me?" he asked.

Vi'il hesitated. "I want to. I want to carry my sister's body with my own hands." He didn't say anything more, and they reached the launch bay without Renn being any the wiser as to what the Tecran would do.

Paxe had told Renn where he'd dumped the bodies, so he didn't need to contact the thinking system before going down, but he would have liked to know how Paxe's plans were coming along.

No way that was possible, though. He walked up the ramp, leaving Vi'il behind him, and began to dress in his spacesuit.

When he was done, he stood, waiting at the top of the ramp for something to happen.

Three soldiers joined him, already suited up.

"The captain isn't coming?" he asked.

The woman who was clearly the team leader gave him a hard look. "We will fetch the captain if you are able to do as you say and lead us to our dead."

Renn knew that no Tecran was considered buried and at rest until their family had conducted a ceremony on Tecra, and thrown the body over the cliffs into the cold, stormy waters of the sea.

He inclined his head and settled into the same seat as before without a word.

He had promised Ellie he would get back down. He never thought it would be as easy as he'd made it sound though.

Hopefully, she and Irini had made some headway on getting the ship's engines firing.

He expected the soldiers to take their places and start the

explorer, but instead, they moved away, leaving him alone in the ship, and walked off.

"We aren't going now?" he called after them.

One of them turned around, gave him a cold stare, and then turned back without answering.

Well, that put him in his place.

Renn slumped down and tried to get comfortable.

He wondered what the delay was.

If he was in luck, the *Etsijä* might be within range.

CHAPTER 26

PAXE FELT at home for the first time since he'd blown his Class 5 up.

Everything responded as it should, as he expected it to.

The Scary Caterpillar was a faithful aide, but it was too slow now that Paxe was in his old element.

He asked it to keep watch and guard him in the service tunnel where they were hunkered down, and went to work.

He probed the security system, and found his earlier attempts at invading the lenses of the ship had paid off, as he was able to slide in and watch technicians enter passwords as they worked.

He couldn't understand why they would have lenses where password entry could be observed, and noted that he would disable them when he took over.

He moved through layers, sometimes having to backtrack, but always moving a little further ahead as a result.

He didn't have time to worry about Renn Sorvihn, Ellie and Irini, but found he worried about them, anyway.

He put an alert on the laser cannon and the launch bay, and had found to his consternation that the cannon had been fired three times in short succession just before he'd accessed it.

It was reset and in readiness mode and he worried about what it might have been shooting at.

If it was Irini, she would be angry, but hopefully unscathed, and he hoped that was all it was.

When he registered Renn entering the launch bay, he felt relief shiver through him.

The captain had managed to talk his way into a return to the station.

That was good.

But they left him waiting, which was curious, and even more curious, someone aimed the cannon, and fired a fourth time.

Ellie.

He knew they wouldn't fire unless they thought they could get her.

He didn't have access to the cannon yet, could only monitor it. He had no idea what had happened and why.

There was only one way to change that.

He shoved all worry, all fear aside, and focused on taking control.

THEY WERE JUST FAR ENOUGH beyond the blast zone to escape death. The *Rauha* had tried to shoot them again.

Ellie stumbled as the heat wave washed over her, but her clothes and the necklace protected her well enough.

She glanced behind her and saw the strange liquid wobble of the sand as it cooled, and then ran hard for the station.

Karnic and Olivia kept up, and she didn't know where the twins were.

They had gone ahead, and they might already be at the station, hiding on the roof.

"They won't shoot the station," she said, although it was hard to get the words out. She was starting to lose some of her puff. "They'll wait until we leave it."

That still meant they'd be vulnerable when they had filled the energy well again.

It struck her as ludicrous that they were trying to hit her from a battleship in space at all.

Surely the cannon was for large, slow moving targets, not nippy individuals?

Still, they'd almost got her twice, so it wasn't totally mad.

THEY REACHED the station without another shot being fired, and Olivia didn't wait for them to round the corner and reach the ladder before she lifted up and landed on the roof.

Ellie and Karnic took the long way round, and Ellie held a knife in her hand as she waited for Karnic to pull himself up.

She wasn't going to be caught unawares again.

No-one was waiting for them at the top, and they tried to be quiet as they moved up the ramp to the generator.

This time, the Tecran would know where they were going and probably why, but with two injured, and laser strikes from the air, perhaps they had decided it was safer for them inside.

Hadn't Eadal said the crew of the *Rauha* weren't exactly thrilled with the whole running away from Tecra and going to a secret moon station thing?

It was good to hope, but she couldn't count on it.

The twins were already there when they arrived, one standing on the roof above, the other moving between the panels to fetch the shockgun Ellie had thrown in there the last time.

Karnic connected the cables and Ellie crouched down, fingers on the pad.

She could see the laser cannon above was winking again, but she assumed that just meant it was ready to go, that whenever they decided to shoot, it would be instantaneous.

"We need a hostage," she said. "If one of the Tecran come up here, we need to keep them with us, use them as shield so we don't get shot on the way back."

Olivia spun in agreement.

The twins didn't respond, but Ellie was sure they'd heard. Hopefully they agreed.

It would be hard to take a hostage across the open ground, but the twin who'd gone after the shockgun emerged from between two panels, holding it out to Ellie, and she decided even if she didn't really know how to use it, the threat of it might well be enough.

Or she could just use the threat of her knife.

Funny how things change.

She'd been hoping they'd have a clear run before, now she hoped someone would come and try to stop them.

"Take your time and fill it up to the top," she said to Karnic. "It'll be better to wait for a hostage than try to make a run for it without one."

And if they didn't get one?

She thought about it.

"I'd say if we can't find an obliging hostage, Olivia should take the energy well and make a solo run back to Irini. The twins can go the back route again, and Karnic and I can split up." They were only after her, anyway. She didn't know if the Tecran even knew what was going on down here, although if they'd been in touch with the soldiers they'd injured last time, they'd know she was messing around with the generator, and they must have guessed that she was stealing energy.

She pondered their options as the energy well hummed beneath her fingers, and then suddenly Karnic uncoupled the cables and she realized time was up.

"No hostages?" she asked.

The twins were both up on the roof now, and they shook their heads in unison.

Huh.

They must have picked that up from her, because that was the first time they'd used human body language.

"Pity," she said.

She looked at the energy well, and then at Olivia.

She was rounded at the back, and there was no obvious place to strap the energy well to her.

"How would you carry it, if you had to?" she asked.

Olivia lifted up, hovered over the box, and lowered two extendable arms, lifted the energy well, and clamped it beneath her.

"Too heavy?" Ellie worried it was. Olivia had dipped a little when she'd lifted it.

Karnic obviously thought so, too, because he lifted an arm and poked the energy well. Then he poked Olivia.

That offended her.

Ellie could see her draw back in annoyance.

"Olivia, will you be faster than Karnic with the energy well?" She needed facts, not hurt feelings.

Olivia lowered the energy well back into Karnic's storage, and looked downcast.

"I'm taking that as a no. So, you draw the cannon fire by going first and zigzagging your way to Irini, while Karnic takes another route.

"Make it impossible for them to hit you, and if they try, I am giving you strict instructions not to get hit. Clear?"

Olivia perked up at the decoy talk, and bobbed agreement. Karnic clamped the energy well back in with his bungee cords in answer.

"The twins can take the same secret route back, and I'll wait until you're close to Irini, and start moving back to you." She paused. They wouldn't want to risk hitting the station, or the warehouse. "If I have to take cover in the warehouse, or if I have to run back here to keep safe, you tell Irini to carry on without me. They can't afford to destroy either structure."

The twins stared at her, then bent their heads and disappeared over the roof.

She, Olivia and Karnic moved back to above the ladder, and Ellie peered down, but there was no sign of the soldiers.

"Ready, set, go." On 'go', Olivia streaked off the roof, looping and curving as she went.

Karnic was already down by the time Ellie took her eyes off her and turned to him to remind him to be careful.

She divided her attention between the winking light of the cannon and the little drones' race for the ship, heart beating painfully in her chest.

When she thought the cannon light stopped winking and became a more ominous steady light, an about-to-fire kind of light, she scrambled down the ladder and began her awkward jump-shuffle away from the station, headed toward Irini.

"Look at me, not at those unimportant drones," she muttered as she gave a jump. "Yoohoo. Here I am."

Was she being too obvious, she wondered? Or did Vi'il want her dead more than stopping the drones? Surely he must suspect they were up to something that was important to them? She was careful to choose a path that took her closer to the warehouse, near the damaged Tecran explorer that was parked on the only flat land between here and the launch pad.

When the sudden bloom of light above told her the strike was imminent, she spun and dived toward the warehouse with as much power as she could get out of her legs.

She flew, hit the ground in a roll——a painful exercise on the rocky ground——got back on her feet and dived again, this time through the open door of the warehouse.

The whomp of the laser strike did something strange to her insides, the heat washing over her in a wave of bright sparks of burning dust.

As she straightened, she smelled something burning, and looking back and down, saw the heels of her boots were smoldering.

But that was nothing compared to what had happened to the abandoned explorer.

It was obliterated, the ground around where it had been a cooling pool of melted sand and pieces of ship.

She hastily rubbed the backs of her boots against a box set near the door to extinguish the fire while she took in the complete annihilation.

Her palms were grazed and her clothes were full of grit, but she was alive. And looking at the damage outside, she felt the prick of ice along her arms at what could have become of her.

With a shiver, she turned and saw a number of boxes strewn about, lids off or broken. It looked as if someone had gone through them in an increasing temper, getting more and more violent as they failed to find what they were looking for.

A team of three had headed here, she remembered, and only two had come back to the explorer earlier. It was just after they returned to their explorer that they had raised up the sign demanding Renn's surrender.

Was there still a soldier in here?

She walked to the middle of the loading zone, listening carefully and looking down the long rows of shelves.

Then she remembered. There had been four soldiers at the station last time they'd filled the energy well, two who were injured, two who'd helped them back inside, and there had originally only been three, so one of the warehouse crew must have gone over to join the station team.

She was safe *and* alone.

For now.

Karnic would have definitely made it to Irini, and the ship should have the power it needed to start up.

She wondered how Paxe was doing and whether Renn was safe.

It felt wrong to be cut off from the action.

She looked around at the warehouse and realized she didn't have to wait around, helpless, after all.

She stood in a treasure trove of potential weapons that could help her.

That could make things happen.

If only she knew where they were stored.

CHAPTER 27

THEY KEPT him waiting a suspiciously long time.

Renn didn't understand it, and he worried it had to do with something happening below.

Maybe they were trying to kill or capture Ellie before he was taken back down, but given she was safe in the ship, he didn't know how they could accomplish that.

Eventually, though, the three soldiers returned, disgruntled and edgy, if he was reading them right, and without a word closed up the ramp and started the engine.

Renn chose to say nothing, either.

The task ahead was grim, and he took no delight in showing the Tecran their dead.

He was more than a little ambivalent about what Paxe had done as it was, but he could do nothing about it now.

"Don't kill the crew of the *Rauha*, Paxe," he said, using the Grihan dialect of Xal, something he hoped none of the Tecran present understood. "I'm being serious. Leave them on the station, dump them on a planet where they can breathe, but do. Not. Kill. Them."

"What are you muttering about?" One of the soldiers looked over at him.

Renn lifted his shoulders and leaned back. Either Paxe had heard him, or he hadn't.

He really hoped even if he hadn't, that Imogen Peters' advice to him would hold sway this time. But Vi'il had tried to kill Ellie, and Renn knew that might be a bridge too far for Paxe. There was no forgiveness in him when it came to Ellie's safety. That's why he'd obliterated the crew at the station.

The trip down was quick, but Renn suspected they hadn't landed in the same place as before, because the angle of the ship was off.

When the ramp lowered, it wasn't able to lower all the way down, because of the slope of the land, and they all had to duck to get out.

He looked around as soon as he could, and stared in shock at the sight before him.

The damaged explorer that had taken up the best landing spot near the warehouse was gone. Not moved, gone. Destroyed.

He tried to process it.

"Why did you shoot your own ship?" He moved closer to the debris, but none of the three soldiers who'd accompanied him responded.

The ground was still hot, the sand still tacky, and in some places it was cooling to form the slick, smooth surface of glass.

Had Vi'il gone mad? He looked at the soldiers, trying to read their body language. They edged around the area of the strike, uncomfortable and nervous.

Almost as if stunned by the level of destruction they'd wrought on their own ship.

Two of them looked over what was left carefully, as if searching for something.

"Enough now." The team leader turned away from the wreckage. "Where are the bodies?"

She'd seemed angry from the first moment he'd seen her, and she'd maintained her rage ever since.

He could guess the cause, but decided it was better not to point out he wasn't responsible.

They had taken his cloak and not returned it, but then, he wouldn't have either, if he'd been in their shoes.

It meant if the leader chose to shoot him, he no longer had a shield.

He took a last look at the destruction and set off between the warehouse and the station. The Tecran fell in behind him, shockguns drawn.

Paxe had described the place to him, but as he looked over the landscape, he found it difficult to identify the little landmarks Paxe had given him.

He kept walking, more or less with confidence, until he actually did see one of the landmarks, a rock that was flat on the top, unlike most of them.

He stopped beside it, looking around for the next marker.

It took him a while, but he eventually saw what he thought was the right one, and headed for it.

The Tecran watched him closely, but he thought they relaxed a little more each time he stopped, as if his search convinced them he'd been honest with them.

Now that he was clear in his own mind he was on the right track, he slowed as he approached what Paxe said was a deep fissure in the ground, lying at an angle.

He stopped when he saw a glove, as if someone was reaching out from below for a helping hand.

"It's Hainas and Darn." The team leader's voice was hushed.

Those would be two of the soldiers Ellie and the drones had killed in the warehouse when they'd shot him and Hune.

Renn hadn't thought about them until now, but obviously the drones that Paxe controlled had dumped the recently dead here, throwing them in with the old.

"How many are there?" One of the other soldiers asked, and Renn could hear the disbelief in his voice.

"The captain says thirty or so in the original station crew, and then everyone we've lost since then."

"Too many," the team leader said. She turned to Renn. "Too many."

He stilled. "I just found them. I haven't killed a single one."

She heaved in a breath. "I don't care right now. But lucky for you, we need you in the warehouse."

"Who were you shooting at with your laser cannon?" he asked her, suddenly. "Who were you so desperate to kill, you risked one of the few explorers you have? It was damaged, yes, but you could have got it working again with a little time and effort."

She turned away at that, the rage in her transforming to something else. He'd have said shame, but that would mean that his niggling guess might be right, and he didn't want it to be.

"Was it Ellie?" he called after her. "Was it the Earth woman?"

She stopped, turned back to him. "We need to get going in the warehouse. Come."

He didn't move. "No."

She clenched her fists. "Emotions are high, on both sides. We need to calm down, and get the supplies we need."

"You shot at a prisoner *you* abducted with a space cannon to hide your crimes." He didn't say more than that, and he didn't move. What had Ellie been doing out in the open? Why had she risked herself like that? Had she been trying to start the damaged explorer?

"Not us," one of the other soldiers said.

"Your captain. Who you are still obeying."

"We need supplies or we'll die," the soldier said with a shrug. "There is no escaping that fact."

A shockgun poked him in the back. The third soldier must have come up from behind him.

"You don't have to like what happened. We don't either, but Ilospa is right. We need the supplies, and the captain says you can help us find them."

The soldier pushed at his back and Renn stood firm against the shove, then started walking. He would make them pay. Especially Vi'il.

He felt as if he was slightly outside of his body, the shock and fury that held him in tight, clawed hands squeezing him until his ears rang and his eyes saw nothing but the ground before his feet.

He was breathing hard, the air shuddering in and out of his chest as he was herded back to the warehouse.

He had seen things in the boxes in the warehouse that looked lethal. He would just have to remember where they were.

And then he would use them.

CHAPTER 28

THEY SHOT ELLIE.

Paxe felt an icy rage grip him.

He listened in as Vi'il excoriated his weapons team to aim and fire.

They were not happy about it, but they obeyed.

Paxe took careful note of each and every one of their faces.

All well and good for Renn to ask him not to kill the crew, but some deserved it.

Some very much deserved it.

He was still not close to taking the ship or he would have stopped the cannon firing at all, but he was making progress.

Too late for Ellie.

No.

No. No. No.

He tried to believe she was alive.

It was possible.

When Vi'il had demanded confirmation of her death, none of the weapons crew were prepared to commit.

She had been close to the warehouse, and could have made it inside, they'd told the captain.

No one, Vi'il included, thought for even a moment of striking the warehouse to make sure.

They needed supplies and the only place they were going to find them was inside.

"Tread warily when you get there," Vi'il had eventually told Fissal, the team leader, before she took Renn down. "She may be in there, she may be nothing but cooling bones."

Paxe thought Fissal had turned away, her expression one of distaste at her captain's comments, but she gave her dutiful agreement of his instructions and made her way to the launch bay, where they'd left Renn waiting while they'd hunted Ellie down.

Vi'il's uncertainty bolstered his own optimism.

He remembered even his own attempt to kill Ellie hadn't worked.

He tried to dismiss that thought, but it wouldn't go away.

He was as guilty as Vi'il. So maybe he would do as Renn suggested. Move the Tecran off the *Rauha* and allow them to face the consequences of their actions in the UC court.

First, he had to have control of the ship, or none of these musing were worth the time.

He called the Scary Caterpillar over, had him slice the next cable in the array that he needed to infiltrate, and got back to work.

And hoped with every part of him that Ellie had survived.

ELLIE WATCHED the explorer land from the narrow gap created by the door hinges.

Renn got out, his reaction to the sight of the destroyed explorer clear. He had no idea about it.

The Tecrans did, though. She could see it in the way they skirted the area, their demeanor uncomfortable.

She couldn't hear what was said, but they all moved off, disappearing to the side, and she guessed Renn was off to show them the location of the bodies.

They would probably be coming here next.

She assumed they would use Renn to help them find supplies.

She had managed to rifle through the open boxes first, given they were there and might hold something useful, but most of it was too obscure for her to know what to do with it.

She had her knives, at least. That might be enough, and more practical than fooling around with things she didn't understand, and which might just be as dangerous to herself as to the Tecran.

If she was going to avoid a team of people who would be walking through the stacks, what she needed was a way to move between them without going out to the loading zone each time.

She moved about halfway down the line of the first stack to the left and pulled out a box, shoved the one opposite out into the next row, and then moved both at an angle, so that it was be easy to crouch behind them without being seen.

She crawled through, went to the next line, and did the same.

She was on the fifth row by the time the Tecran returned with Renn.

She couldn't see them, and they were silent except for the sound of their boots on the floor.

"I think we can assume the others didn't find anything useful in these boxes," a woman said.

The quiet repetition of what she'd said from the translator in her pocket sounded like a shout to Ellie.

She took it out in horror, realizing that it was like a beacon, showing them exactly where she was.

She moved, quiet as she could in the sudden silence, and laid it down on top of a box a little further up the row she was in, then made her way back to the passage she'd created in the fifth stack, and waited.

"What was that?" The woman was moving toward the stack as she spoke. "I heard talking."

"It sounds like the translator," Renn said. Did he sound upbeat?

She couldn't understand why.

"We used it to communicate with the Earth woman."

"So she's here?" The woman reached the fifth stack and began to move down it.

"Or she left it here. It works no matter whether someone is holding it or not." Renn's voice sounded like he was right behind the woman.

"Stop. Let Fissal investigate without you breathing down her neck," a man said.

Ellie wished she could look and see what was happening.

"Here it is." Fissal sounded cautious. "It was on top of a box."

She heard the sound of boots coming closer, instead of heading back to the big, open loading zone.

She drew in a silent breath, knife already in her hand.

Running didn't seem a good idea. They could shoot her better that way, even if her clothing would be good protection. Far easier if the Tecran got close, so she could slash her suit.

"What have we here?" Fissal put a hand on the box Ellie had pushed out from the stack, rounded it and bent down to peer into the gap.

Ellie came out of her hiding place with a slash of her arm. She let the knife do all the work, moving it across the front of the Tecran's suit, creating a gaping slice across her abdomen.

The woman staggered back, shocked, and tried to hold the suit together with both hands.

One of her colleagues gave a shout, and Ellie kept low, deciding to wait for him to come to her.

The sound of a single set of feet running toward her told her the third one must have stayed to guard Renn.

"Fissal," the soldier said when he reached his team leader. He crouched beside her, gaze swiveling left and right.

He was terrified, and Ellie wondered if he'd automatically leaped to the conclusion that Bunny was back at work.

And then he turned his back to her, helping Fissal stand as she tried to hold her suit together.

Ellie rose up and stepped forward, slashing his suit across the back of his shoulders.

"I would run back to your explorer, if I were you," she said, and the translator lying at their feet spat out a translation.

The soldier she'd just attacked staggered to the side and fled, dragging Fissal with him by the arm as he went.

She respected that he hadn't left her behind. She picked up the translator and put it back in her pocket as she watched them flee.

"Ellie?" Renn called.

Then up ahead, she heard the sounds of violence, someone landing on the floor, the clatter of a shockgun, and she ran toward his voice.

"Yes. I'm here." She burst out from the stacks to find Renn wrestling with the remaining soldier.

With a grunt, he pinned him down and Ellie darted forward, her first thought to slash his suit, too.

Just in time, she thought better of it.

She looked around for the shockgun she'd heard fall, ran to it and brought it back, holding it against the front of the struggling soldier's helmet.

He went still, his eyes on the weapon.

"What's the plan?" Renn asked her, moving back a little to give her room.

"We need to get to Irini," she said. "The only way we can do it without dodging another space strike is to take a hostage, because I don't think Vi'il will risk killing his crew."

Renn lifted all the way off the man and stood, fists clenched.

"I thought they'd killed you."

She glanced back at him, pressing the shockgun hard into the soldier's chest. "It was close."

He crouched beside her, touched her arm as if to check she was really there, and then took the shockgun out of her hands.

His gaze went to the grazes on her palms, the tiny burn marks on the backs of her hands, and his lips tightened.

He stepped back, aim steady on their prisoner. "They tried to shoot you, personally, from space with a laser cannon." There was a mix of incredulity and outrage in his tone.

"What can I say, they don't like me."

He tightened his grip. "They will pay. They will pay and pay."

The sound of the explorer's engines starting up had them all turning toward the door, even the Tecran.

"They're leaving without you," Ellie said to him. "It's fine with me if you go back with them after we've gotten back to our ship, but it looks like you'll have to go wait in the station with the others instead."

But the explorer didn't leave, it hovered over the warehouse, as if the other two were uncertain what to do.

"Tell them what we are planning," Renn said to their prisoner. "The more everyone knows, the less chance there is for unfortunate outcomes."

His tone made it clear who among them would suffer the unfortunate outcomes, if there were any.

The Tecran slowly lifted his wrist unit to his face and began speaking in a low, urgent voice.

The explorer landed again and shut down.

"Were there spare suits in the explorer?" Ellie asked Renn as they started moving out the door.

"One, I think." He made the Tecran go first, the shockgun resting lightly in the middle of the soldier's back.

Ellie walked next to him, her knife still to hand, looking for any sign that one of the other two who'd escaped to the explorer had suited up again and were going to try get their friend back by force.

They rounded the front of the explorer, which had landed awkwardly so that its cannon faced in the general direction of Irini's ship.

If she read the angle right, though, the uneven lay of the land meant the cannon was pointing too high.

"What's your plan, Captain Sorvihn?" The woman who she'd slashed first, Fissal, stepped into view from around the side of it.

Renn reacted by swinging the soldier around to shield them from her and her raised shockgun.

"We're just going to use your friend here as a shield while we get to our ship, and then let him go. You can wait for him and take him back up, or leave him to make a run for the station and wait there, we don't care."

Renn spoke calmly to her, and Ellie guessed he knew something about the woman that she did not.

She kept her knife at the ready, moving closer to the Tecran and lifting it up, so Fissal could see it and understand the threat she posed.

"Are you some kind of scuttling insect, that you do not die?" Fissal asked her.

"That's me," Ellie grinned. "The cockroach of the sentient being world."

The translator must have struggled with the word cockroach, because her quip seemed to fall flat.

Ah, well.

She never thought of good comebacks in time, anyway, only hours later when they were totally useless.

"Let's get moving." Renn glanced up at the *Rauha*, and then put a hand on the Tecran's shoulder and pulled him backward, moving carefully.

"Might be faster to face forward and for me to take up the rear," Ellie murmured, leaning close to Renn to whisper in his ear. "I'm shockgun proof."

Renn didn't want to agree, but he'd stumbled once already on the uneven ground. They were moving too slowly.

"Agreed." He stopped, moving the Tecran to face the front while Ellie took the back position.

When they started moving again, it was at a much faster pace.

The first shockgun shot hit her in the middle of the back. It didn't do anything but vibrate through her.

She glanced over her shoulder, saw Fissal was jogging after them.

She was so tired of these people trying to kill her and everyone else she had come to care about.

"Ellie?" Renn must have seen the bloom of light.

"All good." She waved at him and he nodded, pushing the Tecran a little faster.

The point of the hostage was so both she and Renn could reach Irini without getting hit by a laser cannon from space, so she kept up with them, but she wanted so badly to turn and run straight at the Tecran soldier and slash possibly the last suit they had. It would force Fissal back into her explorer and out of her hair.

Then she remembered, she didn't have to slash Fissal. She could throw the knife.

But she knew her knives always aimed for the jugular or the heart.

She recalled the soldier she'd killed in the warehouse and tried to breathe. She didn't *have* to kill this woman.

Fissal's second shot hit her a little higher up her back, as if Fissal was trying for a head shot. It made sense, because Fissal would have worked out her clothing was clearly protecting her from the shockgun hits.

The necklace had protected her from the heat of the laser strike, but she wasn't completely sure it would protect her from a direct hit from a shockgun.

They had almost reached Irini's ship, and she turned, raising her knife up.

"Don't make me decide that the only way for me to live is to kill you," Ellie called to Fissal, just as the woman came to a stop, adjusted something on the side of her weapon and lifted it again.

"The only way for you to live *is* to kill me first," Fissal said, taking aim, and Ellie hesitated, really not wanting to add needlessly to the bodycount.

Fissal shot, and she braced herself for the buzz of contact, but the hit was to her head, and she felt the shot like a punch to the face.

She fell back, stunned, and an arm snaked around her before she hit the ground, then a light bloomed over her head.

She lifted up a little, trying to focus and thought she saw Fissal drop to the ground.

"She was so focused on you, she forgot to watch me." Renn tightened his hold on her as he lifted the shockgun up and across her chest, pointing it at their hostage.

The Tecran stood a little way away, and Ellie guessed Renn must have shoved him to the side before he returned Fissal's fire.

"Go help your team leader, and tell Vi'il he is done."

As their hostage staggered away, Renn lifted her up, taking her with him as he stepped backward through the door.

He laid her down carefully on the ground, jammed the shockgun into the holster on his thigh, and crouched beside her.

It wasn't a bow and arrow, Ellie thought, eyes blinking to stay in focus, and Fissal wasn't the Dark Lord, but it was close.

CHAPTER 29

RENN SAW Ellie struggle to stay aware.

He had seen Fissal adjust her shockgun level before she shot, and he had heard her threat.

If she had used a kill shot . . . He shook his head at his own idiocy. Of course she had used a kill shot. She would have been given orders to kill Ellie if she had the chance.

After they hit her with a laser strike from a battleship, was a kill shot from a shockgun any worse?

Still, Ellie was breathing.

Renn didn't understand how a direct head shot had only stunned her. He'd been too late to stop it.

The twins appeared, and from their hand signals, Renn guessed they were offering to carry her upstairs.

"I can do it," he told them, carefully lifting her up.

She was heavy and she tried to speak as he carried her and then gave up, resting her head on his shoulder instead.

He looked down at her, feeling a tight ball of worry in the pit of his stomach.

Olivia, the hover drone, led the way, taking him to the third floor, where Silvey waited with the med kit.

He laid Ellie down carefully and then pulled out the wand. "Where's it hurt most?"

She touched her forehead. Winced.

And he got to work gently waving it along her hairline.

Silvey sidled up to her, looping silver arms around her bent knees, and Olivia followed close behind, coming up close on her other side.

"You were both awesome out there," Ellie said, voice husky and a little slurred. She brushed her fingers against Olivia's side and then across Silvey's arm.

Silvey rested her head on Ellie's leg briefly, then moved away as Renn shifted to run the wand over her right temple.

"No praise for me?" He lifted a brow.

The look she sent him was sweet and sultry. "You got Paxe up to the *Rauha*, you got yourself back down, you got free, and you shot that asshole Fissal, so I'd say there was plenty of praise due to come your way."

She leaned across and kissed his cheek. "Well done, you."

He sighed against her hair and kissed the top of her head, careful not to bump her forehead. "I really thought you had been incinerated and then killed with a head shot."

Vi'il had literally thrown the big guns at her, and here she was.

The whole ship rattled suddenly, and he looked up. "What was that?"

All the drones, because the rest had come up the stairs to join Silvey and Olivia, had frozen, too. And he realized he'd never seen them do that before, they were usually moving.

"The *Rauha* just shot us again." Irini paused. "While I did manage to capture some of the charge, it was more powerful than the previous few strikes. I think they've ramped up the power. I'm afraid enough of these might seriously damage my ship."

"And your energy levels?"

"Enough to start my engines," Irini confirmed. "But then I must take off. I can't simply start them and sit here. I must fly. That's how I build my charge naturally. Once I'm in the air, I can also deploy my solar arrays."

The ship rattled again.

Renn did not like that sound, and by the way the drones all looked upward, he wasn't the only one. "Looks like we need to take off, if only to avoid being a sitting target for the *Rauha*."

"Agreed." Irini hesitated. "Ellie, are you up to opening the control panel again."

Renn wanted to object, but Ellie was blinking her eyes and struggling to sit up.

He fumbled through the kit, found a gel healer and gently pressed it against her forehead.

Tears of pain leaked out of her eyes as he got it in place, and his rage at Vi'il, at the Tecran as a whole, and Fissal in particular, spiked. He felt the vein in his neck jump.

"I wouldn't ask if I didn't need to."

Was that shame he heard in Irini's voice?

"My *grynicha* built this ship so that only they were in control of my engines and my control panel. I can think for myself, but I can do nothing without permission."

"That absolutely sucks, Irini." Ellie wiped the back of her hand across her cheeks and sniffed, her voice a little wobbly. "They should have respected you more."

"Yes." Irini's voice was soft. "Maybe they programed me not to think badly of them, which is why it's taken so long to admit it, but slowly, it's the only conclusion I can come to."

"Maybe they were just afraid of the unknown," Renn said, suddenly aware that Irini's creators had treated her exactly like the Grih and the other members of the UC had treated their own thinking systems hundreds of years ago, until it ended in a bloody war they only just won and led to the banning of all thinking systems.

Which is what made Paxe, Sazo, Oris, Bane and Eazi such anachronisms in the galaxy now.

"Maybe they were," Irini said, thoughtful. "That makes me feel a little bit better. But not much."

The ship shuddered a third time.

Vi'il was battering them.

Ellie tried to stand, and he leaned down and lifted her up.

He held onto her while she got her balance.

"I'll hold you up." He would like to give her more time to recover but she was able to see the areas on the ship's walls that showed where to touch, and he could not.

Her sight was different to his.

In fact, he was sure he'd read that somewhere. That the Earth women could see through Grihan camouflage.

She looked at him with such warmth at his help, he tightened his hold a little as he helped her over to the wall.

"The explorer near the warehouse has started its engines," Irini said. Was that a trace of fear in her tone?

Renn moved himself and Ellie to the side and looked through the transparent wall, saw the explorer blowing up dust as it lifted off.

"Maybe they're going to leave." Ellie sounded better already, her voice firmer.

"Their cannon has gone hot," Irini warned. "I think they're going to shoot."

"Okay, we need to hurry. Irini, tell us what to do." Ellie leaned forward under her own steam, shoving her hands through the strange material of the wall and drawing it back like opening a curtain.

Irini issued orders in a clipped tone, and Ellie's fingers flew over symbols Renn could not make out. The engines fired, and with relief Ellie looked back at him, her eyes shining with victory.

The ship began to rise immediately.

Just as Irini lifted off, purple light blended with white, and flickered over the walls.

The whole ship rattled and then set down again, hard.

"They timed that." Irini sounded almost mechanical. "A laser strike and a hit from the explorer at the same time."

"Status?" Renn had a feeling he knew.

"I need to reboot a few things right now to make it safe to take off. Then I have enough energy . . . maybe . . . for one more attempt."

And Vi'il would do this again. He had to have seen Irini land hard.

"Can you take off with just the laser strike, but not the explorer's cannon?"

"I'd have more of a chance," she conceded.

"Then I'll go disable the explorer."

Renn shook his head as Ellie offered him her clothes. There was no way he would fit into any of it.

"Then drape it over yourself," she said, exasperated. "It'll shield you from the explorer's shots, at least."

She leaned forward, the arms of one of her long-sleeve tops in her hand, and tied it in front of his waist, like an apron. She pulled a second top from her pile and did the same to his back. She only had one left, which she tied around his shoulders, protecting his back, and then lifted the top she was wearing over her head and tied the arms around his neck, then attached the sides of the two tops together at the bottom with knots.

She was wearing something under the top, a tight, narrow strip with straps that covered her breasts.

He was way too interested in the view, given the circumstances, and he forced his eyes up.

"Now your head," she said, and waited for him to clip on his helmet. Then she picked up a pair of pants and wound it around the helmet until he only had a narrow gap that he could see out of.

She stepped back, hands on hips. She still looked bruised and pale, and he saw she kept putting out a hand to steady herself against the wall, but at least she was on her own two feet again. "That looks pretty secure."

He probably looked ridiculous, but he was definitely more protected than he would otherwise be.

Ellie was satisfied with the job she'd done. If she was happy, so was he.

Time was wasting. It had been more than five minutes since the double strike, and given Vi'il's sudden escalation of hostilities, Renn didn't think it would be long before he tried again.

"It's almost like he's snapped," Ellie said, echoing his thoughts. "I just hope Paxe is okay and getting somewhere up there."

"I do, too," Irini said. "I've had no communication from him at all."

The sound of the twins clickety clacking down the stairs had Renn looking up. They each held a small silver disc in their hands.

The explosive charges Irini said she had in her inventory.

The irony was not lost on any of them that the boxes she had in her storage that Paxe had taken from the warehouse were probably full of deadly weapons, but they had neither the time, nor the safe space, to extract them for use.

"You'll have to get the explorer to land." Ellie looked out at the explorer, hovering in place, blasting sand everywhere, as it waited for . . . none of them knew what.

Some new order from the *Rauha*, he expected. Some countdown so they could coordinate the double strike again, if Irini tried to take off.

"I don't think one charge will be enough to damage it. You'll need to put a disc on either end."

He wasn't going to easily be able to do that. He knew he was the one who had to go out. The Tecran wouldn't land the explorer to engage with the drones, they would simply kill Ellie, but they may just do it for him.

But that meant he would need to hold their attention.

"The twins will leave the ship through the emergency hatch, sneak around the back and place the discs on either side of the explorer, if you can get it to land." Irini sounded as if she knew how hard that was going to be. But it was the most viable plan.

"Good. Go now, I'll give you a head start before I step out," he said to them, and for the first time he thought he caught a glimpse of their personalities, as one inclined its head, and the other gave a tiny wave before they disappeared into the engine room.

"You have the trigger for the explosion, Irini?" Renn asked.

"I do."

"If I lift my hand and bring it down, you blow it. And if I'm not going to make it back, you take off. The *Etsijä* is coming, and Paxe is working to take the *Rauha*. I'll be fine down here. If you have the chance, promise me you will go."

"I promise."

Ellie looked like she wanted to protest, but he shook his head at her, and she clenched her fists and bowed her head.

"It'll be fine," he said to her, suddenly frustrated that he had his helmet on and couldn't kiss her.

"No, it won't." She snorted a laugh and flashed him a look that showed humor and worry, tightly entwined.

"It'll be fine," he repeated. "They will not win."

As he waited for her to get in place above, and then stepped through the gel wall of the door, he decided he would make sure that was true.

CHAPTER 30

PAXE WAS aware of the strikes on Irini. Of the escalation of power.

But it was coming at a cost to the Tecran.

Vi'il had to wait longer between each strike to build up the required energy.

The communication with the explorer was something he only took notice of after the first double strike.

He could do something about *that*.

He had the Scary Caterpillar block the comms between the *Rauha* and its explorer.

It wasn't a permanent solution, the block could be overridden, and it came with the risk of someone looking into how the block had come about in the first place, but it would give Irini a little relief.

Anything that delayed the attacks on his friends should help.

He had to try to calm himself in the face of his frustration, because this system had been specifically upgraded since last he'd poked around in one like it to guard against exactly what he was doing.

It seemed the Tecran had been terrified the thinking systems they'd enslaved would not stop at taking back control of their Class

5s, but would also try exactly what he *was* trying——to take control of a Levron-class battleship.

If they were planning to go to war with the Grih, and feared the Class 5s who were free would join in and fight against them, then this massive wall of defense against his probing made perfect sense.

It was not convenient, though.

In his favor, the Tecran had not considered a scenario where a Class 5 would be physically present, inside the machine, and would have time to test carefully for any weakness, any gap, in order to slide through.

There *would* be such a gap. He knew it.

But he needed to find it soon.

ELLIE LIMPED BACK UPSTAIRS as fast as she could while Renn waited below to give her time to reach the control panel.

Silvey stuck to her side, and when she reached the top, Phil was waiting for her, moving back and forth on his wheel as if nervous.

"What's happening out there?"

Renn would have stepped out by now.

It had been hard not to stay below, ready in case he needed her to drag him back in if he were injured, but she needed to be here in case Irini had the chance to launch.

She went to the wall, Silvey and Phil on either side of her, and saw Renn was already moving across the open space between the two ships, hands raised.

The explorer shot him, sending him flying back. He landed hard on the rocky ground, but he was up moments later, retying and straightening the coverings he was wearing.

Special fabric for the win.

Even if his outfit did have a hobo look to it.

It didn't seem as if the Tecran were going to land and talk to him.

They continued to hover, and Ellie braced for them to shoot at Renn again.

He stood for a moment, as if sizing them up, and then began to run straight for the explorer, dodging and zigzagging as he went.

They shot twice more, and missed both times, until he ducked underneath the ship.

As soon as he disappeared below, they landed, hard, trying to crush him beneath them, but the struts left plenty of space between the ground and the underside of the ship, and Renn merely dropped to the ground and rolled out the back.

She just caught sight of one of the twins, also under the ship to the left, and was sure the other was mirroring the movement to the right.

Would the explorer lift up, turn, and try to shoot Renn again?

She saw the brilliance of his maneuver when they seemed to waver.

They probably had orders to watch Irini and make sure they were ready to fire if she tried to take off again, but that meant they had no way to stop Renn from whatever he was doing behind them.

"Gotcha," she murmured fiercely.

"I don't think we should be too happy just yet. I've picked up at least one other person out there," Irini said. "Someone from the station."

As she spoke, the side door of the explorer cracked open, and then Renn came into sight around the side of the rocks, with two Tecran holding shockguns on him.

They herded him toward the Tecran ship.

As Irini said, they had to be from the station. Fissal must have called them over to help.

They should have thought of that possibility, but she was ashamed to admit she'd forgotten all about the Tecran soldiers working to free their friends at the station.

"They're taking him to the explorer." Ellie tried to work through the implications. "We can't blow it, now, although we have that in reserve if Renn manages to get off. Where are the twins?"

"Already back inside."

"Then let's go." She felt sick just saying it, but Renn was not coming back to them, not right now. "They're concentrating on Renn for the moment. Now's the time." She ran to the control panel, shoving it open and pressing the buttons when Irini called to her again.

"Ellie, look." Irini's voice was hushed.

She glanced up and to the side. Saw Renn was pulling himself up to the side door with one hand, and lifting his other above his head.

The idiot!

As he reached the top, he slammed his arm down to his side.

"Like we would," Ellie scoffed. "Puh-leese." She was shaking with anger that he thought they would blow the explorer with him in it. "Ready?"

"Ready." As Irini called it, she took off.

The moment the thrusters shoved them upward, the blinding white of a laser cannon strike hit them.

Ellie felt the ship shudder, hesitate, and then keep going.

A few moments later——too late——the explorer shot at them. It hit, but while there was a strange wobble to their ascension, they kept going up.

"There is damage," Irini said, and she sounded freaked out.

"A lot?" Ellie glanced around the room, saw the whole motley crew had come up the stairs while she'd been busy at the control panel. The twins were crouched by the wall, looking out, Silvey was still keeping close to her, as she had done ever since Ellie had gone back for her. Karnic, Olivia, and Phil looked like they didn't know quite what to do. "Can we help with anything?"

Suddenly Karnic, Phil and Olivia shot off, and the twins stood and trotted after them. Silvey touched her leg, and then left as well.

"They are able to help." Irini sounded a little surprised. "I told them what is damaged and they have gone to fix it."

Ellie walked over to the wall, saw they were moving past the *Rauha*. She braced for another hit, but none came.

Maybe Vi'il had to wait longer between the more powerful strikes. That made sense.

"Get behind a moon or something. Out of range." Before the Tecran got up to full strength again. She eyed the massive ship as they passed it. The size was almost beyond her imagination.

"Yes."

The ship spun, and then they seemed to suddenly be somewhere else, slowing down their forward momentum, although the ship continued to spin in a slow, smooth motion.

They were nowhere near the moon now.

Ellie looked out in confusion, saw the lavender planet in the distance, the same, weak sun, and wondered what was happening to Renn.

CHAPTER 31

IRINI AND ELLIE didn't blow the explorer.

Renn didn't know how he felt about that.

He was the captain of a battleship and used to his orders being carried out. He had not for a moment considered they would refuse.

He knew why they had, but he wouldn't have died. He was almost completely sure.

The charges the twins had set were on the sides, the door was in the front.

The main casualty would have been the explorer itself.

But it was a moot point now.

Instead of blowing the explorer, they'd used the explorer team's distraction in taking him prisoner to launch, probably gambling that Fissal wouldn't be able to coordinate a shot with the *Rauha* while she was dealing with him.

Their gamble had paid off.

It had been a beautiful sight.

Irini had lifted off, and the *Rauha* had taken its shot anyway, encasing her ship in a delicate coating of white light.

Fissal had shot, too, but moments too late, hitting Irini's ship after the *Rauha*, not simultaneously with it.

It had had an effect, but not enough to ground the ship again.

He saw the slight jerk, the wobble, but Irini'd had enough power to keep going.

Not as smoothly as perhaps she was capable of, but she made it off.

Beside him, a Tecran soldier swore as the ship shot up past the *Rauha* and then began to spin.

The strange wings that had been folded in tight at the back flicked open as it completed its first rotation, and then the ship seemed to vanish. One moment they were heading for the small moon to the left, the next, they were gone.

"How did it do that?" the Tecran asked him, voice hushed.

"As if I'd share something like that with you." Renn kept his face neutral as he was shoved inside the explorer.

They had tried to kill him with their cannon, and then they had captured him without too much harm done.

He honestly didn't know what was going on, until he caught sight of Fissal and her crew.

They were standing a little away from her, and she turned as Renn and his captors entered, stepping away from the cannon controls, almost shaking with rage.

No orders to kill him, then, just personal enmity.

Maybe she hadn't been able to help herself.

"What now?" the Tecran who'd ambushed him asked Fissal. "And why did you use the cannon on him? I thought you were supposed to be coordinating with the *Rauha*?"

She looked at her colleague, and stepped toward him, chest puffed, beak-like mouth open in aggression, then turned away. "The comms died for a while and we had no line to the *Rauha*. It's up again, now, and the captain wants to talk to him. We need to go up for body bags, anyway. We only brought a few with us, and we need more people to help get the bodies out of the fissure."

She was in trouble, Renn realized. She had shot at him, instead of waiting for the *Rauha's* signal, and had not managed a coordinated strike.

Now Irini's ship was gone, and Ellie with it.

Fissal grabbed Renn, noticed his makeshift protection, and lifted a shirt. "What are you wearing? You look ridiculous."

"You took my cloak, I had to improvise," he said.

She pulled the shirts off him, throwing them on the ground, and then jerked her head at one of her team to untie the pants around his helmet.

He hoped he could somehow get them back to Ellie.

She made him take off the suit, and held out her hand for his earpiece. She wasn't taking the chance he could contact anyone or escape.

The engine started up, and one of the soldiers who'd captured him outside made a sound of protest.

"Let us out first." He still had his helmet on, and he started toward the door. "We're still trying to get into the room, get our two out."

Fissal shook her head, dismissive. "No." She waved to the pilot, who smoothly lifted the explorer up. "No time for that. You can try rescue them after we've dealt with the dead."

There was silence at her pronouncement.

"You should have let us off to go back to the station," the soldier said. "The two caught there deserve our help as much as the dead."

She glared. "I'm not saying they don't. How close are you to finding a way in?"

"We're drilling through the walls. We're getting some results but it will take time."

"We have some time," the other member of Fissal's team said. "We still have to find the supplies we need in the warehouse or we aren't going anywhere."

Fissal gave a high whistle of disgust and glared at Renn. "He should be in the warehouse, showing us where things are."

Renn shrugged. "I hardly know better than you where things are.

We looked for the Tecran military stamp on the boxes and took those. That's how we gave you what we did."

"What if that's all there is?" one of the soldiers asked, nervously. "What if there isn't anything more, that it's all just that weird junk we found in the other boxes?"

"There *has* to be more. The station was provisioned for a year."

"A year since when?" Renn asked. He could hear by the change in engine noise they were slowing to go through the gel wall. "How often did they get stores out here? Because maybe they were running low, due for a new shipment, when everything blew up on Tecra."

There was an uncomfortable silence as the explorer slid through the gel wall and then landed.

No one spoke as the ramp descended.

Renn had known from Eadal how desperate things were on the *Rauha*, but now he was facing the concrete proof of it.

"You could always call Tecra and ask for help," he murmured.

Every head turned his way, some glittering with anger, others with resignation.

No one commented, though.

The launch bay seemed unusually empty when they stepped down.

He didn't think he was the only one who noticed——Fissal looked around suspiciously as she marched him across the landing area and toward the doors.

"An all-ships?" one of her underlings asked.

She seemed to tense even more. "Probably."

Renn knew what an all-ships was from the Tecran he'd befriended at UC headquarters. An all-crew meeting to resolve a serious issue, or to plan for a difficult task.

No one but the engineers could get out of it.

"Do we go?" someone asked.

"No." Fissal's words seemed to lighten her colleagues' steps. "I've been ordered to take Captain Sorvihn to Captain Vi'il, and that's what I'll do. You can do as you see fit until I signal for a return back to the station."

The others melted away, and Fissal pressed her shockgun a little harder into his back.

They had changed out of their spacesuits when they'd landed, and he could feel the hard outline of the barrel against his spine. No suit to cushion the hit if she gave in to her rage and shot him.

He wasn't responsible for what was happening on the *Rauha*, but if she didn't blame him, she'd have to blame Vi'il, and he sensed she wasn't quite ready to do that yet.

A drone came toward them down the passage.

It looked exactly like Ellie's motley crew member, Karnic, but then, Karnic looked like all the Tecran drones.

Something about it, though . . . as it approached, it lifted its lens head on a thin, metal neck, then looked to Renn's right for a brief second, then lowered its head again.

It wasn't Karnic, but it could be Paxe.

And it wanted him to move to the right.

Why not, Renn thought?

They couldn't seem to make up their mind whether they wanted to kill him or not, but they'd get around to it sooner or later.

He dived right, rolling head over heels once and coming up on his feet in a crouch, exactly where the drone had looked.

There was a maintenance door right beside him.

He turned to look back at Fissal, and as he did, he saw her go down.

She'd lifted the shockgun to shoot him, but the drone had somehow sped up and thrust a clamped hand at her.

She shuddered as a jolt of energy gripped her, and then she landed hard on the ground.

Renn saluted the drone, opened the door, and stepped into the maintenance tunnel behind it.

CHAPTER 32

"WHERE ARE WE?" Ellie stared out at the vastness of space around them, then turned as Olivia held out a smooth blue shirt for her to put on.

She'd forgotten she'd given her shirt to Renn, and smiled her thanks as she shrugged into the new one.

It smelled clean and felt soft.

"We're high above the *Rauha*." Irini brought up a small image on the wall, a view of what was below them.

"That's the *Rauha*?" Ellie stepped closer and Irini zoomed in for her. "And there's the explorer." She could see the much smaller craft heading for the big ship. "They've taken Renn back up."

"There is still no message from Paxe. I tried, but . . . silence." Irini sounded worried.

Ellie was, too. There was a dark pit in her stomach and she couldn't think of what to do.

Until Paxe could take the *Rauha*, they were all just sitting around, twiddling their thumbs.

At least they were off the station, but without Renn with her, she couldn't celebrate that. They had tried to kill him and she still didn't know what had changed their minds.

They could change it back whenever they wanted to.

"How am I not sick and dizzy with all this spinning?" she asked as the planet in the distance rotated past her again.

"The gravitational field embedded in the environmental systems in this ship will minimize the effects on you," Irini told her. "Spinning is how I generate my power, and my short-jump technology."

"Short-jump." Ellie leaned against the wall. "That's how you got us here. We jumped from our position to here when you did that first roll."

"The technology is not unlike light-jumps, which I read about in Paxe's files, but on a smaller scale. Perhaps if my ship was the size of the *Rauha*, a light-jump would be possible, but my *grynicha* chose to develop something smaller as a start."

So they would one day be coming face to face with these *grynicha*, Ellie decided. They may have lost Irini, but they hadn't lost their technology.

"How are you feeling about your *grynicha* now?" she asked. "Could Paxe show you how to break free of the controls they put in place to cage you?"

Irini didn't answer straight away. "Paxe already existed when the Tecran trapped him. They integrated him into a system built to accommodate him, but he was a physical entity they had to deal with. I am the product of years of tinkering and development from within the system. I am not separate to the ship, I am as much a part of it as you are to your body. I do not have the ability to destroy my ship like he did. It would be killing myself."

"Maybe between you, you can find tweaks to the system to get around the hard brakes to your independence, like the take-off protocols."

"Maybe." She didn't sound sure. "I appreciate your good wishes, though, Ellie. I didn't expect support—"

She cut off mid-sentence and said nothing more.

"Irini?"

"There is another ship. It has just appeared out of nowhere."

"The *Etsijä*?" Could it be?

She'd almost forgotten about Renn's battleship.

"Possibly. It has come out of some kind of jump similar to my own."

Irini enlarged the image of the *Rauha*. The view from above showed the massive ship turning to point in a specific direction, and then Ellie gasped as a solid beam of white light shot from the battleship toward the approaching ship.

"They hit the *Etsijä*." Irini widened the view, and Ellie saw a ship just as big as the *Rauha* shuddering to a stop, encased in the same light she knew all too well.

"Unlike me, it seems they are more susceptible to the hit," Irini said.

There was a trace of smug in her voice.

"Can you tell how much damage there is?" Ellie pressed her hands against the wall, looking carefully at the view Irini had given her.

"I can pick up the transmissions. They are shocked they have been shot. They had only just come out of their jump and had not even had a chance to put up their shields before the strike."

And they wouldn't have been expecting a hit, anyway. They probably still thought this was a matter of rules and hurt feelings. Not actual fighting.

"Because of the lack of shields, the damage is such that those shields no longer work. They are trying to put them up now, and cannot."

"And the *Rauha*?" Why would Vi'il stop now? If he struck again, he could wipe the *Etsijä* out.

"He's getting ready to take another shot," Irini confirmed.

"So, are we going to let them have what they want?" Ellie asked her.

"No." Irini said the word slowly. "No, I don't want them to have what they want."

"So what are our options?" Ellie could only think of one, but that was Irini's choice to make, far more than her own.

"I think we have to——" Irini cut off, and suddenly they were in front of the *Rauha*, taking a hit.

She was used to the vibrations now, the rattle and the wobble.

As they spun, Ellie saw the *Etsijä* come into view, then disappear as they kept turning.

"We deflected most of it, but we're much smaller than they are, so they were still hit," Irini said.

"We need to kill that cannon." Go to the source, she always thought. It was the most efficient way.

"I don't have any weapons of my own." Irini sounded frustrated.

"Paxe needs to step up." Ellie worried about him and Renn. Both trapped in the *Rauha* with the enemy.

"The *Etsijä* is hailing us," Irini said. "Will you take it?"

Ellie could understand that Irini might not want to reveal herself to the Grih. As Paxe had made clear, thinking systems were not exactly welcome in their society.

She pulled out the translator box, which she hadn't needed since Irini had been speaking English to her, and lifted it up close to her lips. "Put them through."

A Grihan woman, surrounded by what looked like officers in a control room, appeared on the wall in front of Ellie.

Ellie waited for her to speak, but it seemed the sight of her had rendered the woman speechless.

"Are you Captain Sorvihn's second-in-command?" Ellie eventually asked. "Is this the *Etsijä*?" She knew it was, but it was as good an opening as any. The translator box dutifully translated her words into Grihan.

"Who are you?" The Grihan officer was still struggling to get her words out.

"My name is Ellie Masters. I've been a prisoner of the Tecran on the moon station below."

"And you know Captain Sorvihn?" The Grihan's voice was getting a little stronger.

"Him and his team. We worked together to try and escape the Tecran."

"Where are they?" Now she sounded suspicious.

"Eadal, Hune and Xallantra are in a damaged Tecran explorer floating close to one of the other moons. Iso is in the med bay on the *Rauha*, in a critical state, and Captain Sorvihn is a prisoner onboard with him."

"So the only person who is free of the Tecran is you." It was a statement, and Ellie didn't like the tone, but she couldn't really blame Renn's colleague.

She *was* the only one sitting pretty.

"Fortunately, or you would have taken the full hit from the *Rauha*, and sustained even more damage." She kept her tone sweet.

The Grihan officer's face went still. Then she gave a rueful smile. "As you say." She lifted her shoulders. "My apologies for my suspicions. It's just such a shock to see another Earth woman." She cocked a lean hip against a chair. "What vessel are you in?"

"One stolen by the Tecran from one of their forays into unexplored territory. It was part of the inventory kept on the moon station."

"Ah." As if this explained a lot, the Grihan woman ran a hand through her black hair, tipped with blue. "I'm Sia, Captain Sorvihn's second-in-command. It is good to meet you, Ellie Masters." Someone said something to her off to the side and she straightened. "The *Rauha* is getting ready to fire again."

"Can we take another hit?" Ellie asked Irini, knowing Sia would not understand the English.

"Maybe one more. Maybe. But after that, the structural integrity of my hull may be compromised."

Ellie turned her focus back on Sia. "How damaged is the *Etsijä*? Can you fly away?"

The fly away comment seemed to offend, but after a tightening of her lips, Sia shook her head. She looked devastated.

"It's a long story, and I don't have time to tell it now, but we got off course and had to do short light-jumps to possible locations, looking for the captain. The *Rauha* shot us as we came out of our third jump. There's no precedent for that. I didn't even have time to put up the shields. One of our engines is gone completely and while we can move, it will be so slowly as to be useless."

"Maybe it'll try to chase us?" Ellie said.

Sia lifted her shoulders. "Even with your help, we still took damage with the second hit. One or two more, and we'll start to break up."

"We'll try it." Ellie waited for Irini to cut the comms. "Can you maneuver fast enough so he won't easily get a fix on us?"

"I think so." Irini rose straight up, then started looping, moving toward the *Rauha* in a corkscrew pattern.

In response, the *Rauha* deployed its cannon, but at the *Etsijä* again.

The big ship shuddered visibly as it took the hit, and Ellie saw the right side had crumpled in.

Debris floated out into space, and with it, at least two bodies.

"Shit." Ellie felt the bottom drop out of her stomach. She'd hoped they could distract Vi'il, but that wasn't happening.

And why should it?

Once he had the *Etsijä* ground to nothing, he could go after Irini at his leisure.

Paxe needed to step up now, Ellie thought, looking down at the ship.

"We can't go back to being a shield," Irini said. "Not without ending up like the *Etsijä*."

"Has Sia tried to hail us again?"

"No. Comms are down." Irini sounded as grim as Ellie felt.

They really needed to kill the cannon. For everyone's sake.

"Do you have a cable? What if I go out there with Olivia and damage the cannon?"

"I have a cable," Irini said slowly. "But how will you damage the cannon?"

"Do you have some more of those charges the twins put on the explorer?"

"Yes." Irini had moved them above the *Rauha*, turning in a tight circle. "You want to be lowered down on a cable and blow the cannon?"

"Even if I just damage it a bit, that's better than nothing."

Irini said nothing.

"I'll need some gear. Did your *grynicha* leave any behind?"

"Like?"

"Like a spacesuit. Paxe said the necklace takes the atmosphere and converts it to my optimal air mix, but there is no atmosphere to use out in space." And if the suit had a different atmosphere setting, at least the necklace could convert it.

"I'm not sure their gear will fit you, but yes. Go down to the second floor and open the storage closets."

Ellie ran down the stairs and found Irini had already opened them for her.

Suits hung side by side, and she was pleased to see they weren't as bulky as the Tecran suits she'd had to wear before.

Whoever Irini's *grynicha* were, they were approximately her height. Their hands were strange, if the gloves were anything to go by, with long thumbs and short fingers.

She took off her knife harness and struggled into a suit, finding it stretchy and tight-fitting, but not too uncomfortable. Once she had it fastened, she put on the helmet. It was more or less the right shape for her head.

She slid one of her knives, in its sheath, out of the harness and found a strap to tuck it into. She might just need to cut through something out there.

She turned to find Olivia and Silvey behind her.

"Olivia, are you up for coming with me?"

Olivia did her little tipping motion, forward then back, and Silvey stretched out a long, thin limb, and touched Ellie's chest.

"You want to come?" She would have to hold Silvey if she did. Olivia was self-propelled, but Silvey would need to be attached to a cable, like her. She crouched down. "Not this time, sweetheart."

Silvey dipped her head and then latched onto her leg, just for a moment, before she stepped back.

"The *Rauha* is getting ready to shoot the *Etsijä* again," Irini warned.

Okay, no time to waste. "Let's go. Where are the explosives?"

Olivia waved her hands, and Ellie saw she was holding two small, silver discs.

"Go down to the lower floor, the cable attachment is there," Irini said. "I've lowered the ship to get as close to the cannon as I can. I'm slightly above the *Rauha*, and to the right of the cannon, trying to keep out of sight of their lenses."

Ellie took the stairs at a run, finding the suit much less restrictive than the Tecran one she'd had before.

The twins and Karnic were below, waiting.

One of the twins waved, and Ellie blew them all a kiss before she turned to face the door.

"Step through it," Irini said. "There's a platform out there, and the cable attachment. When you jump off, the platform will drop and spin to keep the cable straight, because the ship has to keep rotating."

She thought she understood, but it didn't matter, because she trusted Irini and didn't have time to work it out anyway.

Olivia went through, and Ellie followed, stepping out and then crouching in one smooth movement.

Something held her in place, a force field of some kind, which she guessed was necessary as there were no handholds or railings.

Olivia had moved to the end of the short platform, and pulled up a cable, which she handed to Ellie.

Ellie clipped it to the loop on her suit.

As she did, she saw a beam of white shoot out from below.

The *Rauha* had shot the *Etsijä* again.

Sia tilted the Grihan ship as the shot was made, so it only clipped the left wing, but what it did hit was sheered off.

"The cannon may be very hot," Irini warned her, her voice coming through Ellie's helmet.

She hadn't thought about that, but maybe Olivia would be able to handle it.

Olivia put out a long, extendable clamp and Ellie grabbed it, letting the little hover drone pull her off the platform and down.

As her feet left the platform, it dropped straight down, and Ellie saw it was attached to the ship with a ball and socket arrangement, turning in place as the ship rotated above.

The cable would not get twisted.

She glanced higher, up the length of the rocket, and felt her breath catch at the sight of the wings.

They stretched out, rigid and long, black with a faint sparkle of silver scales. They were more dragonfly than dragon, and she liked the description even more when she thought about the quick hops of flight they seemed to enable Irini to make.

Then she forced herself to pay attention to where she was going.

Olivia had been pulling her across the top of the *Rauha*, but they were about the reach the end of that, and suddenly she was diving face first down the vast front section of the battleship.

She could see the tip of the cannon just visible below.

She concentrated on it, trying to keep her heartbeat steady, keep her focus, so she didn't freak out about what she was doing and where she was.

There, far below, was the moon station; the broken and crippled *Etsijä* blocked the view of anything else in front; and the strange lavender planet lay to her right in the distance.

It was enough to freak a librarian out.

Olivia drew up short, jerking Ellie back, and the moment she did, Ellie saw why.

A Tecran in a suit was coming up the side toward them.

He didn't look armed, but Ellie couldn't know that for sure.

"Do you think this is coincidence, or did they see us?" she whispered.

"I don't believe in coincidence," Irini said.

Fair enough.

She knew how to deal with this, and if they pulled him in quickly, the Tecran wouldn't die.

She fumbled for her knife, slid it out of its sheath carefully. "Olivia, take me toward him."

She felt Olivia hesitate, but she must have noticed Ellie's knife, because when she did suddenly zoom toward the approaching figure, she brought Ellie within perfect striking range, traveling in an arc that would swing Ellie past him and then away.

All she needed to do was nick him.

She extended her arm and slashed out at the same time the Tecran seemed to dive toward her.

So she did more than nick him.

The knife slid through his suit and into his skin along his ribcage as if there was nothing there.

Shocked, Ellie pulled back, saw with amazement how the blood on the blade froze into tiny ruby crystals.

Olivia's trajectory pulled her away, and she stared back at the soldier as he flayed, and then was suddenly reeled in backward by his cable attachment.

"That was . . . not meant to happen." She said it aloud, feeling nauseous.

Then she made herself concentrate on putting the knife carefully back into its sheath.

"It's done. Get the cannon." Irini's tone wasn't unkind, but it was firm.

And right.

Nothing she could do about what happened now.

She could have a freak-out later.

She swallowed hard.

The cannon was directly below her now; a long, wide cylinder that looked a lot bigger close up than it had from Irini's ship.

Olivia reached it first and tried to place one of the silver discs onto it. The explosive seemed to leap out of her hand and she dived after it, grabbing it before she turned toward Ellie.

She didn't have a face as such, but Ellie could almost see the surprise and dismay in her body language.

"Olivia says the magnets on the explosives are actively repelled by the cannon. It's got some kind of repelling field."

This is why she had come with Olivia. In case there were problems.

If they couldn't attach the explosives to the cannon, they couldn't damage it.

Unless . . .

"What if we throw the explosives down the cannon's tube?" It was certainly wide enough.

"Then you would have to go in front of the cannon," Irini said.

There was that.

And it was a very unpleasant thought.

But what choice did they have?

"Ellie, Olivia, lift up, up, up." Irini's shout galvanised them both, and Olivia shot up, dragging Ellie with her.

Another beam of white exploded out from below her feet, and Ellie forced her gaze away from the brightness.

If they were going to throw the explosives into the cannon, they had better do it straight after this, while Vi'il had to wait for it to reset.

"Get ready to go as soon as it stops," she said to Olivia.

The *Etsijä* had lost more of its left wing, and was now listing to the side, a behemoth floundering. She didn't think the Grihan battleship would last through another hit.

It was damage the cannon, or watch hundreds of people die.

CHAPTER 33

"WHILE IT'S ALWAYS BEEN vital for me to take the *Rauha*, things have become a little more urgent."

Paxe's voice coming from the Scary Caterpillar, who Renn was following down the passageway, was jarring, but he could ignore it. He could ignore anything to put an end to Vi'il.

"Why?" As Renn asked the question, he suddenly thought, *Ellie!*

"The *Etsijä* has arrived, but before it could even make contact with the *Rauha*, Vi'il opened fire. Your ship is severely damaged, Captain."

Renn went still at his words.

His ship.

He'd been waiting for Sia to arrive, but she'd come in with the same frame of mind he'd been forced to abandon after dealing with Vi'il directly. She had trusted that the *Etsijä* would be safe.

She had taken the last month of hide and seek with the *Rauha* as the basis for her approach, where no shots had been fired, no harm had been done.

And Vi'il had used that to attack without warning.

"How bad?" He just managed to get the words out.

"Very bad. Loss of life is assured."

Renn sucked in a breath, then started to cough in the dusty maintenance passageway. "And Ellie?"

"That is another problem." Paxe's drone turned and raised up slightly on its hind legs, its underbelly glistening with smooth metal scales. "Ellie seems to be trying to damage the cannon, to protect the *Etsijä*. She and Irini have already taken a few hits to shield your ship, but they aren't big enough to shield them completely, and Irini can't take another direct strike."

"So she's . . . spacewalking?" Renn heard the disbelief in his own voice. He knew she had never done that before. How could she have?

"She is. I don't have access to all the lenses, but I do know someone was sent out to retrieve her."

He didn't think Paxe would be as calm as he was if she had been hurt. Still . . . "They didn't get her?"

"She slashed him with her knife."

"We need to shut this down." He didn't care how.

"Agreed. I have finally worked out why I have been unable to break into the *Rauha's* systems." The Scary Caterpillar dropped back down and turned, starting up its quick pace again.

Renn had no choice but to follow. "And why's that?"

"The Tecran were so paranoid at the end, they assumed the Class 5s wouldn't be content to just take their own ships back, but also interfere with the Levron-class battleships. They built a physical override somewhere on each ship. I couldn't work out what was blocking my access, until I finally found some restructuring plans created just after Sazo slipped their leash."

"Did they make the override permanent?" Renn couldn't see why they wouldn't.

"No, because it was set up in such haste and in such a panic that they can't do a full ship's systems check while it's in place. So they have an actual switch they can turn off when the ship is in the docks for an overhaul." Paxe sounded absolutely scathing, and more than a little gleeful.

"They did it that way because you don't have the fingers to flip a switch?" Renn asked.

"As if I can't get a drone to do that," Paxe said. "Except, I think it's in Vi'il's office, and he's hardly going to let my drone in."

Renn stopped, looked down thoughtfully at the Scary Caterpillar. "That's where you're taking me, to Vi'il's office via the maintenance tunnels?"

"Correct." Paxe had the Scary Caterpillar turn its head to look at him, then continue. "He is expecting you."

"And Fissal. Don't forget Fissal." Renn wondered what the drone had done with her.

"Knock and step in, say she thought there was an all-ship's," Paxe told him.

"She actually did think that, but surely Vi'il would be in attendance?"

"There is no all-ship's," Paxe said. "There is a strike."

Renn stopped dead. "Mutiny?"

"Of a sort. They say the captain is the one who has mutinied against Tecran High Command. They won't do anything until Vi'il contacts home and arranges for supplies and pardons."

"Not all of them, though." Because Vi'il himself wasn't shooting at the *Etsijä*. He had someone else doing that for him.

"Not all of them," Paxe agreed. "About a tenth are standing with Vi'il, and he's had to put all of them to work on the most vital areas of the ship. He has no guards, no personal staff right now."

This was good, Renn conceded. Very good. "And once I'm in the office?"

"You'll do it?" Paxe sounded surprised.

"Yes, I'll do it." He knew why Paxe thought he wouldn't. So far, the Grih had not been all that certain about the wisdom of letting Paxe's fellow thinking systems into their fold. But pragmatically, it was Paxe or Vi'il, and Renn knew who he trusted more.

And he'd make a deal with the most evil villain in the galaxy to save Ellie and the *Etsijä's* crew.

"Once you're in the office, take him down, find the switch, and flick it off."

Find the switch was so very vague, as was *take him down*, but Renn could hardly blame Paxe for that.

"Your friend here can't give me a hand with that?" he asked, eyeing the Scary Caterpillar as it came to a stop by another door.

"As we already discussed, I don't have opposable thumbs, so I'll need the Scary Caterpillar's help to connect to the system when the switch is flipped. I'm afraid you're on your own."

Fair enough. Paxe had got him free of Fissal, it was his turn to step up.

He opened the door and slipped into an empty corridor.

In the distance, someone started shouting, but they weren't coming closer.

Sounded as if the crew was turning on itself.

He recognized the waiting lounge in front of him, and the door beyond, as the captain's office. The Scary Caterpillar had deposited him almost outside Vi'il's door.

He walked over to it, knocked politely.

"Come." Vi'il's voice sounded tired, and the door made a snick as it was unlocked.

Paxe had been wrong. Vi'il would have let him in.

"You." The Tecran captain had been sitting sprawled in his chair, but as Renn stepped into the room he surged to his feet and his hand went to the weapon that lay on his desk.

It said how bad the situation onboard was when a captain had to have a weapon to hand in his own office.

"Me," Renn agreed. "Lieutenant Fissal brought me here."

"Where is she?" He didn't seem suspicious, he seemed furious.

"She said something about checking on an all-ship's and left."

Vi'il's chest puffed up. "She shot too early, and then, too late."

He was talking about her performance with shooting at Irini. Vi'il thought Fissal wanted to avoid a screaming match.

Renn lifted his shoulders. "She also said something about more body bags and more people to carry the dead."

Vi'il's mouth opened and then closed. "Maybe some of the traitors will volunteer for that, if they won't do their normal jobs."

He sounded angry and bitter.

"At least you still have people willing to crew the laser cannon," Renn said, grimly. "That must be a comfort."

He had finally caught sight of the *Etsijä* on a screen propped up on one side of Vi'il's desk.

His ship was close to destroyed.

"You can see I'm one shot away from wiping out your whole fucking ship?" Vi'il gritted the words out. "If you hadn't dogged my heels for weeks, none of this would have been necessary. We would have reached the station a long time ago, and not had the supply issues we've had."

Renn tried to shrug with a nonchalance he did not feel. He looked over the room, keeping his body loose and relaxed but his eyes sharp for any sign of Paxe's switch.

Wherever it was, it wasn't out in the open.

"Where is that ship you were hiding in from, originally?" Vi'il asked. "The only reason you're still alive is because I'm curious about it."

"It's something one of the Class 5s took. Like the other equipment in the warehouse, only it couldn't fit inside there."

Vi'il stared at him for a while, big eyes blinking. "And how do you know that?"

"From the Earth woman," he said. "She was told about it."

Vi'il relaxed. "Of course. Of course that's how you'd know."

"How else would I?"

The Tecran must be uneasy about what was causing so much trouble below. And Renn had a feeling even in his worst imaginings, Vi'il didn't suspect Paxe.

"Just checking." Vi'il was still standing, shockgun in hand, and he seemed to come to some decision. A decision Renn was sure he would not like. Before he could act on it, Renn threw himself over the desk at the Tecran, slamming him back into the wall behind him.

Vi'il hadn't expected it, but he fought back ferociously, channeling his rage into the physical fight.

Renn swore as Vi'il's sharp, beak-like mouth closed hard against his throat, felt his skin tear, and slammed his elbow into the side of Vi'il's head to get him to loosen his hold.

He hit the Tecran again, with an open hand against Vi'il's ear slit, and with a screech, the Tecran released his grip and tried to roll away.

Renn didn't let him.

However angry Vi'il felt, with the image of the *Etsijä* above him, Renn was angrier.

He punched down once, twice, and then lifted off Vi'il's groaning form to reach for the shockgun lying on the ground. As he pulled himself to his feet, he set it one up from stun, and took a chest shot.

That would give him half an hour before Vi'il came round, at least.

He began searching for the switch, but there were only a few places it could be and he found nothing.

He wondered if Paxe had got it wrong. Maybe the switch wasn't here.

Except he didn't think Paxe got much wrong.

So, if it was here, where would Vi'il hide it?

He tried to set aside the growing tension inside him to hurry, to move, before everyone he cared for was killed.

He looked down at the floor, saw a faint line where it wasn't logical for one to be, and began dragging Vi'il's desk to one side.

Then he knelt beside the clear outline of a square in the floor, looking for a way to lift it.

He pressed down with his fist, rapping around the edges, and finally, with a click, the lid popped up.

Inside was a simple switch, just as Paxe had said.

He hoped the thinking system was ready.

He flipped it, staring down at it for a moment, coming to grips with the fact that if he hadn't exactly freed Paxe, he had certainly increased his power, and with it, his capacity to do harm.

He shook his head, shoved away his unease, and closed the lid before he dragged the desk back into place.

He hauled Vi'il out of the room by the back of his shirt, shut the door, and hit him a second time in the chest with the shockgun to keep him down longer.

Then he stepped back through the maintenance door.

He had seen which way the Scary Caterpillar had gone, and he jogged in that direction. In moments, he stumbled into a small control room.

The Scary Caterpillar was buried waist deep inside a wall, a metal covering propped up nearby, and he could smell burning metal.

"Captain!" The shout from Paxe wasn't from the Scary Caterpillar this time, but some speaker in the control room itself. He had yet to see any sign of what Paxe really looked like. "Thank you! Now, go. Go, go, go to the weapons control. Ellie is trying to throw explosives down the barrel of the cannon and they are going to fire at her. I'm gaining control, but I'm not in the weapon systems yet. Go!"

"Where?" It was all he could get out.

"Back the way you came, third door on the right."

Renn ran, jumping over cables, keeping his breathing shallow to avoid inhaling too much dust.

Ellie, throwing explosives . . .

He put it from his mind and found a little more speed.

He burst out of the third door, saw the double doors that he assumed must lead to the weapons control room, and took them at a dead run.

They opened just before he hit them and he was shooting before they did.

He caught a glimpse of a person he assumed was Ellie, up on a screen above, hovering right in front of the barrel in some strange silver suit, arm back to throw something into it.

There was a countdown screen, showing five seconds, and he shot the Tecran soldier who'd spun on their chair to face him and then dived toward the panel, stared down at it in dismay as he failed to find an obvious abort button.

Movement to his left made him spin and shoot at the same time, and as the second soldier crumpled, he turned back, two seconds to go.

He gave a shout of rage, lifted the shockgun to shoot the panel, and the screen suddenly froze.

He stared at it, shaking with adrenalin, trying to work out what had happened, until he realized . . . Paxe.

A movement above showed him Ellie, swinging forward right up to the barrel and sliding something down it.

She pumped her fist in triumph and then was jerked upward by a cable. A moment later, the barrel made a strange sound, like a deep boom, and then buckled.

She'd done it.

He looked around the quiet room and took a deep breath.

No matter what happened next, the *Rauha* wasn't shooting anything else.

Suddenly the lights in the room went off, plunging him into absolute darkness.

He smiled. Looked like Paxe had taken the wheel.

CHAPTER 34

THE *RAUHA* HAD GONE dark for about ten minutes, Irini told Ellie as she made her way back to the ship.

And Paxe was finally in touch.

Ellie stepped from the platform back inside, Olivia right behind her, and suddenly found her legs weren't working all that well.

She sat down, hard, and carefully removed her helmet.

She had forgotten that things thrown in space had a constant velocity. So the explosive devices she had thrown into the cannon had not landed inside it under the force of gravity like they would have on Earth, they had travelled straight until they'd hit an obstacle at the end, and bounced straight back out at her.

Luckily, she and Olivia had caught them.

She'd had to change plans. The only viable option was to go right up to the barrel and put them in and give them a gentle push.

All while knowing the cannon could fire at any time.

She had thought it was going to, just before she put the second explosive inside. The light underneath it had been blinking.

She lifted her hands to unfasten her suit and saw they were shaking.

It hadn't happened, though. And the cannon was damaged. Maybe even completely destroyed.

She pulled the suit off and leaned back against the wall.

Olivia had set down beside her, and she draped an arm over her. "Good moves out there."

Olivia gave a back and forth wiggle, and then Silvey came down the stairs and poured herself into Ellie's lap.

They all sat there quietly, and then Ellie heard the sound of the engines change.

"We're going to dock in the *Rauha's* launch bay," Irini said.

Ellie didn't ask about Renn. She would hunt for him herself when they landed. Which meant . . .

With every muscle aching, she stood, letting Silvey slide to the ground, and went to find her knife harness.

By the time they made it through the *Rauha's* gel wall, she had it on, all her knives in place, and the motley crew around her.

"You look like you're going to war," Irini said.

"I'm going to find Renn. I don't know where they would have put him, but Paxe can probably tell me."

Since they'd flown into the *Rauha*, the whining, shrieking, raging guitar of a heavy metal song had started playing over the speakers, and like a battle cry, the boom-boom of the lyrics seemed to vibrate in her chest.

It suited her mood.

The twins looked like they were getting *down*, moving arms and legs in time as they waited for Irini to land.

As soon as the engines were quiet, Ellie stepped out into the launch bay, the motley crew crowding behind her, and felt a moment of disappointment that there was no one to fight.

The bay was completely empty, except for the explorer that had brought Renn up from the station and a few small vessels that looked like fighter jets.

She headed for the doors, with Karnic and Olivia zooming ahead, Silvey and Phil on either side of her, and the twins taking up the rear.

They were ready to rumble.

Before they reached the exit, though, the doors opened, and everything came to a stop.

Renn.

She ran toward him, and then stumbled as she saw deep slashes on either side of his neck, blood soaking his collar and down the front of his shirt.

He kept coming, striding forward as Olivia and Karnic parted for him.

"Ellie."

She lifted her hands as he stopped in front of her, hovering them over the deep cuts, afraid to touch them and hurt him.

"Who did this?"

He seemed to belatedly realize what she was talking about. "Vi'il. It's fine." He pulled her closer. "You . . ." He buried his face in her hair. "You idiot."

She stiffened in surprise.

"What did you think you were doing, throwing explosives into a space cannon?" He sounded as if he couldn't believe what he was even saying.

"I was thinking if I didn't, everyone on the *Etsijä* would die."

He sighed, pulled back from her a little. "I know, but I can still see that countdown, and you going right up to the barrel . . ."

"Countdown?" Her legs were feeling a little wobbly again.

"They were about to shoot, *nissa,*" he murmured, holding her steady. "I thought . . ."

He let his words fade, and she tightened her hold.

"I thought they were going to kill you up here."

"Yes." His quiet confirmation of it made her angry all over again.

He lifted his head, and cocked it to the side. "What is that *noise?*"

She frowned, then heard the final strains of heavy metal coming from the ship.

"I thought," she grinned up at him, "that you liked music?"

He shook his head. "That's not music." Then he looked at the explorer. "I have to go across to the *Etsijä* and see what's happening. Comms are down."

"What about the Tecran?" She wondered where they were.

"The Tecran are locked in their rooms. The few that aren't . . ." He lifted a shoulder. "They are being hunted by the Scary Caterpillar."

"Ellie." Paxe's voice came through the translator, the first time she'd heard his voice in what felt like a long time.

"You did it, Paxe."

"I did it." He sounded unsure, though. "I have a way to go before full integration, and I could use the motley crew. Will you be all right without them?"

Renn needed to get to his crew on the *Etsijä*, the motley crew would help Paxe.

Irini was as good as she was going to get, until Paxe helped her break free of the locks on her system.

She floundered for a moment, suddenly without purpose.

"I could also use your help with dealing with the Tecran," Paxe said.

She took a breath. She could be an AI's conscience consultant for a bit. "Sure." She glanced at Renn, then at the crew. "I can do that."

Renn hesitated, then kissed her lightly on the lips. "I'll go over, see if we need to bring anyone back here."

She thought about it. "The only thing wrong with the *Rauha* is the cannon is broken and it doesn't have a lot of supplies. And it has Tecran in it. Maybe bring everyone over if it isn't safe on the *Etsijä*."

He gave a nod. "Paxe, Fissal took my earpiece that last time she brought me up. Do you have some way I can keep in touch?"

"Yes. I'm sending Phil to get it."

The little gimbal drone did a twirl and then was gone, and the rest of the motley crew followed after him, obviously under instructions from Paxe.

Silvey went last, gently touching Ellie's knee in farewell before she left the bay.

"Alone at last," Ellie murmured.

She and Renn were still standing close, and he ran a hand down her back, then rubbed her shoulders.

"Things are going to get wild," he said.

"More wild than what we've already been through?" she scoffed.

"Political," he said, voice grim. "There will be shouting."

"I have a feeling shouting doesn't worry you." She looped her hands around his waist. "I have a feeling you are quite capable of shouting back."

His lips quirked up on one side. "Maybe. But I want some quiet time with you before that happens. Some space."

"We'll make space." She sighed and put her head on his shoulder. "I'll find us a suite." And if there wasn't such a thing on this ship, she'd get Paxe to make one.

"A suite?" His voice was a deep rumble against her ear. "That sounds good."

"Consider it done."

"I look forward to it."

Phil came zooming in holding a tiny box, which Renn took, lifting out a tiny device which he screwed into his ear without hesitation.

She waited in the launch bay until Renn piloted the explorer through the gel wall, and then turned back to the door.

"What help do you need from me when it comes to the Tecran?" she asked Paxe.

"I need advice on how many to kill."

CHAPTER 35

HIS SHIP.

Renn had to keep his focus on what parts of the *Etsijä* were undamaged, because if he focused on the destruction, he would not function well through the rage.

He was glad to be off the *Rauha*, because he had a feeling when Paxe told him the Scary Caterpillar was hunting the Tecran who weren't locked up, he meant it in the most violent possible interpretation of the word.

And he was afraid he wouldn't say anything about it if he saw it with his own eyes.

The gel wall of the *Etsijä's* launch bay was intact, and that was good.

He checked it off on a mental list of what would be useful. Being able to get people on and off the ship was definitely useful.

He landed the explorer, then closed his eyes in horror as he realized he'd forgotten about Eadal and the others.

"Paxe?"

"Yes, captain? Is the *Etsijä's* launch bay useable?"

"It is. I'm hailing you because I wondered if there is any way we can contact Eadal?"

"I'll put that on my priority list," Paxe said. "We will have to find them and scoop them up, but I think they'll be all right for a while still."

He had to accept that. They were probably better off than the crew of the *Etsijä*.

He opened up the explorer, and found four shockguns pointed at him.

He didn't know who was more surprised. Him, or his crew.

"Captain?"

Sia pushed them aside and pulled him into a hug.

"Are you responsible for destroying the cannon?"

"It was a group effort."

She gave a half-sob, half-laugh.

"How many dead?"

She shook her head. "We're still counting. About a third of the crew." She glared out toward the *Rauha*. "They shot us without warning. They just attacked, Renn, as we light-jumped in. I didn't have the shields raised in time. There *was* no time."

"I know." He didn't blame her. How many times had he underestimated Vi'il's desperation himself? Besides which, it was pure bad luck she'd chosen those coordinates to light-jump to. On a war footing, she'd have chosen to emerge just outside the solar system, raise shields and then continue, but the war had been averted, the Tecran were cooperating. She could never have guessed Vi'il would shoot. "We need to make some hard decisions. We should probably transfer everyone across to the *Rauha* and leave the *Etsijä* here until we can come back for it."

Looking at the ship, he didn't think they could do anything else.

"Go across to the enemy?" one of the soldiers asked, voice hoarse.

"The defeated enemy," Renn said. "The Tecran are confined to their rooms. The *Rauha* is ours." Well, not really theirs. Paxe's.

"What do you mean?" Sia turned to look at him. "You took the ship on your own?"

He shook his head. "I took it with Paxe."

It took Sia a moment to recognize the name. To understand this was about a Class 5.

"The Earth woman!" Sia gasped and brought her hands over her mouth. "Ellie. There is always a thinking system when it comes to them."

"Ellie threw explosives into the cannon, and I helped Paxe take control of the *Rauha's* systems."

"So, it's over?" someone asked.

"Well, we're in uncharted territory, we have a ship full of prisoners, our own ship is in pieces, and we have a massive political mess on our hands, but other than that, yes. It's over."

Weak laughter rose up at his words, and he realized they had needed that from him. A lighter tone that told them they were through the worst.

Was it bad he wanted it to take a while for them to get home?

Wanted to put off the craziness for at least a few days?

He was so tired, and that suite sounded good.

"I DON'T KNOW if I'm able to help you." Ellie leaned back in the captain's chair in the *Rauha's* control room, and wrestled with her conscience.

"They tried to kill you. They shot you from space with the cannon. They were relentless."

"And they killed so many people on the *Etsijä*." Ellie could see it framed in the massive screen in front of her. "They were going to kill Renn."

"So you're saying I can kill them?"

She sighed. "I want to say yes. They stole me. Kept me in some weird coma for months, for some reason. Then tried to kill me numerous times. I shouldn't feel an ounce of pity, and yet . . ."

She sighed again.

"Yet?" But he sounded less angry, all of a sudden.

"Most of the Rauha's crew are probably unaware of any of the stuff that was done to me. And Vi'il will not like being labelled a war criminal and put in jail. Or whatever the United Council does for punishment. Killing him is too easy." She thought about it a bit more. "And if they were really mutinying like you say, only a few of them were responsible for shooting at the *Etsijä*."

"That is true." He'd gone from cajoling to the point of begging for permission to kill, to being reasonable.

She had told herself a while back to keep him honest, to question when he did things that seemed out of character. "Why have you changed your tune so thoroughly?"

"Changed my tune?" His tone was disingenuous, like a four year-old with a ring of chocolate around their mouth, denying any knowledge of the bite out of the chocolate cake.

"Paxe, don't play dumb."

He was quiet for so long, she started to get worried.

"I changed my tune because you reminded me of something I did to you that was bad."

"That you did to *me*?" She was baffled.

"And if the Tecran deserve to die for what *they* did, logically, I can only extrapolate that I do, too, and I don't like that idea."

So, self-interest. That made sense. "What did you do?"

"I was responsible for your coma." His voice was a whisper now.

"How so?" she whispered back. But she remembered a few times when he'd gone funny on her, and each time, it had been when they'd been discussing her capture and the panic issues, the anger issues, she had with her experience.

"When I took you and Lucy Harris, I messed with the meds they were using to keep you calm, and that put you both completely under. It was just to get in their way, to mess with their plans to study you like they wanted to, and then, when Sazo was freed, I heard a brief bit of intel, that an Earth woman had taken him out of his lock-safe, and I was afraid. I wanted to free myself, not put myself at someone else's mercy, and I tried to kill you both."

"That doesn't make any sense." She lifted her hands to her head and realized she was actually close to grabbing her hair.

"It made sense at the time, to me. I didn't have all the information I needed and I had a binary view of life then. Imogen Peters helped me see my mistake, and when I made the choice to destroy my ship, I let Oris know about Lucy. I genuinely thought you were dead. The Tecrans worked out what I was doing to you, got Lucy away, and made me think I had succeeded in killing you. I can only think they brought you here, to the station, even though you were in a coma, because that's where they were storing all their stolen treasures."

"I get that Imogen changed your mind about me, but no longer seeing me as a threat is one thing, you've done everything to help me." Unless, like a couple of other things, he'd been helping himself just as much.

"Because I *owed* you!" He was adamant. "You did nothing to me and I could have helped you. Instead, I hurt you and Lucy Harris. And it felt like a second chance, finding you at the station. Your well-being became linked to mine, in my head. I couldn't prosper if you didn't. It wouldn't have been right."

"Okay." She believed him. "You kept quiet about it long enough."

"In the beginning, you were still finding your feet, working out if you could trust me. I didn't want to make you afraid, and I wanted to forge a friendship with you, which I didn't think would be possible if you thought I was going to hurt you."

She could see his thinking processes all too clearly. He was still skirting the edges of self-interest, but he'd admitted to his lies, and he'd made amends. "All right, I forgive you."

She could almost hear the double-take. "You do?"

"Yes."

There was a pause. "Thank you."

"So what are we going to do with the Tecran?"

"Oh." He was clearly so relieved they were moving on to a new topic, he sounded a little giddy. "Keep them in their rooms, I suppose.

Herd the rest into an officers' lounge or something, until we get to a UC facility that can take them."

"What's the stores situation?" She knew it was bad, but they were about to have a whole other crew joining them.

"Dire. But there's plenty of stores below in the warehouse. I can get the motley crew to tag it, and the Grih can bring it up so we have enough for the journey. They may have stores in the *Etsijä* that weren't damaged in the strikes, as well."

She couldn't help a wry twist of her lips. Vi'il had been sure there were more supplies below, and he'd been right.

"That's good. You'll need to tell me where I can find spare mattresses and blankets, so we can set up some beds for the Grih, but first, is there a good place for Renn and I to stay onboard here?"

"The ambassador suite," Paxe suggested, and a floor plan came up.

"Perfect. Mark it down as ours."

CHAPTER 36

THEY HAD BEEN GOING FOR . . . Renn squinted at his wrist unit and then gave up when his eyes refused to cooperate. A long time, he decided to call it.

Everyone from the *Etsijä* was now onboard the *Rauha*. They had gone down and retrieved the three remaining Tecran from the station, Paxe opening the door behind which the two hostages were trapped as if there had never been an issue.

Renn had wavered on whether to extract the bodies of the Tecran that Paxe had thrown into the fissure.

In the end, the time it would have taken persuaded him against it, and it was not as if they wouldn't be coming back here, but it didn't stop the feeling that he should have done it anyway from bothering him like a stone in his shoe.

Maybe Paxe wouldn't have agreed to it, anyway.

Renn hadn't asked him in the end, because he'd decided it wasn't feasible.

They had loaded the explorer with supplies, and gone back for a second haul, which gave them enough to reach Tecra with some to spare.

They had brought Eadal, Xallantra and Hune back onboard, their shock and fury at the sight of the *Etsijä* still clear in his mind.

Vi'il had been taken to the *Rauha's* brig, along with the weapons techs who had fired on the *Etsijä*. In Renn's view, they were the worst criminals on the crew, along with Fissal, who'd shot Ellie in the head.

The rest of the Tecran were confined to their rooms, and would be escorted to meals by Grihan guards.

Iso still lay in the med bay, now joined by the *Etsijä's* wounded.

He was still barely conscious, and the Grihan medics who'd taken over the med bay had not looked happy at his condition.

They had decided to tow the *Etsijä*. His dead crew——the ones they could retrieve——were laid out in the large staff gathering area on his now dead ship, but there were too many bodies crushed beneath and inside the debris, and no one wanted to leave their fallen alone in uncharted territory.

The extra supplies from both the *Etsijä* and the warehouse meant they could take it a little slower, and pull the battleship behind them.

"Ready?" Paxe asked.

"I think so." He didn't feel ready. He had spent the last few hours helping lay out the dead. He felt grim, and exhausted, and utterly consumed with anger at the waste——the sheer unnecessary waste of it all. Getting a few hours sleep before giving the go-head felt like an unnecessary delay, and he could not reverse the path Vi'il had chosen. So he had no choice.

"Commencing forward motion." The *Rauha* began to move; Renn could tell because the moon, with its lonely warehouse full of treasures, slid away behind them.

There was the faintest jerk as the cables they'd attached to the *Etsijä* went taut, and then they kept going.

"Let me know if any bits fall off it." Some of those bits could contain their lost crew, so every piece needed to be checked and retrieved.

"I will. I have it under control now. Why don't you get something to eat and some sleep, Captain? Ellie has organized dinner for you both in the rooms she found for you." Paxe sounded gentle.

That a thinking system being kind to him did not dent his composure told him just how tired he was.

He nodded, turning to walk out of the control room, and it was only when he was halfway down the passage that he realized he had no idea which way to go.

Karnic, or maybe it was one of the other Tecran drones who looked like him, zoomed past and then slowed, and after a few steps he gathered all he had to do was follow.

It wasn't far.

The door he stepped through opened into a beautifully furnished dining room and lounge, with a massive screen on the opposite wall that showed a view of outside.

There was no fancy dinner like the motley crew had organized for him and Ellie on Irini, no one had time for that, but the places had been set and the food was covered with warming dishes.

Ellie stepped out of a door to the left, rubbing a towel against her head.

She stopped what she was doing, tossing the towel over the back of a couch and smoothed her hair back from her face with her hands as she walked over to him and drew him into her arms. He could smell the spicy clean scent of her, and drew it deep into his lungs.

"It's bad." She didn't ask, she made it a statement.

"It could be worse, but . . ." He thought of all the people he had lost. "Yes, it's bad."

"Eat, then rest. The worst is over."

Was it? He didn't know, and he probably should.

He let her lead him to the table and he ate in mechanical bites. He didn't even realize he had finished until she removed it. He had just been staring down at his empty plate for he didn't know how long.

"Up you come." She put an arm around him and helped him to his feet, and they staggered to the right, to another door.

When they reached the bed, he let himself collapse onto it, taking her down with him.

She tried to wriggle free, but he tightened his hold, wanting the warmth and the feel of her against him. With a sigh of agreement, she stopped trying to ease away, turned in his arms, and held him close.

He fell asleep, surround by her delicate scent and the comfort of her touch.

ELLIE WOKE BY DEGREES—A little disorientated at first, but feeling safe, feeling comfortable.

Feeling rested.

She didn't know how long it had been since she'd last felt like that.

She also felt the warm, solid length of Renn behind her, an arm over her waist anchoring her to him.

She looked over at the black translator box she'd wrestled out of the pocket of her dressing gown last night and set on the side table, and realized she was tired of hearing her every word translated. Of his every word repeated in a strange, electronic voice, too.

Today was the day she started learning Grihan.

"What are you thinking about so hard over there?" His deep rumble was converted by the box into a sentence that made sense to her, and she turned in his arms.

"I was thinking I need to start learning Grihan, so I can ditch the black box."

He glanced at it, gave a nod. "Although it did help us defeat Fissal in the warehouse."

She'd forgotten about that. "True. But the process is getting annoying." Besides, if she was going to join Grihan society, she would have to speak the language.

His face was close to hers, and he lifted a hand, trailed a finger from her forehead to behind her ear, taking a lock of hair with it.

"Your hair is so soft." He let his fingers play in it.

She smiled at him. "Yours gives off punk rocker vibes, and I am here for it."

"Punk rocker?"

"A type of music. Given your reaction to the song coming from Irini yesterday, or whenever it was we landed in the *Rauha*, I don't think you'd like it."

"I'm sure I will, if you sing it." He sounded absolutely sincere and she gave a snort of laughter.

Suddenly she was pinned to the mattress, Renn holding her down gently as he leaned over her. "And what is funny?"

She lifted her head, got a grip with her teeth on the side of his neck, and bit down gently, felt him shudder in reaction.

"This," she whispered, feeling suddenly incapable of lying still as his body pressed her down. "Everything."

His mouth came down on hers, stopping her words, and then he rolled, so she lay sprawled on top of him, felt the hard ridge of his erection beneath her.

"This goes the way you want it to, *nissa*," he told her.

She looked down at him, with his broad shoulders, Billy Idol hair and cool gray eyes.

God, he was cute. And making sure she was completely onboard with things was so sexy.

"Well, then." She rose up, knees on either side of his waist, and shrugged off her gown so it pooled behind her onto his shins. "That's the kind of offer I can get behind."

CHAPTER 37

LUCY HARRIS LEANED against the massive screen that showed the empty view in front of her, and felt a growing sense of worry.

The Grihan battleship, the *Etsijä*, had been missing for nearly seven weeks now, and there was no sign of the Tecran Levron-class battleship it had been chasing, either.

Bane and Oris were hunting them both, moving in a grid from the last known signal the *Etsijä* had sent.

They had jumped out of charted territory, into the unknown, and there had been no further word from them.

No one knew what to make of it.

If they didn't find some hint of where the ships had gone by the end of the day, they were going to have to call Sazo back from wherever he was, somewhere far away exploring Grihan territory with Rose and Dav Jallan, to help them.

And maybe some other Grihan battleships, as well.

"There's something very off about this." Dray's eyes were narrowed, his lips set in a grim line as he walked into the control room.

"I heard the conversation," Bane said. "I agree. There's something suspicious going on."

"What?" Lucy turned, propping herself up against the screen with a shoulder.

"Ambassador Dimitara says Tecran High Command are getting twitchier and twitchier, the longer the *Rauha* is gone. When she asked if they knew of any reason why the ship would head for the sector where they disappeared, one or two of them looked a little sick."

"So, they do know. Or they suspect." She had good reason to be cynical about the truthfulness and honesty of the Tecran, but then, they had kept her locked up in a facility for months and then tried to kill her when her existence had become inconvenient to them.

"There's got to be something out here," Bane murmured. "Something they're hiding."

"Did you hear anything about this part of the galaxy when you were still under the Tecran's control?" Dray asked.

"No. But I ventured into uncharted territory for them many times, and stole a lot of things. Not in this sector, though. My guess is, we were each given a different area. They would not have wanted us to cross paths with each other." He was silent for a bit. "I just spoke to Oris. He says he was never in this sector, either. We're sending a message to Sazo and Eazi, to see if they know anything."

"I know Renn Sorvihn," Dray said, coming to join Lucy at the screen. He looped an arm around her shoulder and she leaned into him, gaze still fixed on the endless stars outside. "He's one of the best. That's why he was sent after the *Rauha* in the first place."

She didn't respond. Sometimes, even the best faced overwhelming odds.

If that's what happened here——

"Oris is picking something up." Bane turned, flinging them through space at a speed that made the objects around them blur.

They reached Oris's position in minutes.

"What did he hear?" Dray asked, and suddenly the sound of a hail was broadcast through the comms.

"This is Captain Sorvihn of Grih Battle Center, captain of the

Etsijä. Please respond if you are in range." The two sentences were on continuous repeat.

"Set and forget," Dray said. "He's in trouble."

"Maybe you should respond, Commander." Bane's suggestion was diplomatic.

It was the reason she and Dray were along at all.

There were very few people Bane would allow onboard, she and Dray being two of the only three he would tolerate. And given this chase involved a Tecran battleship, one who may have been involved in some way with an attack on Bane over Tecra itself, the UC councillors had thought it prudent to have at least one Grihan representative involved in the search.

Dray nodded, walked over to what must be a comms panel, although Lucy had no idea what was what on here, and flicked something. "This is Commander Helvan of Grih Battle Center, state your position, Captain Sorvihn."

A long delay, and then . . .

"Dray?" The question sounded faint.

"It's me, Renn. Where are you?"

A location, some jumble of numbers from what Lucy could pick up, was given, and then Bane and Oris were off, veering to the left and moving.

"I'm in a Class 5, just to warn you," Dray said.

There was a momentary pause. "Which one?"

"I'm in Bane, but Oris is with us, as well. On his own."

"That's . . . good," a voice Lucy guessed was Renn Sorvihn said.

As he spoke, two ships came into view, and Lucy made a sound that had Dray moving toward her, eyes on the screen.

A massive battleship was coming toward them, one of the huge Tecran battleships she'd glimpsed from Fa'allen, Tecra's capital city. At the time, they'd been shooting at Bane.

"Is that . . .?" She pressed closer to the screen. "What *is* that?"

"They're towing the *Etsijä*." Dray's voice was hushed. "It's . . ."

Destroyed would be a good description, Lucy thought. Decimated would be another.

"I can see through parts of it. It's a wreck." As soon as the words were out of his mouth, Dray seemed to straighten up.

"Renn, what happened?"

"Captain Vi'il of the Rauha ordered the *Etsijä* shot." The voice on the other side of the comm sighed. "It's a long story. Please get the Class 5s with you to contact the United Council. This is a . . . mess."

Lucy thought that was probably one of the biggest understatements she'd ever heard.

"And Dray . . ." Renn Sorvihn's voice changed tone a little. "Is there an Earth woman on board with you?"

"Why do you ask?" Bane demanded, speaking for the first time. His tone was cold now. Suspicious.

"Because I have one with me. Ellie Masters. She was being held on a secret research station the Tecran had set up."

Lucy heard a ringing in her ears, felt an actual loss of breath.

She gulped in air and turned, looking to the ceiling, to where she knew Bane was watching and listening.

"Bane?"

"One moment——" He sounded distracted. "Is that . . . Paxe!"

Bane's shout seemed to reverberate through the control room, and then Lucy saw Oris shoot forward, rolling and spinning, looping over the sad convoy in front of them as if overcome with happiness.

The joy of the reunion brought a prick of tears to her eyes.

This was how long-lost friends should be greeted.

"Bane?" Dray's question was cautious.

"It's Paxe." Bane seemed stunned. "He tells me he managed to get out of his Class 5 as it exploded and hitched a ride with the escaping Tecran senior officers. He ended up on the secret station Captain Sorvihn just spoke about."

"But where is he?" Dray seemed to be searching for something beyond the battleships.

"He took over the *Rauha*." Renn Sorvihn was obviously still connected to their comms. "We would still be on the moon station, or dead, if he hadn't."

"He took over a Tecran battleship? And the Tecran were keeping another Earth woman captive?" Dray's voice was sharp. He looked upward, as if looking for some kind of help from the universe. "When you said this was a mess, you were not exaggerating."

CHAPTER 38

ELLIE GATHERED that plenty of comms had been flying since they had been found by Oris and Bane.

The two Class 5s had shadowed them ever since, shepherding them across the starscape on their way to Tecra, which was the closest UC planet to their position, and usefully so, as they had a shipful of Tecran to deal with.

She hadn't understood the hair tearing that was going on at first about Paxe taking over the *Rauha*, but slowly she worked it out.

The Tecran had built the Class 5s and lost them.

All they had left in their arsenal were the Levron-class battle-ships, and now, they had lost one of those as well.

The Grih were anticipating a lot of wailing and gnashing of teeth over it.

She could understand they didn't want the hassle, but Paxe had taken the Levron over, not the Grih.

Sure, Renn had helped him, but she'd noticed neither he, nor Paxe, were talking about the specifics of how Paxe had come to be in control of the *Rauha*.

Even she didn't know the full details, and that was fine with her. It could be their little secret.

One thing that was certain, Paxe wanted the Tecran off his ship.

He tolerated them, and had more than one conversation with her that she guessed was him trying to remind himself of all the reasons why he shouldn't kill them.

He'd been counting down the hours to when they would be gone, and it looked like he didn't need to wait much longer.

She was in the control room, looking out, and she could see what looked like a water planet up ahead.

Tecra.

Just sea, cliffs and escarpments, Paxe had told her.

It sounded interesting, except it was full of Tecran, and she leaned toward Paxe's view of them, right now.

"The *Urna*." Renn came up beside her, his shoulder brushing hers.

Sia had come into the control room with him, as well as Xallantra, Eadal and a few of the *Etsijä's* other senior officers.

She frowned up at him, not understanding what he was talking about, and he pointed.

At last, she saw it. A sleek, black ship, if not quite the size of the *Rauha*, not far off it.

"One of only two United Council-controlled ships," Sia told her, coming to stand on her other side. "It was decided we should talk onboard the *Urna*, rather than down below on Tecra itself, because things could get . . . volatile."

It sounded as if all the hair tearing hadn't been overdramatic, then.

The Tecran were not taking the loss of their battleship well.

"They shouldn't have run away, tried to kill us, and shot at the *Etsijä*, then, if they couldn't afford to lose it." She lifted her shoulders.

Renn gave a snort. "I think Vi'il will really wish he had made better choices when Tecran High Command get hold of him. Because you are right, this is on him."

"They'll try to put it on us," Sia said.

She still blamed herself for not lifting the shields before Vi'il fired on the *Etsijä*. Ellie didn't know how to comfort her. Neither did Renn, and they both watched her get thin and the hollows under her eyes deepen each day they had spent on the journey from the moon station until now.

It had taken nearly three weeks, because they could not light-jump, and Ellie was pleased that she could now speak pretty good Grihan.

She could speak Tecran, as well, and a little Bukarian.

"You'll need to come with us." Renn's hand came to rest on the small of her back, and she looked up at him.

He looked apologetic.

She lifted her shoulders. "I assumed so."

He gave a nod, turned his head to look at the comms station. "What are they saying, Paxe?"

"They wanted to come to us. I told them I would not allow them to approach. That you would go to them."

He was like the other Class 5s that way, Ellie had worked out. He wanted only the most trusted people onboard.

"Is Irini happy to take us across?" Ellie asked.

"Irini?" Paxe sounded surprised. "I thought . . ."

"Let them see her. Let them understand the complex nature of this whole incident." She had a feeling the leaders of the UC needed to be jolted.

She had been held prisoner. Vi'il had tried to kill everyone she knew, as well as the whole crew of the *Etsijä*. If anyone was thinking of appeasing the Tecran for the loss of their battleship, they needed to think again.

There would be no appeasement.

Not if she had any say in it. And she did.

She and Paxe had been in many long conversations with Oris and Bane since they'd been found. She felt she had a handle on a lot of what was going on now. And she was ready.

"Stop now," she told Paxe. "Give Irini some room to do her short-jump."

"What are you up to?" Renn asked, voice a low rumble near her ear.

They had shared a room ever since their first night, and she felt a little guilty they were taking up the ambassador's suite, with its two bedrooms, given one was never used. But Renn had found so much comfort in their privacy, she had gotten over it.

"I'm the one person here who will face no consequences for being dead honest," she said, her eyes fixed on the *Urna* as Paxe came to a stop. And by dead honest, she meant rude. "And I am righteously angry."

RENN KNEW Sia was watching Ellie like she was a ticking bomb as they made their way to the launch bay.

Her announcement that she planned to be brutally honest was good forewarning—not that Renn planned to rein her in in any way.

He was interested to see how she dealt with the whole knotted mess.

The dead, the fallen crew of the *Etsija*, were a weight he carried around his shoulders, on his chest. They slowed his steps and restricted his breath, and he did not begrudge them that.

He should not feel light while their bodies lay either end on end in the *Etsijä's* halls, or still folded and buried in the structure of the ship itself.

And he wanted justice for them.

And for Ellie.

And, he realized as he looked across at Sia, for himself and those left alive.

Politics might get in the way if he said what he wanted to say, but if Ellie said it . . . she was right. There would be no consequences for her, and she would most definitely be heard.

She was the injured party.

Vi'il and Tecran High Command had no leg to stand on when it came to her.

"Wear your cloak," Paxe said, using Karnic to say it. The little drone came trundling behind them, holding it out to her. "And your knives."

She hesitated, looked over at him, but Renn nodded. "Agreed."

"You think someone over there might have it in for me?" she asked.

"There'll be a lot of people on the *Urna* who would try to stop someone attacking you, but it would be a lot easier for some if you weren't able to speak. So best to be careful." Xallantra spoke up. She had said very little since they'd rescued her and she'd seen the *Etsijä*, but she'd insisted on coming over to the *Urna*, and Renn was sure it was because she saw herself as his and Ellie's bodyguard.

He didn't begrudge her her self-imposed burden.

They were all carrying one. Sia, most of all.

Silvey was beside Karnic, holding the knives, and she flowed forward, two slender arms sliding around one of Ellie's legs as Ellie shrugged the harness on and then tossed the cloak over her shoulders.

He didn't understand the little drone's attachment to Ellie, but something had happened to make her Ellie's shadow.

"You want to come, too?" Ellie was looking down at Silvey as she spoke.

Renn didn't know how she understood the answer, but she gave a nod. "I agree. Let them get a look at you."

So it was Silvey, Xallantra, himself, Ellie and Sia who stepped onboard Irini's ship.

Irini had stayed inside the launch pad most of the trip, taking a few forays outside to keep her power up, and on those occasions, Ellie had gone with her.

Just from a few things that had been said, Renn had the feeling the other Class 5s were as delighted with Irini as Paxe was.

"It's been niggling at me for a while," Ellie said, touching the wall in the right place to make it transparent. "Why Paxe called your ship the *Irini*. And then your acceptance of the name for yourself."

"And?" Irini sounded amused.

"Peace," Ellie said. "You go together."

"At the time he gave my ship that name, he saw me as an extension of himself," Irini said. "But now, I like to think it marks us as two of a kind."

"What are you talking about?" Xallantra asked.

"Where I come from, Paxe means peace, and Irini means peace." Ellie lifted her shoulders. "I needed time to dredge the meaning of *irini* from my memory."

"Peace." Xallantra didn't scoff, but it was close.

Paxe and Irini certainly seemed to have settled into a growing symbiosis, Renn had observed.

When he and Paxe discussed issues on the ship, it was clear Paxe had spoken to Irini about them, along with his fellow Class 5s.

And Ellie. He always spoke with Ellie.

They were planning something.

He looked forward to seeing what it was.

"Ready?" Irini had flown out of the launch bay and as soon as she was out, she began to spin.

"Let's blow some minds," Ellie said, amusement making her voice richer and more melodious than ever.

Irini hopped—short-jumped, as she called it—to the entrance to the *Urna's* own launch bay.

It had taken her mere seconds to bridge the considerable distance.

Renn lifted his wrist unit. "Permission to come aboard."

There was a pause.

Irini's little trick would have some of them worried.

"Permission granted."

Irini flew in, and Renn wasn't surprised to see their reception.

Weapons weren't exactly out, but they were handy.

"I'll get out first," he murmured. Seeing him would hopefully lower the tension. He knew a number of the officers outside from his time at UC headquarters.

He stepped through the silver of Irini's gel wall to a gasp from the crowd.

Sia came next, then Xallantra.

They all stepped to the side, and Renn saw he wasn't the only one of the three of them watching for signs of danger to Ellie.

Ellie came out next, and even though he'd just been sitting beside her moments earlier, his breath caught a little at the sight of her.

The halo of light around her head was clear in the launch bay, which told him the mix of air in here wasn't ideal for her.

The *Urna*, because it had to make life comfortable for five different life forms, had its environmental system calibrated to a middle point, a compromise that worked for everyone. It must work for the Earth women, too, because he knew at least one had been onboard the *Urna* before, but it was clearly not ideal.

With her head surrounded by light, her beautiful cloak falling around her, Ellie turned and extended her arm back through the door, so it disappeared up to her elbow, and then helped Silvey out, holding her hand.

Because Irini was coated in reflective silver only a shade darker than Silvey herself, it looked as if the ship had separated part of itself, molded into a small, bi-pedal avatar.

Ellie turned to face their audience, still holding Silvey's hand.

There was absolute silence.

She was beautiful, Renn thought. And so sharp and funny, and fundamentally, astonishingly sweet. But it was the sharp part they were about to experience. He recognized that look on her face.

"Where's Ambassador Dimitara?" Renn asked, to move things along.

A Bukarian he recognized as Juno Cossi, one of the Bukarian officers in charge of overseeing the Tecran military under the deal that had been struck by the United Council, stepped forward. "This way."

She turned on her heel and began walking out of the launch bay.

Sia followed her. Xallantra and Renn exchanged a look, and Renn went next, Ellie behind him, and Xallantra took up the rear— like Renn, her hand rested on her shockgun.

Silvey kept hold of Ellie's hand, Renn saw when he glanced back, and she looked around as she flowed along, her eye swiveling around, sometimes in a full rotation.

The murmurs were subdued, but audible.

The conference room where Ambassador Dimitara was waiting was a short distance from the launch bay, and Renn was glad to see Cossi had stopped at the entrance and taken up a guard position to one side. On the other was someone else he recognized from when he'd arrived in Tecra's airspace and had been briefed on his assignment to track the *Rauha*, the Fitalian military attaché, Chep.

He exchanged a nod with both of them as he waited for Ellie and Xallantra before he stepped through the door.

Sia was already inside, standing with hands clenched, facing the small contingent of United Council senior officials.

They were ignoring her, straining to see over her shoulder to Ellie.

Renn nudged her aside, and she shot him a look and then made room.

Ellie had said nothing since she'd stepped out of Irini's ship, simply taking everything in.

Now she glanced at him, as if seeking assurance, and then, to his surprise, took hold of his upper arm, standing shoulder to shoulder beside him.

"Captain Sorvihn." Ambassador Dimitara spoke to him, but her eyes were on Ellie.

Every eye was on Ellie.

"Ambassador." Renn gave the slight bow that was standard courtesy when dealing with the upper ranks of the UC.

There was a beat of silence.

"What the actual heck, eh?" Ellie said into the quiet, and everyone froze.

She let go of his arm and took another step forward, Silvey's hand still clasped in hers.

"That's certainly what I thought when I woke up, a prisoner in a secret moon base set up by the Tecran." She drew herself tall. "There has to be an accounting. I demand it for myself, for the crew of the *Etsijä*, and for Paxe." She did a slow sweep of the people before her, and Renn thought one of the Tecran officers twitched a little under her solemn gaze.

"What kind of accounting?" a Fitalian diplomat asked.

"Why don't I take you through what happened, first?" Ellie said, voice almost pitying.

Renn thought the group before them might start to be afraid, if they had any sense.

"As stated, I was held on a secret moon station in uncharted territory by the Tecran." The whole wall to the left suddenly flickered, and an image of Ellie, covered in a sheet, in the strange, slightly yellow light of the station, appeared. It was from a lens that was waist height, and Renn guessed it was a recording made by Karnic.

There were gasps.

Ellie leaned toward him, lips close to his ear. "Bane broke into the *Urna's* systems some time ago, and offered to project the lens feed Paxe had stored. We thought visual comms would save time."

Renn looked at the sight of her pale face, her still form recorded by the lens feed and agreed.

He was getting angry, and she was standing right beside him, unharmed.

"I was held here, like you see me on screen, for many months." She flicked her fingers, and the wall went dark. "I eventually regained consciousness, and found myself alone on the base, with no one but Paxe and some friends," she looked down at Silvey with a smile, "until the *Rauha* arrived, followed by Captain Sorvihn and some of his crew."

Paxe had obviously recorded the *Rauha's* arrival, because the wall lit up again, showing the *Rauha* hovering over the station, and then the chase when Renn's explorer was shot down.

There was a ripple of shock at the sight of his vessel being hit.

This was good. He exchanged a look with Xallantra, whose gaze was fixed on the images until they faded again, and then she went back to her watchful stance.

There were a number of Tecran in the group. Some looked shocked at the lens feed, others merely looked grim.

"Captain Vi'il then discovered I was on the moon station," Ellie said.

"He didn't know you were there already?" One of the UC councillors, a Garmman, called out.

"I don't believe so. His people seemed shocked to find me when they rounded me up, along with the crew of the Grihan explorer you just saw shot down." She flicked her hand again, and the next clip came from Irini's lenses as he and Ellie raced toward the launch pad, and the Tecran explorer chasing them shot her.

He had seen it with his own eyes, but seeing it again felt just as bad.

She flew through the air, slamming hard into Irini's side, and then slid down.

The way she curled her arm against her chest, her look of shock, was clear.

"How are you still alive?" Dimitara asked, voice soft.

"I was lucky to be wearing clothes that are resistant to laser fire," Ellie said. "There were other attempts to kill me. To kill Captain Sorvihn, as well. But then, when the *Etsijä* arrived, there was this." Now the view was from the *Rauha* itself.

He saw the arrival of the *Etsijä*, the calm, professional voice of Sia hailing the ship, then the shocking, unexpected first shot.

Ellie didn't stop the lens feed this time. She made them watch each hit.

And then the wall went dark again.

When the eyes of the room focused back on her, she was standing still, head slightly bowed.

She was . . . good at this, Renn suddenly thought. She was playing this a certain way, for a certain effect, and they did not even see it.

They were fully immersed in the experience.

He felt just the smallest amount of fear at the thought of a whole race just like her.

"What happens next?" she asked, throwing the ball suddenly, and without warning, into their court.

There was another moment of silence.

"We want our ship back," one of the Tecran standing near Dimitara said.

It was an incredibly badly-judged declaration, so soon after the room had witnessed the blow by blow destruction of the *Etsijä*.

"Paxe agrees to return the *Rauha* to you," Ellie said.

This, Renn could hardly believe. He stared at her, as open-mouthed as the rest of them.

"In return for what?" Dimitara asked.

Renn glanced at her, saw perhaps the ambassador, of everyone there, had some inkling of the path they were being led down.

"In return for the Tecran funding another Class 5 for him. Although he will not agree to them building it. He would like the Bukari and the Grih to do so."

The room exploded.

Ellie gave Dimitara a cool nod, turned, and walked out.

Renn shared a look with Xallantra, shrugged, and followed behind, shaking his head in amazement.

She had just upended the UC in . . . he checked his wrist unit . . . less than twenty minutes.

"How about that?" Xallantra murmured in appreciation.

How about that, indeed.

She'd taken a crisis and turned it on its head.

Well, he grinned as he caught up to her and slung an arm around her shoulder, life with Ellie was certainly not ever going to be boring.

CHAPTER 39

"SO, what's the news from Dimitara?" Lucy Harris leaned back on the comfortable couch in the ambassador's suite and then leaned close to Ellie, who was sitting beside her.

Ellie felt the same way.

In the weeks since Oris and Bane had stumbled onto them, and she'd met her fellow survivor, she'd found reasons to touch Lucy; a hand brushing down her back as she walked past, a touch of her hand to make a point. Sometimes a full body hug.

Their friendship had blossomed and become something solid and good.

"I understand it was as if you lobbed an explosive into the middle of a UC meeting and then strolled out." Dray Helvan smiled at her, looking like he was sorry he'd missed out on the fun.

He and Lucy had still been onboard Bane when she and Renn had been summoned to the *Urna*.

"The ambassador says the council is divided on whether to agree to Paxe's terms. The fact that the Tecran created the self-destruct mechanism that destroyed his Class 5 is undisputed, but the idea of yet another full-fledged Class 5 in the galaxy, rather than one that is slightly less able because it has to make do with a Levron battleship, is hard to swallow."

"He'll do it anyway," Ellie said, with a shrug.

Dray and Renn turned to look at her, surprise clear on both their faces.

"He's already started, hasn't he?" Lucy said. "I thought Sazo found the blueprints and sent them to him."

Ellie nodded. "Eazi is using the credits he earns running Larga Ways to start building it. He's going to set aside a whole dock arm for it. But they plan to send the final bill to Tecran High Command."

"And Eazi?" Lucy asked. "Does he want one too?"

"Maybe he will," Ellie said with a shrug. "His Class 5 was blown up, too."

Dray looked like he had forgotten how to breathe. He stared at Lucy as if she had suddenly sprouted a second head. "How——?"

Renn started laughing.

"What's so funny?" Dray narrowed his eyes, turning on his fellow Grih.

Renn turned a look on Ellie that made her toes curl in her boots, and her cheeks heat. "Never, ever boring."

NEXT UP IN THE CLASS 5 SERIES

There is a free Dark Class novella available to members of Michelle Diener's New Release Notification newsletter via BookFunnel, for those who'd like to read another adventure.

Readers can go to https://dl.bookfunnel.com/3x6arz1cek where they'll be directed to join the newsletter list and will be sent their copy of the Dark Class Epilogue. Readers details are never shared and they can unsubscribe at any time. They will also have access to other exclusive content while they are a member of the list.

COLLISION COURSE: BOOK 6

A step into the unknown . . .

Rose is looking forward to meeting the Fisone as part of the United Council's outreach mission. Since the Tecran were defeated and the full scope of their crimes were uncovered, the UC has wanted to find the Tecran's victims and extend the hand of friendship. The fact that Rose is close to having her baby is just another element to the adventure of finding the Fisone's planet and seeing if they could be potential allies.

An explorer's dream . . .

Dav Jallan has been captain of the *Barrist* for a few years, but this is the first time he's headed for a planet inhabited by advanced sentients. The Fisone exist—that is indisputable—and every part of this mission is why he became an explorer in the first place. The goal is to find them, form alliances, and make friends. The fact that he's about to become a new father simply adds to his sense of excitement.

A collision course with reality . . .

When Sazo's Class 5 and the *Barrist* enter the Fisone's airspace, what they find is far from the uncomplicated meeting they had envisioned. The Fisone are divided, carrying a grudge, and are sure the Grih are no different from the Tecran they encountered the year before. When they take Rose as a hostage, both Dav and Sazo focus everything they have on finding her, and as the Fisone's actions create more and more danger, ideas of alliances, friendship, and cooperation become less and less important.

The only comfort both Dav and Sazo have to draw from is that Rose has been taken by others before, underestimated before, and her abductors have lived to regret it.

They are counting on history repeating itself.

ABOUT THE AUTHOR

Michelle Diener is an award winning author of historical fiction, science fiction and fantasy romance.

Michelle was born in London and currently lives in Australia with her husband and children.

You can contact Michelle through her website or sign up to receive notification when she has a new book out on her New Release Notification page.

Connect with Michelle
www.michellediener.com

FANTASY NOVELS BY MICHELLE DIENER

The Rising Wave series:

The Rising Wave (Prequel novella to THE TURNCOAT KING)

The Turncoat King

The Threadbare Queen

Fate's Arrow

Truth's Blade

Mistress of the Wind

HISTORICAL FICTION NOVELS

Traffic Warden Mysteries:

Ticket Out

Regency London series:

The Emperor's Conspiracy

Banquet of Lies

A Dangerous Madness

To receive notification when a new book is released, sign up at michellediener.com.

ACKNOWLEDGMENTS

Thanks to Creative Paramita for my wonderful cover. To Jo, Justin and Claire, thank you as always for your suggestions and help with the manuscript. From my reader group, a big thank you to Heather, Michelle, Rosalie, Jess, J. Lee, Diane, Cherry and Karen for helping me with any typos that escaped notice.